Acclaim for

The Sweet By &

"A heartwarming collaborative debut."

— Publishers Weekly

"Enter the magic of Whisper Hollow and open your heart. Like Sara Evan's bittersweet songs, the notes and melody of Jade Fitzgerald's past sing a new future. In a world of wounded souls, forgiveness and redemption are the lyrics of this enchanting story."

— Patti Callahan Henry
New York Times best-selling
author of *Driftwood Summer*

"*The Sweet By & By* is the flowing story of a family struggling across the generations for redemption and reconciliation. The women in this novel are sometimes funny, sometimes serious, but always interesting. I was hooked from page one."

— Homer Hickam
best-selling author of *Rocket Boys*
and *Red Helmet*

". . . witty dialogue, believable characters and a page-turner of a plot. Just what I look for in a good book!"

— Cassandra King
author of *The Same Sweet Girls*

"Conveys a meaningful message about forgiveness."

— CBA Retailers +
Resources

"Beautifully real characters shine in this even more beautiful story. A wonderful first novel."

— Eva Longoria Parker
actress and model

"Wow! I am completely inspired by this book. I have always admired Sara's ability to tell stories through her music, and now I can say wholeheartedly that she is able to make a great story sing on the pages of this book. This is a beautiful, breathtaking novel full of redemption, reconciliation, and grace. I fully recommend it!"

— Robin McGraw,
#1 New York Times bestselling author

The Sweet By & By

SARA EVANS
WITH RACHEL HAUCK

THOMAS NELSON
Since 1798

NASHVILLE DALLAS MEXICO CITY RIO DE JANEIRO

The Sweet By & By

Published in Nashville, Tennessee. Thomas Nelson is a registered trademark of Thomas Nelson Inc.

Thomas Nelson, Inc. titles may be purchased in bulk for educational, business, fund-raising, or sales promotional use. For information, e-mail SpecialMarkets@ThomasNelson.com.

Scripture quotations are taken from the following:

Published in association with the literary agency of Alive Communications, Inc., 7680 Goddard Street, Suite 200, Colorado Springs, CO 80920.

This novel is a work of fiction. Any references to real events, businesses, organizations, and locales are intended only to give the fiction a sense of reality and authenticity. Any resemblance to actual persons, living or dead, is entirely coincidental.

ISBN 978-1-59554-778-1 (trade paper)
ISBN 978-1-4016-8582-9 (value edition)

Library of Congress Cataloging-in-Publication Data

Evans, Sara, 1971–
The sweet by & by / Sara Evans with Rachel Hauck.
p. cm.
ISBN 978-1-59554-489-6 (hardcover)
I. Hauck, Rachel, 1960- II. Title.
PS3605.V3765S94 2009
813'.6—dc22 2009022210

Printed in the United States of America

11 12 13 14 15 QG 5 4 3 2 1

To Olivia, Audrey, and Sarah Ashlee

"And our spirits shall sorrow no more."

—"The Sweet By & By,"

lyrics by S. Fillmore Bennett, 1868

Prologue

Summer '77

The stage lights were down, but then an electric guitar buzzed from the darkened stage, igniting the crowd gathered in the Iowa State Fair grandstand.

Chills multiplied down Beryl's legs as she glanced over her shoulder to a sea of cigarette lighters raised toward the twilight sky.

She leaned against Harlan as he swayed back and forth with his arm around her hips. For the first time since Woodstock, she was at a concert with no intention of getting high-as-a-kite, or leaving with the last man she'd kissed.

Her senses felt heightened by love, in tune with the frenetic energy around her and the music to come.

Rumor had it that this was the largest concert gathering in fair history. Fans stood shoulder-to-shoulder, cushioned by the heat-infused air.

Whistles pierced the night, followed by cheers and shouts: *Stevie, Lindsey, . . . Mick.*

Another guitar lick reverberated in the air with a shrill that hit Beryl in her chest. She cupped her hands around her mouth and yelled from the deepest part of her belly. She wanted to be heard.

Harlan's call for the music bellowed after hers, then his warm kiss blessed her ear, then her cheek.

When a drunken fan stumbled against her, sloshing beer against her sweat-dampened shirt, Harlan grabbed the man by the collar.

"Watch what you're doing."

The drunk moved on without a word.

"You all right?" Harlan asked Beryl.

"I'm perfect."

Until Harlan Fitzgerald, Beryl had been a wanderer, a traveler, a liberated woman with no visions of picket fences, rocking babies, and happily ever after.

Then he came along, a ponytail-lawyer from Des Moines. He rescued her from legal trouble—arrested at a sit-in—and stole her heart.

"Ladies and Gentlemen—" The announcer's mike screeched, settling the crowd down to a hovering din. "Fleetwood Mac."

Beryl's cheer erupted with the rest as she applauded with her arms in the air. Harlan's chest swelled as he drew a long breath and let go a deep, resonating holler.

The lights came up with the opening bars of "You Can Go Your Own Way." The grandstand seemed to move with a life of its own—the crowd swaying and clapping. Beryl moved in time with Harlan and the music.

If I could, baby I'd give you my world . . .

Beryl stretched to see over the fans in front of her.

"Jump up," Harlan said, then caught her midmotion and hoisted her to his shoulders.

Lifting her arms, Beryl let them sway freely with Harlan's motion. When the song ended, she bent forward to kiss his forehead. He was one of the truly good ones.

Harlan pressed something into her hand.

"What's this?" Beryl lifted the lid of a small black box. "Harlan—"

He helped her slide down from his shoulders. "It's an engagement ring, to seal our deal. Since you're not a traditionalist, I figured a *diamond* wouldn't be your thing—"

Even in the dim light, she could see the blue spark in his eyes. He looked cute and shy as he tried to explain himself.

"An engagement ring, huh?" She grabbed his neck and pulled him down for a kiss. "Very cool."

"It's a jade stone. The green matches the flecks in your eyes." He brushed her flyaway hair from her face, then took the ring and slipped it onto her finger. "Will you marry me, Beryl Walker?"

She didn't have to wait a week to give her answer this time like she did a month ago when Harlan took her by surprise and proposed under the moonlight, his voice textured with emotion. "Yes, Harlan Fitzgerald, I'll marry you."

One

Whisper Hollow, TN

The October sun warmed the Blue Umbrella's office. A pool of light washed over Jade's paint-chipped desk and the box of ruby-red invitations shoved against the windowsill.

"Here you go, Liz. Eighty-five dollars for your aunt's antique bread box." Jade pushed the box out of the way so she could grab the check she'd printed for her customer, exposing a solitary, displaced red invitation.

Beryl Hill, Prairie City, Iowa.

"Bless your heart, old Aunt Ginny, for never making friends with the garbage can." Liz Carlton blew a kiss at the check before folding it into her purse. "Jade, I've got plenty more items to consign with you."

"I'm always interested." She patted the small, spry woman on the shoulder. "And don't forget you can sell some of your valuables on eBay."

"On eBay? Goodness, child, I'd have no idea how to—"

"And there's the county dump." Jade walked her across the bright, polished shop to the front door.

"The county dump? I do believe you don't sound a bit grateful, Jade Fitzgerald. I bring in my precious family treasures for you to sell, sharing the profits with you, and what thanks do I get? A recommendation to the county dump."

"Liz, I appreciate your business. You know I do. But the Blue Umbrella is looking for timeless pieces, items with a story and a history. Last week you brought in a bag of peeling costume jewelry and some moth-eaten sweaters."

"Those sweaters had a story, Jade. I told you my great-great-granny knitted them by a coal fire."

Jade gently slipped her arm through Liz's. After all, she was a valued client, despite her lack of vintage prowess. "I'm looking for quality, not quantity, Liz. But I do admit"—Jade paused at the door—"your items always come with interesting stories."

Liz opened the door. "You wait and see what I dig up next."

"I'm holding my breath," Jade said with a grin.

Back in her office, Jade dropped to her desk chair, sighing. Liz was entertaining if nothing else.

She surveyed the row of lime-green sticky notes running along the top of her desk. Her to-do list. Her eyes fell on one sticky note, the one with the curled edges where her arm grazed over it:

Mail invitations.

Jade snatched up the note. The gummy adhesive was dotted with dust and lint and no longer adhered to the desk's surface. The lump she felt in her chest every time she moved the note had grown from a pebble to a rock. How much longer could she stall? The wedding was five weeks away.

"Hey, boss, what's up for today?"

Jade glanced up at Lillabeth, her sole and treasured part-time assistant. "You're early today."

"Coach rescheduled the team meeting for Friday." The seventeen-year-old folded herself into the rickety metal chair beside the desk. Her blonde ponytail swished over her shoulder, and a pair of tiger-striped Oakley shades rode atop her head.

"It's slow-day Monday. Why don't you work on the Baker estate inventory?"

"Shouldn't you have mailed these already?" Lillabeth slipped a wedding invitation from the box.

"You sound like my future mother-in-law." Jade took the envelope and jammed it back with the others.

"What about that one?" Lillabeth pointed to the banished invite.

"This one is special. Sort of." Jade tucked it a little farther under the box. "Tell me, what do you think when you hear the word *invitation*?"

"'You're invited,' I guess." Lillabeth shrugged, making a face. "'Come to the party. We want to see you.'"

"Come and participate? Your presence is requested?" Jade had been thinking about this for a while.

"Pretty much." The Whisper Hollow basketball star nodded. "Is this a trick question? Do I win a prize for answering right? Money?"

"Money? You're on the clock; you're getting paid." Jade got up and headed toward the storeroom. "Come on. Let me show you the Baker stuff."

On the opposite side of the shop was the old Five & Dime's storeroom, cool and dark with cinder-block walls, a cement floor, and a row of random old calendars hanging on the back wall.

When Jade set up the Blue Umbrella, she left the calendars for posterity's sake. A piece of the building's history. The first calendar was 1914. Then 1920, followed by 1929. There were calendars from 1945 and 1950, 1963 and 1967, 1980 and 1988, 1996 and 2001.

Jade planned to add her own, but she wanted to wait for a really cool year.

Though so far, the one she lived now had been fairly stellar. When she moved to Whisper Hollow, a close-knit, small Southern town up the mountain from Chattanooga, she'd expected to moonlight for her former boss writing promotional copy for Smoky Hills Media. But the Blue Umbrella thrived its first year, ending in a lovely shade of financial pink.

Then she met Max—love wrapped in olive-toned skin, hazel eyes, strength, and kindness. Yes, this calendar year just might be worthy of the wall.

"Okay, where's this *famous* Baker inventory?" Lillabeth dropped to the stool in front of the antique-white secretary hutch Jade used as the storeroom desk and jiggled the computer's mouse. "Odd question about the word *invitation*, Jade."

"Yet you still answered it." Jade pushed a crate toward Lilla with her foot. "These are leather-bound, mint condition, first editions."

"Books? Since when do we take books?" Lillabeth angled to read the gold-imprinted spines while absently launching iTunes, then hunted for QuickBooks in the Mac's dock.

"Since these are worth money. A friend from college knew the family and hooked me up." Jade gave her a cheesy thumbs-up. "Jessup Baker was a Tennessee governor and his wife, Cecelia, earned all kinds of humanitarian awards for establishing reading programs in the hills."

"Who's going to read these?" Lillabeth wrinkled her nose as she examined one of the books, the spine creaking, the pages crackling.

"Plenty of people. We just need to figure out how to lure book snobs to Whisper Hollow."

Lillabeth settled the book on the secretary. "Who don't you want to invite to your wedding?"

"Someone. So, get to inventorying these and listen for the front bell. I'll be in the office." Jade paused in the doorway. "The camera is in the file cabinet. Take pictures of the books for the website."

"I'll crash your wedding if you didn't invite me." Lillabeth started typing in the publishing information. "I witnessed your first meeting with Max, right here in the shop. I should get a finder's fee or something."

"What is with you and money today?" Jade propped herself against the door frame.

"Nothing." The girl's light dimmed.

Jade regarded her for a moment. "Hey, if you need to talk . . ."

"I know."

On her way back to the office, Jade checked the shop for customers. It was quiet, like last year this time, and she welcomed the reprieve. Gave her time to catch up from the busy summer, scout out new inventory avenues, advertise for new consignment clients. It wasn't like vintage merchandise came with manufacturer sales reps.

Jade stood by her desk and scanned her sticky note to-do row.

Call Henna Swift about exhibiting at February's Country Home Antiquing Festival in Nashville.

Upload new images to website.

Call Ilene to pick up her consigned items.

Dress fitting at 2:00 next Monday.

Set appointment for trial wedding hairstyles.

Pick up prescription for Max's back.

Mail invitations.

She couldn't get past *Mail invitations.* Not today. She had been ignoring that particular note, despite her future mother-in-law's constant, "Please mail the invitations."

Beryl Hill, Prairie City, Iowa.

A snort resounded from under her desk. Jade took her seat to peek underneath, nudging the sleeping dog with her foot. "Wake up, Roscoe, and give me some advice."

The sprawled-out German shepherd lifted his head, viewing her with his one good eye.

Jade flashed him the red invitation. "Do I invite her to the wedding? What would you do if, say, dogs got married?"

He exhaled, tucked up his paws, closed his eye, and dropped his head back to the floor.

"And after all I've done for you." Jade tapped his belly with her foot. "Don't expect me to share my pizza crust next time, buddy." The threat carried no authority, caused no shiver of trepidation. One wink of his big brown eye, and she'd hand over a whole slice without hesitation.

"Okay, Roscoe, how about this. Heads, I invite her; tails, I don't." Jade fished a quarter from the stash she kept in the middle drawer's paper clips slot. "Lift your head for, well . . . heads. Wag your tail for tails. Here we go."

Before she settled the quarter on her thumb and forefinger, a squeaky, airy sound emitted from Roscoe's hindquarters.

"Oh, dog. Phew." Jade fired her rolling chair across the floor, crashing into the filing cabinet. "Why don't you tell me how you really feel?"

He snorted.

"I need a soda." Lillabeth burst into the office, going straight for the quarter stash. "My throat is clogged with book mites."

"Wait." Jade rolled back to the desk and slapped her hand over Lillabeth's as she retreated with fifty cents. "Heads or tails?"

"What?"

"Call it. Quick." With a flick of her thumb, Jade launched the coin high in the air. "Heads or tails?"

"Heads, no . . . tails. Tails."

The coin rotated in midair, a silver glint slicing through warm afternoon sunlight, then fell to the floor, landing on its narrow edging with a *ping*, and rolled across the floor. Jade and Lillabeth hunched over and followed it until the quarter hit a crack in the floorboards and disappeared.

"Ack." Jade dropped to her knees and slapped the floor with her palm, then thunked her forehead against the wood to peer through the dark slit. "Get me a flashlight, Lilla. I want to see if it's heads or tails."

"You've gone crazy, Jade. What are you trying to decide?"

"If I should dye my hair pink for the wedding." Jade held up her hand, wiggling her fingers.

"Liar." Lillabeth snatched the flashlight from the leaning bookshelf and slapped it into Jade's palm. "Pink's not vintage."

"I do have more than one string on my violin, Lilla. I play contemporary now and then." Shining the round beam through the narrow slit, Jade tried to see how the coin had landed, but she couldn't even find it, let alone discover if it was heads or tails.

"Contemporary, maybe, but not 1999 punk. Too tacky. Dark brown hair suits you fine."

Jade sat back with a heavy exhale. "There goes twenty-five cents and the answer to my problem."

"Is this about the invitation? Jade, you have the answer." Lillabeth tapped her chest. "In your heart."

"Don't you have work to do in the storeroom?" Jade returned the flashlight to the shelf.

"Hey, you asked me. Heads or tails. Remember? I just came in for soda money." Lillabeth rubbed her two quarters together. "For what it's worth, I think you should send it. I mean, unless you're inviting an ex-lover or something. Or an ax murderer."

"Can I pretend she's an ax murderer?" Jade plopped onto her chair and stared out the window. *The trash guys forgot to empty the Dumpster again.*

"Who is this horrible person?"

"Someone." Raking her hair back from her face, Jade dug around her soul for a thimble's worth of emotion that might tell her what to do.

"Ah, the elusive someone." Lillabeth lowered herself into the rickety metal chair. "Hey, Jade, can I ask you something?"

"Sure. What?" Jade drummed her fingers over the invitation. If she sent it, the issues of her life she'd carefully dubbed "unusable vintage" would recycle through her heart and resurrect all kinds of ugliness. Liz Carlton's great-great-granny's moth-eaten sweaters had nothing on Jade's tattered past.

The teen inhaled long and slow, tapping the edge of one quarter against the face of the other. Jade watched her, slipping the invitation onto the desk.

"Must be hard to talk about. Usually I can't get you to shut up." Jade smiled and kicked the air in front of Lillabeth.

"Yeah, well"—big exhale—"let's say you did something you didn't mean to do and the result—"

"Good afternoon, ladies." A svelte, tan June Benson, outfitted for golf, swooshed into the office with a wide smile and grand gestures. "Lillabeth, goodness, how are you? I didn't see your mother on the tennis courts all summer. Here it is fall. Tell her we could use her on the golf course. We're missing a fourth."

"She's into Pilates these days." Lillabeth held up her quarters and motioned she was going back to work.

"Take me with you . . . ," Jade called after her, then laughed for June's sake, but the woman was focused on the invitations.

"As I suspected. These lovely"—June patted the box of invitations—"unique . . . very red invitations are still here. We can say one thing: the envelopes will stand out in the mail. So what do you say we mail them, hm? Time is running out, Jade. Please let me take them. Except your mother's. You can keep that one until you decide."

"I haven't told her yet." Jade wadded up the lime-green sticky note. *Mail invitations.*

"Then call her. Land sakes, you're a grown woman." June collapsed in the metal chair Lillabeth had just vacated, catching herself when it listed to starboard. "What will people think if your mother is not at your wedding?"

"That I'm wise and gutsy."

June straightened the hem of her madras golf skort. "Or petty and childish."

Roscoe peeked out from under the desk, his eyebrows twitching as he scanned the space between Jade and June. *Ladies, keep it down. Let sleeping dogs lie.*

"If you'd let Max and me get married in a small ceremony up on Eventide Ridge at dusk like we wanted—"

"And have my only child married without a proper ceremony?" June propped her hand on the edge of the desk and leaned toward Jade. "No ma'am. And you'd regret it, too, in time. Trust me."

Jade matched her future mother-in-law's hard gaze. "Trust me. I wouldn't."

"Send the invitation, Jade, because *these*"—June rose, switching her handbag from one shoulder to the other and tucking the box of invitations under her arm—"are going out whether you're ready or not. I'm sorry, but time is running out. I don't mean to be so bossy . . . goodness, I can't imagine what angst exists between you and your mama. Were you abused? Pardon my frankness."

"No."

"My granny, bless her soul, used to say, 'Whatever ill you have against someone isn't worth sending the Lord Jesus back to the cross.'"

"I don't even know what that means." Jade faced her computer screen and clicked on an unread e-mail. "But I'm not sending Jesus anywhere."

"It means Jesus' love and forgiveness is sufficient for any wrong or violation done to us, Jade. Don't you think it's powerful enough for you and your mama? This I do know"—June stood just beyond Jade's peripheral vision—"you need to forgive your mother for whatever it is that she did to you." She paused. "Believe me, holding a grudge does nothing but deepen and widen your hurt."

"I appreciate your input, June, but forgiveness has a twin: forgetting." Jade waved Mama's invitation in the air. "Which is what I'm trying to do."

The only way she figured she'd come close to forgiving was to forget her past, which included her mama.

"I won't argue with you. You know your own heart better than I do, but I wish you'd reconsider." June pressed her hand gently on Jade's shoulder. "See you at seven? Diamond Joe's, meeting with the wedding planner?" She leaned to peer at Jade's to-do list. "I declare, I don't know how you run a business this way."

"My system works for me." Jade rolled her chair away from the desk, giving June a *good-bye, have a nice afternoon* smile. "See you at seven."

"What's this?" June invaded "the system" and snatched up a sticky note. "A prescription for Max?"

Nosy. Jade took the note from her. "You have my wedding invitations; now you want my sticky notes too?"

"What's wrong with Max?"

"His back is out again, and the doctor called in a prescription to the pharmacy up here. He asked me to pick it up."

"I didn't know he hurt his back. What'd he do?" June snatched the sticky note from Jade, her expression drawn, her tone laced with concern. She seemed a bit ruffled.

"Sneezed wrong or something. It just happened yesterday."

"His back's been a mess since high school football and track." June stuffed the sticky into her bag. "I've got to run by the pharmacy anyway. I'll pick this up for him. You're so swamped here."

"June, I'm not *that* swamped."

"Well, like I said, I'm on my way to the pharmacy anyway. See you at seven." And June was gone.

Okay, then. Thanks. Despite June's overreaching into Jade and Max's wedding plans, and, well, most everything around Whisper Hollow, the Bensons were good people. Floured with Southern charm and tradition and deep fried, June and Rebel were Whisper Hollow pillars. Both sets of Max's grandparents were descendants of the town's founders.

Her people, on the other hand . . . a dad she hadn't heard from in years, and a flower-child mother stuck in the dried-up soil of the '60s.

Jade knocked off her clogs and dug her toes into Roscoe's warm, thick fur.

He sighed and kissed her ankle with a lick. Her vision of her wedding had been a handful of friends and family gathered around as she and Max pledged themselves to each other in a peaceful, solemn, simple ceremony. Jade had never imagined she'd find true love again. But Max had captured her heart.

Why should she invite the one woman who could destroy it all?

Two

Amber hues muted the last of the Iowa blue day as the sun rounded the horizon toward the west, taking with it the last bit of warmth. An icy breeze nipped Beryl's face as she fumbled for her house keys, her arms loaded with mail and groceries, a pack of hungry dogs swirling around her feet, panting and yipping, splashing drool on her shoes.

"Willow?" That girl, where'd she run off to today? "Willl*oooow*?"

Between the doctor's appointment, the aggravating man in front of her at Prairie City Foods—who paid his fifty-dollar tab in quarters—and the crowding of her daughter's mangy mutts, Beryl was fresh out of straws.

Willow, please suddenly appear. Open the door. Help me inside. Beryl's arms were starting to tremble from balancing her bags. And she craved a cigarette. Her mind's eye pictured the pack she had stashed in the back of the pantry.

Dr. Meadows had demanded she quit, but right now, he could stuff his no-smoking advice. Beryl would smoke him right along with her Virginia Slims.

"Willow!" As she stretched to slip her key into the lock, Beryl's packages crashed to the gray porch boards. Her key slipped from her fingers.

She swore and kicked at the mail. A slick ad for cheap pizza sailed over the yard. Pepper, the little Jack Russell, bounded after it, yipping and snapping.

The remaining dogs watched with heads tilted and tails wagging. "Yes, she's one of you," Beryl said. "Embarrassing, isn't it?"

Stooping to retrieve her keys, purple and brown spots swirled before her eyes and she stumbled forward as a ringing sounded in her ears. "Mercy . . ." Beryl drew a deep breath, sitting and propping her back against the kitchen door.

Sooner or later Willow would come along. Not to check on her mother, but to feed her dogs.

Pepper returned with the pizza ad, wrinkled and frayed, sticking out both sides of her jaw. She dropped it on Beryl's lap.

"Thank you, Pepper. Now, if you could, please open the door."

The dog sat, panting, grinning. Beryl lifted her hand to brush the pooch's head. The wind had swept away the warmth of the afternoon and a fall chill seeped beneath her skin, but Beryl couldn't motivate her old, tired bones to move. When did fifty-nine start to feel like a hundred and nine?

"Beryl, what the heck?"

Willow stood on the bottom step eating a red apple, her T-shirt askew and her hair tousled. Next to her stood Lincoln, Beryl's occasional handyman. A long, yellow piece of straw stuck out from the side of his head, and he was smiling to beat the band.

Darn it, Willow. Leave the help alone.

"Your stupid dogs knocked me over."

"Why didn't you call me?" Willow wedged the apple between her teeth and offered her mother a hand. Lincoln steadied Beryl once she got on her feet.

"I did. But you were"—she looked at Lincoln as she unlocked the kitchen door—"*busy*. How about teaching your canines a few manners?"

"I'll see what I can do." Willow took a final bite of her apple and tossed it into the yard. "Read to them from Emily Post tonight or something."

"Oh, please, not Emily Post." Beryl gathered her purse and one of the grocery bags. Every joint ached. "Bring in the mail and groceries for me, Willow, please. Lincoln, how about seeing to the busted porch screens I've already paid you to repair. Maybe I can enjoy a few nights of fall before winter drives me inside."

"I'm on it right now, Mrs. Hill."

In the boxy, warm kitchen, Beryl dropped her things onto the red, cracked-ice Formica and chrome table, an antique from her childhood, and snatched up the teakettle. She hankered for a hot cup of sweet tea. Then a cigarette. Yes sir, tea and a cigarette.

Still outside on the porch, Willow laughed low to the rhythm of shuffling feet. Lincoln responded in a deep, muffled tone.

"I'm not paying you to make out with Willow, Linc." Beryl called as she stuck the kettle under the faucet and cranked the water.

"Leave him alone. He's not robbing your paid time." She dropped her arm-load of packages to the kitchen table. The canned beans tumbled from the plastic sack and rolled to the edge.

"Willow, please don't ding the table." Beryl could still see Paps' face the night he brought the table home to surprise Mother. The summer of '56. Or was it '57? Elvis had been on the *Steve Allen Show* that night.

"I didn't ding the table." Willow stacked cans in the center. "I'm going to help Lincoln."

"He don't need your kind of help. I want my screens fixed." Beryl fired up the burner under the kettle, thinking she'd best put the groceries away while she had the energy. Sliding the mail away from the table's edge, she reached for the bean cans. "It's not like me to tell you who to be with, Willow, but at least let him take you to dinner first."

"Dinner? This is a fling, Mama. No big deal." Willow swung open the pantry doors, searching. "If I let him take me on a date, he might start thinking I'm his girlfriend."

"Heaven forbid. Does Linc know it's just a fling?" Beryl shoved Willow aside and set the cans on the middle shelf, then turned to the table for the bread, spaghetti, cereal, and two-liter of pop.

Willow shrugged, taking the pop bottle from her mother and setting it on the pantry floor. "If he doesn't, he will soon enough."

"Do what you will, but be honest." Beryl retrieved her favorite teacup—a gold-rimmed Lennox with holly leaves—from the cupboard, then stared out the window by the sink, waiting for the water to boil.

Tank Victor's harvested field ran along the hem of the fading-green backyard like a pleated, coffee-colored skirt.

This view always took her back to the summer of '67. She'd been standing by the same field when Mother agreed to let her spend the summer in San Francisco with her college-age cousin, Carolyn. Mother's reluctant yes dropped Beryl into the heart of the Summer of Love, an inaugural member of the counterculture that permanently inked her life.

"You miss it?" Willow fell against the counter next to Beryl, peeling cellophane away from a Twinkie.

"Depends. Miss what?"

"Farming."

"No, not really. I'm not sure you can call three seasons of corn planting 'farming.' I did like driving the tractor. Actually, I was thinking about my first summer in California."

"The year of the hippie. Paps had to drive out to San Francisco to bring you home for your senior year." Willow stuffed half the Twinkie in her mouth and tossed the wrapper in the bin under the sink.

"So you've heard the story. Sorry to bore you." Beryl glanced over. "How can you eat those things?"

"You were an original wild child, weren't you, Beryl?" Willow munched on the second half of the Twinkie, dusting her hands against her jeans.

"Not wild. Free. Different from Mother and Paps. They were so square-thinking and backward."

"Compared to you, maybe, but it doesn't mean they were wrong, Beryl."

"I thought you were going to help Lincoln." Beryl reached for the ceramic blue canister and lifted the lid for an English Breakfast tea bag.

"You told me to leave him alone."

"Now I want you to leave me alone."

"I called you at work today." Willow didn't leave but remained propped against the counter, picking at the jagged edge of her broken thumbnail. "They said you were on leave or something."

Nosy little girl. "I'm taking some vacation, getting some things done that I needed done." Beryl scooped sugar into her teacup, two teaspoons tonight instead of one—hot tea was no good unless it was sweet—and resituated the ancient art deco napkin holder Mother owned when Eisenhower was a mere general.

"What things?" Willow opened the kitchen's junk drawer and picked around the pens, pencils, bread ties, glue, safety pins, and what all.

She was fishing in the pond of none-of-her-business. "I'm a senior teamster, Willow, and your mother—even if you do call me Beryl—and I don't have to answer to you." The kettle started a slow steam. "What are you looking for in that drawer?"

"A nail file."

Beryl stepped beside Willow and dug to the back of the junk. "Here." She cut the air with a well-worn but sufficient emery board. "Ask Lincoln to chop some wood before he goes home tonight. I might like a fire." Lately, she craved the simple, homey things she'd once found confining and antiquated.

"Yeah, okay." Willow filed her nail and dropped the board back into the drawer, then reached for the mail. "Is everything okay, Beryl? You seem edgy these days. More than usual."

"I'm fine." Beryl snapped off the burner under the kettle and filled her cup. "Can't a woman take a few days off without the third degree? My stars—"

"Whoa, she *actually* sent it."

"Whoa, what?" Beryl stirred as she carried her cup to the table, her rattled nerves calming. She didn't want Willow to know. Not yet. There was time.

Standing by the table, Willow stared at a ridiculously red envelope. "Good for her."

"Good for who, girl? What are you yammering about? Is that a Christmas card already? It's only the first of October."

"Uh, I'm going to see if Lincoln is ready for dinner." Willow tossed the envelope to the table. It landed in front of Beryl.

"Dinner? He just started working." Beryl slid the chair away from the table and angled to sit down, reading her name inked in gold across the front of the plush linen envelope. "And wouldn't that be like a *date*?" Lincoln's music drifted through the house as the front door squeaked open.

The kitchen light faded as evening shoved the sun westward around the curve of the earth and Beryl inspected the suspicious letter. Sipping her tea, she turned the invitation over. *Jade Fitzgerald.* Her fingers let go. *Don't it just figure.*

"Well? Aren't you going to open it?" Willow had returned and stood in the doorway.

"She's getting married, isn't she?" Beryl gripped her teacup to steady her trembling hands.

"November fourteenth." Willow opened the silverware drawer before sitting in the red-ice and chrome chair across from Beryl. She slit open the invitation with a butter knife.

"Haven't heard from her in three years, and the first I do, it's this." Beryl slid the invitation free and stared at the embossed script.

"Last I looked, your dialing finger wasn't broken."

Jade Freedom Fitzgerald and Maxwell Charles Benson along with Mr. and Mrs. Rebel Benson . . .

"Have you met him?"

"At Christmas."

"And?" Beryl didn't expect to read her name on the invitation, so the sting of disappointment surprised her.

"He's great, sweet, charming, good-looking. Seems to really love Jade." Beryl's youngest child shuffled the salt and pepper shakers between her hands. "He's a lawyer."

Beryl peered up from the five-by-seven card. "You're kidding."

"His family's firm has been around, like, seventy years. Full of Southern charm and good-ol'-boy power."

"So she found a man like her father after all. My efforts wasted." Beryl clicked her tongue against her teeth.

"Some effort," Willow scoffed. "All two ounces of it."

Let her be. She had a right to speak her mind. Even if she had no idea what she was talking about.

. . . cordially invite you to stand in witness as they exchange marriage vows Saturday, November 14, 6:00 p.m. First Baptist Congregation Church, Whisper Hollow, Tennessee. Black tie required.

"Fancy wedding, I see. Black tie." Beryl tucked the heavy card back into the envelope and laid it on the table with a pat of her palm. "How long have you known?"

"Six months. I'm her maid of honor."

"Does she really want me to come?"

Willow shrugged. "She mailed it, didn't she?"

"Someone did." Probably not Jade, if history was any indication. Beryl sipped from her teacup. "Were you going to go without telling me?"

"No . . . well, actually . . ." Willow eased back, hooking her elbows over the top of her chair. "If she didn't tell you, yes. I've never understood what's between you two, and I'm not going to get in the middle."

"She's never said?"

"Neither have you."

Beryl set her cup in the saucer and pushed it away. The tea had already cooled beyond her liking. "Why don't you and Lincoln run down to the Dairy Queen for dinner? Bring me a small chocolate shake."

"That's it? All you have to say?" Willow rose from the table, sliding the chair underneath. "Bring me a chocolate shake?"

"Remember, a small shake. A medium is too much." She got up and headed for the kitchen staircase. "Do you need money?"

"No, no . . ." Willow patted her jeans pockets. "Beryl, you okay?"

"I thought you wanted to go to dinner. Get going." Beryl climbed the back staircase to her room as Willow's "Dinner break, cowboy" resounded through the house.

Gripping the faded quilt draped over her bed, Beryl knelt to the floor and peered underneath. Between the dust bunnies and storage bins she spotted the old sewing box stuffed with pictures, her old memories rising and etching the fiber of her soul.

~

Des Moines, March 1980

A slice of yellow light from the hospital hall fell over Beryl as her room door eased open.

"Is it safe?" Harlan's angular face peered around the door.

Beryl smiled, trying to shift upright, but her body wouldn't cooperate, exhausted from ten hours of labor. She slumped down on the pillow as Harlan tiptoed across the tile to her bed. His kiss was warm.

"Did you see her?"

"Yep, all bundled in pink and sleeping." He sat on the edge of the bed and gripped Beryl's hand. "Six hours old and still an ugly little fart."

"She looks like you." Beryl squeezed his fingers. "How's Aiden?"

"Already spoiled. Your Paps has him holding up one finger telling everyone, 'I one. I one.'"

"Tell Paps to bring him by, please." Beryl sighed. "So what's with the suit coat, lawyer Fitzgerald? You didn't have to go to court today, did you?"

"No, I wore it to hide this . . ." Pulling aside his suit jacket, Harlan revealed a Dairy Queen cup. "Contraband."

"A chocolate shake." Beryl pushed herself up from her pillow. "Now I remember why I married you." She drew a long, cold, sweet taste. The best, absolute best. Harlan *and* the shake.

He laughed. "Keep that in mind, will you? Listen, I couldn't stop them, but your mom has a crew of women from her church dropping off dinners and diapers and offers to clean."

"She's determined to get us *saved*—one way or another."

"Christmas is coming in nine months. We'll make our church appearance then."

Beryl grinned, chewing on the tip of her straw. "Harlan, how'd savvy people like you and me end up with two babies in two years?"

He drew a deep, long kiss from her lips. "Darling, if I have to tell you—"

"You know what I mean." She tapped his nose with the white straw. "I was breastfeeding—"

"Are you sorry, Beryl?"

"Just an odd place for two people who didn't want children."

By the time she realized she was pregnant, it was too late to consider another option. And her wide-eyed, towheaded son, who fit perfectly in the cradle of her chest and brushed her chin with his fingers when he nursed, had awakened her maternal desires. "I'm just wondering how we're going to manage. The apartment is so cramped—"

"Maybe we don't have to worry about the apartment anymore." Harlan brushed her hair back from her forehead.

"Uh-oh, what?" She wrapped her lips around the straw and a chocolate chill hit the warm middle of her tongue. Beryl shifted carefully to face her husband. Oh, she was still so sore. "Did Family Aid lose more funding? Did you lose your job? We can't move in with my parents, Harlan. We can't."

"I quit," he said, without flinching or a second of hesitation.

Beryl's mouth dropped open as she lowered the cold cup to her lap.

"I took the job with Bernstein & Lowe . . . as a junior partner."

"A for-profit firm? Harlan, no, I won't let you. We can stay in the apartment. It's not that cramped. How can you abandon your work, your principles, for corporate hypocrisy? What about the job with the ACLU?" Passion flooded her weary muscles.

"I still plan to use the law to help the poor and discriminated. Bernstein & Lowe require so many pro bono cases a year. But I'll earn four times what I made at Family Aid. And that's just the beginning. Next year it'll be eight times, including bonuses. I can do more to help people this way."

Was this her Harlan Fitzgerald or a stranger? "How could you do this without talking to me?"

"The offer came today." He paced to the edge of her bed, hands in his slacks pockets. "They called and asked me to meet with them. Beryl, I'd be a fool to pass on this. I've not changed; I've grown smarter. Time to consider our future as well as the rest of the world's."

She swirled the straw through the thick drink, shaking her head. "It feels cheap, as if we've surrendered. Given in to The Man—"

"I put a bid in on the farmhouse. Looks like they're going to accept."

Beryl stopped stirring. "The one on Highway 117?"

"The rambling two-story you love, with the wraparound porch and twenty acres. Two miles from your folks, I know, that's the downside, but you can farm, grow your own garden . . . Shoot, create your own Prairie City commune for all I care. As long as I have my own bathroom." He held his palms wide, grinning at his simple concession. "Beryl, two months ago the house was a pipe dream. This job makes it a reality. What good are dreams if they have no chance of coming true?"

"Don't paint your sold-out soul pretty colors and tell me it's a rainbow." She pinched her lips together, trying not to smile, resisting the sweeping tide of his enthusiasm. "You gave up your principles, *our* principles, about money and *things*. We're now a part of the world's problems. Another rat in the maze, grubbing for money and power."

"A house isn't a *thing*, Beryl. It's a necessity. Isn't this the very issue we fight for? The right of every person, no matter race or creed, to have a house, a little slice of the American dream? Now it's our turn. If we can't succeed, how can we encourage others?" He gestured toward the window and looked out. "There's a whole world out there, baby, with all kinds of possibilities. Look at it this way: Bernstein & Lowe sold out when they hired me, a ponytail-lawyer with a fierce record on social justice."

"But now you're the establishment, the other side, the type of people we loathed and protested."

"You're looking at it wrong, Beryl." Harlan came back to her bed and the light behind his eyes was like a hundred Christmas trees. "Don't you see? Hiring me affirms all we've stood for, Beryl. We've made a difference. And will continue to persuade society. One day, one person, one case at a time."

His broad smile defused the last of her resolve. "You do this to me . . . win me over with your reasoned speeches and charm." Beryl rested against her pillow.

"It's why you married me." He kissed her hand, then reached for the shake, taking a long, smiling sip.

"It's one of the hundred reasons why I married you."

From the moment she met him—in a Des Moines jail, arrested for a slaughterhouse protest and sit-in—she wanted him to be more than her lawyer. Her lover, certainly. But her husband? His out-of-the-blue proposal shocked her. She'd never had visions of white picket fences and jolly family dinners, and Beryl took the better part of a week to say yes. Then he surprised her with the jade ring at the Fleetwood Mac concert and she'd wondered why she ever hesitated.

But Harlan's dashing manner had hooked her heart. The night he'd gently pressed her for an answer, she knew she belonged to him. Everything in her detested the idea of institutionalized marriage, but she ached to *be* with him, to be his heartbeat, his missing rib.

"Your dad's already offered to help buy some hens and a noisy rooster, a couple of cows and a pig or two . . . if they're not too stinky. Come on, Beryl sweetheart, what do you say? It's good for us. Good for our future. Our values haven't changed. If anything, we're sinking them deeper into the soil."

The door creaked open and a nurse peeked inside. "Feeding time, Mrs. Fitzgerald."

Harlan tucked the chocolate shake underneath his jacket as the nurse rolled in the bassinette. Beryl plumped the pillow behind her back, snickering at him. Big-time lawyer hiding a frozen treat from an LPN.

A second nurse rolled in the bassinette for the mother sharing Beryl's room. "Feeding time, Mrs. Ainsworth."

The woman groused and rolled onto her side, away from her blue bundled child. "I told you, I'm not nursing this one. Keep him in the nursery, please. I want to sleep."

"It's her seventh one, and we got a pool going to see if she's even going to remember to take him home," Beryl's nurse whispered as she passed over the pink bundle. "I'll be back for her in an hour or so."

"Jade Freedom Fitzgerald, how are you liking the world so far?" Harlan asked, shoving his thick finger into her tiny grip.

"She's getting prettier by the minute, Harlan." Beryl smoothed the tuft of brown hair trying to spring up from Jade's crown.

"Looking more and more like her mom." He peered at her. "Still want to name her for a gemstone?"

"Yes. And when she's older, I'll give her the ring you gave me. We're going to be the best of friends, aren't we, little Jade-o?"

Three

Jade spotted Max waiting for her between the stone columns of the First Baptist Congregation portico. His smile reminded her why she endured his mother, let her have her way for their wedding. Love.

"The shop busy today?" He winced as he leaned to kiss her.

"Tourist bus with vintage shoppers from Atlanta." She curled into him, drawing her sweater tight against the evening's dewy chill. "The shop's a mess, but the cash register is happy and full."

"That's my smart entrepreneur." Max slung his arm around her shoulders as they headed for the giant sanctuary doors, leaning against her. "I love how you make old things new, babe."

"Someone has to . . . Your back is still bothering you?" Jade grabbed the wrist of his arm draped over her shoulder. "Aren't the meds helping?"

"Meds?" Max winced as he reached to open the sanctuary door. "Mom hasn't handed over the prescription yet."

"Talk to your mama. She came by the shop to hijack the invitations, got nosy with my sticky notes, and took the one about going by the pharmacy. She didn't give them to you?"

His jaw tightened. "No."

"But you're in pain." Jade paused in the foyer. He was agitated. "She seemed so intent on helping."

Max motioned for her to go inside the sanctuary. "I'll talk to her again."

"It's a prescription, Max." Jade tried to see his eyes as they walked down the aisle toward the church offices. "What's the big deal?"

"Nothing. Except for the occasional shooting pain down my leg." Max tried to straighten his back, air whistling through his teeth as he did. "And my meddling mother."

"Meddling? Okay, what's up? Do you want me to just call your mom? We can meet her—"

"I've got to go by the house tonight anyway." Max leaned against the office door.

"Evening, folks." Reverend Girden emerged, his long and lean runner's build moving in graceful synchronization. He watched Max carefully. "Max, what's with your back?"

"Whisper Hollow High versus East Ridge, playoffs, fall of '90." Max eased forward to shake the reverend's hand. "You remember my fiancée, Jade."

"I do. Nice to see you again." Reverend Girden stood aside for Max and Jade to enter his office. "Ah, yes. The old East Ridge game. If I recall, you ran for ninety-five yards, Max."

"And *sooo* gone are the glory days." Max winced.

The men reminisced for a few minutes, exchanging football battle stories, then recounting the fourth-quarter tackle that sent Max to the ER.

Jade hung onto Max's fingers, listening, loving stories that deepened her understanding of the man she loved.

Besides, it took her mind off being behind the reverend's closed office door, from treading on holy territory—churches and ministers, God and holiness. The whole deal made her uncomfortable and threatened her sense of worth.

Reverend Girden reminded her of her granny's preacher back in Iowa—soft and unassuming, but with a laserlike gaze.

"How are things at Benson Law, Max?"

"Busy, really busy. Named best law firm in the Southeast by a couple of trades and associations."

"Means you can charge more now, right?" The reverend sat behind his desk, motioning for Max and Jade to take the frame and leather chairs across from him.

A nervous flutter hit Jade. For the first time since learning of this meeting, she considered the implications. The reverend wanted to *meet* with them.

Next to her, Max didn't appear tense or anxious. He'd moved from talking football with the holy man to golf and his new graphite clubs.

The reverend's office was masculine and dark, with only a single floor lamp lit behind the desk. The walls were lined with bookshelves, double-stacked with books. Jade imagined it was impossible for one man to read so many.

But the room was hot. The books and heavy furniture sucked up all the light and air. Digging her fingernails into the wood tip of the leather arm, Jade's heart rate spiked. Why did the walls choose now to close in on her? Maybe she shouldn't be here, chatting with God's representative about marrying marvelous Max. She didn't deserve him. At all. Breathing deep, Jade glanced at the exit. Could she make a run for it? But the door was closed. Her pulse drummed in her ears. *Trapped.* If she ran, she just might never come back.

Max was standing now, his hands wrapped around an invisible golf club. Would he understand if she bolted? Or be embarrassed? Think she was crazy?

The reverend watched Max go through the elements of his swing, chin in hand, humming.

Breathe, Jade. Breathe. She focused on the reverend's credenza and his arrangement of pictures. A mountaintop scene of blue sky and white peaks freed her thoughts from the claustrophobic space of her mind.

"Is that your family?" she blurted. Max snapped his gaze from the imaginary golf tee.

The reverend did a double take between Jade and the pictures to his back. "Oh, those, yes, my wife and children." He pointed to the frame on the left. "The rest are the grandkids."

So the reverend was a regular man, a family man.

Max lowered his arms and took his seat. "Guess we didn't come here to talk about golf." He winced. "My back is really unhappy with me now."

"Sorry, Jade," the reverend said.

"No, no, it's okay." If that was the worst that happened . . . Jade relaxed her shoulders. The room opened up. The air circulated, and her heart ceased to throb.

"So how are the wedding plans coming along?" The reverend folded his hands on top of his cluttered oak desk.

"Good, good." Max shifted his position, stretching his left leg. "Jade?"

"I'm a two-witnesses-and-justice-of-the-peace kind of girl. Max's mom has done most of the planning."

"You're marrying a wise woman, Max." Reverend Girden gave her a knowing smile.

"I don't know how I deserve her."

No, it's me. I'm the lucky one.

"Haven't seen you two at church lately." The reverend got right to business.

"No, I guess we've . . ." Max shifted carefully again with a side peek at Jade. Why look at her? She didn't have an excuse. "Uh, we've been busy."

"My wife, Darnell, raves about your shop, Jade. She bought an antique grandfather clock from you."

"I remember. One of my first big spenders."

"And me on a minister's salary." He chuckled. "Darnell captured my heart the first time I saw her, and I've found it hard to deny her anything ever since. She's a good woman."

"I fell in love the first time I walked into the Blue Umbrella." Max cupped his hand over Jade's. "That old Five & Dime where I used to buy jawbreakers and ice cream now had the most beautiful woman."

"But I wasn't for sale."

The reverend rocked back in his chair, fingers clasped over his middle.

"I had to ask her to dinner to get her to even look my way." Max grinned.

Jade's eyes watered. If he only knew. The night he pushed open the Blue Umbrella's front door and asked her to dinner, the brittle bandages wrapped around her scarred heart had finally begun to fall away.

"What about you, Jade? Was it love at first sight?" The reverend peered at her.

"Me?" She tightened her fingers around the tips of Max's. "He was standing in front of Sugar Plumbs, holding a tall coffee and telling stories that made Mae Plumb belly laugh."

"Love is a wonderful thing . . . a wonderful thing. And weddings . . ." The reverend searched through his desk drawers. "Ah, here." He held up a compact black binder. "Weddings are my favorite part of the job."

"Better than funerals," Jade said, running her moist palm over her jeans.

"Not always." Reverend Girden flipped open the notebook. "We had a parishioner pass about four or five years ago of cancer. Never saw such grace and peace on a person. On hard days, I'd stop by her place just for a bit of sunshine. Even in her pain, she reflected the light of Jesus. During her funeral, for about a good thirty seconds, I was physically jealous. Mrs. Dover stood in the full, unveiled presence of Jesus. And I was stuck on earth."

Full, unveiled presence of Jesus? What was he talking about? Jade ached to ask, but when he looked at her, the flutter in her chest stole her voice and tugged her gaze to her shoes.

"This is my marrying book," he said, patting the cover, "with different ceremony and wording options."

"I don't think we want anything fancy, do we, Jade?" Max slid forward slowly, a pinch in his expression, angling to see the book.

"I just want us to be honest and sincere in what we pledge." Once, she'd fiercely loved a boy who'd promised his love *forever*. But his *forever* only lasted six months.

"Whatever you think is best, Reverend," Max said.

The reverend jotted a note. "How are you two doing otherwise? Getting along all right? Weddings can be trying on a relationship."

"We're doing well." Max squeezed her hand. "What do you think?"

"I think November fourteenth can't come soon enough." Allowing a stranger, a holy man, to probe into their relationship made Jade uncomfortable.

"Have you talked finances? Who does which chores? Where to spend holidays?"

"Max can do the finances," Jade offered. "I have my fill with the shop."

"We seem to have a good routine." Max shrugged. "When we're at her house, she cooks and I clean. At my place, I cook and she falls asleep on the couch."

The reverend laughed.

"I'm close to my brother and sister, but"—Jade glanced at Max, squeezing his fingers—"holidays aren't a big deal in my family. The Bensons' home seems to be a nice place for holidays."

The reverend rolled out his bottom lip—*I see*—and jotted a note. "What about children? Believe it or not, a lot of couples get married without talking about children. How many and when?"

Jade drew her hand away from Max's and sat stiff-backed against her chair. *Is this where it all hits the fan?* She tightened her jaw and chest, dug in her heels, and leaned against her soul's closet door.

"We've discussed children as they relate to the big picture," Max said, "but without details. I'd like children anytime, really. I'm thirty-six . . . Jade?"

"Sure." She tipped her head. *Anytime.*

"Do you have children from past relationships? Max, I know you don't, but Jade? Any ex-husbands, fiancés?"

"No. None." How was this any of his business?

"You two have discussed past relationships, hurts, and pains?" Reverend Girden's fire-blue gaze burned through her.

Jade felt exposed, and as if her Secret roll-on was completely letting her down.

"We've talked. Some." Max rubbed his hands together, resting forward with his forearms on his thighs.

"Our pasts don't matter much to us, Reverend," Jade said with a rise of confidence.

"Right," Max said. "We consider our relationship a clean slate. Who she was with before me doesn't matter."

So he *was* listening that evening she rambled on about her life beginning the day she met him and the past being more of an anchor than a revelator. It sounded so wise and philosophical, but the dozing Max had merely muttered "Mm-hm" from a subconscious state of twilight.

"Interesting." The reverend rocked back and forth in his seat. "So Jade doesn't know you've been engaged, Max?"

"Well, yes, she knows about Rice, yes." Max rubbed his thumb over hers. "Kind of hard to hide it since Rice grew up here . . . but Jade knows that relationship is ancient history now."

"How about you, Jade?"

"You mean besides grade-school crushes?" Jade laughed, flipping her hair away from her face, shrugging with her palms open. "I've been waiting all my life for Max."

Max stretched across his chair and kissed her cheek. "Thanks for finding me."

"I understand where you two are coming from, and I've seen cases where couples talk too much about their past loves and experiences, but communication is the key to a strong relationship. If I had a dollar for every couple who could solve their problems with honest, open conversation, I'd be sailing my yacht in the Caribbean. Don't be too cautious with this past thing." He shook his head, searching under the papers on his desk. "Hidden things have a way of coming to light. Ah, here it is." He flashed a gold pen.

"I'm confident in our relationship and communication, Reverend," Max said.

"Good, good." The reverend shuffled through the papers again. "I'm not usually this disorganized. Here we go." He held up a printout this time. "Your wedding is on the fourteenth; all set, ready to go. Just one thing—Max, I'm sure you're aware of the church's desire to unite men and women in marriage who are of the same faith."

Max tipped his head to one side and scratched behind his ear. "Y-yes."

"Jade, do you have a certificate of baptism confirming you've accepted the tenets of the Christian faith?"

"Certificate?" Once again, her Secret roll-on was breaking down.

"Yes. Or a letter from your pastor confirming your profession of faith."

"Reverend, just take her word. Jade's a good woman." Max patted her arm. Made her feel like the old gray mare.

"What's the name of your home church, Jade?" Reverend Girden scribbled on the found paper with his found gold pen.

"Um, it was, um, my granny's church. Prairie City Community Church in Iowa."

The reverend gazed at her from under his brow. "Have you been baptized, Jade? Made a profession of faith?"

"Formally? No. But I do believe in God, Reverend."

"I see." He closed his marrying book. "We don't like to unite people merely because they are spiritual or believe in God, but because they have the common foundation of a profession of faith in Jesus Christ."

"Reverend." Max rose to his feet. "Where are you going with this?"

"Max, I know you've professed faith in Jesus Christ as a boy, but I'd like to know where Jade stands before I unite you two in the covenant of marriage before God and the congregation. Certainly, you understand faith is an essential part of a successful marriage."

"Jade can believe whatever she wants." Max maneuvered around to the back of the chair, bending slightly forward until he could square away his back. His pain didn't seem to hinder his defense abilities. "I'm not demanding she convert."

For a long, hard moment, no one spoke. Jade perspired and shot Max a dozen mental messages. *Let's go.*

"I'm not trying to be the bad guy here, Max." Reverend Girden flipped open his Bible and handed it to Jade. "I just want Jade to know Jesus loves her. He has a destiny for her. Read verse seventeen. Yeah, there, Psalm 139."

Her voice didn't engage at first, a swell of emotion crashing over her. Clearing her throat, shifting in her chair, Jade blinked her eyes clear. "'How precious also are Your thoughts to me, O God! How great is the sum of them.'" She closed the book.

"You're always on His mind, Jade."

She nodded, a cold tear slipping down her cheek, dropping from the edge of her chin.

"Reverend." Max white-knuckled the back of his chair. "We're less than five weeks away from the wedding. I don't want you or anyone coercing Jade into a belief system just so we can get married in the church."

Reverend Girden rose, shoulders taut as he towered over his desk. "I can't ask her to make vows before God if she doesn't believe." He tapped his gold pen against the desk absently. "I need to know where she stands. Perhaps you'd be happier with a civil ceremony. Judge Anders does a fine job."

"I told you, I believe in God." Jade shot to her feet. "I do, Reverend. I attended church with my granny, attended Sunday school." She lifted a medallion from beneath the ridge of her sweater. "My Paps gave me these praying hands so I'd remember Jesus prayed for me."

"Jade, can you tell me what's in your heart? Do you know God is glad over you?"

The reverend didn't get it. God would never want her. Not if He was truly good. He couldn't possibly. Inviting her in would darken the splendor of His beauty.

"What's in my heart? That I love Maxwell Benson. That I want to spend my life with him. I can't believe how lucky I am to have found him."

Max wrapped her in his arms, kissing her cheek.

"Why not take a few classes with me, Jade? Be sure of your salvation," the reverend said.

"Jade, no, you're not required." Max shoved her chair aside and opened the door. "The Bensons founded this church. Paid to have the west wing addition. And I believe we can be married here if we want."

"Max, yes, but there is a requirement for a religious ceremony—"

Down the main sanctuary aisle, his footsteps echoing, and out to the parking lot, Max fumed. He aimed his key fob at the Mercedes like a light saber.

"Max, calm down." A sour taste swirled in her throat. "I don't mind taking classes if—"

"He's got some nerve." Max fired up the engine.

"For what? The reverend seems to think marriage is more than pomp and circumstance. Why can't he ask his questions?"

"Because he challenged our integrity."

"And you challenged his. Call it even." Light from streetlamps fell over Jade's legs as Max turned out of the parking lot, heading toward Main Street. "He's a man of the cloth. Wouldn't you check a new client's credentials, or make sure a new attorney actually passed the bar?"

"It's not the same." Max stopped at the four-way, gunned the gas, then fired across the small intersection.

"Not to you and me, maybe, but to him."

"Don't defend Reverend Girden, Jade. Are you hungry?"

"A civil ceremony is fine. I have a frozen pizza at home."

"I know, I know, but the Bensons and Mom's family, the Carpenters, have been members of First Baptist Congregation since 1890-something. It would feel cheap to not include God somehow. I'm okay with your faith. Why can't he be?"

"What you told him about me made me love you more." Her eyes welled up.

"All true, babe." He looked over at her. "I love you. Guess that's why it bothers me he's making such an issue of whether you profess faith in Jesus Christ or not." One of Whisper Hollow's two traffic lights caught Max with a red at Divine Drive and Cherish Hill. As they waited for green, Max turned to Jade and pressed his lips to her forehead. "I think I'm addicted to you."

Jade settled into the plush leather seat as the light turned green and Max eased toward the Blue Umbrella. She hung Max's confession in the secret room of her heart, and she'd visit there on the hard, blue days.

He loved her, and she was counting on him.

Four

Saturday morning, Beryl woke with a hankering for something she couldn't explain in a single word. Phantom scents and sounds from the old house lingered around her—the clatter of her mother in the kitchen frying eggs and bacon, the scent of brewing coffee and a hickory fire.

She drew the bedcovers over the pillow and padded to the bathroom. Her bones creaked in harmony with the dry, splintered floorboards.

In the bright, bare light, her complexion appeared more sallow than she remembered. And her breasts sagged under her nightgown. Turning sideways, she tried to hike them up, but they didn't stay where she shoved them. Forty short years ago, she'd been a tight-bodied flower child without one thought of ever being fifty-nine.

In her day, they believed the world wouldn't survive 1984 and 1999. Beryl drank from life's cup by the moment and never danced with regret. Then she met Harlan, fell in love against her better judgment, got married—a move that surprised even herself—and populated the globe with two kids. Then she'd married Mike and produced one more.

Pots clattered from the kitchen beneath her feet, followed by a crash. *Willow. Her child with Mike, and most likely to burn the house down one day.*

"Beryl, I'm making pancakes," Willow called up, her voice seeping through the old walls and floor.

Beryl forgot the thinness of the old house until Willow came home from school or from one of her road trips across country with friends. Willow still got her to laugh with her bit about hearing the ants' dinner table chatter.

Raided a great picnic this afternoon, Marge. Carried off a whole watermelon.

Did you hear about Frank? Bug-sprayed.

No. Poor Frank.

Fugetaboutit, he went quickly.

"Did you hear me? I said I'm making some 'cakes."

"I'm getting in the shower. I'll just have coffee."

"I'll save you some." Willow always heard but never listened.

After showering, Beryl snapped on a pair of jeans that rode low around her waist, but not like the hip-huggers she wore in the '70s. The sweater she tugged on swished loose about her waist.

She regarded her reflection before twisting her long gray hair into a braid. Today might be a good day to wander into Des Moines for a bit of clothes shopping. Or head out to the old place on Highway 117. She'd heard the house was being condemned.

Down the back stairs to the kitchen, Beryl found Willow gyrating her hips to a bass beat while flipping pancakes onto a plate.

"I'm going for a drive." Beryl lifted her keys from the hook by the kitchen door. "What's the weather like?"

"Sunny but cold. Where are you going?" Willow shot her a quick glance. "I got your 'cakes here."

"I told you only coffee." Coffee. Beryl took the travel mug from the cupboard.

"So where are you going?"

"Nowhere and everywhere."

"Fine, don't tell me."

"Now you know how I feel." Beryl sugared the coffee and snapped on the mug cap.

"And how I felt *my* whole life. Aiden and Jade too." Willow sliced the air with her batter-tipped spatula.

"So you're speaking for them now?" Beryl refused to hear another installment of Willow's you-were-never-around speech.

"Did you decide about the wedding yet?" Willow shoved the pancake plate into the oven, then leaned against the counter.

"Are you going to eat all of those yourself?" Beryl moved toward the door.

"Lincoln is coming over with some of his friends."

Beryl frowned. "Don't trash the place. Clean up when they leave."

"You're getting good at evading. Are you going to the wedding or not?"

"I don't think Rolf will let me off. It's a busy time for Midwest, and I've been on vacation a few weeks already this year." Darn doctor appointments eating up all her time. "I really need to get back to work." Beryl set her mug on the table, then fished around the back of the pantry for her Virginia Slims.

"That's your excuse. Come on, Beryl. You can do better than that."

"Who's walking her down the aisle?" If Willow said Harlan . . . Impossible. Beryl couldn't imagine that Jade and her dad had repaired their relationship. But what did she know? Certainly not that her daughter was in love and getting married.

"Aiden's walking her down the aisle." Willow started flipping the pancakes bubbling on the griddle.

Beryl tapped a cigarette out of the pack. Big brother giving her away. It made sense. Jamming the cigarette between her lips, she dug around in her purse for a pack of matches.

"Junk drawer," Willow said without looking.

Beryl pulled out the narrow drawer, found the matches by the emery board, and struck a flame. "I'll bring home supper."

Willow came around the table. Dark blonde flyaways curled about her face, and her narrow features were pink from the kitchen heat. The girl had the aura of a kite caught in a current.

"Last semester I took a government class. Snore bore, right? But then one day they showed us old news clips of the sixties, the great counterculture, and I realized something."

"What would that be?"

"For a generation who claimed to be all about peace, you sure started a lot of wars. Not with guns and bullets, but with words and ideology. With your parents, your kids. Your generation didn't bring anything together. You tore everything apart."

"What's your point?" Beryl inhaled, filling her lungs with smoke, and opened the back door to exhale. Once in a while, Willow came up with an original observation. Wrong, but original.

"Make peace with Jade, Beryl."

Five

Servers in black tie and tails passed under the crystal light of the chandelier, carrying silver trays of champagne to the Bensons' two dozen guests. In the main hall, a pianist played Chopin.

Jade sipped her chilled champagne, wondering where Max had disappeared to and wanting to be home, curled on the couch with her cold toes tucked under his knees, reading a book and playing Name That Tune with Roscoe's cacophony of snorts.

Definitely the opening bars of "Smoke on the Water."

What? You're crazy. That's the bass riff to "Brick House."

"This music makes me feel as if I should be doing a relevé or a plié." The egg-shaped Nettie Hargrove bumped up next to her. "Jade, sweetie, what's this music?"

Jade swigged her bubbly. Imagining the round-hipped Nettie at the ballet bar with her toes and knees pointed out was too much.

"It's Chopin, Nettie." June broke through a circle of guests, coming toward them.

"Chopin, Toepan, who cares? It's making me relive my worst childhood memory. Mrs. Weiner tapping her cane on the floor, insisting, 'Nettie, put down that hot dog and plié. I said *plee-ay*.'"

"You did not go to ballet with a hot dog." June punctuated her skepticism with a flick of her hand.

Jade laughed. "That would've been fun to see."

"Oh, honey child, believe me." Nettie offered Jade a half smile while working to maintain her facade. "Please, June-bug, do us all a favor. Tell that man to play some jazz or a sanguine version of the Beatles. Or Elvis. Better yet, how about 'Great Balls of Fire'? If he flips his hair like Jerry Lee and plays with his feet, I'll tip him a hundred dollars."

"Mind yourself, Nettie." June backed toward the marble and glass hall. "But I'll see what I can do."

"All right, tell me about *you*." The hot-dog-eating ballerina hooked her arm around Jade's with a force that caused her champagne to slosh around the cut-crystal flute. "The woman who stole my Max's heart. You know, he was going to be my male companion, all perfectly on the up and up, of course. Travel Europe with me. Then you came along and stole his heart." She sighed dramatically. "So goes my last hope of ever being seen with a gorgeous man."

"I can lend him to you now if you want." Jade set her champagne flute on a passing server's tray. "For a few minutes."

"What's the use?" Nettie exhaled with exaggeration. "He'll merely pine for you. I'm left to do the bidding of *that* man over there." Nettie pointed to the lean figure with a thick handlebar mustache.

"He's quite handsome," Jade said.

"Don't lie, girl. It's not Christian. With that mustache, Carmen appears confused about the era in which he lives."

If Nettie's humor cost a hundred dollars an ounce, Jade would find a way to purchase a gallon.

"Maybe I could hire him to model in my vintage shop," Jade teased. "Charge up the atmosphere a bit."

"Tell me the day and time, sugar. I'll make sure he's there."

"All right, Nettie." June Benson powered her way toward them. "Abel will play some Beatles just for you. But he's not too happy about it."

Nettie cocked her head to one side as "I Want to Hold Your Hand" rose from the hall with a distinct Chopin accent. "No, no, still makes me feel as if I should plié."

"You're impossible." June snatched a fresh flute of champagne from the passing server. "You plié, Nettie. I'll see about dessert."

"Look there, I'm being summoned." Nettie gestured toward her husband. "Off I go like a well-groomed, highly trained pet."

"I don't believe it for a moment." Jade grinned.

"Shh." Nettie pressed her finger to her lips as she wove her way through the guests, displaying a bit of her ballet grace. When she pecked her man's cheek with a kiss, he wrapped his slender arm around her shoulders.

Jade searched the room again for Max. Was he going to be gone all night?

"Is this your first Benson soiree?" A feminine voice floated over her shoulder.

Jade turned to see a sleek-haired brunette with sharp eyes. "My second. I attended the Christmas party last year."

"Ah, the coveted Benson Christmas bash. Sorry to have missed it. I was skiing in Aspen."

"And you didn't take me with you?" Jade raised her eyebrows, grinning. She liked this woman, whoever she was, with her clipped, fresh manner.

"You're funny." The woman offered her hand. "Rice McClure."

Jade hesitated as she took her hand. *Max's ex.* "Jade Fitzgerald."

"So, you're the one." Rice's broad smile fit her bold features. "Congratulations. Max is an amazing man."

"Yes, he is." Jade tapped the base of her glass, glancing around. Where *was* the man she'd snagged, by the way? "So, Rice, what do you do?"

"I'm a patent attorney at Benson Law. Just moved back from New York to head up the new patent department."

"Really?" Jade narrowed her gaze. "Well, then, congratulations to you too."

"Ah, this is news to you, isn't it? Max hasn't said much about me, has he?"

"No, he hasn't."

"Understandable. It was painful at the end. It's why I went to New York. I needed a fresh start, you know, a way to break away. For a long time, I thought we'd make it, but he was so in de—Listen to me, going on about *your* fiancé. I'm so sorry." Her voice drifted and she stared into her champagne glass as if looking for answers. "So, tell me, where did you get your wedding dress?"

"On Market Street, BoutiqueCouture." Typically all vintage, Jade decided her wedding dress must be "something new."

"I've heard fabulous things about them. How has your—"

"Rice, there you are." June broke through a circle of women all wearing black gowns. "I've been looking all over for you. I promised to show you my Paris purchases. Excuse us, Jade."

"Now? Well, okay." Rice reached around Jade and set down her flute. "Off to Paris. Say, Jade, maybe we can have lunch sometime?"

"I'm at the Blue Umbrella every day."

"I'm sure Max has your number." Rice started off, then paused, looking back at Jade. "The gown you're wearing. Is it vintage?"

"An Irene Lentz." Jade brushed the light velvet of her skirt. "She was—"

"A costume designer in Hollywood's golden age." Rice backed away, smiling, her heels leaving the rug and clicking against the hardwood. "Yeah, I know."

Jade watched June and Rice round the corner of the hall leading to the stairs. Max was in . . . what? Denial? Demand? De— What?

"Can I get you anything?" A server paused in front of Jade.

"Please, a Diet Coke would be lovely." She set her champagne flute on the tray next to Rice's, then wandered across the room to the wall of windows overlooking the valley.

Max had a right to his past secrets. Same as she. They'd agreed. It was a new day when they'd met each other. The past stayed where it belonged—behind them. Skeleton doors were locked. Chained. But Rice brought Max's past to life, flesh and bones, with a stunning smile.

"Here you go." The server handed Jade a glass with fizzing soda. "Lovely dinner, isn't it?"

"Yes on all counts." Jade held up her Diet Coke. "Thank you for this."

Sitting on the leather bench, Jade peered down to the pool deck, the wood and stone construction designed to be one with the mountainside.

White stars salted the black sky, but below the window, between the blues of the pool luminaries, five small hot orange glows burned in the blackness. Cigars.

Jade identified Max by his wounded-back silhouette, his posture angled a bit forward and to the right, his foot jutted out.

An explosion of laughter reverberated against the windowpane. Jade thought to go down and join them, but a crystal chime pinged from the front of the great room.

Rebel Benson hopped up on the stone hearth.

"Gather 'round, folks, gather 'round." He tapped his Duke Law class of 1970 ring against his flute. The Chopin music faded. The guests gathered and quieted. "Now that we've stuffed ourselves on June's famous beef Wellington and are awaiting dessert, we shall get the fun started."

He sounded like a circus ringmaster. *Ladies and gentlemen, in the center ring, we present to you the most magnificent, stupendous . . .*

Jade moved to the edge of the room, curious. Rebel defied her understanding. She liked him, sort of a larger-than-life patriarch, but she had yet to figure him out.

"Hey." A soft kiss touched her cheek. Warm, smoky breath grazed the nape of her neck.

"Where have you been?" Jade whispered.

"Outside, inhaling secondhand cigar smoke."

"Don't even try it." She peeked up at Max. "I saw you out the window, holding your own cigar, regaling your friends with a story."

"Shh, Dad's fixing to talk."

"Tonight we celebrate my son's impending doom . . ." Rebel bowed toward Max and Jade as laughter pinged around the room. Next to him, June beamed at the guests, hands clasped at her waist.

"I thought you hated smoking," Jade whispered.

"I took one puff. One." He grinned, slipping his hand around her waist. "Burl insisted."

From his makeshift stage, Rebel bantered back and forth with hecklers, most of the ribbing coming from his golf buddy, Bump Davis.

"Please don't tell me you submitted to peer pressure at thirty-six" She jabbed his ribs with her elbow. "Dork."

"Once a fraternity man—"

"Always a frat boy." Jade pillowed her head against his chest, easing against him. Her frat boy.

"Don't bust me just because you were always the good girl," he murmured in her ear.

"All right, now, back to the purpose at hand." Rebel easily took back the reins of the room. "June and I are so happy Jade has agreed to take Max off our hands." Laughter peppered Rebel's words. "With that in mind, y'all know why you're here. June made every serving of beef Wellington with her own hands, even killed the fatted calf, I believe, in honor of tonight and our son.

So let's get going. Be generous. It's not every day a man gets to partake of June Benson's cooking. I should know."

"Can't afford to be generous in case there's a doctor bill, Reb. Last time I had June's beef Wellington—"

"Tom Floyd"—June pressed her hand to her flushed cheek, smiling—"don't shame me now."

"Exactly, June-bug. An insult adds an extra zero to your most generous gift, Tom, my Scrooge friend," Rebel said. "And that's *after* the comma."

"What insult? I got the doctor bill to prove it." Tom was a short, balding man with round shoulders, a round chin, and a round belly.

The guests erupted and Jade watched June roll with the merriment, though Jade guessed she didn't really find the moment funny.

Max bent to Jade's ear. "Tom owns the Floyd Banking Association."

"Max, I don't get it. What's going on?"

"Watch and see."

"For the rest of our esteemed guests . . ." Rebel gazed around the room. Someone had handed him a cigar and he held it between his fingers, unlit. "I've been to these same parties for your children and grandchildren." He jammed the cigar between his lips and puffed out his belly. "Don't think I haven't kept records of my own donations over the years."

"We wouldn't expect anything less of you." A masculine quip fired from the back of the great room.

"Keep it up, Harv." Rebel jabbed the air with the cigar. "You owe me since I fixed your grandson's mess."

"All taken care of, Reb." A white envelope appeared above the guests' heads.

"June, where's the basket?"

She stepped up on the hearth. Rebel steadied her. "There are two baskets on the sideboard in the front hall. One for your gift, another for notes of encouragement."

"There you go." Rebel wrapped up her instructions. "Don't forget the notes, folks. I know the kids will appreciate all your fine wisdom and advice. And Bump, don't write 'your wife is always right,' because we know how well that philosophy has worked for you."

Laughter exploded, filling up the high ceilinged room.

"I still say my advice is good." Bump moved toward the hall, pausing in front of Max and Jade. "And one of these days, I'll prove it."

Max's chest rumbled against Jade's back. "In the meantime, what do I do, Bump?"

The silver-haired man winked at Jade. "Let her think she's always right."

Rebel hopped off the hearth. Couples huddled, laughing and murmuring, then filed into the hall.

"I met Rice," Jade said, turning to face Max.

"Oh?" His grip around her waist slacked. "She missed dinner. I wasn't sure if she was coming."

"Well, she did. You never said she was a lawyer, or that she moved back to Tennessee to work at Benson Law."

"Dad wanted a patent department." Max kissed her forehead. "He called Rice and invited her down. I found out a week before she walked into the office."

Couples breezed by them, waving white envelopes and smiling. Jade smiled back. What was it Rebel said they were doing? Her mind had been wandering, thinking about her conversation with Rice, not really listening to Rebel's speech. Must be taking a collection for a Benson charity. They used every occasion to raise money.

Back to Max. "She said your relationship was hard at the end. Something about hoping it'd work out."

"Rice says a lot of things." Max affirmed Jade by pulling her closer. "This is our night, Jade, and I don't want to talk about Rice. Now, or ever. Our relationship is over, buried in the past. What matters is you and me"—he touched her lips with his thumb—"and new beginnings."

"Max. Son, over here," Rebel beckoned.

Max lifted his lips from Jade's and peeked across the room. "Shoot, he's with Dickson Waters. Potential client."

"Work never ends, does it?" Jade commented. The slender, bearded man with Rebel wore a vintage Pierre Cardin tuxedo. "See if he wants to sell his tux."

"Want him to take it off so you can carry it home?"

"Oh, could you do that for me? Thanks." Jade kissed his cheek and shoved him toward his dad and the client.

"Careful, babe. My back." Max covered his lower back with his broad hand.

Jade winced. Three trips to the physical therapist hadn't done much for the pain. When Jade asked him about the pain meds, he changed the subject.

Over by the kitchen, Rice talked with June, patting her shoulders while nodding, her lips forming short phrases. After a moment, June hugged her, then slipped inside the kitchen.

Well, enough of this wing-ding. Jade was ready to go home. The lovely evening and gracious company no longer distracted her from the pinch of her dress's waistband. She was ready for baggy pajamas and an old movie on TMC.

Max appeared to be finishing up with his father and vintage-tux man. Jade decided to deposit her glass in the kitchen and tap his shoulder as she passed. Their signal for "time to go."

"Jade, over here." An inebriated man propped against the wall by the kitchen door *pssst*-ed her. Sloppy and slow, he tapped a blank check. "I don't have a wife to tell me what to do. What do you think? One, two? Five?"

Jade peeked at the check. "I can't tell you how much to give." She glanced around. "Maybe one of your friends can help you . . . what charity is this for anyway?" She didn't bring her checkbook, but she'd bring a check around tomorrow.

"Come on, Jade, don't be shy. This isn't for charity. You're why we're all here in monkey suits listening to parlor music. Five? Is that good? Y'all need a house, don't you? Can't live in his bachelor condo forever. There's no place for kids." The man jammed his hand inside his tuxedo jacket. "Do you got a pen?"

"What do you mean, I'm why you're all here?"

"Ah, here it is." The man lifted a ballpoint from his side pocket. Jade watched as he wrote *five thousand* in a large, loopy script. "For you and Max. Seed money."

"Five thousand?" she said, the words coming out more loudly than she intended. "Dollars?" Her words billowed, stopping all commotion. "For Max and me?"

"Should it be more?" The man eyed her with a cloudy gaze before pointing with his pen across the room. "Bump Davis, don't cheat the kids now."

"You worry about yourself, Taylor."

"Wait, everyone, please. Stop!" Jade charged into the middle of the room. "Is this why you came here tonight? To give us money?"

"Babe . . ." Max gently tugged her from the middle of the room, whispering in her ear, "It's okay."

"No, it's not." Heat rolled down her neck, across her torso. "Put your checkbooks and wallets away, please."

"Jade, sugar, settle down." Rebel chewed on the tip of his unlit stogie. "This is our tradition for our kids and grandkids."

"Whose tradition, Rebel? Yours? Bump's? Tom and Taylor's? Nettie's?" The burn on her face intensified, and she began to tremble. "Certainly not mine."

"Jade." Max's fingers bit into her flesh. "Shh."

He walked her to the edge of the great room and said in a low voice, "These people are my parents' friends. My friends, soon to be yours. Not to mention, your business demographic."

"This is humiliating, Max." Her whisper was too loud. "Do they think I expected this? Wanted it? We don't need their hard-earned money. I saw your last bonus check, and the shop is holding its own. We don't want for anything."

"It's not about how well we're doing or not doing. It's about tradition. My parents and their friends have been doing this for their children since I was a kid. I'm not the first recipient. In fact, I'm one of the last."

"So that man Tom, the Scrooge, who has to add an extra zero after the comma, has to give us at least a thousand dollars? That's absurd."

"A thousand? More like ten thousand," Max said, shaking his head, smiling. "Tom's the most generous."

"Ten thousand dollars?" Hot embers burned between Jade's ribs, and without looking, she could sense the guests' curious stares. "I don't even know these people."

"But I do." Max's tight-lipped response lacked patience.

"I can't do this, Max. It's embarrassing. These people are my clients and customers. How can I look them in the eye after this? I'll feel as if they think I'm charging prices based on the size of their wallets. Or as if I owe them something. Money changes relationships and people. Trust me, I know. Max, we're fine without being beholden to tens of thousands of dollars from the Whisper Hollow elite."

Jade was a bit of a chip off her mama's shoulder. She had no desire for things, or wealth, or the attached strings.

The kitchen door burst open with a wide swing and June's petite form created an angular silhouette in the block of light falling on the imported wool rug.

"Jade." June jerked her into the kitchen, away from the guests. "Would you please be quiet? Who do you think you are? Coming into our home and insulting our friends."

"I'm not insulting anyone." Jade's pulse thickened in her veins. "But I'm trying not to be indebted to half the town. This is ridiculous, coercing people into giving Max and me money just because you served homemade beef Wellington."

"It's not the beef Wellington, Jade. It's the tradition, the friendships, how we do things in the Hollow. Something you know nothing about."

"Mom." Max stepped between them.

"Rebel and I have given thousands of dollars to *their* children and grandchildren." June pointed toward the door. "Tonight is our night, our season to celebrate our only son's wedding with them. Then you come along, and—"

"Calm down, Mom. She didn't know."

"Don't speak as if I'm not here, Max." Jade glowered at him. "June, the Hollow is my town too. And this is my wedding."

June closed her eyes, inhaling deep. "—and you stand there, Jade, in all your vintage shop glory and demand they put away their checkbooks, insisting their money isn't good enough for you."

"I never said their money wasn't good enough." Tears washed her eyes and she shivered a bit from the confrontation despite the warmth of the kitchen.

"Your actions spoke loud and clear." June trembled as she clenched her hands into fists. "In the twenty years we've been celebrating in this way, no one has ever protested our generosity. Not even the Pryor girl from up the mountain, the one Clyde Jones' boy married."

"All right, Mom, enough, we get it. Don't make more out of it than it is. At least she had the courage to stand up for her convictions. Your friends"—Max motioned toward the great room—"will understand. Half of them wish they had her boldness."

"*Our* friends, Max?" She crossed her hands in the center of her chest. "Yours too. And will they understand? I can just imagine the conversations driving home tonight, while lying in bed, in the morning over coffee." She wagged her finger at him. "You're partly to blame. Why didn't you tell her?"

"I don't know . . ." He reached for Jade's hand. "Didn't seem like such a big deal."

Jade tightened her fingers around his when she caught the spark in June's eyes.

"Big *deal*?" She punched "big" and "deal" with a one, two of her lips and tongue. "How could you not know it was a big deal? This was a dinner party, in your honor." June deflated and turned away, the chiffon skirt of her wine-colored gown whirling a half second behind. She pressed one hand to her forehead, another against the kitchen island.

"Mom." Max stretched his hand to her shoulder, and the movement made him moan and wince.

"Max." June faced him, her pink-ringed eyes dark with concern. "Your back? Still?"

"Yeah, Mom, still."

June pinched her lips into a thin, pale line. "Jade, can you give us a moment?"

"Mom, no, she doesn't need to leave."

"I need to speak to you alone."

A server smashed through the dining room side door. "Mrs. Benson, dessert is ready and the guests are leaving."

"Oh, shoot." She upbraided Jade with a single glare. "Serve those who remain. Freeze the rest. Now, Jade, please."

"Mom," Max protested, hands on the island as he gently stretched his left leg.

"Max, I'll get our things." Jade brushed her normal sense of self.

As the kitchen door closed behind her, Jade collapsed against the wall. Except for a faithful few guests, the great room echoed with clicking glasses and silverware as the servers cleaned up. Trays of chocolate mousse remained untouched.

Jade had ruined June's evening without intent. How could she make it right without taking their friends' money? Ever since the first Christmas after Daddy left, she wondered if she'd ever resolve her feelings about Mama signing them up for charity gifts at school.

"Aiden and Jade Fitzgerald," Mr. Ellison called over the squealing loudspeaker at the end of the school Christmas pageant. "Here are your Christmas gifts from the Salvation Army."

Her classmates' snickers seeped out through hand-covered lips and burned Jade's skin.

Jade glanced at the dark door haloed by the kitchen light. What was June saying to Max in there? *Dump that girl.* Jade's nerves twitched. Her track record with mothers was less than stellar.

Jade had tried to erase the twenty-year-old Christmas memory, but it had found a permanent place in the front of her soul, pulled up a comfy chair, and ordered a tall latte.

She and Aiden had been the only ones in the whole school who received charity presents that year—and for three years after.

Jade pressed her hand over her middle. Miserable memory. She wanted to go home.

"Caught you off guard, did we?" Rebel walked over and stood beside her.

"A bit." Jade stood straight, gathering her composure, putting elementary school behind her, scraping together her normal sense of self.

"Get used to it." He inhaled from his unlit cigar and blew a fake stream of smoke over Jade's head. "I'm sure it won't be the last."

Six

The conversation between Max and Jade on the short ride from the Bensons' to the Blue Umbrella faltered.

"I'm sorry, Max, about the money," Jade said absently, staring out the passenger window. Max had exited the kitchen, after talking to his mom, stiff and closed.

"So you've said."

"Your mom—"

"Forget it." Wincing, Max shifted sideways in his seat, gripping the steering wheel. "Oh, man, pain shooting down my leg." He popped the wheel with his palm.

"Max, aren't you taking the pain pills?"

"Mom still has them." Another moan pinched his expression. He barely made the turn down the alley behind the Blue Umbrella.

"Why?" Jade sat forward, away from the warm leather seat. Max had fired up the seat heaters to relieve the leathery chill and soothe his back.

"I'm fine, Jade, just need to keep working with the physical therapist." Max slowed at the Blue Umbrella's delivery door and shifted into Park, leaving the engine running. He jerked the bow out of his tie.

"You're not coming up?" Jade's chilled fingers gripped her pocketbook.

"I have an early appointment with a client." He shifted in his seat again, his face tight, one hand squeezing his leg.

Jade popped open her door and gathered her skirt, moving with hesitation. "Max, if you—" She hated being here, feeling isolated and on the outside.

"Jade, don't push. You do that sometimes, you know?" He sighed, rubbing his forehead with his fingers.

Out of the blue, it happened. The dormant sensation of dread awakened, possessing her from the inside out. The light of her emotions flickered, trying to hang on, before a whisper of hopelessness puffed it out.

Jade flinched, straining her shoulders, squirming to stay above the pool of darkness, holding on to her bag as an anchor. "Please, Max. Stay." Her fingers glided over the skin of her neck. She hadn't worn Paps' praying hands tonight.

"Jade, I need to think. I have a lot on my mind, never mind this pain." He snapped his gaze to her face. "Why don't you want the money?"

"Please." She gazed in the opposite direction. "Come up for a minute or two." Her rapid heartbeat stole her breath, and her request sounded weak and needy, clinging. "I won't be able to sleep otherwise."

"Won't sleep? What are you talking about?"

"Nothing." Trembling, she forced herself out of the car.

"I'll call you later."

Jade stooped to see inside the car. "Max, if you're going to break it off with me, do it now." Cold vibrations surged through her veins like an electric pulse, increasing in intensity as she waited, exposed. She tried to surface her thoughts from the blinding deep by searching for a lifeline of happy emotions—like the feel of snuggling between clean sheets, the security of sinking into a mound of pillows, or the hope of cradling Granny's tattered old Bible to her chest.

"Sheesh, Jade." Max thumped the gear shift with the flat of his hand. "I'm not going to break up with you. You think I'm that shallow?"

"You smoked a cigar tonight, something you hate, because a frat bro teased you. How much more power does your mother have? I have no idea what she told you, Max, but it must be pretty bad for you to barely speak to me on the ride home."

A stream of cool mountain air threaded down from the top of Eventide Ridge, and as quickly as the dark panic hit, Jade's jitters and spiking sensations began to ebb.

"Mom is . . ." He shook his head. "Mom. She worries. Sees and believes what she wants." Max leaned against the headrest and peered at Jade. "Don't worry; she doesn't have that much power over me. I'm tired, irritated, in pain, and need some space. Is that all right?"

"Then why do I feel like the enemy?"

"Jade, you're not the—"

"Good night, Max." She clapped the car door shut. No, she wasn't the enemy. But did June realize it? Jade had been on this ride before—the girlfriend caught between mother and son. Maybe she should wake up, see the signs, and be the first to walk away.

Through the Blue Umbrella's storeroom and up the loft stairs, Jade's heart ached as Max's high-octane engine revved down Main Street.

Five large scoops of vanilla. No, six ought to do it. Jade scooped another ball of Breyer's from the carton and dropped it . . .

On the floor. Nice.

She grabbed the dish towel hanging from the oven handle and swiped the cold blob into the sink. Turning on the hot water, she melted it down the drain and once again scooped vanilla from the carton. This time into the blender.

Next, a cup of milk. Maybe a dash more. Finally, chocolate syrup. Jade squeezed the Hershey's bottle over the concoction until syrup ran down the sides of the blender jar.

Slapping on the lid, Jade mashed the Liquefy button. The KitchenAid motor grunted as the blades struggled through the wad of ice cream. Maybe six scoops was a bit much.

At one a.m. she'd accepted that she couldn't sleep. The events of the evening ran through her head like high-pitched munchkins from Oz. The dinner party, meeting Rice, the money, June's reaction, Max's sudden silence. And her bout with panic.

She'd gotten out of bed to draw a hot bath when she was hit with an overwhelming craving for a chocolate shake. When she was a girl, her daddy sometimes drove her to the Dairy Queen, just the two of them, until . . .

Jade straightened her pajama pants, tugging the hem over her heels, and pushed the Stir button.

If Froggers had been open, she'd have hooked Roscoe to his leash and jogged over to Laurel Park—PJs and all—and ordered an extra-large double chocolate shake with whipped cream. But they closed at nine in the fall.

Her own mixture would have to do, and so far, the blender contents swirled together nicely. Jade's tongue buzzed with anticipation. She cut the motor and tiptoed for the old-fashioned soda fountain glasses she kept in the cupboard.

Grabbing a long spoon and a handful of treats for Roscoe, Jade wandered into the living room, dropping to her 1930s beige channel back sofa.

The first drink of her shake tasted creamy and sweet. Just the right amount of chocolate and ice cream. Roscoe sat patiently at her feet. Jade tossed him a meaty bone, setting her heel on the low cherry coffee table.

But the soul-drink didn't cool her hurt or settle her thoughts. She debated calling Max, yet what if that didn't go well? What if he didn't confess the reassurance she longed for from him? His grumpiness had to be the back pain, and maybe a response to whatever meddling thing June said to him in the kitchen. Of course, making a scene out of the gift money didn't help. She'd explain tomorrow. To Max. Apologize to June.

Jade glanced at her cell phone, wanting company. She could call Daphne or Margot. Wake them up. Margot, the dentist, would be asleep at this hour, but she'd hop out of bed and drive up to the Hollow with more chocolate just to talk it all out.

Daphne, the psychiatrist, also asleep, would chat with Jade incoherently, rattling off solutions. Probably tell her, "Stop eating chocolate, go to bed, and be at my office by ten a.m."

Jade tossed Roscoe another dog bone, deciding not to call her college friends. She didn't have the energy to explain. So at the wee hour of one-fifteen, the only sound in the loft's still atmosphere was the crunch of Roscoe's munching.

Jade romanced her milkshake for a few minutes, then reached for Granny's Bible. Closing her eyes, she cradled it against her chest.

What was the prayer Granny always prayed? Grant to her . . . wisdom and revelation . . . something, something of You. Roots and love. She knew the words were from Scripture, but she couldn't remember where.

And Paps. He prayed for Jade to have praying hands. *Oh Paps, you died before teaching me.*

The Book was comforting and solid in her arms. She liked holding it. A longing for home, for Paps and Granny, colored her emotions. Jade snatched her cell phone from the end table and hit the number four on her keypad.

"What are you doing awake?" The voice on the other end was slow and sleepy.

"Wow, what are you doing in bed already?" The milkshake spoon clanked against the side of the glass.

"Catching up on sleep. Got to do it every once in a while. What's up?" Willow's voice gained energy. Jade needed to hear her sister, to care for someone other than herself for a moment.

"Are you with Linc?"

"Now or in general?"

"Whichever." Jade tipped up the glass for a gulp.

"In general, yes. At the moment, no."

"Willow, be careful. I'm not sure it's wise to—"

"*Mo-om*, I *am* being careful."

"Don't 'mom' me. Someone has to keep you in line. So are you being careful with your body *and* your heart?"

"It's just a fling, Jade."

"And that changes your answer in what way? You've been *flinging* a lot lately, Willow."

"While I still got something to fling." She laughed. "That was a joke, big sister, a joke. Enough snooping into my life. What are you doing awake, and why are you calling me?"

"Just am." Jade set the glass on the end table coaster, then cuddled a throw pillow.

"Vintage shop stress?"

"No, more like mother-in-law stress." Jade ran the pillow's fringe through her fingers. "Fiancé stress."

"Ooo, dish."

"Wills, I—" Jade slid to the edge of the sofa, tossing the pillow aside. "I sorta felt panicky again."

"Sorta? Did you have a panic attack? Get a text message from one? What?"

"Your compassion moves me. It's scary, Wills." Her sister's flippancy reminded Jade the panic was only a shadow. She was fine . . . just fine.

"Why don't you talk to Daphne, Jade? Can't she prescribe a good drug?"

"I don't want drugs." Jade ran her fingers through her hair. "I thought I was past this."

"You are, you just had a bad moment. Don't wrap your life around it. Sheesh, if I got all bent every time I had a bad day, I'd be a living pretzel."

Jade laughed. Willow had a way of throwing her a lifeline, adorned with gold charms and white lights, and perhaps a fuzzy pink boa or two.

"I made a chocolate milkshake." Jade had created her own type of lifeline.

Willow's laugh went down smooth for Jade. "There you go, the best comfort food on earth. Beryl sent me to get her one the other day. In fact, the day she got your invite."

"So she got it. What's she going to do?"

"You tell me, Sherlock. She acted weird, hinted at an issue between you two, then clammed up like always. Like you do."

"Is she coming?"

"She's not sure you want her to come, Jade." A *crack-pop* sounded in Jade's ear, followed by a fizzy, slurpy sip.

"I sent the invitation, didn't I?" Jade reached for her milkshake and took a deep drink.

"Do you want her to come? Really?"

"What I want is for you and Aiden to be here, and Granny. Do you think she would've liked Max?"

"She'd love any man you loved. Hey, I took a break from school, so I'm thinking about coming down a few weeks early, and—"

"Willow, you had a scholarship and your dad was paying for the rest. Why aren't you in school?"

"It's boring, Jade."

"Boring? Get over yourself, Wills. People should be so *bored* as you." A light rapping sounded through the loft. Jade glanced at Roscoe. He remained asleep in the narrow space between the coffee table and the sofa, so she went back to her conversation. "You're the smartest of us all, and look at you. Wasting time. Go back to school."

"Are you sure you're not my mom instead of Beryl?"

"Technically, yes, but—" The rapping echoed again, louder this time. Roscoe bounded to his feet with a low grumble.

"Jade?" Max's muffled voice seeped through the door. Roscoe trotted across the loft, wagging his tail.

"Max?" She jumped over the coffee table, phone still to her ear, her bare feet thudding against the floor.

"Hey," he said when she opened the door.

"Willow, call you later."

"Have fun. Say hi to Max for me."

Jade clapped her phone shut. "Willow says hello."

"Hello to Willow." He'd worn jeans and a cotton pullover under his tan barn coat. His blue eyes were clear with repentance. "I'm better now—"

She lunged into his arms. He *oomphed* as she knocked him into the wall. "I'm sorry, so sorry."

"Careful," he managed to say before her lips covered his.

"I didn't mean to . . ." Her eyes watered.

"Me neither." He pulled her against him. "I'm sorry too."

"It's just that when I was a kid, my mama put Aiden and me on a charity list—"

"Hey, it's okay. The past is the past, right?"

"Yeah, the past is the past," Jade echoed.

"We can give the money away if you want."

She held his face in her hands. "Want a chocolate shake?"

"Best offer I've had all night." He stepped into the loft, kicking the door closed with his foot.

Seven

On the corner of Madison and Washington, the Midwest Parcel offices sat in the shade of towering silos. Beryl parked and cut the engine of her '82 Corolla.

The fall air, scented with grain and dying leaves, had grown colder since sunrise. Taking the familiar walk to the front door, Beryl's middle fluttered. *It'll be good to return to work.*

Rolf Lundy motioned for her to come in when she tapped on the glass pane of his door and waved.

"To what do I owe this privilege?"

"Well . . ." Beryl took the wooden chair across from his desk. "I'm ready to be behind the wheel again."

Rolf's light faded. "Beryl, all the routes are taken. I had to fill—"

"I'm a senior teamster, Rolf. You can't take away my job while I'm on vacation."

"Don't you mean a leave? I know the rules, Beryl. Shoot, I hired you."

"Like you'll ever let me forget." After Harlan left, Beryl had been desperate for a job. Thirty-eight and living back home with Paps and Mother with an eight- and nine-year-old. She almost went crazy with domesticity until she ran into Rolf at The Tavern one night.

She begged him for a job. Flirted and tempted. One all-night with him was worth the price of her freedom.

"I love the I-80 corridor to Chicago," she said. "But I understand that route might have been reassigned."

"Dr. Meadows won't release you to drive, Beryl."

"You've talked to him?" Her shoulders slumped as she gazed at her feet. She'd been so pushy and cocky, coming in here, all ready to work. But Rolf knew all along.

"You mean he didn't tell you?" Rolf sat on the edge of his desk.

"Maybe. I'd sort of hoped he hadn't told you. I only fainted a few times, Rolf."

"I can't let you drive, Beryl. Not with lives on the line. But I can keep you in the office, working administration. Mindy goes on maternity leave in a few weeks."

"No." She'd rather be on the disability list. Besides, "You remember when I broke my leg and worked a few weeks in the office?"

Rolf flicked his hand dismissively. "Doris recovered fine from the stapler injury. Beryl, let me put in your retirement papers. Let's do it up right. Enjoy what you've worked so hard for."

And what would that be? After twenty-one years on the job, three kids, and four husbands, what did she have to show? A worn-out Toyota and her parents' old farmstead. "No thanks, Rolf. I'm not ready to retire yet."

"Where's the Beryl who used to tick me off when she requested leave for three or four months so she could travel with a carnival or go on the road with her musician husband?"

"Grown up, finally. A bit wiser for her troubles. Gig squandered half my pension on his so-called *music.* I'm just now back to where I was when I met him."

"Ah, so loving a music man ain't always what it's supposed to be?" A laugh drifted behind his quote.

"Thank you for that bit of insight, Steve Perry and Journey. Since when did you start quoting song lyrics? Look, Rolf, I like my routine and steady job. The mundane has lost its chains. Shoot, if they tear down the BP at the I-80 Newton exit, I won't be able to sleep for a week."

Rolf regarded her for a moment, resolve in his gray gaze. Beryl released the tension in her back and shoulders, reclining against the chair's spindles.

"What's this I hear about Jade getting married? Congratulations. You must be thrilled. Are you looking forward to the wedding?"

"To be honest, I was looking forward to getting back to work." Beryl rose, hitching her bag over her shoulder. He didn't have to paint with such bright colors. "Is Sharon here? Thought we'd go for some lunch."

"She's around. Beryl—"

"I'll let you know when Dr. Meadows releases me to drive again."

"Have a good lunch."

Beryl found Sharon out back on the smokers' porch. Sliding on top of the picnic table, she dropped her bag to the bench seat.

"Let me bum one of those."

Sharon exhaled a stream of smoke and passed Beryl a pack of Marlboro Lights. "Aren't you supposed to be quitting?"

"I did. From around eight a.m. till now. What is it, noon?"

Sharon flicked her ashes in her soda can. "Rolf said the doctor wouldn't release you to drive."

"Not yet. You want to go to Goldie's for lunch?"

"Sounds good." Sharon doused her cigarette in the last of her drink. "I hear Jade's getting married."

"Was it in the paper or something?" Was Beryl the last to know?

"My son heard from Willow." Sharon tossed her soda can in the trash by the porch post. "You're going to the wedding, aren't you?"

"I'd hoped to be back to driving by then."

"Listen . . ." Sharon scooted in next to her. "Don't hate me for this, but you've been stubborn about her long enough. Beryl, look at your life. Is this what you want?"

"She's the one being stubborn." The cigarette tip burned and crackled as Beryl took a drag.

"From where I sit, you've been pretty stubborn too."

"I thought she'd grow out of it."

"Maybe she thought the same about you." Sharon pulled her cell phone from her pocket. "If we're going to lunch, let's go now. Goldie's fills up so quick."

Beryl picked up her bag, stamping out her cigarette in the glass tray. "I'm not even sure she wants me to come. Too much water under the bridge." And a whitewater rapid of memories.

Sharon stepped off the porch. "Come by the house tonight. I'll loan you my canoe."

~

September 1992

Beryl sat with her knees against her chest on the fading summer green Iowan burial mound that snaked along the line between Mother's backyard and Paps' cornfield.

The prairie breeze, woven with a bric-a-brac fragrance of warm grass and moist soil, tangoed with her loose hair. If she looked down, Beryl could catch the red reflection of the setting sun in her golden strands.

Tonight was her last night. Hallelujah and pass the peace pipe. Maybe she could convince Jade to braid her hair. *One, two, three, right, left, middle.*

"Aiden said you wanted to see me."

Twelve-year-old Jade stood next to her in shorts and a top, her bare feet tanned with play-day dirt. Wild wisps of her walnut-colored hair danced around her face and over her head, freed from her untidy ponytail. Beryl patted the ground. "Nothing like a summer night on the Iowa prairie."

"Yep." Jade dropped to the ground, body posture as stiff as her tone.

"I'm leaving in the morning." Beryl closed her eyes and tipped her nose toward the breeze, feeling the light of sunset on her skin.

"All of us, or just you?"

"Carlisle called and needs a driver for her carnival truck until the end of the season. You remember Carlisle, don't you?"

"The lady with the black-and-white hair and spooky eyes."

"Spooky? Carlisle will like that one when I tell her." Friends since her Haight-Ashbury days, Carlisle visited Beryl on the "Fitz Farm" every year with her traveling band of beatniks and hippies. They pitched tents in the backyard until Harlan, when he was around, blew up and tossed them off *his* land. Such a big deal because Jade caught Mama's friend Eclipse naked, showering outside.

"You have a job at Midwest Parcel." Jade sounded so prissy and adult, so much like Mother.

"I'm taking a two-month leave."

"Then Aiden and I are going to see Dad in Washington. And Willow? Is she going with you? She's only two, so you can't leave her—"

"I know how old she is, Jade." Beryl glanced at her through the blowing strands of her hair. How she loved the prairie wind. "She's staying here, with Granny. I need you to help out."

"I ain't her mother. Where's Mike?"

"Don't be smart. If Mike comes 'round here for Willow, call the police. He'll take her, and I'll never see her again."

"Like you'd care. If he comes around, I'll give him Willow." Jade shot Beryl an optic fireball. "Then I'll go live with my dad." Her words were laced with venom.

Jade, Jade, Jade. Why did she push and push? Harlan didn't want his kids invading his busy, snooty, political Washington life. His silence spoke a thousand words. Maybe Beryl *should* let Jade call her dad, hear how truly uninterested he was in her. In Aiden.

"I know you're upset about your dad, but he's got a very busy life. It doesn't mean he doesn't love you, Jade-o." It was a lie, but for the good of the cause. "Now, listen. There's diapers for Willow in the crawl space between your room and the attic stairs. And in my top dresser drawer, there's a wallet with three hundred dollars. Use it on the extra stuff you guys need. Don't spend it all on pop and movies. If you start your period, there are pads in the bottom of my closet."

"Mama." Jade jerked up clumps of grass.

"Maybe you don't understand, but trust me, baby. If I keep hanging around here, I'll go mad. I need space, get my head on straight, soothe my soul from the damage done by that rancid Mike Ayers."

"He's gone because of you, same as Daddy." Jade plucked more grass, digging her thumbnail into the dirt.

"It may seem that way to you, but it takes two people to make or break a marriage."

"My friends' parents stay married. How come it's so hard for you?"

"Yeah, you want me to be like all the other kids' parents? Hm? You and Aiden have it pretty easy. Are your friends allowed to go to bed whenever they want? Play outside until the sun is down, have liberty to visit their friends whenever? Not clean their plates at dinner? Or do they get yelled at, grounded, get a whipping or two? As long as you and Aiden act responsible, you guys are free to come and go."

"Except when you want me to babysit Willow so you can go off and do whatever you want. Besides, I'm not supposed to get my way. I'm twelve. You're supposed to ground me when I'm bad, stay home to take care of us."

"Yeah? Tell your little friend Rachel's mother to keep her parenting advice to herself." Beryl popped open her cigarette case.

"At least she's still married to her first husband and takes care of her kids."

"Do you *want* to be grounded, Jade?" Beryl shook the match, extinguishing the tiny flame, and exhaled a stream of smoke. "Cause we can arrange that if you want. I'm just saying—"

"I'm not watching Willow. Take her with you. Mr. Wimple said Rachel and I could help out at his country store."

"You can work in the store on Saturdays or after school, but be back by the time Mother gets home. She'll be tired from working. Jade, I know it seems like the sky is falling—after all, you *are* twelve. But you can do this. Aiden will help out, and he's already volunteered to take care of the yard and garbage. You two get along, no fighting."

God didn't make sons much better than Aiden. Thirteen going on twenty-five. Harlan didn't know what he was missing by ignoring that boy.

"If you're not here, I don't have to mind you."

Beryl spit out a laugh. She tapped her ashes into the wind, watched the floating flecks with orange edges twisting then fading as they fell to the grass.

"I reckon you don't, but don't think Granny will put up with much. She still believes in that 'spare the rod, spoil the child' crap."

"Yeah? Seems it didn't work so great on you."

Let her be. She's young; she'll learn. Beryl let the silence defuse the atmosphere. For a long three or four minutes, only the wind spoke, whistling through corn silk and evergreen leaves.

Finally, Jade gathered the grass she'd been plucking, held up her palm, and let the blades blow into Beryl's hair and face. "You're so selfish."

"Back at you, Jade-o."

The girl jumped up and ran toward the barn.

"I'll write," Beryl hollered. "And call."

"Don't bother. We won't answer."

Eight

"What do you think?"

"I think it's . . . empty." Jade turned a small circle in the hollow, dark, and musty River Street space with a view of Coolidge Park. The floor was cement. The open ceiling's steel beams stretched toward the water-damaged, cracked plaster walls. "And it would need a lot of work."

One thing she loved about her shop in Whisper Hollow was it required very little renovation. Her biggest expense was refinishing the wood and painting the walls.

She'd considered several downtown properties when she began the journey of opening her own place. But she'd wanted to live in Whisper Hollow. Discovering the availability of the Five & Dime was a divine kiss on her dream.

"Where's your imagination, Jade? Picture it finished, painted, filled with your tasteful inventory."

"June, what's going on? I thought we came to have lunch at Aretha Frankenstein's."

"Nothing's going on." June pulled together the edges of her scarlet pea coat and crossed her arms. "I think this would be a great space for a second shop. Blue Umbrella Two."

"Blue Umbrella Two?"

"You're going to be a Benson, Jade. You need to learn to think big, think corporate. Legacy. Tradition."

Despite heavy tourist traffic up in the Hollow today—the fall colors were spectacular—Jade had closed up shop when June called last minute for a lunch date. She'd hoped to make amends for her dinner party blunder. What she didn't want to do was property shop.

The heels of June's black boots scraped the floor as she walked. The flare hem of her gray slacks almost touched the cement. "I like this. It feels good."

"But I'm not interested in a Blue Umbrella Two." In fact, Jade had never mentioned expanding to anyone except—

"Well?" Sean Dunham, of Dunham Development, entered through the glass and metal front door. "Jade, what do you think?"

"I think it's nice." Big mouth. Teach her to trust a father-like stranger. "But not for me."

"She's being stubborn, Sean." June crossed over to him, shaking her head.

"Actually, I'm being practical." In the spring, Jade had met the Chattanooga developer, a longtime friend of the Bensons, at a charity cookout. Over grilled Johnsonville brats, Sean coaxed her into dreaming about a second shop.

"I suppose practical is wise." Sean shoved his suit coat back, settling his hands on his belt. "But this is a great location at a great price. The space is perfect for vintage retail. Right on the Tennessee, across from Coolidge Park, in the heart of the downtown revival and art district." Sean arched his silver eyebrows.

"I appreciate you thinking of me, Sean, but I'm getting married in three weeks and Blue Umbrella *One* is barely making money. I couldn't afford this place even if I was desperate for a Blue Umbrella Two."

"Rebel and I are thinking of investing in your business, Jade."

"I see." Was June testing her? If she wouldn't accept their friends' money, would she accept theirs?

"No pressure, Jade, but just to make you aware, I have several bids on this space." The heels of Sean's loafers echoed among the beams as he walked.

"I think you should do what you have to do, Sean." She tried not to feel set up, but she did.

"Tell you what, Sean." June brushed her hand against his sleeve. "Send the details over to the office. Reb will have Lance Olin take a look and advise Jade."

"I'll do it." Sean turned to Jade. "What do you say?"

She liked to think she learned from her mistakes. With a nod, she said, "Send it on over." She'd worry about saying no later.

"Good." June popped her hands together, looking as if she'd won. "Now let's eat. Sean, we're going to Aretha Frankenstein's. Care to join us?"

"My mouth is watering for one of their 'waffles of insane greatness,'" he said, holding open the door, slipping a key from a large ring into the lock. "I'll meet you ladies there."

Walking to June's Audi, Jade struggled to keep her thoughts to herself. But once they were in the car, June kicked the door wide.

"Could you be a little more gracious?" June adjusted the heat blasting from the vents as she backed out of the parking spot. The noon sun had defrosted the cold morning. The deep chill rolling down from the hills had melted in the city's warmth.

"About being railroaded?" Jade snapped her seatbelt in the lock. "I'm not even sure what happened back there."

"I brought you an excellent investment opportunity." June headed east on Tremont, toward Aretha Frankenstein's.

Jade cradled her handbag. So far, none of the responses running through her head were appropriate.

"June, don't take this wrong, but no, you didn't bring me an investment opportunity. You brought me along for one of your ideas. I've got enough going on with one shop. If I opened a second, I'd have to hire a manager, divide my time, increase my inventory. It's not like manufacturing reps come knocking on my door. I have to go out and find what I sell, look for consigners. Besides, I want my first year of marriage to be about Max and me, not a Blue Umbrella Two."

"Are you adverse to any help? Or are you so self-sufficient you don't need others?"

"Is this about the other night?"

"You tell me."

If she only knew. "June, you've done so much for me already . . . planning the wedding, paying for most of it, welcoming me into your family and circle of friends. Can it just be simple and straightforward? I don't want another shop."

June cruised up to the curb by Aretha Frankenstein's, shut off the Audi, and set the emergency brake. "Yes, it can. As long as you know it's fine to be independent, but it's also wise to know when to say 'Yes, thank you very much.' To know when to speak, and when to hold your opinions to yourself."

Jade paused. "We're not talking about the property anymore, are we?"

"There are things, Jade . . . Expectations." June combed the ends of her hair with her fingers.

"Like?" Small knots floated through Jade's emotions.

"Like understanding the way the game is played."

Jade reached for the door handle. "I'm not playing games, June."

Sean Dunham was in the waiting area of the colorful restaurant, converted from an old neighborhood house. If Jade had rattled June with her comment, the elegant woman hid it well.

"How about the corner table, under the window?" Sean led the way, motioning for the waitress to come over. He had a commanding air; he obviously knew which privileges to expect.

After ordering lunch, the table conversation started off slow, with chit-chat about the weather and UT football, and Sean's season tickets on the fifty yard line. He'd already invited Reb to the Florida game.

Then one of them mentioned the city council, and the conversation raced down the political track. Jade mentally checked out.

Really, what was June's motive today? Hijacking their lunch for a real-estate pitch. Jade uncrossed her legs and shifted sideways in her chair, peering out the window. Did June want to make a point about her control? Her power and position?

It'd been over a week since she'd rebuked Jade for protesting the gift-giving dinner. Since then, Max had been busy with a client and a weekend seminar in Atlanta on blogging law. They had yet to talk in-depth about his conversation in the kitchen with June.

June's laugh rose above the din of the dining room and cut into Jade's musings. Across the table, the woman pressed her hand against Sean's bicep, then squeezed his chin with her fingers.

"I don't believe you. No sir, not the great Sean Dunham. There must be dozens of eligible women for you to date. You just don't want to see—"

"Excuse me." Jade slid away from the table. "I need to make a call. June, I'm meeting an estate broker from Kentucky at two, so we should leave by one thirty."

"All right, dear, whatever you need," she said, propping her elbow on the table, resting her chin between her fingers. "Fine."

Was she flirting? With Sean? Right in front of her? There was Southern-charm flirting, and then there was make-your-husband-jealous flirting. And June flirted with the line.

Cheating on Rebel wasn't June Benson's style. She had her rules and traditions, her very strong opinions, and her flirtatious charm. But she was faithful.

Walking toward the ladies' room, Jade autodialed Max. A longing for him made her heart pump, and she wondered what he'd think about her adventure with his mom today. He was good about giving Jade perspective.

"Hello?"

Jade stopped. "Max?"

"Hey, Jade, what's up?"

She whirled around. "Why am I hearing you in stereo?"

"Stereo? What are you talking about?"

Jade scanned the dining area. Because it was a converted house, the room wasn't exactly square. There. She spotted the tip of his dark head and started weaving his way. "Are you at Aretha Frankenstein's?"

"How'd you know?"

"Because I'm here too." Jade stopped just shy of his table. His head was tipped toward a dark, feminine one, and his hand rested on a woman's slender forearm.

"Where are you?" Max jumped up, whirling around, almost colliding with Jade.

Rice McClure looked up at Jade, her eyes watery and red.

"What's going on?" Jade gazed between Max and Rice, who stared at a wadded napkin. The scene made Jade feel as if she were on the outside peering in, like the scorned girlfriend trying to win back her man.

"No-nothing's going on. What are you doing here?" Max peered down at Rice.

It started with a thought. *What if he still loves her?* The notion exploded in Jade's mind, scattering fear fragments over the valleys of her heart. The light of her soul flickered.

She'd been here before . . .

Don't . . . think . . . Sinking . . . No, no . . . Jade shifted her weight, taking a step backward. Her eyes darted about the small room. *Alone, they want to be . . . alone. Where to . . . focus. Daphne said . . . the window . . . light . . . focus on the window.*

The clanking sounds of dishes faded to the background. Jade's fingers gripped the praying hands medallion hanging around her neck.

Don't want . . . to go . . . crazy.

"Jade?" Confusion, no, impatience darkened Max's expression.

Rice rose from her chair, her eyes red, her brunette hair neatly tucked behind her ears. "Jade, are you okay?"

"I'm fine . . . fine." Jade pulled her arms tight against her torso and moved backward, bumping into the table behind her. Water and tea sloshed over the tops of the diners' full drink glasses. A bully-faced man jumped away from the table, knocking over his chair.

"Babe, babe." Max lunged for her, apologizing to the Aretha Frankenstein's patron. "Your lunch is on me."

Jade peered at the man. *I'm sorry. So sorry.*

"Jade, sweetheart, what's going on?" Max grabbed her by the waist and steered her to a nook in the back of the restaurant.

The walls gathered around, the ceiling hovered just over her head . . . *Out . . . I want out . . . Need air.* Jade broke free from Max and bolted between the tables and out the front door. The golden afternoon sun cut a bold light across her vision as she stumbled down the stone steps. His footsteps crunched behind her.

Where did she park? Darkness slashed through her thoughts, raiding her sense of self. Her car. Where was her car? Jade wanted to go home, to the Hollow, to her safe boundaries.

"Jade, tell me, what's going on?" Max handcuffed her wrist with his tight grip.

"You, Rice, your mom . . . I, I . . ." Jade shook her head gently, releasing her arm from Max's hand, and teetered on the edge of reason.

"Mom? She's here?"

"What are you doing here with Rice?" Jade tore off her jacket, letting it slip down her arms and hang from her wrists. The cool air felt perfect against her hot skin.

"She wanted to talk."

"You work at the same office, Max—on the other side of the river I might add. You had to come here to talk? You had to hold her hand?"

"I wasn't holding her hand. She's upset about her boyfriend in D.C., and she asked if we could go to lunch."

With a deep inhale, Jade peered at Max. "Do you love her?"

"No." Max propped his hands on his leather belt, eyes narrowed at her. "Is that what this show is about?"

"Show?" He had to hate seeing his fiancée insecure and clinging. Jade stepped off the curb. "I need to go. An estate broker from Kentucky is meeting me at the shop."

"Jade, is everything all right?" June asked, with Sean and Rice following.

Max slipped his arm around Jade. "Mom, she's fine. Sean, how are you?" Max clapped his hand into the developer's.

Jade's pulse slowed as reason gained ground, and she rested her head against Max's shoulder. Rice stood off to one side, her eyes narrowed and observing. She smiled with a mini wave when Jade's gaze crossed hers.

"What are you and Jade doing down here, Mom?" Max said.

"Blame Sean here. He has a property on River Street he thought would be great for a second Blue Umbrella."

"You want space in the city?" Max peered down at Jade, his smile rescuing her from the muddy emotional pit.

"Your mom thinks I should open up a second shop."

"But do you?" Tender, patient, focusing only on her.

"No, actually." There, she confessed it for June and Sean to hear. "Maybe someday." Jade pulled Max away from the watching gallery. "It's you I want.

Not a second store. Not your parents' friends' money. Just. You." The confession came from a deep, secret place in her heart, where only a few treasures lived. Paps and Granny, Aiden and Willow. And now Max.

His lips brushed her ear. "It's you I want. Just. You. Not an old fiancée who couldn't stick around when the going got tough. She was always more like a buddy than a girlfriend. And don't let Mom's ideas become yours . . . unless you want."

"I'll stick with you, Max, I promise, if you'll stick with me." She whispered her promise against his chest, the pound of her pulse matching the easy pulse of the breeze.

"In a few weeks, I'll say it in front of Whisper Hollow and all of heaven."

She wrapped her arms around his waist, clinging to him as her will and emotions rebounded from the raw bomb of anxiety. She'd work every day of their marriage to deserve him.

"Jade, darling, it's one forty." June started for her car. "We'd better get you back to the shop."

"See you tonight?" Max said, still holding her close, kissing her softly.

"See you tonight. And Max"—she brushed her hand over his thick chest—"if your mother doesn't make it home . . ."

"Benson Law has a fine capital defense team."

"Thank you." She smiled, everyday brightness returning to her internal world.

"Back there . . ." Max walked with her to June's car. "That was about more than me talking with Rice, wasn't it?"

"Back there was just a little bit of my old life trying to cheat the new."

Nine

Riding ten hours in the car with Willow from Prairie City to Whisper Hollow wore every fiber of Beryl's being down to a bare thread.

"Why didn't we rent a car? It's a hundred degrees in this death trap." Willow hooked her bare heels over the edge of the seat and hung her head out the window of Beryl's Corolla as it clattered and rattled toward Whisper Hollow. "Sorry we didn't make your wedding, Jade. We spontaneously combusted."

"Would you please, please, for the love of Pete, shut up?" Beryl swore, white-knuckling the wheel. The Corolla was a good, solid vehicle. So a little hot air blew in from the engine. And the floorboard was like a griddle when the muffler pipe heated up. At least it was warm. "I didn't see you forking up the money to rent a car."

"Hey, I'm a poor college student."

"Aren't you throwing the word *student* around loosely?"

"I'll go back to school. Sheesh, between you and Jade." Willow picked at the exposed foam in the torn vinyl seat. "I need a little time to find myself."

Beryl squinted at Willow as if seeing herself forty years ago. What could she say? *Do what I say, not what I did?*

"We should've flown, Beryl. This is ridiculous. Aiden said he'd buy our tickets."

"Can you complain a bit more, Willow? I'm not quite sick of you yet." Beryl had refused her son's offer. The least she could do at this stage of her life was pay her own way to her daughter's wedding. "What would we do for wheels once we got to Whisper Hollow? You want to be cooped up in a bed-and-breakfast for three weeks?"

"Have mercy, no."

"Try to sleep," Beryl said in a softer tone. "You're driving in an hour anyway."

"It's too hot to sleep and the seat doesn't even go all the way back. And look, this side is broken. My face falls against the door. Hello, white trash, your name is Beryl Hill."

"Willow." Beryl sighed, holding back the rest of her rebuke. The girl was right; the car was hot and old, with broken, battered seats. Beryl just couldn't see paying good money for a new car that devalued the moment she drove it off the lot.

"Wake me when it's my turn." Willow stuffed ear buds into her ears and scanned her iPod for a playlist selection.

"Sleep well." Beryl recognized her daughter's unique way of saying "I'm sorry."

With Tennessee a few hours away and night beginning to fall, Beryl let her thoughts wander, moving between anticipation and indifference. *Seeing Jade tomorrow will be the first time since Mother's funeral.*

Bearing down on the gas with the vibrations of the old car in her chest, Beryl took an I-24 curve and headed south, her thoughts drifting, her mind wandering time's old corridors.

~

Prairie City, August 1998

Sitting in the kitchen with Mother, Beryl raised her coffee mug to her lips with a glance at the ceiling. Directly above them, Jade packed for college, the radio blasting. In between dragging her suitcase across the floor and the metal clap of dresser drawer-pulls, she answered the incessant phone calls.

Her excited conversations drifted down through the floorboards and boxed the silence hovering between Beryl and Mother.

"I'd forgotten how you can hear the gnats gnawing in this house," Beryl said.

"Paps and I never could figure out why they built this place with paper walls. But it was forty years old when we bought it, so who knows what the builder had in mind."

"Do you want more coffee?" Beryl got up, her empty mug hooked over her finger.

"I'll never sleep if I have another cup. Beryl, how's Gig? I haven't seen him in a while."

Gig was gone, but Mother didn't need to know right now. "Did I tell you I'm back at Midwest Parcel?"

"Rolf let you come back again, did he?" Mother twirled her cup, a gold-trimmed Lennox with the holly leaves, against the saucer.

"Whether he liked it or not. Union rules." The phone rang again. Jade's footsteps thundered over their heads. The bed squeaked as she landed on the mattress, probably diving for the phone. "Seems all of Prairie City is calling to say good-bye."

"You're upset she's leaving, Beryl? Mercy knows I didn't sleep the entire summer you were in San Francisco. Paps would turn on the news so we could see what was going on out there, and . . ."

"It's not *that* she's leaving, Mother, but *how*." Beryl popped open the bread box. A piece of toasted bread sounded good.

"I've prayed a lot of prayers for that girl. She'll be fine."

"Because you prayed?" Beryl shoved down the toaster lever. "Who knows, maybe. More likely, she'll be fine because she's a smart girl."

"Even the wise need wisdom."

Didn't Beryl know it. Growing up, she resented her parents' religious beliefs. *Do this; don't do that.* She fought them. Quit church at her first opportunity. But in the past few years, there'd been nights when Beryl's only comfort was the thought of her parents' prayers.

"Think she'll ever come home?" Beryl opened the drawer for a butter knife, the cupboard for a small plate. "From school?"

"She best come home. I'm here, and Willow and Aiden. You work out your differences with her on your own time. Besides, Beryl, can she ever really leave? This is her home, where her heart lives."

What girl did Mother observe around the house these days? Jade was already gone in mind, soul, and spirit. Tomorrow, the body.

"Why isn't she down here asking for help? Doesn't she need something washed or ironed? Or mended?" Beryl carried her buttered bread and coffee to the table.

"She's been shopping for clothes and supplies all month," Mother said. "I gave her some money from what Paps set back for the kids' college. Good thing she and Aiden earned scholarships. I hated using the savings to replace my dead car, but I have to get to work."

"Is Daddy's old truck running? I might like to drive it for a while."

"It runs . . . barely." Mother held her gaze for a moment, peering a bit too close. "Keys are where they always are."

Beryl nodded, knowing the keys hung on the wall hook. "Thank you."

"You'll always have a home here, Beryl. You know that, don't you?"

"Yeah, Mother, I know." After all Beryl's rebellion, Mother's kindness was humbling.

The phone chimed again, and Jade caught it on the half ring. Beryl munched her toast, debating if she should just go upstairs and talk to her daughter. Help her out, make sure she had everything she needed for her future in Knoxville and the University of Tennessee.

Brushing bread crumbs from her fingers, Beryl got up from the table, carrying her coffee mug. "I'm going to see if she needs help."

"All right, but Beryl, Jade hasn't needed your help since she was about nine."

Mother's hint triggered the dull ache in the middle of Beryl's chest—her baby was leaving home for good. Always before, Beryl had been the one leaving, but she knew Aiden, Jade, and Willow were home safe with Mother. Now, she didn't know exactly where Jade would live or with whom.

At the top of the stairs, Beryl gazed down the hall toward Jade's room. Her long, lean shadow moved against the wall. Thankfully, she wasn't on the phone.

"Need any help?" Beryl called, cat-walking toward Jade's room.

Silence. Beryl braved a stance in the doorway, leaning against the wood frame so it fit perfectly between her shoulder blades.

Several taped-up boxes of Jade's things lined the wall, ready to go.

Last year, when Aiden packed and headed off to college, Beryl had been on the road with her third husband, Gig. But she didn't worry about Aiden. At nineteen, he was a man and beyond competent. She was proud of him.

Jade, however, fluttered around Beryl's heart like a wounded little bird, and she didn't want to let her go.

For the past two years, since Dustin Colter and *that* whole ordeal, Jade had posted an emotional Do Not Enter sign between her and Beryl. Respecting her daughter's boundaries, Beryl figured she'd get over it soon enough. So she continued to wait.

"Your room looks so empty."

Jade surveyed the wall and floors, her gaze skipping over the door and her mother. "I'm only taking a few things, really."

"What time do you leave tomorrow morning?"

"Six. Marilee's parents want to get to Knoxville before dark. I'm spending the night at their house. Her dad's coming to get me soon."

Beryl swirled her coffee, fighting sadness. *So she was leaving tonight.* "Do I need to give him money for gas?"

"Nope. All taken care of."

"Can I pay you back, then? Or Mother."

"It's all good."

"I feel like I've hardly seen you this summer. With you working two jobs, and—"

"You off with Gig and his merry band of idiots."

"We've been around a good bit this summer. Most of July, in fact." Then Gig decided he needed to travel light and drop a hundred and thirty pounds of Beryl.

The phone rang, and Jade snatched it up. While she bubbled and talked, Beryl braved another step into the room. *Show her your feelings with actions, not words.* Peeking into the oversized leather case that used to belong to Paps, she found Jade's tops and sweaters wadded and mashed instead of folded and organized. Beryl set her coffee on the end table and reached into the suitcase.

". . . Yeah, it does seem like a long time until Christmas, but the time will go by fast."

Beryl snagged the comment and stored it for her own comfort. *She'll be home for Christmas.*

"I know, I can't wait. College is my ticket out of this hole in the wall . . . Absolutely I have football tickets. Yeah, it's a long drive from Knoxville to Prairie City."

Beryl snapped the top straight, laying it out on the bed, folding the sleeves in, then the bottom hem toward the neckline.

When she was Jade's age, she believed that her ticket out of Prairie City was protesting the war in 'Nam, marching on Washington, living in communes, and avoiding The Man named corporate America.

"What are you doing?"

Beryl glanced up to see Jade wide-eyed. "Folding."

"Well, I don't need you to fold." Jade tossed the phone to the bed and took the top Beryl had in her hands.

"I'm just trying to help."

"You're meddling." Jade smashed the shirt into the suitcase.

"You're going to college, Jade, so I bet you know the true definition of *meddling*."

"Yeah, and it has your picture beside it."

All right. This conversation wasn't working. "Isn't Paps' old case great?" Beryl patted the leather edge.

"Yep." Jade dumped a wad of underwear between the tops, mashing them into place with a glare at Beryl. The praying hands medallion dangling around her neck swung back and forth.

"Once a year, Paps would pack up this bag and drive off to some fishing cabin in Canada. He'd come back relaxed and happy. Mother started teasing him about having a secret lover."

"Paps would never." Jade snapped around from the dresser, her arms loaded with jeans. Some still with the tags.

"It was Mother's joke, Jade."

"Paps was the finest man I've ever known." She dropped her jeans into the suitcase. "Why did you tell me that, huh? To make yourself feel better?"

"It was a joke." Beryl sat on the bed out of Jade's way, reaching for her coffee, which was now lukewarm.

"I'm taking the video player," Jade said, lifting jackets and coats out of the closet. "I bought it with my money."

"I'll buy a new one for Willow."

"She likes Mary Kate and Ashley Olsen and VeggieTales movies. Granny has some old cartoons on tape, Bugs Bunny and that lispy cat, but don't show her anything scary, including *The Wizard of Oz.* She'll have nightmares. I'm not kidding, Mama. Don't turn it on thinking I was exaggerating. There's something about Winnie the Pooh that frightens her too."

"She's eight, Jade. Good grief—"

"Who cares how old she is? If it scares her, don't put it on."

"All right, I hear you. Be mad at me all you want, Jade, but Willow's still my kid. And it wouldn't hurt you to show me some respect."

"Respect is earned." Jade stopped jamming her coat into the case long enough to peer at her. "Willow likes to write to Aiden at school. We've been coloring pictures for him on Wednesdays before she goes to bed. We call him once a week and send e-mails."

"I don't have an e-mail account."

"Yes, you do. On AOL. Willow wanted one for you so she could e-mail you when you're gone with Gig or Midwest Parcel, or wherever you've run off to." Jade's voice and expression were rock hard. "Pretty sad when your eight-year-old feels she has to e-mail you to keep in touch. She has four e-mail addresses: Aiden's, mine, her dad's, and yours. She'll show you how to use it when you're home long enough."

"Gig's gone. I'm home now. Back at Midwest." Beryl smoothed her hand over the worn quilt.

"Do you have something against marriages lasting longer than two years?" Jade went to her desk, opened drawers, and picked out pencils, pens, and other office-type supplies. "By the way, Willow's been asking to see Mike."

"I've called him already. Do you think it's wise for me to let her go with him?"

"About as wise as it is for her to live with you. He is her father. And he's married now. He came by with Vickie a few weeks ago. She seems nice enough, and Wills liked her." Jade stood in the center of the room, a collection of pencils and pens in her hand. "I'd never wish it on any girl to grow up without her dad."

"Don't judge me with that tone of yours, Jade. Harlan wasn't exactly calling up begging for you and Aiden to visit. Sorry if that sounds harsh, but it's the truth."

With Mama, the truth was always someone else's fault. Jade unplugged her alarm clock and bedside lamp, adding them to the box of bedroom items. "Sorry about Gig, Mama."

"Yeah, well, it was fun while it lasted." For a quick second, their eyes met.

"Hey up there!" Mother called from the bottom of the stairs. "Joe Farrell and Marilee are here."

Jade ran to the banister and bent over. "Be right down. Go Vols!"

"Hurry," Marilee called. "Mom's making lasagna for our going-away celebration. And a bunch of people called to say they're coming over."

Jade barreled back into the room, slamming down the lid of Paps' suitcase. Mother hurried in, breathless from the stairs, and without a word fell into rhythm with Jade.

"You've got your money in a safe place?" Granny asked.

Jade snatched her backpack off the floor, still with the store tags dangling from the straps. "In here, in my wallet. I've got my credit card in there too."

"Just send me the bill." Beryl watched as Mother lifted the suitcase lid, her hands deftly rearranging, folding, and organizing. "I'll cover up to two hundred a month, but Jade, make sure it's for school stuff, or clothes. Not pizza for your dorm floor."

The girl kissed her granny's cheek. "Promise. And thank you."

"All right. Shoes." Mother glanced around. "Do you plan on going to school barefoot?"

"Shoes. I forgot." Jade dropped to her knees in front of the closet and started shuffling out sneakers, loafers, boots, clogs, flip-flops, discussing with Mother what she'd need and when, deciding what items could wait until she came home for the holidays.

Beryl headed down the hall. She'd call Willow home from the Pattersons', then wait in the living room with the Farrells to say good-bye to Jade.

But at the bottom of the stairs, she sank to the bottom step. Her girl was going off to college, leaving home. Beryl brushed her cheeks with the back of her hand. Four months until Christmas. Already it felt like an eternity.

Ten

"That's the last one, Jade." Harvey Roper jumped down from the flatbed he had double-parked in front of the Blue Umbrella, wiping his forehead with his red checked sleeve. "What in tarnation are you going to do with two dozen pumpkins?"

"Decorate the shop. Give it a fall look."

"You wouldn't be waiting for the Great Pumpkin to appear now, would you?"

"Not since . . . hm, never."

"Well all righty." Harvey jerked open the passenger side door and took out a slip of paper. "Here's the invoice. I'll be along later for the money. No hurry."

"Are you sure? I can cut you a check now." Jade motioned for him to come inside, cradling the last pumpkin he'd handed her in the crook of her arm.

"Naw, best get these pumpkins off the sidewalk before someone trips and sues you."

"Yeah, well, I know a good lawyer."

The Indian summer day was perfumed with the sun-browned, dying fall leaves. And the subtle mountain chill made the day perfect for opening the shop door to do a little hauling. The Victorian-style street lamps were adorned with gold, red, and brown leaf wreaths.

"Need some help?" Mae called from across the street where she stood in front of Sugar Plumbs.

Jade squinted in the light. "Yeah, I do. Come on."

"Ah, sugar, now why'd you have to go and say that?" She cupped her hand around her ear, turning toward the diner door. "What's that, Al, the kitchen's on fire? Jade, got to run."

Jade laughed. Mae would give a person the shirt off her back, but not an ounce of muscle.

When she'd moved about half the pumpkins, Max appeared in the doorway, his suit coat hanging open and free, his tie knot cocked to one side.

"Hey," he said, carefully stepping through the pumpkin patch.

"What are you doing here? You're wearing an Armani. Were you in court today?"

"Until two thirty."

"Is it that late already?" She was meeting Daphne and Margot at five to try on their dresses.

"Three o'clock. The judge recessed, and I didn't have anything pressing this afternoon." He slipped his arms around her and bent his head toward hers.

Jade loved the taste of his kiss. And the treat of seeing him in the middle of the day.

"Can you take a break?" He held her hand, glancing around the shop. "I mean, if these pumpkins don't need you."

"Well, I don't know." She gazed around, hands on her hips. "Pumpkins, what do you think? Should I go with him?"

"Jade, sorry I'm late." Lillabeth burst into the shop from the back room, scooping back her hair with her Oakleys. "I'll make up the time."

"Yeah, that one minute is really going to cost you."

"But if you need me to work extra hours . . . Oh, pumpkins." She smiled, rubbing her hands together. "What are we doing?"

"Decorating. Why don't you see if you can make twenty-four pumpkins—and no, I didn't really think this through—look appealing while I am whisked off by my handsome fiancé?" Jade tugged him toward the door. "We only have about an hour. I'm meeting Daph and Margot at five. Call my cell if you need me, Lilla."

Max suggested walking to Laurel Park. Jade suggested shakes from Froggers. They ordered—strawberry for him, chocolate for her—and sat at a round stone table.

"Did you really come home just to see me?" Jade tore the paper from her straw and wadded it into a ball.

"Yes, and to talk to you about some stuff."

"Ah, stuff." Her eyes met his for a second, then she focused on mixing her shake with the straw. She didn't want to talk about her episode at Aretha Frankenstein's. The memory embarrassed her. How could she let panic win? Even for a moment?

"I talked to Mom." Max shrugged off his suit jacket and folded it over his legs, then spread a napkin on the table and set his shake in the middle. "I wanted to know why she thought you should open a second shop. Why on River Street."

"What'd she say?"

Max drew long on his straw. "The usual, she was just trying to help. Jade, she really does thrive on helping others. She's the ultimate team player. Coaches, cheers, reminds everyone of the rules."

"Then why'd she send me out of the kitchen the night of the party?"

Max set his cup on the table and stared out over the green lawn of the park. "That's a different story. Mostly, she worries. Do you know a mom who doesn't worry?"

"Yeah, one." *Beryl Walker Fitzgerald Ayers Parsons Hill.* "What's the story?"

"First, she was upset the Reverend Girden suggested we have a civil ceremony. I'd talked to Dad about it during lunch the other day, and he mentioned it to Mom." Max sighed. "You'd think he'd know her better by now. Anyway, church is important to her, and her standing in the community. It upset her that her only child won't have God in the wedding. She said marriage is hard enough, and couples need all the spiritual guidance they can get. I know this is all about what Mom thinks and feels, but she does so much for people, Jade, Dad and I try to humor her." He reached around for his ringing iPhone. "Max Benson."

He stood, lowering his chin to his chest, his countenance fading. "When? Yeah, I'm on my way." Clapping his phone shut, he walked his shake to the trash. "The judge turned down a motion for continuance. I've got to go back to the office, babe. I'm sorry."

Jade tossed the rest of her milkshake into the Froggers trash can and fell in step with Max as he headed toward Broadway, slipping on his jacket. "So, you're telling me that June kicked me out of the kitchen because Reverend Girden suggested a civil ceremony? I'm not buying it, counselor. There's more to this story."

"Yeah, well, June's not exactly a closed book. Look, Jade, she stood by me through a hard time in my life and she gets a bit protective, worried."

"When you broke up with Rice?"

"In a way." Max picked up the pace as they crossed the street. At his car, he paused to regard Jade. "This is not a two-minute conversation. Can we talk about it later?"

What was the resonance in his tone? The shade over his eyes? "Yes, of course."

Jade stood in the lane, watching Max drive down the hill, until Arthur Kettle rolled his produce truck right up to her and blasted his big-honking horn. "Jade, girl, what are you, crazy?"

~

Jade met Daphne and Margot at the Read House Starbucks for lattes before heading to BoutiqueCouture. Rain clouds ballooned above the Cumberland Mountains, leaving the air wet and frosty.

"The bride cometh." Waiting by the register, Margot smiled as Jade entered Starbucks, sweeping the air with her arm.

Daphne met Jade with a one-armed hug as she snapped her wallet shut. "Still going through with it, Jade? The whole marriage thing?"

"Bitter, oh so bitter." Margot leaned over the counter to place her order. "Grande latte please, size zero."

The barista made a face. "Zero?"

"Skinny, sweetheart. No fat."

Daphne picked napkins from a dispenser and gathered yellow packets of Splenda. "You could dump Max the day before the wedding, and the three of us could go on the honeymoon trip and write a book about it, titled something like—"

"*Two Stupid Women and a Shrink*," Margot offered.

"We'll go on *Oprah*—"

Jade ordered a latte, staying tuned to her friends' banter.

"I'm telling you, Daph," Margot said, shoving her wallet into her overstuffed Coach bag. "Oprah won't launch your dream of being the female Dr. Phil."

Jade led the way to a table while they waited for their names to be called. "I'm marrying Max, Daph. You'll have to find another way to get on *Oprah*. I love you, but I don't plan to honeymoon with you."

Starbucks was quiet and calm, a peaceful reprieve for Jade from a busy afternoon of pumpkin hauling and hearing that her intended had an issue that still worried his mother.

But then again, it was June . . . who still pressed her hand over her heart when she recounted the story of Max falling off his first bicycle when he was six and breaking his arm. The issue had to be nothing. And, if it was something, did it matter? The ordeal belonged in the past.

Half listening to Margot go on about a skittish patient, Jade assured herself Max would cling to their bargain—the past made no difference to their future.

Because if he started snooping around the secret areas of her heart, he'd find things he never imagined.

"You okay?" Daphne asked.

"Yeah, I'm fine." Jade smiled, flicking her gaze over her friend's assessing stare. "Just ready for a latte and to try on my wedding dress."

Daphne had teased her about buying a new wedding dress when she was the one aiming to be the queen of vintage. But Jade chafed at the idea of wearing another woman's wedding gown. She wanted to glide down the aisle in something uniquely hers.

The barista called Daphne's order, then Margot's, and finally Jade's. The friends stirred sweeteners into their lattes and eased into a chat about past friends' weddings—the good, the bad, and the very ugly.

"Man, remember when Tricia Palmer's ex-boyfriend busted into her wedding, drunk?" Margot smacked the table with her palm. "I was like, 'Oh my gosh, where is my video camera?' A ten-thousand-dollar moment happening right before my eyes."

Closing her eyes, Jade visualized Tricia's face, shaking her head. "I felt so bad for Tricia, and for her ex. What was his name? Elio or something?"

"Leave it to you to want to capitalize on someone else's pain." Daphne *tsked, tsked* Margot.

"Me? Have you watched those home video shows? People are back-flipping off trampolines and landing on their heads, or crashing into barn doors going twenty miles an hour, belly flopping into pools, and everyone's laughing. Shoot, they add canned laughter. So don't talk to me about capitalizing on people's pain." Margot waved her finger under Daphne's nose. "Besides, I didn't say it was funny to see Tricia's ex stumbling down the aisle right when the minister asked does anyone object. Ooo"—Margot twisted around to face Jade square on—"That's not going to happen to you, is it, Jade?"

"No, and why would you ask such a thing?" Jade squinted at her, making a face.

"If I remember your story right, your old flame Dustin—"

"You're crazy, Margot. Dustin was a gazillion years ago," Jade insisted. And could they please change the subject?

"I'm hiding a camera in my bouquet. Just in case." Margot blew over the surface of her coffee before taking a sip.

"If anyone is going to have an ex-boyfriend crash her wedding, it's you." Jade tipped her head toward her bottle-blonde, red-lipped friend.

"What *did* Max say about your relationship with Dustin?" Daphne, ever calm, always soothing, lobbing cherry bombs.

"He doesn't know." Jade avoided visual confrontation by gulping her latte, her very hot latte. She twisted the cap off the water she'd also purchased and took a long swig.

"Max and I made a pact about our past . . . it doesn't matter. Especially relationships. Our lives began when we met."

"Dustin did a number on you, Jade." Margot shook her head and played with her stir stick, bending it between her thumb and forefinger. "Tell her, Daphne. She needs to get it all out before Max touches an old wound or something. Right?"

"I'm not wounded, Margot. Some people grow up and get over their hurts. So don't shove your issues off on me."

"Max deserves to know. Daph, back me up here." The dentist and her five cents of advice. "I took psych in college; I remember a few things."

"The psychiatric world thanks you for going into dentistry," Daphne said. "I'm with Jade on this one. There are benefits in *not* dragging out all the skeletons in our closet. Might be the best decision you've made for your marriage."

"What about you and Rainy, Daph?" Margot began with a smirk on her lips. "I seem to recall you guys 'talking all night' and 'sharing your hearts.' And he was the poster boy for lying scoundrel."

Daphne snarled at Margot. "Forgive me for being trusting and not asking if he had a wife and family on the other side of the country."

"Jade, have you asked Max if he has a wife and kids?" Margot teased. "Not if he has ever been married, but if he *is* married?"

"No, but I'll clarify that with him." Jade laughed low, winking at Daphne.

"You two are just cruel. Cruel." Daphne smiled now, but it'd taken two years before her eyes didn't glisten when she heard a romantic melody or the words *love* and *happily ever after.*

Tender and kind, with a wide open heart, Daphne had never suspected the sincerity of the eloquent and august Rainy Collins. She'd found her Mr. Darcy. But he turned out to be a Mr. Wickham.

"Jade"—Margot held up her BlackBerry—"It's five fifteen. What time is our appointment at BoutiqueCouture?"

"Five thirty." And it was only a minute's walk away in the lobby of the Read House. So—"I met Max's ex-fiancée at his parents' house, the night of the infamous money-giving dinner party."

"What's she like?" Daphne said.

"What you'd expect as a potential Benson wife. Athletic, beautiful, educated, accomplished, blah, blah." Jade stared toward the window, the pink of twilight reflecting in the glass. A river of red taillights flowed down Broad Street.

"You think she'll be the one crashing the wedding?" Margot laughed, but the comment pinged Jade's fears.

"I caught them at Aretha Frankenstein's—" She hadn't planned this confession, but hearing her words caused the air in her lungs to feel lighter.

"Across the river from Benson Law? Hm, some sort of secret meeting . . ."

"Margot, you make everything sound suspicious."

"What? You're the one who said you 'caught them.' Is it Margot-is-the-bad-guy day or something?"

"It's just that—" Jade had trusted a man before, and . . . "Nothing. Max said they're just friends, and I have no reason not to believe him."

"Any word on your mom coming to the wedding?" Daphne asked.

"Willow said Mama got the invite but doesn't know if she's coming."

"Can I ask you something?"

"Uh-oh," Margot moaned. "Every time she prefaces a question with 'Can I ask you something?' she's in headshrinker mode. You have to cut this out, Daph. You don't see me walking up to people asking to see their molars."

"That's because your job is disgusting. Mine is about healing people's souls."

"Disgusting? Who else can turn the world on with a smile?" Margot threw her arms wide. "A big, bright, white, perfectly capped smile?"

"Mary Tyler Moore."

"Deflect if you want, but I'm on to you, since our freshman year. You secretly want to tell everyone how to think and feel."

"On to me? Freshman year?" Daphne countered. "You were so into Chris Herman you couldn't walk across campus without hitting a tree."

"At least he was human. What was that science project you dated—Rico somebody?"

"What's your question, Daph?" Jade waited.

"Why don't you just call your mom? Ask her to the wedding."

"Because . . ." She fiddled with her napkin. "I don't know if I want her to come."

"Is there *anything* you like about this woman, Jade? Other than her giving birth to you?"

Jade's thoughts shot through her heart. Sweet, gentle, dangerous Daphne and her cherry-bomb questions.

"When I was a girl," she started slowly, digging deep, "Mama taught me to braid her hair. I loved running my fingers through the long silky strands that shone like gold threads when the sun hit them. She was larger than life, so alive and free with these unique, interesting friends. She would throw these grand parties at our farmhouse in Iowa, and her hippie buddies would pitch tents and park their vans. Then one day, it all changed, at least that's how it seemed to me at eight years old. I thought Mama and her friends were magical, but now I know they were high and out of it."

Jade rubbed the lipstick stain from the rim of her latte's lid. Daphne and Margot waited, listening.

"One summer, Mama threw a party every weekend, and a deputy would come around about sundown every Sunday to shut her down. By then, at nine, ten, eleven, I realized how stupid she was behaving."

"But look, here you are, Jade." Daphne gripped Jade's arm with her steady hand. "Successful, smart, about to marry one of the most eligible bachelors in the Southeast. What a blessing."

Jade exhaled a staccato laugh. She didn't deserve any blessings.

"Aiden and I watched the parties from my bedroom window. I had the large room in the back of the house. Daddy stood guard by the bonfire, arms crossed, feet apart. Now I know it was the beginning of the end." She peered into Daphne's olive eyes and absently touched the praying hands medallion at the base of her throat. "Granny and Paps made life stable for Aiden, Willow, and me, and then I went to college and met you and Margot. You became my family."

"Remember when Daphne found you in our room, practically paralyzed by a panic attack?" Margot recounted the memory as if discussing an all-night study session.

A gray sensation doused Jade. She'd never forget that afternoon. It was terrifying, and even now it haunted her. She stirred herself. "What time is it? . . . Five twenty five. We'd better go."

Jade followed Margot out Starbucks' front door, stepping into the cool evening. Daphne walked alongside, linking her arm through Jade's.

"Max's capped teeth will drop right out of his head when he sees you," Margot said, the skip of her heels on the sidewalk moving in rhythm with Jade's.

"He doesn't have capped teeth."

"I'm a dentist, Jade. Trust me." Margot tipped her head to see Jade's face. "Maybe you don't know everything you need to know about this man."

"I'm telling you." Daphne pulled up before going inside and gestured at their reflection in the glass. "This could be the cover of our book. Just leave Max at the altar."

Margot backed away. "No way is my face appearing on a book cover with the word *stupid* in the title. Not even for a chance to be on *Oprah*."

"Hey, it was your title idea."

Jade swung open the door. "You two can fight among yourselves, but I have an appointment inside to try on my wedding dress. I'm getting married in three weeks."

Mama or no Mama.

Eleven

She passed the Blue Umbrella for a third time.

"Beryl, *helloooo*." Willow waved and pointed her hand out the window like it was on fire. "Where are you going?"

Home. Prairie City. To blackmail that crazy Dr. Meadows into giving her a release to go back to work. Coming to Whisper Hollow was a stupid idea. Jade didn't want her at her wedding. And her first night at the "cozy and quaint" Magnolia Tree Bed and Breakfast was loud and uncomfortable. Beryl had slept for two seconds.

"Hey, kids, this is your brain on drugs . . ." Willow knocked the top of Beryl's head.

"Stop it." Beryl smacked Willow's hand away as she downshifted, braking for the stop sign at the bottom of Main Street. The old Toyota's gears groaned.

"The street is what, three inches long? How can you miss the Blue Umbrella? It's right there."

Beryl swerved, pulling off into a muddy patch marked with tire treads. "Get out."

"Gladly." Willow smashed open her door. "Do you want me to tell her you were here, or just pretend—"

Beryl gunned the gas, kicking up a bit of mud with her tires. Willow was too bright and too stupid for her own good. One of these days, she was going to have to choose a side.

All Beryl wanted was a moment of quiet, a chance to think, to go over what she wanted to say when she saw Jade for the first time in three years. Turning left at a light, Beryl circled through a park parking lot, came out on a side street, and once again crept up Main toward the Blue Umbrella.

Choosing a spot in front of the diner, Sugar Plumbs, she parked the Corolla, cut the engine, and set the brake.

Yep, there was the Blue Umbrella. And inside, her girl. Girls, for that matter. Dropping her forehead to the dry, peeling steering wheel, Beryl gathered an arsenal of small talk to use when the conversation began and ended with "Hello."

"Sugar, you okay?" A sparkling cherub face peered through the passenger window.

"Yes, I'm fine." Beryl rubbed steering wheel dust from her forehead.

The woman came around to her side of the car. "Mae Plumb." She nodded toward the diner. "Are you Jade's mama?"

Beryl crinkled her brow. "I might be. Why?"

"I see it in your eyes. Same shape and color, yeah, and the same . . . same . . . I don't know. Sadness."

Same sadness? "Beryl Hill, nice to meet you."

The woman shook her offered hand. "Listen, I own Sugar Plumbs, so you come on over to lunch or supper. On the house. We love Jade around here.

Her pretty little shop has already helped tourism. And marrying that Max Benson ain't hurting nothing neither, you know? How do you like him?" The diner owner was chattier than Willow, but twice as nice.

"I haven't met him yet."

"No fooling? Well, you'll love him. He's a catch, a mighty fine catch."

With her fingers on the door handle, Beryl listened to the woman—Mae, was it?—go on about the Indian summer weather and how the town planned to really do up trick-or-treating for the kids this year.

But past the round, pink woman was the Blue Umbrella's front door. By now, Willow had informed Jade, "Beryl's here."

So what was her delay? All she had to do was walk across the street and say hello.

Then somehow build a bridge across a deep valley of whys.

~

"What's she doing now?"

"Sitting in the car, drinking coffee. Mae just brought her a cup."

Jade fussed with the pumpkin display, moving the biggest one in the front to the back. And the cluster of small ones Lillabeth had arranged in the back to the front. *There. Perfect.* Then she gazed out the front picture window over Willow's shoulder. "Why won't she come in? It's been over an hour."

"It's Beryl, Jade. She's been even weirder than usual lately."

"Weirder than usual?" Jade fluffed the orange tabby cat pillow sitting on the banister-back rocking chair. "How could she get more weird?"

"Different weird, like taking long vacations. Agreeing to come down here three weeks before your wedding. I mean, what's up with that? Wonder if she's on the outs with Rolf again."

"After all the abuse she's given him . . ." Jade peered across the street again. Navy blue clouds rolled in with the noon hour, and a stiff wind blew rain sprinkles against Main Street's windows.

Mama sat behind the wheel of her Toyota, windows rolled up, sipping Plumbs' coffee, looking straight ahead, her silver braid slinking down over her shoulder. Stubborn woman.

"Jade, are these Calvin Kleins?" Willow had wandered from the window to the clothing racks. She was holding up a pair of jeans with gold stitching on the hip pockets.

"From the 1980s. There are a couple of pairs. The lady who consigned them wore them when she went discoing in Manhattan during the Studio 54 days." The shop's phone rang. Jade leaned over the counter for the portable receiver. "Thank you for calling the Blue Umbrella."

"What in tarnation are you doing?" Mae asked. "Get on over here and greet your mama."

"Is her leg broke, Mae?" Jade straightened the small stack of Blue Umbrella business cards by the register. "I don't see her walking inside."

"She just drove eight hundred miles to see you. I think you can hike your hindquarters across the street to say hello. Come in the diner and have an early lunch. Everything gets smoothed over with a good slice of pie."

"Does the UN know about you? Mae Plumb's solution to world peace? Pie."

"You surprise me, Jade. I've seen you put up with June Benson's silliness, smiling against the urge to pluck her eyes out. Mercy knows, she can grind your last nerve into the dirt, but this is your mama."

Jade collapsed over the counter, propping her forehead against her palm and sighing. "It's complicated, Mae."

"I understand that, girl, but leaving her sitting in the car when it's fixing to pour buckets ain't going to make it uncomplicated, is it?"

Jade went to the door. Mama still sat behind the wheel of the Corolla. She was nuts. Reaching for the knob, Jade looked at Willow, who added a pink tie-dyed top to the clothes draped over her shoulder, and whispered, "Help me." Then with a resigned sigh, she stepped outside.

Mama cracked her car window an inch when Jade rapped lightly, hovering against the chilly wind. "You can't sit out here all day."

"I thought I'd go back to the bed-and-breakfast."

"Are you coming into the shop or not?" Two cars lined up at Main Street's single traffic light. The drivers stared.

"What's Willow doing?"

"Shopping."

Mama rolled up the window, then popped open her door. She followed Jade inside, the large leather bag slung over her shoulder, banging against her hip. She wore a pair of loose jeans with a hem that bounced around her ankles, a tucked in T-shirt with a large, loose sweater, and a pair of white sneakers.

"So this is it?" She surveyed the Blue Umbrella, turning in a small circle.

"There's a storeroom in the back and a loft upstairs, but yeah, this is it."

Mama's gaze stopped on Jade. "You look well."

"You came."

"You invited me, didn't you?"

"To my wedding, yes."

"Jade, I'm going to try these on," Willow said. "About time you came in, Beryl."

"I needed a break from you."

Jade glanced at her sister. "Not the beige dress. Wrong color for you."

She dropped the dress over the rack. "What about this teal?"

"No," said Jade.

"Yes." Mama's yes crashed into Jade's no.

Jade peered at Mama, then Willow, who draped the teal top over the rack. "Hang them up when you come back."

"I will. Are you buying? It's my birthday soon."

"No more than a hundred dollars."

"Cheap-o." The door to the small dressing room, a former broom closet, clicked shut.

"Will you talk to her about going back to school?" Beryl said.

"She said she was bored." Jade walked slowly toward the sales counter, offering Mama the stool.

"Everything bores her." Mama remained standing, arms folded over her middle. "She gets bored two seconds into her morning shower. She's too brilliant for this game. Talk to her for me, will you?"

"Haven't I always?" Jade moved to the clothes rack, hanging up the teal top and the beige dress. "I was there for her when you weren't, reading her stories, tucking her in—"

Twelve

Prairie City, June 1996

"Willow, come on, which jammies?" Jade held up Ariel in one hand, Barbie in the other. "Granny said Mama might call tonight."

Jade leaned to see Granny's hall clock. Ten minutes. Dustin would be here in ten minutes. It was an hour's drive over to Deep River with no minutes to spare. A quiver weakened her knees. Tonight all their plans came together.

"I hate her." Willow fell on her bed, tugging on her yellow lace panties, her wet hair tangled about her shoulders, then reached for a book under her pillow and held it over her head, flipping the pages.

"Don't say 'hate.'" Jade yanked the book from her sister's slender fingers. "Which pajamas?"

"Hate, hate, hate, hate." Willow kicked her feet against the mattress.

Jade raised her hand. One pop on the behind, just one. Willow could be so impossible. "I said, don't say 'hate.' Here, you're wearing Ariel."

"You say 'hate.' I heard you." Willow sat up with her arms raised, and Jade slipped the nightie over her head.

"I was mad at Mama."

"Me too."

"Mad at her for what?" Jade shoved onto the bed next to Willow, surfing under her pillow for the rest of the books she'd stashed there. Most six-year-olds slept with dolls or stuffed animals. But Willow curled up with *The Little House in the Big Woods*, *The Secret Garden*, and Granny's worn copy of *Little Women*. The little bugger could read them herself too.

"'Cause she's never here. Always going off with some stupid man, or asking Rolf for long trips in the truck. Or going with Carlisle. She doesn't care about us."

Oh, boy. "Pick a book." Jade spread them across the bed. Willow had just rattled off every word Jade had said to Granny last week when she thought Willow was in bed.

"This one." Willow tapped *Blueberries for Sal*, by Robert McClosky.

"What? You've read this a hundred times. You recite the next part of the story before I can turn the page."

"It's my favorite."

Jade curled her arm around Willow's narrow frame and, kissing her forehead, opened to the first page. "Willow, we don't hate Mama, okay? You're only saying those things about Mama because you heard me say them."

She stretched out her long, lean legs, arching her feet and spreading her toes. "Why'd you say them?"

"I was just upset. Listen, you, Aiden's bringing home ice cream from Kroger when he gets off work tonight. If you go straight to sleep after reading, I'll tell Granny to let you have chocolate ice cream for breakfast."

Willow stiffened her arms and squeezed her eyes shut. Jade wanted to laugh, but that would start a whole other routine of Willow-as-entertainer and she didn't have time for that tonight.

"How's it going in here?" Granny walked through the door, shoving her rinsed-red hair away from her high forehead. She sat on the edge of the bed with an exhaled *oomph* and squeezed Willow's toes.

"Jade's reading to me," Willow said without moving, but cracking her eyes just enough to see Granny through long-lashed slits. "She says for you to let me have ice cream for breakfast."

"Oh, she did?" Granny angled her head back to see Jade.

"Only if she's good and goes to sleep after this story."

"All right, but you have to let me listen."

"Certainly," Willow said, closing her eyes tight again, stretching her body taut. She looked ready for a coffin.

Certainly? Where does she get this stuff? "Here we go."

Willow opened one eye. "Show me the picture."

Jade showed her the book with a glance at Granny. Her eyelids fluttered closed and her hand was limp over her middle.

She was so tired. Raising Mama's kids for her so she could do what she wanted. The latest being a "rock tour" with a musician she'd met in Omaha.

Gig Parsons.

Gig. What kind of name was that for a grown man? A sour shiver crept through Jade whenever she thought of the gregarious, chain-smoking guitar player. He was too young and too smarmy for Mama.

"Have you heard from your mother?" Granny said from her half-sleep.

"We hate her." The parrot, Willow.

Jade tapped her leg with the spine of the book. "Stop saying 'hate.' No, we haven't."

"I saw Rolf in town today, and he's pretty upset she isn't back from her leave of absence. It's been three months and counting."

"She's a teamster. He can't fire her."

"He can lay her off."

"You think she'll care?"

Granny sighed. "Not until that musician husband of hers dumps her for someone younger and prettier."

"Mama's ugly."

"Willow, that's enough. You're not allowed to say another word unless it's nice."

"Nice." She giggled and snorted into her palm.

"Your mother . . ." Granny's voice faded. "She listens to a different beat than the rest of us, especially your Paps and me."

The lullaby of tenderness in Granny's voice touched Jade. Granny loved Mama—despite all the pain.

"Granny," Jade started, her plans with Dustin surfacing. She hated deceiving her. "Dustin and I—"

Shh. Don't tell. She'd made a pact with him.

"Dustin and you what, sweetie?"

"Are, um, watching movies at Rachel's tonight. Stu's coming over. Like a double date. I'm going to spend the night there, if it's okay."

"On a school night?"

A thump of Jade's heart jolted her pulse. "My homework is done."

"Well . . ." Granny's voice faded again as if thinking this issue through wasted her last ounce of energy. "If Bonnie is okay with you staying over . . . I trust you."

"She is. W-w-want me to have her call you?" *Please no, please no, please no.* Jade thumbed the pages of the book, her pulse carrying an anxious beat through her ears. Next to her, Willow was already halfway to dreamland.

"Don't bother her. But listen, I do need you to come straight home from school tomorrow and get supper. I'm working late again. Aiden's going to pick up Willow from after-school care since the babysitter can't keep her late on Tuesdays. Mercy, sixty-eight is too old to be working overtime."

"Why don't you retire?" Jade closed the *Blueberries* book and tucked it under the pillow. Willow made a small, kittenlike noise and curled up on her side. "You talk about it."

"Then what? Sit in my rocking chair and rot? I'd rather complain about being too old to work overtime."

"Can Dustin come for dinner tomorrow?" Jade slipped Willow's legs under the covers.

"He's always welcome, Jade." Granny smiled, her eyes still closed. "He's a honey, isn't he? I remember him from Sunday school. 'Hello, Mith Walker.'" Her laugh fell over Jade like a gentle summer rain.

"He loves you, Granny."

With a sigh, Granny pushed off the bed, eyes bleary. "Better get ready for bed. My program's on soon, but I'm not sure I can stay awake to the end." Yawning, she walked around and kissed Jade's forehead. "You're a good girl, Jade-o."

Jade's eyes watered and she squeezed Granny's hand as she walked away. "I love you."

"I love you too."

Watching Granny's rounded back disappear around the corner, Jade smoothed her hand over Willow's damp, curly hair. She should've blown it dry for her. Tonight's plans had her so distracted . . . excited.

Kneeling beside the bed, Jade plugged in the string of Christmas lights that Willow had draped over the dresser last Christmas and clicked off the bedside lamp.

Easing out of the room, Jade peered out of the upstairs hall window just as Dustin's headlights turned into the drive. "He's here. Night, Granny."

"Have fun." Granny came out of her bathroom rubbing a thick white cream on her face. "Remember, straight home tomorrow."

Down the stairs with her insides congealing like cold Jell-O, Jade ducked into the bathroom off the kitchen and changed into her skirt and top for her date. In an overnight bag, she had a change of clothes for school and—her breath went shallow, her cheeks burned—something *special* for later in the evening. Tingles chased shivers down her spine.

Hurry, Jade, Dustin is waiting. Granny will be coming down any minute. She tugged the top over her head. Dustin liked this one with the scoop neck. Said it made her look sexy.

At her neck lay the praying hands medallion Paps gave her so long ago. Jade unhooked the clunky clasp and slipped the medallion into her bag.

In the halo of yellow porch light, Dustin waited against the rail wearing jeans and a starched button-down. "Hey," he said, low and warm, pulling her toward him.

The fragrance of Dial and Obsession seeped through her pores and into her memory bank. She wanted to remember everything about tonight. How he looked, how he smelled, how he tasted.

"You're wearing my favorite top." His nuzzles against her neck were hot and inviting.

"Well"—she kissed him—"it's a special night."

His hand slipped low on her hips, pressing her into him. "I love you, Jade."

She pressed her forehead to his chest. "I'm counting on it."

Thirteen

Music floated from under the door of the Blue Umbrella's storeroom. The faint tunes of Don McLean's "Tapestry."

Jade knocked softly before opening the door. Mama sat in the pea-green and brown recliner circa 1974 with her head back and eyes closed, her toes tapping out the beat against the air.

"Excuse me. I just need to check something." Jade jiggled the mouse of her inventory computer. A customer had e-mailed about the Baker book collection, and she'd forgotten the price.

Mama lowered the footrest and lifted the needle from the vinyl LP. "Where did you find this old album?"

"I have a connection in Memphis. Rumor was Elvis owned the album, but—" Jade made a face. "Who knows."

"Well, that proves it. He's not alive. If he were, he'd not let this album go."

"Alert the media. Mystery solved." Jade shuffled paper and pens around the desk without purpose.

"Do you have any Fleetwood Mac?"

Jade shook her head. "Never considered you for a Fleetwood fan."

"Harlan and I saw them at the state fair right after we were engaged."

"Really? So, you're feeling sentimental?" Jade remained focused on the computer, her tone bland and disengaged.

"Just about music. By the way, June has invited me to lunch."

"Max told me." The bent metal chair tossed Jade forward a bit when she moved.

Last night, the Bensons met Mama for the first time over pie at Sugar Plumbs. And so far, nothing between Jade and Mama had changed. Mae knew nothing about pies and peace.

"June's a bit over the top for my taste, but she seems likeable." Mama slipped the record into the jacket.

"What time is lunch?" Jade ran her palms against her jeans. Mama needed to know something before dining alone with June.

"Twelve thirty. Guess I should get over to the B&B, get cleaned up." Shoving out of the chair, Mama teetered for a second, hand to her forehead.

Jade stood, hand out to steady her. "Are you okay?" Mama's cheeks were bland and pale.

"Head rush. Moved too quickly."

Jade paced around to the back of the recliner and brushed her hands over the wooly upholstery. "Mama, remember the night Mr. Barlow came to the house with his gun, ready to shoot the hide off Daddy?"

Mama turned stiffly. "What makes you bring that up?"

Jade shrugged. She'd been remembering a lot of things the past few days since Mama had shown up, fragments of her past. "Aiden and I were so scared." Jade walked over to a stack of boxes and began to sort—which ones to keep, which to break down for the Dumpster.

"How could I forget? I was furious at your dad. That night was the final straw in our relationship."

"Yeah, well, here's the thing. The Bensons sort of think Daddy's dead."

Mama frowned. "How do they sort of think a man is dead?" She tucked the album under her arm, walking slowly toward Jade.

"Funny you should ask."

"Jade."

See, mail one invitation and everything tucked away and hidden worked toward center stage. Might as well fire up the spotlight and write a musical score.

"That's what I told them."

"Why on earth—?" Mama stopped. "I guess I don't need to ask why."

"My freshman year of college, someone asked me about my dad. It just came out. 'He's dead.'" Jade ripped apart a damaged box and tossed it on the Dumpster pile. "Not a thought or plan ever to say it. People seem reluctant to pry about dead parents. One line about how painful it was, and no one ever asked me about my father again."

"Was I ever dead?"

"No."

"So why tell Max your dad's dead?" Mama's feet remained planted. Not moving away, not moving closer. "New town, new friends. Start clean."

"Same scenario. It just came out. Kind of a natural story after a while." Jade picked up another box. It was good and solid. She added it to the keeper pile. "I knew Max was special, but I didn't imagine marriage. Besides, it's not like I'll ever see Dad."

"Let me guess. You don't want me to tell June?"

"If she finds out Dad's alive, she'll probably demand I invite him to the wedding. On top of everything else—" What in the world? Something sticky coated Jade's hand when she reached for the next box. "Max took a class from Judge Harlan Fitzgerald when he was at Duke and thinks the man is brilliant."

"I see."

"Have you talked to him?" Jade wiped her hand on a towel, then broke down the sticky box and surfed it over to the trash pile. "Dad?"

"Not in the past nineteen years or so, since you and Aiden were ten and eleven." Mama perched on the arm of the recliner, smoothing her hand over the blue and brown Don McLean album. "I can't think how I'd do anything different, Jade. Between your dad and me. The marriage had run its course."

"Is that why you came down early?" Jade tossed another broken box to the trash pile. "To defend yourself?"

"Am I defending myself? You brought up your dad. Not me. I'm merely telling you how it was, if that's okay with you—or do I have to stand against the wall like a flower until your wedding?"

"I didn't tell you to come down three weeks early."

"I foolishly let Willow and Sharon talk me into it."

"Willow and Sharon? You listen to those two?" Jade jerked the broom from the corner. "What happened to Rolf?"

"Nothing. Unfortunately." After a delay, Mama laughed low. "Rolf's all right. Certainly put up with me over the years."

"Just don't tell June about Daddy." Jade swept box particles into a pile with quick, short strokes.

"Are you planning on keeping this secret forever?"

"Worked well for the past ten years." She lifted the dustpan from the nail on the wall by the broom's corner.

"I loved your dad, Jade," Mama said. "I didn't talk to you kids about our divorce because I didn't want to complicate matters. How do you divorce a man you love? The father of your children? We wanted different things. Our marriage simply ended."

"Aiden and I heard you two arguing that night after Mr. Barlow left. You were on him pretty hard. You forced him out, Mama." Jade gripped the broom tighter, sweeping farther out from the pile, reaching under the shelves along the wall, filling the dustpan with dust bunnies, paper bits, and torn cardboard.

"He wanted to leave, Jade. For a long time. He just didn't have the courage."

"Well, thank you so much for giving it to him." She dumped the dirt into the large trash can by the back door.

"He took the job in Washington without a thought toward me and you kids. That was the second time he'd taken a job without discussing it with me. What does that tell you? He knew how I felt. On top of that, he helped Land & Farm Bank take Mr. Barlow's place away from him. A farm that had been in his family for a hundred and fifty years. He betrayed our friend and neighbor, not to mention what we stood for as a family."

"What about standing for love and marriage, commitment? You picked Todd Barlow over Daddy, Aiden, and me."

"Is that why you've been so mad at me all these years?"

"Mama . . . if I have to tell you . . ." Jade tossed the broom into the corner and hung the dustpan on the nail. "Just don't tell June."

~

Jade walked with Max against the throng of exuberant trick-or-treaters—four-foot superheroes, princesses, cowboys, and angels.

Whisper Hollow had designated Begonia Valley Lane, a magnolia-lined street with some of the Hollow's most treasured old homes and cottages, as Halloween Alley.

Max ducked under a crooked swag of orange pumpkin-head lights dangling from a branch of reddish-gold-tipped magnolia.

"I think they hired third-graders to hang these things."

"I love this." Jade tapped a masked monster on the head as he, she, *it*, ran by. "It's like a big street party."

Despite the dark side of Mama's parties, Jade grew up loving the sound of laughter behind good music, the shriek of freedom from the day's cares.

Tonight, the air was heavy with the steady sound of children's voices and music. Residents on the lane had gone all out. Bright orange inflatable pumpkins and scarecrows loomed and swayed in almost every yard—and old Clint Smith had hitched up Bessie and Boss for hayrides.

Jade swerved into Max, avoiding a run-amok Stormtrooper.

"Careful." Max caught a drip of mustard from his Froggers corn dog with his tongue.

"I can't believe you're eating that thing." Jade counted the lazy scrape of Max's loafers against the sidewalk—one, two, three, *scrape*, one, two, three, *scrape*. His back was better, so he insisted on a Halloween night stroll.

"What do you mean *that thing*? This is dessert." Max shoved the last of the corn dog in his mouth and chewed with his cheeks puffed out.

"Your mom served lamb with rosemary potatoes. And you top it off with a cheap hot dog rolled in cornmeal."

"*Mm*, good." His goofy grin made her laugh.

"A coffee from Diamond Joe's would've been a lovely dessert."

"But Diamond Joe's is not in the direction I want to go." Max continued down the lane, pushing against the trick-or-treaters.

"Do you have a specific direction in mind?" She thought he just wanted to stretch his legs, buy a corn dog.

"You . . . with all your questions." He stepped aside to let three elbow-linked ballerinas wearing fuzzy crowns pass. He bowed. They giggled. "So what'd you think? About Beryl meeting the Reb and June-bug."

"I was too busy hoping she'd not be Beryl Hill, hippie first-class." She slipped her hand into his. He leaned toward one of the city trash cans and tossed in his corn dog stick.

"The hippie and the socialite seemed to gel a bit. Reb was his usual charming self. Seemed to take to Willow."

"Doesn't everyone?"

"Not everyone." He scooped her into him, kissing her temple. "Too bad your dad isn't around. I'd like to have met him. Beryl was saying he was a good man. Did I hear her say he was a lawyer?"

Jade didn't know how it had happened, but right in the middle of dinner, Beryl launched into a grand story about the greatness of Harlan Fitzgerald, only she called him "the kids' daddy," and how he loved the law. . . . About then, Jade's glass of red wine mysteriously tipped over.

"Jade, hey Jade." Lillabeth dashed across the lane wearing the '50s house dress she'd bought from the shop, low-heeled pumps, a short-haired silver wig, pearls, and white gloves.

"Who are you supposed to be?" Jade said.

"June Cleaver." Lillabeth motioned to her friends. "Tabby's Carol Brady and Anne is Rosanne Barr."

Max laughed. "Lose a bet, Anne?"

"*Noo*." Anne curled her lip.

"Jade, I was wondering if you had any extra hours for me this week?"

"You're already working every afternoon."

Lillabeth glanced at Tabby. "Maybe I could come in before school, help clean or do inventory. Work after closing, go on pick-up runs."

"What about basketball?"

She jiggled her ankle from side-to-side. "I can miss a few practices."

"Lillabeth, what's going on?"

"I owe someone, is all." She and the other girls backed away. "So, can I come in early on Monday?"

"I'll find something for you to do."

"Thanks, Jade, you're the best."

"Wonder what she's up to?" Jade stared after her, straining against Max as he tried to steer her down the lane.

"Babe, come on, one foot in front of the other. Let's go, we're almost there."

"There? Where?" Jade stopped to peer through the bars of the wrought-iron fence surrounding an old gabled house at the end of the lane. "I love this place."

The three-story with a wraparound porch sat in a weedy, overgrown yard, looking neglected and alone, but Jade thought it was magical.

Max enclosed her between his arms, his hands gripping the bars. "It's gorgeous on the inside. Hand-carved trim and molding, jib windows, open floor plan. Unusual for the day. Huge eat-in kitchen. Living room and family room. A den. Six bedrooms. Forest Wesley built it in 1898. He hired an Italian carpenter to install all the wood and design a curved staircase with a carved walnut banister."

Jade turned toward the gate. "You've been inside?"

"Last week." Max dangled a brass key in front of her. "Welcome home, babe."

Jade twisted out from under his arms. "What? You're lying."

Max slipped the key in the lock. "Am I?" He swung open the gate.

She couldn't move. "You bought this place? For me?" The subtle knot of tension she'd felt during dinner, trapped between his family and hers, loosened.

"Remember the call about the judge throwing out our contingency motion?" He shook his head. "It was the Realtor. Part of the inspection failed, and he asked the seller to lower her asking price. She agreed, and I needed to get the paperwork going. Do you like it?" Max tapped the keys against his palm.

"I can't believe it." Chills slipped down her arms and legs as she walked through the gate.

"It is okay, isn't it? I wouldn't have bought it if I didn't know how much you loved it."

Jade collapsed against him. "This is the nicest thing anyone has ever done for me."

"It was my pleasure, babe." Max curved his arm around her back to draw her close, resting his cheek against her hair. "You are so welcome."

"Max . . ." Jade sniffed. "You smell like mustard."

He bent to kiss her. "Get used to it."

She laughed, her lips against his. "Can we go in?"

"All yours." Max handed her a set of keys, then grabbed the flashlight he'd stored on the porch for this special occasion.

Inside, he moved the light beam along the walls and windows, up the curved staircase to the open second floor, and along the walnut crown molding.

With a slow turn, Jade took in every detail. She was home, finally home. It was as if Forest Wesley had built the house for her. "It's beautiful. Musty smelling, but beautiful."

"Yeah, it's been closed up for a few years. All the bathroom fixtures need replacing. The kitchen needs to be modernized—"

"Modernized? Max, no. You can't *modernize* a vintage work of art."

Max laughed. "Spoken like the true queen of vintage. We have to do some work, Jade. When I turn on the shower, I'd like a steady spray of hot water. Not a sprinkle of green mold."

"You're so demanding, Benson."

"What can I say, I'm a product of my upbringing." Max nuzzled her neck, leading her to the steps. "Want to make out? In our new house?"

"What are you? Fifteen?"

"Yes. All guys are basically fifteen. We only pretend to be mature so you'll like us." He kissed her softly, pulling her to him as he sank to the steps.

Jade swam into his affection, her heartbeat reminding her of how good he was, how much she needed his love. She didn't deserve him, nor this crafted house of beauty and history.

Fraud . . . A prickly sensation gripped Jade and she pushed out of his arms.

"Hey, that was some of my best kissing." Max ran his hand over his hair, breathing deep. "What's wrong?"

"I need to tell you something." Max deserved the truth. How could she go into marriage with such a big lie on her conscience? Deadbeat, albeit alive, dads didn't fall under the 'past was the past' clause. "My dad . . . Max."

"What about him?"

Jade paced the open, high ceiling foyer, the hem of her skirt brushing her calves. This would be Max's first memory of her in this house—discovering his wife was a liar.

"Jade?"

"My dad." She pulled her hair away from her face with her hands. "He's . . . you're going to hate me."

"Hate you? What are you talking about? Come here and sit with me, please."

But Jade remained by the door, peering out the side light. The houses along the lane were starting to dim as the hour grew late. The horde of kids had diminished to a few stragglers, mostly teens who didn't bother with costumes.

"He-he's not dead, Max." She glanced back at him.

He remained on the bottom step in the glow of the flashlight, with his elbows propped on his thighs. After an intense silence, he said, "Why'd you tell me he was, then?"

"It started in college when a friend asked me about him. It just came out. Seemed so simple and uncomplicated." She walked to the edge of the foyer, glad to hide her shame in the shadows. "Only Daphne and Margot know the truth."

"That he's alive."

"Yes. He lives in Washington, D.C. You've met him, actually."

"How would I have met—?" Max stood, balancing the flashlight on his shoulder, shining the light on Jade's face. Squinting, she shielded her eyes with her hand. "Fitzgerald. Judge Harlan Fitzgerald is your dad?"

"One and the same."

Max lowered the light so the white circle haloed their feet. "Oh, man. Jade, you've heard me go on and on about him. Why didn't you tell me?"

Jade tried to think of a good reason why she'd let the lie continue, but nothing came to mind. Tension gripped her neck and shoulders. "I've never talked about him with anyone. I barely know him. He left when I was eight, Max. Aiden and I visited him, like, three times, then we never saw him again."

"Well, when did you see him last?"

Details. She hated digging up the details. "I was ten, I guess."

"Phone calls? E-mails?"

"Not after I turned twelve. I think Aiden called him one Christmas."

"Unbelievable." Max's familiar steps skipped over the foyer floor. The flashlight's beam swished back and forth, sending the light to and fro. "He's a conservative judge, noted for his stance on family values."

An ember of ire flared in Jade's chest. "Are you saying you don't believe me?"

"His papers and decisions on family law, children, divorce, and marriage are becoming a part of the American legal system. But you're telling me he abandoned his family and never looked back?"

Jade stiffened. "You're surprised a man's professional life doesn't match his personal life?"

"He's a fraud then."

"Maybe he really believes all he's said and done in the legal world, Max." Jade came up beside him and pressed her cheek to his back, circling her arms about his waist. "But he just couldn't live it."

"I've argued cases based on his writings and decisions."

She tugged on his arm gently, turning him to face her. "Because you believed in what you were doing, Max. Not because some other man said it."

"How? I mean, what happened?"

"With Dad leaving? You'll have to ask Mama if you want the partial truth."

"No, you tell me. What do you remember?"

"I was eight, but in my mind, it all started with Mr. Barlow losing his farm."

"I know the case. *Barlow vs. Land & Farm*. That case set precedent and launched your dad's career."

Jade sank back down to the broad, smooth, hardwood steps. "The night the case was decided, Todd Barlow showed up at the house with a shotgun."

Fourteen

July 1988

"Harlan Fitzgerald, get yourself down here. Now!"

Jade's eyes popped open. Darkness cloaked the walls of her room.

"Did you hear me, you lying coward?"

Jade rolled onto her belly and peered over the windowsill. The glow from the utility lamp by the edge of the driveway haloed the ground with a triangle of light. Who was out there?

Angling sideways, Jade tried to see around the side of the house, but her bedroom was in the back, and—

"Fitzgerald!" The cock of a shotgun cracked against the air. Jade's pulse surged as she ducked beneath the window, burying her face in her pillow. "I'm calling you out."

Sliding out of bed like a snake, Jade crawled across the floor, careful of splinters, and eased open her door. The hall was black, but she could see enough to crawl toward Aiden's room.

"Shh," he said as she eased onto his bed. His room was hot, the hum of the floor fan barely stirring the summer's moist night air. The fragrance of corn and barley drifted through the skinny screen.

"Who is it?" Jade asked, stretching out next to her brother and peeking out the window with her eyes barely above the sill.

"Sounds like Mr. Barlow."

"Is he loaded?"

"Don't know about him, but his gun is sure cocked and ready to fire."

A man in coveralls stood just beyond the porch steps, silhouetted by his truck headlights, a shotgun hooked over his arm. Jade had seen Paps holding his gun the same way when he went hunting.

"I got all night, lawyer. Thieving, robbing lawyer." The man's words swam together. He wiped his face with his sleeve.

"Yep, he's loaded." Aiden pushed himself deeper into the mattress.

"Think he can see us?"

"Naw. Don't mean he won't aim for the house, though. Get away from the window."

"He's mad, ain't he?"

"Like a stirred-up hornet's nest."

"But he owed money. Lots of money."

"How can he pay his bills if he can't farm, Jade-o?"

Jade set her chin on her fist. Aiden argued like Mama. She was fit to be tied when she found out Daddy's client was the bank.

"You're helping the bank take away a man's livelihood?"

"Beryl, he sold off his collateral, took the money, and never paid one dime against his loan. The bank is out three hundred thousand dollars with no recourse."

The shotgun blasted, rattling the windows. The inside of the house came alive. Doors opened and closed, light eased through the crack of Aiden's closed door, footsteps powered down the hall.

"Beryl, call 9-1-1."

"Wait, Harlan . . ."

The gun cocked and exploded. Jade screamed and buried her face into Aiden's arm. Her legs shivered so hard she couldn't control them.

Be a bad dream, please. This is just a bad dream.

The bedroom door flew open. "Both of you, get on the floor now," Mama commanded. "Jade, stop screaming."

"Harlan!" Another shot exploded, reverberating in the house, echoing across the fields.

Covering her head with her hands, Jade's silent screams billowed in her lungs. *Don't hurt Daddy. Please, don't hurt Daddy.*

"Todd, get off my property right now and we'll forget all about this," Daddy called from the porch under Aiden's room. "You're drunk."

"He's plastered," Aiden whispered to Jade, lying beside her on the floor by the bed.

"We've called the sheriff," Daddy said.

"Does Daddy have a gun, Aiden?"

"Mama said guns kill people, but Dad laughed and said something like, 'Not law-abiding guns,' and she had a hissy fit."

Jade moved so close to Aiden she could hear his heartbeat. Mr. Barlow had a gun. Drunk Mr. Barlow. But not her kind, sober Daddy? Tears slipped down her cheeks.

Talk to Jesus when you feel scared, Paps always said. Jade rolled over and started crawling toward the door.

"Where are you going?"

"To get my medallion from Paps. The one he wore in the big war. Said it kept him alive."

"Jade, no, wait. Come back."

By the time she snuck back into Aiden's room with the medallion around her neck, she'd begged Jesus to help her Daddy, uttering the prayers Paps taught her. But nothing had progressed between Daddy and Mr. Barlow.

"We can do this nice, Todd. It's your choice. Put the gun down."

Mr. Barlow rattled off some words Jade had never heard before. Aiden whistled. "He's ticked."

Jade looped her finger over the leather cord holding the medallion. *Can't you hear me, Jesus? Please help Daddy.*

"They took my farm, Harlan. And I have *you* to blame for it."

"Blame yourself, Todd. You put up your stock and equipment as collateral, and the bank loaned you money based on the value of those things. Then you sold them. Refused to pay your note."

"I have to live, don't I? Feed my family, buy more seed?"

The sirens wailed long before blue flashing lights colored Aiden's dark wall.

"You also have to pay your bills, Todd, meet your obligations."

In the next minute, police cars surrounded Mr. Barlow.

"Listen," Aiden whispered.

Jade breathed long and slow, rising up toward the window. But all she heard was the *thump-bump* of her own blood in her ears. "What is it?"

"Crying."

Jade stretched her ear closer to the screen. Watery, muffled cries blended with the cadence of the flashing lights. "Poor Mr. Barlow." Her heart twisted, watching the deputy cover his head and fold him into the sheriff's car. "What do you think they'll do to him?"

"Put him in jail, probably." Aiden balanced his chin on top of his fist.

"First his farm, now jail. Not a good day for Mr. Barlow." Jade squeezed the water from her eyes. *He tried to kill Daddy.*

In the next few minutes, the blue lights stopped bouncing and the squad cars cleared out of the yard. The air around the house hovered, empty and eerie. Not even the locusts were singing.

Jade's stomach contracted as her emotions deflated, like the night Paps was lowered into the ground. Batting away the sting of tears, she jumped off the bed. "I want Daddy."

Just as she reached the door, Mama stepped in, clicking on the dresser lamp. "Are you two all right?"

"Is he going to jail, Mama?" Aiden asked, scooting to the edge of his bed.

"For now."

Daddy stood in the door. "How's everything in here?"

"Daddy." Jade jumped into his arms, clinging to his neck, inhaling the starched fragrance of his shirt. "I prayed for you, like Paps taught me."

"Did you now?" Daddy wrapped her tight. "You know I can take care of myself, Jade-o. Especially when I buy a gun—"

"Harlan." Mama sighed. "You're not getting a gun."

"It's not 1967 anymore, Beryl."

"No, it's 1988, and the world is even more dangerous. But I'm still a pacifist." Mama helped Aiden under his sheet. "Go to sleep now, if you can."

"Then you face Todd Barlow's shotgun next time." Daddy carried Jade to her room. "Don't be afraid," he said, settling her on her pillows. "I'm here."

"I heard him crying."

"Forget about him, baby." Daddy straightened her nightgown, then kissed her cheek. "He should've thought about his actions before he got liquored up and drove over here with a loaded gun."

"Are you going to get one? Really?"

"Is this fun bedtime talk?" Daddy tickled her ribs. Jade giggled and squirmed, kicking away her sheet. "Now, you go to sleep. In the morning, I'll get up and make my famous waffles."

Jade tightened her expression. "Daddy, you never make waffles."

"There's always a first time."

She rolled over on her side, curling her legs. "Night, Daddy."

"Night, Jade-o." He powered her fan up a notch on his way out, clicking her door shut behind him.

Even with her door closed and the fan humming, she could hear the roar of Mama and Daddy fighting.

"He could've killed your daughter and son. *Killed*, Harlan."

"You think this is my fault? Beryl, the man is in charge of his own actions. Tough times don't change men's hearts; they only reveal them."

"Do you see what you're doing? You're becoming one of them."

"Them who? People who want to build a future? Earn a good living for their families? Send their kids to college? Live by the integrity of their word? Beryl, he put up his stock and inventory, then sold it out from under the bank."

"I know what he did, Harlan. I'm not stupid. You could've found a better way."

"Like what? Payments? Todd blew that option."

"It's the money, isn't it? The bank has deeper pockets so you sided with them."

"The bank was my client. And I would've sided with Todd if he'd had a case, if he were right."

"How much, Harlan?" Mama's tone was the one Jade hated. It meant trouble.

"How much *what*?"

"How much is the bonus for winning this one? The money you're starting to make is near obscene."

"Me? What happened to 'we,' Beryl? And this wasn't about the money, but about my client's rights."

"A bank? Rights? I never thought I'd hear you side against the working man. Makes me sad. You've lost yourself, Harlan. It's evil what you're doing. Money has made you blind and stupid."

Jade's door creaked open, and Aiden crawled into bed next to her. "They're fighting like two toms."

"Do you think Daddy's evil?" *Evil* was one word Mama used that Jade understood. "Mama called him Hitler the other day."

"He's not a Hitler. Paps said that Hitler was the devil himself in the flesh."

There was a crash and Jade ducked under the sheet, gripping her medallion and whispering to Jesus, the God and friend of Paps.

~

Max's cell rang, interrupting Jade's story. She collapsed against the banister spindles.

"Jade, sorry, I need to answer this." Max held up his iPhone, brushing his hand down her arm. "It's the third time he's called."

"Take it, please." She needed a minute to reset her boundaries, to get away from the story, away from the aching tenor of Barlow's sob and the slice of Mama's anger tearing down Daddy's argument.

Letting go of the lie was freeing; reliving the reasons *why*, draining.

Max wandered from the foyer into the great room, his footsteps bouncing against the high, sculptured ceiling. Jade rose from the stairs, her hip cramping from the hard surface.

Walking into the great room, she gazed through the jib windows into the front yard. It was overgrown and needed weeding. Like her. But she was glad to whack at some of her secrets today. Max needed to know about Daddy. In letting go, she'd cut a shackle.

"Sorry, babe, work . . ." Max touched her shoulder.

"I was thinking we should hire a landscaper." Jade faced him as she settled against the window frame.

Max peered beyond her to see the yard. "I'll call Doug Hogan tomorrow. He did Dad and Mom's garden." Then he settled next to Jade. "So what happened after that night?"

Jade sighed. "Barlow went to jail . . . for a long time. Two months after his arrest, Mama and Daddy were fighting. The tension was like cold peanut butter, even to an eight-year-old. Aiden and I tiptoed around the house, hiding, trying not to upset Mama or Daddy."

~

Prairie City, August 1988

Jade dropped her bike by the back porch, her stomach growling, cocking her ear to the door, listening. Daddy's new Porsche sat in the curved driveway, and it wasn't even dinnertime yet. Jade feared she'd walk into an explosion between him and Mama.

While the fighting had become more familiar than frightening, she still never felt safe.

"Jade-o." Eclipse waved from his army-green tent. "How's school?"

"Good." Jade waved, wishing he'd go away.

He and Carlisle, Paul, and some bony girl named Sabrina had driven in during the night a few days ago and set up tents while they slept. Boy, Daddy was ticked when he woke up the next morning.

"Just remember, tune in, turn on, and drop out." Eclipse grinned, giving Jade the peace sign.

Jade jerked open the screen door. She never knew what he was talking about. *Mm*, the kitchen smelled good, like cinnamon. Did Mama make cookies? Sniffing, Jade trotted across the uneven linoleum to the counter. But it was clean and cleared.

Her head jerked up when Mama's light footsteps moved across the upstairs. Daddy's longer, heavier steps followed.

". . . It's an incredible opportunity, Beryl."

Jade curled up on the sofa, covering herself with the throw pillows. *Shoot.*

"Oh, really? For who? You? What am I going to do in Washington, D.C., among all those lying politicians and their fake wives? Or their mistresses pretending to be wives." Mama slammed a drawer shut. "And once again, you made a major decision without consulting me, Harlan. Like that ridiculous car."

"I see. It's fine for you to make decisions without consulting me, but—"

"What decisions?"

"Um, like having kids."

Mama's laugh was sharp and not funny. "Having kids. You were the one who—"

"Said the world was too troubled to bring more children into it, and you agreed. No babies. I wanted a career and you wanted to farm, or go back to school, whatever you felt like doing. It was going to be just the two of us."

Jade gasped, trembling. Mama and Daddy didn't want them?

"Yes, and I told you I wanted to do a physical cleanse and was going off the pill. You agreed to be responsible for birth control."

"So it's my fault?" Daddy's footsteps hammered above the ceiling. Jade covered her ears to block out their voices, curling on her side. Oh, her tummy ached.

"It happened on your watch. Both times. Draw your own conclusions."

Daddy growled, "Fine, whatever, but here we are with two kids, Beryl, and I'm doing my best to give them a future, a chance at a good education, or are you suddenly against that too?"

"No, but I'm sure as heck not moving to Washington, D.C."

Jade snatched up the remote and powered on the TV as a creeping chill worked its way over her skin, freezing her brain. She stared at the TV until the edges of the big box blurred.

"What now?" Aiden appeared and plopped onto the couch next to her, his camera dangling from a strap around his neck.

Jade focused on him. "I thought you were spending the night with Sticks."

He shrugged, peering up at the ceiling. "Changed my mind."

She understood what he felt without words. The Fitzgerald household was about to change.

"I don't want to move to Washington," she said.

Aiden put the camera to his face and pointed it at Jade. "I'm going to stay here and live with Granny and Paps."

The argument upstairs got louder. Bigger. "Get off your high horse, Beryl. You knew I wanted this job with Mitchell & Peterson. You ironed my shirt while I packed."

"I didn't think you'd say yes without talking to me."

Click.

Jade shoved Aiden with her foot. "Don't take my picture. Does Dad know you have his camera?"

"He don't use it."

"I'm walking into Mitchell & Peterson a partner. Next year it'll be Mitchell, Peterson & Fitzgerald. Beryl, this is a great move for us, for Aiden and Jade. Not to mention getting inside the system where we can effect real change. Not just protests and sit-ins."

Jade glanced at Aiden. "What do they want to change?"

"Mama says the world. Daddy says himself." He fiddled with the film winder. Clicking it over and over.

Mama's footsteps landed hard against the stairs. *She's coming down.* Aiden and Jade scrambled off the couch and out the front door. To make herself move fast, Jade pretended Mama was the Wicked Witch of the West.

Aiden ran off the porch, gripping the camera. But Jade froze, flattening her back against the boards of the house beside the window.

"This move is about your career and prestige, Harlan. So you just go on to Washington, live your life, leave me stuck here with the kids . . . Forget about what I want out of life."

Jade squeezed her eyes shut. If she were a bird, she'd fly away.

"Ah, here we go. Back to the women's rights speech. You pull this out every time something doesn't go your way. Well, Beryl, wake up, it's 1988. If you want to do something with your life besides minding kids and cleaning house, get out there and do it. Who's stopping you?"

The muscles in Jade's jaw tightened until her temples throbbed. *Fly away* . . . But she couldn't move.

"How can I do anything for myself if I'm following you around?" Something thumped. A chair or table? "Get out, Harlan. Just get out."

"You're not even going to consider Washington? You spent most of your twenties protesting on the Washington Mall. Now you have a chance to get inside, and you refuse."

"*You* have the chance to get inside. Not me. If you want to go, go. Take the kids with you, and I'll make my own next big move in life."

"I can't take Aiden and Jade to Washington if you don't come."

"And if you leave? What will I do with them? Leave them here by themselves so I can get a job—"

"Would you stop all this, Beryl? You're being stubborn for stubborn's sake. Just come with me. Then neither one of us is stuck with the kids."

Trembling, Jade gazed over the darkening landscape, salty tears running under her nose, gathering around the corners of her lips.

The front door jerked open and Jade fired off the porch, running toward the cornfield, raising her arms to her sides. She was flying, flying away.

~

"Wow, he actually said he didn't want kids?" Max found a movers blanket in the foyer closet and had spread it out on the great room floor. He propped the flashlight against the stone fireplace, the yellow beam glowing against the vaulted ceiling like a paper moon.

If she thought too much on it, Jade created a kettle of anxiety in her heart and mind. Thinking about it now made her want to run away, like she did that evening.

"How can you not want your own kid?" Max reclined on his side with his head propped in his hand.

Jade winced. "How many family law cases does your firm take every year, Max? Come on, it happens every day. People are selfish, whether they mean to be or not."

Max smoothed his hand over her hair, then cupped her head, drawing her to him for a kiss. "I'm sorry, Jade. I can see why you said your dad was dead."

"Doesn't make it right. As far as I know, he's a good man."

Max fell back on his elbows, stretching his legs the length of the blanket. "How can he be good? He abandoned you."

The dull ache in Jade's soul throbbed. "I like to think he didn't mean it. There's this father in my memory who loved me and cared for me. One time, he found me when I was scared and lost."

"Yeah." Max tapped her leg gently with his toe. "Go on, little bird, how'd he find you?"

Fifteen

Prairie City, August 1988

The sharp leaves of the August cornstalks sliced at Jade's arms as she pushed deeper into the field.

Stuck with . . . kids . . . Didn't want babies. Go, go. Take the kids and go.

Running, running, running so hard she couldn't breathe, Jade aimed for the heart-shaped clump of trees on the edge of the field.

Aiden, where are you?

Catching her toes on a root or vine, she stumbled forward, arms flailing as she pounded to the hard, dry dirt. She wouldn't cry. She wouldn't. Birds don't cry; they fly.

Jade hopped up, ignoring the warm trickle of blood down her calf. In a minute, just a minute, she'd break into the open and fresh air around the trees.

She hunched down and ran, the heat among the cornrows stifling. Where were the trees?

Fear blipped over her skin along with the trickles of sweat. Someone moved the trees or she'd be able to see them by now. *Aiden, which way to the trees?* Slowing her pace, Jade twisted around to see if she could see the trees or the gabled tip of home. But all she could see was golden silky tips of corn. Rows and rows of corn.

"Aiden!" Her scream rose to the tips of the corn, then fell back to her chest, barely disturbing the still air around her.

Cutting to the left, Jade hunched down, trying to run under the tall stalks, but the leaves slapped against her face. When she felt she'd run far enough without breaking into the tree stand, she cut to the right and continued to run.

Sweat stung her eyes. Her shirt stuck to her skin. When she stopped to breathe, Jade collapsed to the ground, whispering, "Daddy . . . Daddy."

Did he see her when he came out the door? Because she wasn't really flying, only running.

Boon-Doggle, Aiden and Stick's friend, once glared at Jade with his yellowish eyes and hissed, *"If you miss the patch of grass leading to the tree stand, you're as good as a goner. Won't come out of the corn until harvest time."* His vicious laugh resurrected in her soul and chased her fears through her mind down to her heart.

"Daddy."

A shadow fluttered across the corn, blocking the sun. Jade tipped back her head to see a throng of birds riding the current. Big ones, little ones, soaring and looping over the field.

"Birds, I'm down here. I'm down here." Jade jumped and waved, her words drifting to the top of the corn and down again. "Tell Daddy, please. No, Aiden. Tell Aiden."

One or two, she couldn't tell really, flew away, she was sure of it, leaving the rest to watch over her. Jade plopped to the hard ground, the sweat gelling on her arms. Her pulse no longer drummed in her ears.

It was dark when she woke up, shivering. The hot afternoon had faded to cold. Aiden hadn't come. Or Daddy. Sitting up, pulling her knees to her chest, Jade searched the moonlight for signs of her winged friends.

They were gone. She was alone. Panic pulled her to her feet as a bucket of tears splashed her face. "Aiden."

Didn't they miss her at supper? Who set the table? It was her turn this week. Daddy and Mama were probably glad she was gone. What if Daddy already moved to Washington, and Mama got a job? Did they leave her behind?

"Daddy, don't go, please." Jade stepped forward, shoving the cornstalks aside, seeing nothing in the dark. Her feet felt like bricks, too heavy to lift. Sinking to the ground, she dropped her forehead to the dirt, her tears forming rivers in the cracked, dry soil.

A fluttering sound batted the air above the field, followed by a twittering song. Granny said it was the melody of the nightingale. Lifting her head, she listened closely before whispering, "Bird, did you tell them about me?"

Wings beat the air. Following the rhythm, Jade caught the silhouette of a small bird in the wispy light as it lifted from the stalks right over her head.

A sharp call sounded on the edge of the silence. It sounded like her name. Jade jumped up. "Aiden? Daddy?" She strained to hear. There it was again. And the faint *snap-clap* of a screen door followed by a shout.

A rumbling motor disturbed the still night air.

"Daaaddeee!" Jade pressed the call from her lungs until she ran out of air. She inhaled deep and let go again. "Daaaddeeee!"

A hound bayed.

"Daaaddeeee!"

The corn rattled and shimmied, then a wet nose tapped Jade's leg. "Snoops, old Snoops, you found me." She dropped to her knees and crushed her cheek against his saggy, furry neck.

Dropping his rump to the ground, Snoops lifted his nose and bayed, long and loud. Jade's deep Daddy-shouts accompanied him, arching over the field. Bright lights snapped on and washed the corn with pure white beams.

Snoops sounded his alarm twice more, then settled at Jade's feet. She stood stock still, waiting, listening to the rustling corn leaves.

"Jade? Baby?"

"Daddy?"

Suddenly he appeared between the corn stalks and the light, scooping her into his arms. "Baby, you had us worried sick."

She buried her face against his neck and sobbed. Now that she was safe, she was terrified.

When they came out of the field, the deputy who took away Mr. Barlow signaled to cut the big lights. "She's out. Snoops found her."

Mama teetered on the edge of the porch as Daddy carried Jade home. "Jade Freedom, what on earth . . . ?"

"Leave her be, Beryl. She's been through enough." Daddy cupped his hand over the back of her head and carried her into the house, sitting with her on the couch. "We thought you were in your room, asleep. Mama went to check on you and your bed was empty."

Mama came toward Jade with cotton balls and peroxide, dabbing at the cut on her leg, her fingers trembling. "What on earth possessed you to run into the cornfield?" She glanced at the open screen door. "Eclipse, is that you? Come on in, Jade's doing fine."

Daddy brushed the sticky strands of hair from Jade's cheeks and eyelids. "Did Boon-Doggle or Sticks put you up to it? Aiden?"

"No." She cast her eyes down, picking at the dried wound on her knee. "Hey, Eclipse."

"Hey, kiddo." The strawlike man with greasy braids knelt beside her. "Did you hear the nightingale sing for you?"

Jade sat up. "I did, I did. The birds watched me. I told them to get Daddy."

Eclipse closed his eyes and brushed the air with his palm. "The earth is one, Jade, the earth is one."

"All right, Eclipse, that's enough." Daddy stood. "Thanks for stopping by."

"Harlan—"

"Fix Jade something to eat, please, Beryl. I'm taking her up for a bath." Daddy carried her upstairs to the bathtub, singing, "When Irish eyes are smiling, 'tis like the morn in spring."

Later, when he tucked her into bed, he stared at her for a long time. "Is there anything you want to tell me? Why you ran into the field?" Daddy curved his arm around her head and leaned against the wall.

"I just ran." Jade stared at the ceiling, inhaling Daddy's end-of-day scent. She liked his cologne. It was her favorite smell.

Daddy sat forward, clearing his voice. "Jade-o, Daddy has to, um, well . . . go away on business for a while."

"To Washington?"

"So you know. Of course, you're smart, aren't you? Yes, to Washington. But I'll see you real soon. You go on to sleep now." Daddy tucked the sheet in around her and turned on the floor fan. "Remember, I love you."

"I love you too." She rolled onto her side but didn't fall asleep, listening to the sounds of the house. She reached to the fan and clicked off the motor.

Bump, bump, bump. Footsteps pounded the stairs.

"Did you tell them?" she heard Mama ask.

"I said I was going away on business."

More bumping sounds. Suitcases.

"Harlan, don't leave this for me to handle alone. It's not fair. You're the one—"

"No, you're the one, Beryl. Tell the kids I'll call them later."

"Harlan, could you find a worse way to do this? Talk to them. I bet they'll understand."

"Beryl,"—Jade scrambled to her door, cracked it open, and crawled into the hall. *What happened to Daddy's voice? It sounded like the rain dripping from the eaves*—"I can't."

Aiden crept down the hall. "He's leaving."

The peace and security of thirty minutes ago leaked from Jade's pores. "Shh, you're lying. He's going away on business. He told me."

"Are we really doing this?" From the top of the landing, Jade could see the shiny black of Daddy's head. He was angling toward Mama; Jade could only see the tip of his shoulder.

"We're different people than we were ten years ago, Har."

"At least one of us is." Daddy stepped out the door, onto the porch. Jade caught the tips of his Nikes in the yellow porch light.

"Daddy," Jade murmured, crawling down the hall to Aiden's room so she could peer into the front yard. "Don't go."

At his car, he lifted his suitcases into the trunk, gazing back at the porch as he walked around to the driver's side door. "I'll send for the rest of my stuff."

"I told you," Aiden whispered in her ear. "He ain't coming back."

Jade smashed her fists into his arm. "Shut up."

"There's money in the account. I'll call you about details. Beryl, are we—?"

"See you, Harlan." Mama's voice came from the porch, the voice she used when she asked if they wanted pizza for dinner because she was too tired to cook.

Daddy hesitated by his open car door, playing a jiggling melody with his keys. *Don't leave, don't leave.* Jade dug her fingernails into the paint of the windowsill. He glanced toward the second-floor windows, lifted his hand halfway, as if wanting to say good-bye, then slipped into the Porsche and fired up the engine.

"Told you." Aiden rolled onto his back, away from the window.

"Wait, Daddy. Wait!" Jade stumbled from the bed, her toes caught in the hem of her nightie. "Daddy, wait!"

"It's too late, Jade."

"I want to go." She tripped as she flew down the stairs, her gown too tight around her legs. "Wait for me, Daddy. I want to go with you. I promise to be good. I promise. You'll be glad I'm born." Jade smashed open the screen door. "Wait, Daddy, please. Don't leave me. Please!"

Pumping her legs, wishing for wings, Jade raced to the end of the drive, the soles of her bare feet pierced by the sharp-edged gravel.

But Daddy didn't even slow down. Jade watched until his car disappeared around the bend, his red taillights swimming at the end of her vision. She crumbled to the asphalt and became one with the grime and the pebbles.

Sixteen

By Wednesday afternoon, shop details had stacked up on Jade. Four messages from estate brokers, seven from consignment clients, and an in-store shopper asking for the history of the banister rocking chair.

In the loft, Willow surfed cable channels while waiting for Jade to go with her to BoutiqueCouture for her fitting.

"What do you want me to tell Mrs. Ellison about the rocking chair?" Lillabeth followed Jade to the office.

"Tell her it has a history. We just don't know it yet." Dumping the mail on the desk, Jade reached into Roscoe's treat bin and tossed a soft bone to his spot under the desk.

Jade snatched up a sticky note and maximized QuickBooks. Ah, Luella Wentworth. That's right . . . She needed to print a check for her.

"The chair is eight hundred dollars. She thinks it's a lot of money unless there's some story behind the chair. She's worse than you about wanting a history with her antiques." Lillabeth and the rocking chair.

"Okay, yeah." Hands on her hips, Jade gazed out the alley window. "Here . . . How about I found it in Atlanta. Is she a Rebel or a Yankee?"

"Transplanted Yankee."

"Okay, good. Found it in a house once occupied by Union troops during the war. It's believed General Grant used the rocker during his nightly prayers."

"Ooh, good." Lillabeth started out of the office. "I like it."

"Wait." Jade grabbed her arm. "Don't tell her unless she presses. Start with finding it in Atlanta and go from there. If she starts to negotiate, go straight to General Grant."

"I'm on it." Lillabeth hurried through the shop. "Mrs. Ellison, I just read up on the chair's history."

Jade stooped to say hi to Roscoe. "We're busy today, old boy. But soon, you'll have a house with five acres all to yourself and a fenced yard. You won't have to fear runaway trucks." She massaged his neck and front quarters.

Three thirty. Where did the day go? She had to get Willow and head to the city. "Lillabeth, thanks for holding down the fort for me. I should be back to close." Jade crossed the shop, heading for the loft stairs. "Mama."

She was seated on the bottom step.

"I'd like to go with you." She reached for the rail to pull herself up. "Willow thought it'd be all right. After so many years on the road, sitting in a B&B all day gets a bit tiring."

"You can come to the shop anytime, Mama. No one said you had to sit at the B&B. And Max promised you a tour of the house tomorrow, didn't he? You should call him—"

"I just meant I'd like to go with you this afternoon, Jade. Don't need a lecture."

Jade bounded up the steps and rapped on the door. "Willow, let's go. Bring my truck keys."

Just as they stepped out the storeroom door, Jade's cell rang from her hip pocket. It was Max.

"I'm on my way to see you."

"Now? We're on our way to the boutique for Willow's fitting."

"Have her handle it without you."

"Why? What's wrong?" The edge in his voice disturbed her. She knocked her toe against the surface of the blacktop.

"Wait for me at the shop. I'm in the car. Be there in ten." His cell went silent.

Jade glanced at Mama, then Willow, the palm of her hand sticking to the phone. "Max." She held up the phone as if were exhibit A. "He's on his way. Needs to see me about something important."

"Like what?"

Jade tossed the truck's keys to Willow. "Take Mama and go. The boutique is on Market Street by the Read House." She eyed Mama. "Do you have a dress for the wedding?"

Mama sliced her fingers through the tip of her braid. "Hadn't thought much of it until now."

"Help her find one, Wills. Charge it to the account."

"Right-o, Jade-o. Let's go, Beryl-o." Willow looped her arm around Mama's shoulders. "Feeling a bit boney today, are we?"

Standing in the alley, Jade watched Willow drive down the hill with Mama, her arms folded, hunching against the nip in the air. Curly, puffy clouds drifted between the Appalachian peaks and the pale blue sky. *What's up with Mama?* Showing up for the wedding, unannounced, three weeks early, contrite and quiet. She'd been distant and curt at Granny's funeral, but today Jade noted a softness about her and a poised expression as if she was about to speak.

"I sold it." Lillabeth skip-jogged over the pavement to where Jade stood.

"The rocker? Fantastic."

"For the whole price, but only half the story."

"Double fantastic." Jade slapped her a low-five.

"I think I'm salesgirl of the year." Lillabeth started back toward the shop. "I thought you were going to the city."

"Willow took Mama. Max called. He's on his way here."

"So, do I get a commission?"

"On?"

"Selling that chair. Full price." Lillabeth stood in the storeroom door, angling to see into the shop. "A workman is worthy of her hire."

"I'll see." It was unusual for Lillabeth to be so concerned about earning money. It's not like she needed it. Her family was part of the Whisper Hollow elite.

Jade wandered back into her office to work, but her mind drifted. What could drive Max from his office in the middle of the afternoon to talk to her? She tried to discern her thoughts by rattling the bag of bones stored in her emotional closet.

"Max just pulled up," Lillabeth announced.

Jade met him in the middle of the shop with a casual, "What's up?"

"Can we talk in the loft?"

Jade's mind twisted with the purpose of this demanded meeting. Was it the house? Did the deal fall through?

Wait, was this about her dad? Oh please, don't tell her Max went looking for Harlan Fitzgerald. Jade would wish she'd left him dead if that were the case.

Was it something to do with June? Maybe Rice? A chill numbed her thoughts.

Max shut the door as Jade entered. "You're scaring me." She fingered Paps's medallion, wishing she had the courage to pray. But she'd surrendered her rights and any possible access to Jesus thirteen years ago.

Max stood on the other side of the coffee table. "Why didn't you tell me?" He locked his eyes on her, piercing and drilling.

"Tell you what?" Jade sank to the edge of the sofa and picked a loose thread from her sweater. "That Mama was weird? What? Is this about my dad? I don't—"

"I feel like such a fool."

"Max, enough, what are you talking about?" Jade tightened the loose thread around her thumb until the tip was blood red.

"I bought into your line, Jade, about the past being in the past. Hook, line, and sinker. Deaf, dumb, and stupid."

"Like you don't have a few skeletons to hide?" Jerking her thumb free, Jade rubbed it until the skin was normal and pink. The direction of the conversation made her shiver. "Like the real reason you and Rice broke up. She told me she wanted it to work, but you were in something . . . denial, deceit, something. And your mom being all funny about your back problems and your meds, refusing to talk in front of me. What's going on there, huh, Max?"

"Never mind me. You're married, Jade. Mar-*ried*."

She rose slowly to her feet. "What?"

"Yeah, you're married." He faced her, chin out, feet apart, arms akimbo. "My secrets have a long way to go to top yours, babe, trust me."

The blood drained from her head and gathered in her toes. Purplish-red spots swirled before her eyes. A cold sweat dotted her forehead and neck.

"No. I'm not married."

"You sat in Reverend Girden's office and lied. I defended you when he questioned your spirituality, told him you were good and honest. Do you make a habit of lying about your past?"

"I'm not married, Max." She balled her hands, gripping them in her lap. "I'm not. Stop saying I am."

"Does the name Dustin Colter ring a bell?" He pulled a paper from his pocket, unfolded it, and dropped it to the coffee table.

No, no, no. Jade knocked the paper to the floor. "I'm not married."

"Well the state of Iowa sure thinks you are. How did you get married in '96 anyway? Did Beryl give you permission?"

No, no, no, no. This isn't happening. Jade scooped her hair back from her face and stormed into the kitchen.

"Jade?" Max came in, flipping on the overhead light. "You lied to me about your father. How do I know you're not lying about this? This is insane, Jade, I trusted you. Is there anything else you need to tell me?"

Covering her head with her hands and arms, she sank to the floor, sitting on her heels. "I'm not married, Max." She shook her head, chasing wild thoughts, trembling. Puffs of warm breath filled the pocket between her legs and torso. "I'm not married."

"Tell me what happened." His voice softened as he moved over to her. She felt his presence kneeling next to her.

"Do you love me?"

"What?" He bent to see her face. She tucked her forehead tighter against her arms.

"Do you love me?"

"Yes, I do, but I'm not sure I *know* you."

She sprang up, wiping her face with her hands, yanking a paper towel from the roll. "I can't believe this . . ." How could she mess up her life like this? Was she not destined for love and happiness?

"Jade?" Lillabeth's knock was tentative. The loft door eased open. "Luella Wentworth is here."

"Her check's on my desk." Jade sniffed. "Tell her thanks for the business."

The door clicked shut.

For a long moment, Jade could only look at her shoes while Max waited against the counter, his legs crossed at the ankles. She wanted to reach for him but feared being shoved away.

"Do you still love him?" he finally asked.

Jade tossed her head back with a watery laugh. "No, double no." Worst decision of her life . . . No, second worst.

"How'd you get married at sixteen?"

"I lied." As the truth left her lips, Jade buckled with the weight of her confession. More lies for Max to see. "We forged our parents' names. Used an eighteen-year-old friend to witness getting the license." She shot a brave glance at him. "How'd you find out?"

"Let's just say your mother had lunch with mine." Max walked to the fridge and took out a bottle of water.

Mama . . . "The marriage was annulled, Max." How did she end up with so many lies to cover? Jade had been so worried Mama would spill the beans about Daddy, but she never dreamed the name Dustin Colter would come up in conversation.

"Jade, the state of Iowa has no record of an annulment." Max twisted the cap from the water and tossed it in the trash. "My paralegal spent half a day searching."

Jade snatched her phone from her pocket. "Willow, put Mama on . . . Nothing. It's nothing, but please, put Mama—Okay, then go into the dressing room."

Max gulped half the bottle of water, then wandered into the living room. Jade brushed her eyes with the back of her hand, her insides turbulent.

"Mama, the Colters . . . they annulled the marriage, right? Yes, *the* Colters, Dustin's parents . . . Didn't you see a form . . . sign something? I don't know, you said you'd handle it. Well, didn't you ask when you came off the road with Gig?" Jade brushed the heel of her hand over her forehead. "Yeah, okay, thanks. I guess it was too much to be concerned about your daughter's life for five minutes."

Snapping the phone shut, Jade yanked her jacket from the hook, threw open the loft door, and hammered down the stairs. The walls were closing in up there. Closing in.

"Jade, where are you going?" Max thundered after her.

"Lillabeth, close up, will you? Yes, yes, I'll pay you extra." Jade shoved out the front door, the cords of fear and anger tight around her chest as she headed toward Laurel Park. There was a merry-go-round on the west side, and she had an urge to ride.

"Jade." Max caught up to her, walking stride for stride.

"I should've known." Balling her hands into fists, Jade punched the air. "The fates can't rest unless they're tormenting me."

"Don't blame the fates, Jade. Own up to what's yours. Maybe you didn't know about the annulment, but you could've at least told me you were married before."

"And then what?" She stopped so fast he almost bumped her. "Would you have done some PI work on your lying little fiancée to make sure she was indeed single?"

She started walking for the park's merry-go-round. *Midmorning, there had better not be a crowd.*

"I might have checked it out, just to make sure."

"Ooh, I bet your mom is loving this." After the merry-go-round, a chocolate shake from Froggers. A big one. Maybe two.

"She doesn't know, Jade. She mentioned to Dad how interesting it was that you'd been married before, and he mentioned to me—"

"So you opened the investigation?" Jade whirled toward him, faking a belly laugh. "What great communication you have in your family. Does Rebel relish being in the middle? The stoolie? 'June, Max's fiancée is a heathen.' 'Ooo, Max, your little girlfriend was married.' And by the way, Señor Nosy, did it occur to you to call and ask me before you went snooping into my business?"

The music from the merry-go-round spurred her forward. Under her heavy stride, yellow-brown leaves crackled.

"Did it occur to you that being married before, at sixteen no less, might not fall under the past-is-the-past clause? And why is this bothering you so much? Why can't you just say, 'Gee, Max, yeah, I was married. Sorry, I thought it was annulled.'"

"Hm, I did say that, and you called me a liar."

"You admitted to lying."

Jade swung around. "To the state of Iowa, not to you."

"Yes, to me. You sat in Reverend Girden's office and said, 'Nope, I've never been married.' Let's just clear the air, is there a kid or two you haven't mentioned?"

"Yeah, Max, I hid them in my bedroom, taking them out to play when you're not around."

He pinched her arm. "You could've put a baby up for adoption."

"There's no baby, Max." She held steady. "No adoption."

Mr. Hannity, the park's maintenance man and merry-go-round jockey, spotted Jade as she pulled away from Max and waved her over. "Come for a ride, Jade? Not many more nice days like this left. That you, Max? Haven't seen you in the park on a weekday since you was in high school."

"Ah, Mr. Hannity, now that's downright depressing," Max said, keeping up with Jade as she picked up her pace.

A couple of moms were herding their little ones toward the mechanical horse race. Beating out a couple of dirty-faced rug rats, Jade hopped on a chocolate brown pony with a red saddle. Max threw his leg over the pink one next to her. The *short* pink one.

"Why did you say no in Reverend Girden's office?"

"Mr. Hannity, let's go." Jade smacked the neck of her fiberglass steed.

"Jade, I know I came on strong at the shop, and I'm sorry. But, babe, you need to know we have a technical difficulty." Max rested his forehead against the gold-plated pony pole. "We can't locate Dustin Colter. And if we can't locate him, we're not getting married a week from Saturday."

"See what happens when you go snooping?" The ride lights flashed; it was getting ready to begin. "If you'd have left the past in the past, this would've never come up and we'd be getting married, no worries."

"And claim innocence if caught? I suppose so. But we did find out. I could be disbarred if I knowingly marry a married woman."

Jade sat on her stationary mount, silent. The breeze cooled her face and cleared the heat from her eyes. "Why'd you do it? Investigate without asking me."

"Didn't even occur to me. I asked Stella to run a check, and once she discovered your marriage intact, the process took on a life of its own. I wondered, who was this man, this boy, who captured Jade's heart before me? What was his name? Where did he live? How old was he? The news left a pit feeling in my stomach."

She couldn't look at him. "Getting over Dustin was the hardest thing I ever had to do, Max. He caused me a lot of pain. More than anyone knows. And frankly, I planned to never think about him again." She tapped her engagement ring against the pole. "Hey, Mr. Hannity, is this thing ever going to start spinning?"

"Simmer down, girl. Give a man a chance."

Two little girls raced across the grass, yelling for Mr. Hannity to wait. They jumped on the platform and stopped by Max and Jade, staring at them with Precious Moments eyes.

The brown-eyed girl gazed at Jade. "That's my favorite pony."

"So? I was here first. Get another pony. Look, there's a red-and-black one over there."

"But I like chocolate."

Meanwhile, the hazel-eyed child glowered at Max. "The others are too big for me."

"Well, we're riding these ponies this time." Jade shooed the girls with a flick of her hand.

The girls' eyes welled up, and Jade gave the brown-eyed one a twisted-lip expression. *Might as well learn now, life isn't fair. In fact, it can be downright painful. Best to learn it when you're young. Walls take time to build.*

"That's it." Max grabbed Jade by the waist and lifted her off her horse.

"Hey!"

Holding on to her, he motioned at the horses with his chin. "You girls can have our horses."

"They aren't real horses, you know!" Jade called over her shoulder, squirming, working her elbows into Max's ribs. "And that one's not real chocolate!"

"What's the matter with you? Act your age." Max steered her toward one of the sleighs and shoved her in.

"You act yours." She thumped down on the seat, crossing her arms, setting her stubborn chin away from Max.

He sat next to her as the merry-go-round lights went up and the music began.

Dustin. Of all the blasts from the past. He was not supposed to be in the middle of her relationship with Max. His name didn't deserve the honor of her breath.

"The other night," Max started, "you trusted me enough to tell me about your dad. Can't you trust me about Dustin?"

"It's not about trusting you, Max. It's about forgetting. Leaving the past in the past." She gazed down at her hands. "Guess that's becoming a cliché by now."

"What are you trying to hide?"

"Nothing." She shook her head. All her emotions were settling at the bottom of her soul and the waters of her heart began to calm. "I just want to be happy, Max."

"I want you to be happy, too. Very. Look, I don't want you to slice open a healed wound just so I can have the details." He turned her chin so she'd face him. "But I want you to know, I'm here for you. I'll always be here for you. Please, tell me what happened."

She peered into his eyes, feeling his words. "No offense, Max, but you don't know you'll always be there for me. Daddy said he loved me, then he left. Dustin promised me forever. Shoot, even Mama ran out on us kids from time to time. What really scares me though . . . maybe it's not you who will run one day, but me."

Seventeen

Prairie City, June 1996

Jade clung to Dustin's hand. They'd driven all the way to Deep River without saying a word, just listened to the radio. But they were *actually* going through with their plan.

A shiver caused her legs to twitch.

"He's finishing his supper. Two shakes and he'll be right out." The wife of the justice of the peace scrutinized them from the kitchen doorway, arms akimbo, lips pinched tight.

"Thanks." Dustin's voice cracked.

"Go on in the parlor." She motioned to the boxy room to the right and disappeared.

The parlor was cluttered with magazines and newspapers, a couple of old radios and two TVs, powered on but muted. The pungent odor of sauerkraut stung the air.

"Are you nervous?" Dustin whispered, hugging her to him.

"A little." Jade's knees shimmied with a nervous chill.

"Are we really doing this?" Dustin released her, peering out the side window.

Stu and Rachel waited outside.

"Well, don't you kids look nice." The JP appeared in a faded plaid shirt and worn dungarees. His wispy gray hair was combed forward from the crown of his head, and wiry whiskers grew from the sides of his ears.

"I'm Dustin." He stretched to shake the man's hand, his words fast and shaky. "This is Jade. You married my cousin Bart and his wife two years ago."

"Good for me. Sorry about the mess. The missus is a collector." The JP shuffled through a stack of books and binders by a wooly brown easy chair. "Gwyn, where's my book?"

"How should I know?" came through the wall.

"Here . . ." The JP offered up a worn leather binder. "Do you have the license? The Bulls play in fifteen minutes, and I'd like to see the game if it's all the same to you." The man scratched his protruding belly.

"Yes . . . yes." Dustin patted his pockets. "You think the Bulls will win the championship with Jordan back on the team, sir? I must have left the license in the truck." He started out the door, Jade on his heels.

"Bring the signed notes from your parents. I'm guessing neither of you is eighteen." The JP arched his eyebrows as he dropped his chin to his chest.

"Yes, sir. Our parents gave their permission. We do have the notes, and a license."

"Yet you came to see me, a Deep River JP."

"Yes, sir. My cousin recommended—"

"So I heard."

Jade squeezed Dustin's arm. Blowing out a long breath, he squeezed her hand three times. *I. Love. You.*

"Our best man and maid of honor are outside. They can come in, too, can't they?"

"Unless they have X-ray vision and can witness through the walls."

"Right." Dustin took a step and banged into the door, nodding to the JP. "Be right back." He smashed the handle on the screen door and darted onto the porch.

Scurrying down the steps, Jade laughed. "Are you scared, cowboy?"

The JP poked his head out the door. "Don't forget the fifty-dollar fee."

At the truck, Dustin opened the driver's side door, then swooped her into his arms. "No, I'm not scared. We're getting married, baby."

"Pinch me, I'm dreaming." She buried her face against him, inhaling all of his goodness.

Could this boy really want her? Straight-laced, smart, clever Dustin Colter, last year's prom king runner-up and, as he said, "wrestling stud"?

Stu, his best friend, and Rachel, Jade's best friend, jumped out of Stu's Camaro.

"Stu, I need the license." Dustin dug around his glove box. "Didn't you see me put it in here?"

"Look at you, Jade-o. Last fall, he'd just asked you to homecoming." Rachel slipped her arm through Jade's, smiling her trademark hooked smile.

"Shannon Bell cornered me in the restroom. Remember?"

"She was so jealous." Rachel laughed. "Thought she had Dustin in her hip pocket."

"This is insane." Jade's legs shook, and the hem of her flared skirt brushed her knees. Wild. Exciting. But insane.

"I need the parents' notes. The JP wants to see them." Dustin's head popped out from the other side of the truck. "Rach, weren't they with the license?"

"Men, good grief. Step aside." Rachel crawled into the cab, her feet sticking out over the seat, her flip-flops slipping from her toes.

Looking back now, Jade knew she'd fallen in love with Dustin during homecoming. He never left her side that night, refusing to let other boys cut in. Turning down girls who asked him to dance.

When the DJ played Elvis singing "I Can't Help Falling in Love," Jade nestled her head on Dustin's chest and whispered the lyrics to his heart.

As he drove her home that night, she convinced herself the midnight hour had come and her Cinderella evening was only a fairy godmother dream. Monday morning, she'd be girl-in-math-class again.

Eight months later, he proposed by a moon-washed lake after prom. Watching him by the truck, laughing over something with Stu, Jade's muscles twitched under her skin and the ground seemed to shake beneath her feet. As much as she wanted nothing—no fears or doubt, no Granny-tainted wisdom—to rob her of this perfect night, she had to remind Dustin one more time.

"Let's go." He grabbed her hand. "Got the license, the signatures, the money. Times a-wasting. Bulls are about to tip off."

"Dustin, wait." Jade tugged on his belt loop, dragging him toward the thick-rooted tree in the front yard. "Let me talk to you for a second."

"Gorgeous, can it wait?" He walked with her, stealing kisses and sneaking peeks down her top.

"Stop, listen." She wrestled with his hands. He'd better pay attention, because after tonight, she'd never mention this again. He'd have no excuse. "Dustin."

He backed up with a heavy breath, fixing the tuck of his shirt. "What's up? Make it quick. I'm ready to get married."

"I just, um, wondered, you know . . ." Jade's urgent, desperate statement caught in her throat. "You could have anyone, Dustin. Any girl in Prairie City. Are you sure you want to marry me?"

"Is that what this is about?" He sobered, sliding his fingers around her neck.

Heat bumps ran over her skin. "I love you, Jade. I want to marry you." His kiss was soft at first, then hungry, wooing her to him.

When he released her, she felt mushy and ready to surrender. "But marriage?" She stammered out the last of her argument. "You're only seventeen. I'm sixteen. This is your senior year." The power of Jade's challenge startled her, and she understood her words could convince him to change his mind.

"So what? I've always known what I wanted. Be the baseball team's pitcher? Earned the spot in one season. Want a new truck? I tossed hay bales for three summers to pay for it. When I switched from football to wrestling, everyone said I came too late to the game. Went to regionals my first year. I knew, Jade, here." He slapped his hand to his heart. "I could do it."

"But this is marriage, Dust. Not sports. Not a truck."

"The first day I met Stu, I knew we'd be best friends for life. And that was way back in fourth grade. I signed up for AP classes, and everyone said it'd be too much with sports. My parents, my counselors, my coach. So far, I've never gotten anything below a B."

Jade tugged at his shirt sleeve, loving his reasoning and that it was overpowering hers. "Marriage, Dustin. *Marriage.* Fifty percent of them fail in this country. My mom's on her third."

"My parents were high school sweethearts. They're still going strong. Jade, I'm telling you, I know you're the one I'm meant to spend my life with. I have no doubt." He kissed her with a confident touch. "Outside of Stu, you're my best friend. I wake up thinking about you. Go to sleep wondering if I'll get to see you before the first bell. Last week I had Mom take the phone out of my room so I could study without being tempted to call you every five minutes."

Her heart bounced at his confessions. "I kiss your picture at night and pretend you're holding me, telling me everything is going to be all right, that I'm safe with you. I love you, Dustin. But I'm not so rosy-eyed to believe young love always lasts." *Jade, don't blow this. He loves you.* What would her days be like without him? Brooding and dark, a Transylvanian dungeon.

"Remember during homecoming? You asked me why I invited you," Dustin said gently, running his finger under her chin and along the edge of her jaw.

"Yeah, and I still can't believe you chose me." His touch created chills on her warm skin and caused her eyes to mist.

"I asked you because I was tired of watching you from afar." He grinned. "The girl I pushed out of a corn field when she wrecked her granddad's truck. The girl I tried to casually bump into between classes for the next year, or sit next to during lunch. I changed math teachers so I could be in your class. Should've seen the counselor's face when I gave her my reason. Something stupid like, 'Ten o'clock is my best hour for math. Peak time for my brain.' By homecoming, I'd just gotten tired of pretending. Jade, you don't know it, but you're one of the coolest girls in school." He grinned, entangling his fingers with hers. "It's one of the reasons you *are* so cool. Beautiful, wide-eyed, innocent. Listen, I'm sworn to secrecy as a guy, but the locker room talk . . ."

"I'm talked about in the locker room?" *Ew.*

Dustin held up his free hand. "You're the girl all the guys want to end up with one day. I just discovered you first."

"Hey, you two, save it for the honeymoon. What's going on over there?" Stu banged his fist against the side of Dustin's truck. "Let's go. I'm hungry."

"Stu—" Rachel's smack and his "ouch" punctured the night. "Does everything have to be about you?"

"Be right there . . ." Dustin tugged Jade toward the JP's porch. "Stu's right, we can talk on the honeymoon. All one night of it."

"Dustin—" Jade planted her heels, ready to march out her final thought. "You can have me without marrying me." Did he get what she was too shy to say? In their eight months of dating, they'd come close to making love many times, but Dustin was always the one to stop, shove away. *Not like this, Jade.* "We don't have to be married, you know. We can . . . do it."

Mama's over-the-shoulder advice was a distant echo in her mind. *Jade-o, explore your sexuality. Sixteen isn't too young. I was seventeen in the Summer of Love, you know.*

"I know." Dustin bumped her body with his. "But I don't want it to be that way, Jade. You deserve better. You're worth more." He squeezed her fingers. "I want you, bad. Lots of nights I wondered why we didn't . . ." In the light from the porch, she could see the shine of his eyes. "But it never felt right. Guess it was the way I was raised, going to church and all. This feels right. Marrying you. The way it's supposed to be. I don't want to just 'do it.' Any lug head can 'do it.' I want it to mean what it's supposed to mean."

His confession smashed her last clump of doubt. Except . . . "Dustin, I want everything you just said, but what about waiting until you're eighteen?" She couldn't help it; she had to make sure, hear his confidence one last time. "Your parents won't be able to stop you, and I'll be seventeen a few months later. I'm sure by then Mama would give me permission or tell Granny to sign for me."

"No, Jade, no." Dustin gestured toward the house. "We're here now. We've thought about it, planned it. Come on"—he tugged her toward the porch—"trust me. The JP's waiting."

The porch light flicked off, on, off, on. "Tick tock, kids, let's go. Game time."

"Jade?"

In the small span of space between them, she could feel Dustin's heart beating. "Yes, let's go." She threw her arms around him. "We're getting married."

For the first time since Todd Barlow fired shots into the night, calling out her daddy, Jade Fitzgerald was completely safe.

~

After the JP made it official, Stu and Rachel treated the newlyweds to dinner at Maid Rite in Newton. It was out of the way, but everyone agreed it was the perfect reception location.

Rachel raised her pop in a toast. "To Dustin and Jade. Many years of love and happiness. May we be so lucky, Stu."

"If only you were as sweet as Jade."

"What? I am sweet—"

"Like a sweet tart." Stu grinned and bumped her with his shoulder.

"You're so mean. To Dustin and Jade." The four thunked their glasses together.

"Forever." From the moment Dustin pledged to love her until death—forever—his love removed all shadows from Jade's consciousness.

Peeking at her hand in her lap, she twisted the Irish claddagh ring he'd slipped on her finger. He wore an identical one on his hand. One day, when he had more money, he promised her a diamond.

Eating baskets of loose seasoned-beef sandwiches and fries, loving the feel of Dustin's hand on her leg, Jade laughed at Rachel and Stu. They argued about everything—when and if they would *ever* get married, who would drive Stu's car home tonight, who had the best grades, who knew more funny lines from *Seinfeld.*

When Dustin moved closer, running his hand up and down Jade's thigh until she thought she'd go crazy, Rachel and Stu didn't seem so entertaining.

Finally, Stu went to pay the check and Rachel ducked into the ladies' room, leaving Dustin and Jade alone. He nuzzled her ear. "You're my wife. Mrs. Dustin Colter."

Chills swirled over her skin. "You're my husband."

"I appreciate Stu and Rachel, but I wish we'd turned them down." He ran his hand around the back of her neck. "We'd be on our honeymoon now if we'd gone on."

"Ah, come on, this is our reception." Laughing, she kissed his cheeks. "You only get married once."

"Once. Just once."

In the parking lot, the friends gathered in twos. Dustin and Stu by the tailgate, Jade and Rachel by the passenger door. Chitchatting.

Rachel grabbed Jade in a hug. "Are you nervous?"

"A little," she whispered. "It's not like we—"

"Right, right." Rachel gripped her shoulders. "Relax, he loves you."

"I'm counting on it."

"Ready?" Dustin unlocked the passenger side door and held it open for Jade.

She hopped inside. "Remember, Rach, if Granny calls—"

"You didn't feel good and went to bed early. Oh, wait—" Rachel ran to Stu's car. "I want pictures."

Stu groused while Rachel posed everyone, setting the timer so she could duck into the shot. Then she posed Dustin and Jade, Dustin with Stu, and finally handed the camera to Stu. "Take one of me and Jade, and it best be in focus."

He clicked the shutter without checking the view finder.

"All right, one last shot of the happy couple." Rachel aimed the camera just as Dustin scooped up Jade in his arms. Laughing, she tossed her head back and flung her arms wide.

The camera clicked.

"That'll be one to hang on the wall, show your grandkids."

Stu was shoving Rachel toward the Camaro.

"Bye, you guys. Have fun."

By the time Dustin fired up the truck, Stu had powered out of the parking lot, his red taillights slicing the darkness. Shifting into gear and slowly backing out, Dustin peered at Jade, grinning, a lock of his brown hair dipping over his forehead. "How are you?"

"I'm good, really good." She slid under his arm as he steered down the road. "It was a lovely wedding, wasn't it?"

"Perfect in my book. Stu paid for dinner, and in the eight years I've known him, I've never seen him pay anything for anyone."

"Love has strange powers." Jade set her head on his shoulder, a small cloud of regret threatening her sunshine. "Dust, I feel sort of bad that we lied, though."

"Yeah." He rubbed her arm, braking as the car in front of him turned right. "It's the downside, but nothing can change my mind. Tonight was right, Jade."

She kissed his jawline. "I love you."

Driving west, Dustin announced he'd committed one more little indiscretion. "I used Dad's credit card to book a room at the Des Moines Hilton. But I'll pay cash when we leave, so no sneaking anything from the mini bar, just in case."

"The Hilton, hey, big spender." Jade was glad Rachel had talked her into buying something special to wear for the evening.

"Getting married by the JP was fine by me, but I thought we'd want to remember a nice, fancy wedding night."

"Do you think the room will have one of those Jacuzzi bathtubs?"

He wiggled his eyebrows at her. "Why don't you just sit back and enjoy the drive, Mrs. Colter?"

"As soon as you turn eighteen and we tell our parents, I'm changing my name."

"Until then, it's our little secret."

Driving with one hand, holding her with the other, Dustin stole kisses as they sped along I-80, both of them singing to the radio this time, laughing.

Jade repainted the evening's details as they came to mind, hanging the vivid memories on the walls of her heart. The color of Dustin's shirt, the feel of his hand resting on her back as they stood before the JP, the wash of emotion when he said, "I now pronounce you husband and wife," and the scent of sweet corn and honeysuckle that hit her when they ran out of the house, married. Dustin had picked her up and whirled her around, head back, shouting to the stars.

If she loved him any more, her heart would burst.

Dustin swerved into a CVS parking lot on the edge of the city. "I'll be back," he said with a kiss, leaving the truck motor running.

"Where are you going?"

"To get stuff, you know"—he bobbed his head from side to side—"for tonight."

Her eyes widened, and she ducked into the shadow of the store light. "Oh, yeah, right."

At the drugstore door, Dustin looked back at her. Snickering, Jade slumped down against the seat and watched him. A few minutes later, he tossed a small paper bag into the truck like it was on fire. "Next time, you're going in with me."

"Oh, no, I'm not." Jade peeked inside the bag. Lotion too? She had a lot to learn.

"Yes, you are. I felt like a perv."

"Fine, then you go in with me when I buy tampons."

He fired up the truck. "Man, married life is already complicated."

"Wimp." She fell into him with her kiss.

When she lifted her face, he pressed his hands over her hair and down her back. "This is forever, Mrs. Colter. You and me."

"Forever and a day."

Eighteen

The music of the merry-go-round faded as Jade finished her story. Max sat forward, staring at the painted rump of the horse pulling their sleigh, the sleeves of his blue dress shirt straining against his arms.

Rubbing the fingernail imprints from the palms of her hands, Jade watched Mr. Hannity weave his way through the horses toward them.

"Must have been some conversation. Y'all rode for almost thirty minutes. Listen, I can fire her up for another go-round, but after that, I'm taking my dinner break."

"Thanks, Mr. Hannity, we're fine. Please, take your break."

"Suit yourselves. You can sit as long as you need, but I'm shutting down the lights."

Sitting on the motionless, dark merry-go-round, Jade waited for Max to speak. In the park oval, after-work joggers kicked fallen leaves from the cement walks.

"Aren't you going to say anything?" Jade said, breaking the silence.

"Just processing."

Let him be. The memory of that night had burned through Jade's heart and leaked emotion through her words.

Max stood after a second, exiting the sleigh. "It bothers me, Jade. I don't want it to, but when you were telling what happened—"

"I don't love him."

"Sure felt like you did." Max stepped off the ride.

"I don't, Max. Believe me." Jade followed, standing next to him on the walkway. "I haven't seen him in thirteen years."

"You're married to him, Jade. Your first love. Most people never forget their first love. I've seen it . . . in the practice. People divorcing after ten, twenty years of marriage because they ran into their first love at a high school reunion." He stared toward the green oval instead of at her. The wind looped his caramel-colored tie over his shoulder. "Being married to him has surely added a layer of emotional complication."

"He may have been my first love, Max, but he destroyed my heart." The word *destroy* sounded like an exaggeration, but she was desperate for him to hear how much she didn't love Dustin Colter. "What about those cases you've seen where love is lost because one spouse obliterated the trust of the other?"

"I've seen it, but"—he shook his head—"it's not entirely the same."

"No, it's worse. If love and marriage were so binding, people would never divorce. Haven't you seen cases where high school marriages ended in hate and disgust?" Jade closed her eyes, exhaling. *Believe me.* "Until I met you, I didn't want to fall in love again. No man was worth my heart. I didn't believe in happily ever after."

In a quick, jerky move, he snatched her to him, roping her into his arms. "I can't stand the thought of you loving someone else who hurt you so bad, Jade. I don't know what he did to you, but I don't like him. Not at all."

"That makes two of us. It's you and only you for me, Max. This is why the past is the past. It never happened. It doesn't matter." She tipped her face to see his.

"Are you sure?"

"Oh, Max, so very sure. But what about you? Do you think about Rice? You were engaged."

"No, but sometimes I think about the first woman I ever truly loved."

"Oh?" Jade took a step back, gauging his tone and expression. She couldn't ask, not really, if the past was the past.

"And the best part?" Max brushed her hair aside, kissed her temple, and enveloped her in his embrace. "She's standing in my arms right now."

Nineteen

Prairie City, November 1996

Long shadows crept across the living room from the south-facing windows. Curled on the couch, Jade surfed afternoon programs, her thumb rapid on the remote's channel button.

Eighty channels and nothing decent on. She tossed the remote to the end of the sofa. Willow had some program she watched at five thirty anyway.

Granny had dropped her off after picking her up from the babysitter and before making a run to the market, and asked if Jade was going to be home for dinner. She wanted to know how much chicken to pick up.

No, Gran, Dustin was picking her up after football practice. Restless, Jade picked up the JC Penney catalog on the end table. Flipping through the pages, she paused at the ones Willow had already marked for Christmas.

"What are you doing?" Willow bolted into the room with a pageant of Barbies in her hand. Mama brought her a new one every time she and Gig stopped by on their way to another show.

"Waiting for Dustin."

"He's late again, ain't he?" Willow dropped to the floor and started lining up her dolls.

"Isn't he. No."

"You can watch Mary Kate and Ashley with me and the Barbies. Shh, Miranda, you can't talk during the show." Her finger to her lips, Willow bent toward one of the dolls. Then she aimed the remote and clicked on the television.

"Who do you like best? Mary Kate or Ashley?"

Willow shrugged. "They both leave something to be desired, but they're good entertainment."

Jade laughed. "Where'd you hear that?"

"Read it in *People*."

"Does Granny know you're sneaking into her magazine stash?" Jade brushed her hand over the girl's long, tangled hair before rising from the sofa and grabbing her jacket from the hook by the door.

Walking out to the porch, she leaned against the post. The scene before her had changed since Dustin picked her up in June and carried her away.

Summer green had given way to fall gray. The forecast predicted snow tonight. She and Dustin were going to build a fire in his parents' basement—his parents always turned in early—and watch a video.

A tingle tightened her skin. Living apart, keeping their marriage a secret, made the relationship both exciting and frustrating.

It was hard to be with him and then have to stir herself to go home. Especially now that the weather was growing colder and snuggling was more fun. But Granny's curfew was nonnegotiable. Even Mama couldn't override her.

Mr. and Mrs. Colter had a different approach with Dustin. They'd just say, "Don't stay out late, son."

After five months Jade had zero regrets about marrying him. If possible, she loved him more every day, but . . .

They had their trials—Dustin getting distracted by football and the guys, and the Northern Iowa University recruiter who offered him a wrestling scholarship.

Even now, the idea of him going away to college muted all the colors in Jade's world. When he proposed and they talked through their plans, he'd promised to wait a year for her. He'd work at the plant and on the farm with his dad, then they'd go to college together. She'd spent hours researching married housing and off-campus rentals.

Then there was the week his dad grounded him for back-talking his mom—no truck, no phone, no visitors. That was a long, hard week, but Dustin spent the entire time planning their reunion.

The memory made Jade smile.

So they'd weathered a few storms and were stronger for it. Then last night, during a gin rummy match with Aiden—

The screen door clapped, and Jade looked down to see Willow hanging over the porch rail next to her. "Those twins are insipid."

"Willow, do you know what *insipid* means?"

"No, but I like saying it. Insipid, insipid."

"Better not let Granny catch you out here without your jacket. Oh, look, is that her car?"

Willow was a dirty-blonde blur. Her feet thudded. The door slammed. When she returned, her jacket was zipped to her chin and her hood rode low over her forehead.

"I don't see Granny's car."

"Hm, must have been one that looked like hers."

Willow stuck her feet through the porch rungs, bending her waist over the rail, eyes toward the road. "I'm waiting for Aiden. He's taking me to church tonight."

"Is he?"

"They give kids cookies and Kool-Aid."

"I bet."

Aiden attended church with his girlfriend's family. A few months ago he got baptized. Jade went to witness with Dustin, Willow, and Granny. When Aiden disappeared under the water, Jade touched her praying hands medallion as her belly did a free fall with hot tears chasing. Next to her, Granny cried, covering her nose with a tissue, and Willow pestered Dustin about how long Aiden could hold his breath underwater without croaking.

When the pastor lifted Aiden from the water, declaring all his sins buried with Christ, a lump formed in Jade's chest. Her brother looked different, his simple happiness boosted by a spiritual experience.

She'd leaned against Dustin. Aiden had Jesus, and she had her husband.

"What else do they do at church?" she asked Willow.

Willow spotted a fleeing spider on the porch rail and puffed it over the side. "Talk about Jesus."

"Yeah? Do you like Him?"

"He seems like a good guy. I'd like to spit in the dirt and stick mud in someone's eyes too."

"And who might that be? Billy Spangler?"

"Yeah," Willow said low, out the corner of her mouth, cheek against her palm. Billy taunted Willow regularly. So much that Granny had to call the school. "But I'd have to poke his eye out first."

Jade swung her up in a hug and sat with her on the porch swing. "You just tell Billy when you're grown up and drop-dead gorgeous, he'll be sorry."

Willow frowned, leaning against Jade. "I want him to be sorry now."

"Yeah, well, me too." Jade pushed her toe against the porch and set the swing in motion. "But trust me, it'll mean way more when he's sixteen and you won't give him the time of day. By the way, what time is it?"

"I'll go see." Willow hopped down, running inside. "You want a snack, Jade?"

"Just the time, please." Riding the swing back and forth, she surveyed the road. Football practice ended at five-thirty. She expected to see Dustin's blue truck coming around the bend any time now. Jade gathered her jacket around her. Cold anticipation prickled up her arms and down her legs as her mind upped the volume on last-night's conversation with Aiden.

"So, what do you think of Dustin's news? Northern Iowa is not that far. I think Paps' truck could make the trip without falling apart."

"What are you talking about? He's not taking the scholarship . . . He's going to work for a year, then go to college with me."

"It's all over the locker room. He took the scholarship. He'll be road-tripping to NIU with Hartline this weekend."

"You're lying, Aiden."

"Why would I lie, Jade-o?"

"Don't come in here all holy and mighty, Saint Aiden, and rain on my world. Dustin wouldn't leave without telling me."

His wife.

"Whatever, take it up with him. Are you playing cards or not? It's your turn."

"I don't want to play."

She'd tried during school today to talk to Dustin, but a net of emotion trapped her words.

Willow thundered back out to the porch. "Dustin wants to talk to you."

Jade jumped from the swing. "He called?"

Willow hung on the porch rail, gazing down the road. "Don't see him standing here, do you?"

"You watch too much television, Wills." Jade steered her sister back inside and picked up the living room portable. "Hey, where are you?"

"I'm at Hartline's house." Booming voices trampled over his.

"Hartline?" Ben Hartline, the one going on the supposed road trip. He was a burly defensive end who thought a good time was shooting BBs at dogs and cats. "You're supposed to be here, picking me up."

"I was planning on it, believe me, but . . ." His voice faded like he'd dropped the mouthpiece below his chin. "Hey, don't start the film without me . . . Jade, Coach gave us film of Mid Prairie. We're ordering pizza, going over their plays and key players. If we beat them, it's Division for us."

"Colter," a bass voice interrupted. "Cut the ball and chain and let's *goooo*. Daylight's burning. Did anyone order the pizzas?"

"Ignore Brill . . . you know how he gets when he's hungry." Dustin's laugh burned her ear like a hot prairie wind.

"Is that funny? Calling me a ball and chain?" Brill was another player with a bit too much *Animal House* going on.

"He's had a few too many."

"Too many? Are you drinking, Dust?" She hated drinking. Observed too many of Mama's parties to see any use for alcohol.

"No." His tone was defensive.

Jade debated. Back off or push? Let him do his football thing now, then press him later with the questions burning in her heart? Forces beyond her control threatened her happiness, so she'd best be wise, think this thing through.

For now, she had to trust his pledge. His promise of forever.

"Don't be mad, Jade. This is my last high-school football season. I want to have fun, make it count. Most of us have played together since Pop Warner."

"I'm sorry, but I am mad. Football buddies or not." Jade lowered her voice. "I'm your wife, and I haven't seen you for four days, Dustin."

"So I can't hang with my friends my senior year? Maybe Brill had it right . . . the old ball and chain."

The words smacked. This wasn't happening. Jade jumped from the sofa and stood in the middle of the living room. "A ball and chain you begged to wear. Now you're acting like an immature—"

Jade caught Willow glancing up from her circle of Barbies, eyes rounded and scared. She flashed her a smile. "Willow, why don't you go grab me a Diet Coke, okay?"

"Is that still Dustin? On the phone?" She pushed up from the floor, a Barbie trapped in each hand.

"Everything's okay. We're just working something out. Go on now. And get me a cup of ice." When she disappeared, Jade fired the rest of her thought into the phone. "Jerk. An immature jerk. And now you've got Willow upset."

"Me? You're the one going off."

"Because my husband"—she clenched her teeth—"is avoiding me."

"No, I'm trying to make everyone happy, including you."

"Including yourself." Jade snapped on the end table lamp. A V-beam fell across the end of the sofa.

"Jade, look, Sunday I'm all yours."

"Sunday? What about tomorrow night's game? And all day Saturday? We were going to study, then go to the movies." Since the first game of the season, they'd developed a tradition: dinner at Dairy Queen with their gang after Friday night's game, then hauling off to be alone, curling up in the bed of his truck until Granny's curfew.

"Some of the guys want to drive up to Cedar Falls after the game to check out Northern Iowa."

"Did you accept the scholarship?" She was losing all firepower.

"Let's talk on Sunday, okay? Jade, it's good, I promise. I've got a plan."

Willow crept across the living room, carefully placing one foot in front of the other, balancing a Diet Coke can and a tall, very full cup of ice, her Barbies tucked under her arms.

"Plan? *You* have a plan? What happened to *our* plan? You made promises to me, Dustin." Jade cradled the phone against her shoulder and reached to help her sister.

"Hey, don't be like—" A high, rolling laugh filled Jade's ear from Dustin's end of the phone line. "Looky here, it's Kendall-wendall."

"Kendall's there?"

"Of course—she's Hartline's sister," Dustin said with a tussle in his voice. "His *ugly-mugly* sister."

"Look who's calling who ugly, Colter." More tussling with laughter.

Jade sank to the edge of the coffee table. Kendall Hartline was beauty defined. Not cheerleader plastic as in Shannon Bell, but an athletic, strong, barefaced beauty with sleek dark-brown hair that glistened like a Pantene commercial.

"Hey—" Feeling very beige and nagging, Jade deployed a new tactic. "Why don't I come over, bring brownies and ice cream?"

School rumor was that Kendall had had a crush on Dustin since last spring. Jade put Rachel on it, but the most reliable sources clammed up whenever she went snooping.

"Ah, thanks, Jade, but this is a team thing. Besides, they don't . . . you know . . . know about us, and it'll just look like I'm whipped."

"Dustin, hang up. Jade, give the boy some breathing room," a host of male tenors chimed in.

Jade slammed the phone to the base, her hands icy and moist. She was losing him. Dustin had convinced himself after his junior year that he'd missed out on a wrestling scholarship.

Then in October, the future he never imagined knocked on his door.

It made sense now. He wanted to go to college next fall. Wrestle at college level. Jade wondered if he'd seized this opportunity like all the others, like he seized her. Only this time, going for what he wanted had a catch.

A wife.

"Willow, Granny will be home any minute." Jade started for the kitchen, her untouched Diet Coke still fizzing in the glass. "Stay inside and watch TV. Unless Aiden is ready to take you to church." Where'd she put her book bag with her wallet? "Don't light candles or the fireplace . . . just don't play with matches at all."

"Where are you going?" Willow turned from her row of Barbie dolls that toppled every which way on the floor.

"To take care of something."

"Are you mad at Dustin?"

Jade walked across the room and kissed her sister's hair, smoothing her cheek with her hand. "Don't worry about Dustin and me, okay? We're together forever."

Snatching Paps' truck keys from the hook, Jade burst out the back door, jogging toward the barn. The crisp evening cleared her thoughts, cooled her emotions. Everything was going to be fine . . . just fine.

Backing down the driveway, Jade figured she couldn't very well drive to Hartline's. Even she'd be embarrassed to show up while the team watched game film. So she drove to the next best place, the home of her heart for the past year: the Colters'.

The golden glow of the living room light falling through the windows welcomed Jade, soothing her angst as she rang the doorbell and lined up her toes along the line where light sliced the darkness.

"Jade, you have a sixth sense," Mrs. Colter said when she answered the door. "I'm just about to take a cake out of the oven." The cropped-haired brunette was fragrant with flour and vanilla. "Come in, come in. I guess you know Dustin's off with the team."

"I thought I'd wait for him here, if you don't mind."

"Don't be silly. I could use some girl talk." Mrs. Colter shuffled Jade into the kitchen with her arm around her shoulders. Jade discarded her anxiety as she walked by the curio cabinet stuffed with Precious Moments figurines and framed pictures of gaped-tooth Dustin and his sister. "What's new with you these days?"

"School mostly. Still working for Mr. Wimple. He gave me a raise." Jade perched on the counter stool, tugging her jacket sleeves down over her hands.

"Good for you, Jade sweetie. So—" Mrs. Colter turned from the oven with a cake pan in her mitted hands. "What do you think of our boy getting a scholarship? Rowdy and I are so proud. We overindulged Sydney when she wanted a fairy-tale wedding three years ago and we still haven't recovered. Then she got pregnant, and Blain got hurt on the job—" Mrs. Colter dumped the cake upside down on a plate and hovered her hand over the white sponge. "Gotta let it cool a bit. We were so concerned Dustin wouldn't be able to go to college."

"Yeah, it's exciting. I'm proud of him." Jade rubbed her thumb over the gold flecks of the countertop, afraid to look up. Dustin had never talked about wanting college very much. But Jade was beginning to realize how much he wanted to go.

"Oh, honey, are you crying? Don't worry, there are plenty of fish in the sea." Mrs. Colter came around to squeeze her shoulder. "Dustin's not the only man in the world. You'll be the queen of PCM high school next year and forget all about him." She winked.

"E-excuse me?" What was Mrs. C talking about?

"I guess I should let you know Dustin told us, honey."

"W-what did he tell you?" About them being married? No, she said something about Dustin not being the only man in the world.

"Well, that you two broke up." Mrs. Colter touched the cake with the tip of her finger, then opened the lower cupboard by the oven, her voice all sad. "I know it's hard, but I think you two did a wise thing." She plopped a mixing bowl on the granite counter. "There's nothing like your first true love. Rowdy and I understand that, but the world is different today. It's best for kids to break apart, and if it's right, they'll find their way back."

"Right, take a break." Jade jerked her claddagh ring from her finger, her eyes blurring the edge of the counter with the far wall of the kitchen. What had she done? Why did she listen to Dustin . . . trust him? Stupid, stupid girl.

"But he said you two were still best friends." Mrs. Colter unwound the cord of her hand mixer, smiling at Jade. "I'm impressed, sweetie. If Rowdy had broken off with me in high school, I'd have dented his car and slashed his tires."

Don't tempt me. Then the walls of the room inched closer, closing her in. Jade's pulse surged and her breathing got shallow, and it was as if she were all alone in the world.

Sitting in the cozy, bright kitchen, alone. Jade gripped the counter, afraid she'd topple off the stool. Her heart beat so hard the edge of her top fluttered.

Mrs. Colter gathered ingredients—powdered sugar, vanilla, Crisco—her lips moving, yet Jade's ears were filled with the sound of her own blood.

After an eternity of seconds, the walls of the room inched back into place. Jade breathed, deeper and longer, and her white-knuckled grip on the counter eased to pink. The rushing sound ebbed from her head.

"Carla, what is that heavenly smell?" Mr. Colter crossed the kitchen smiling and kissed Jade on the cheek, ruffling her hair. "Don't tell me, I've figured it out. It's Jade."

"Stop bothering my help, Rowdy." Mrs. Colter reached over and smoothed Jade's hair into place, then turned her husband toward the living room. "I'll bring you a piece of cake when it's ready."

"How are you, Mr. Colter?" Jade felt watery and weak.

"Good, now that you're here."

And now that you *are here.* The resonance of his voice comforted her.

"Hurry with that cake, Carla." Mr. Colter winked at Jade with a crinkly blue eye and patted his flat belly. "The diet gurus say you shouldn't eat too late at night."

"And what do you know about dieting, Rowdy?" Mrs. Colter pressed her hand over Jade's and peered into her eyes. "You are always welcome here. We just love you, and who knows?" The woman smiled. "You and Dustin might find your way back to each other one day."

The kitchen door flew open and an energetic, laughing Dustin burst into the kitchen with the bubbly and brunette Kendall draped over his back.

"Are you sure your mom won't mind?" She was trying to cover his eyes with her hands.

"No, Mom won't mind. She loves you." Dustin grabbed her hands, hooking them over his shoulders and to the front of his chest. He smacked his mother's cheek with a kiss. "Mom, we're going to—"

When his gaze fell on Jade, it took several seconds for Dustin to exhale her name. "Jade."

It took all her courage to hold his gaze, but she broke after a few seconds. Kendall's presence made Jade feel bland and beige, like she was a boring piece of kitchen furniture. Absently, Jade smoothed her hair, licked her dry lips, and squared her shoulders.

"Kendall, look at you, all this long, gorgeous hair. I'd kill to have hair like yours." Mrs. Colter popped open the fridge for the jug of milk. "Jade, isn't it gorgeous?"

"Yes, gorgeous." Her eyes met Dustin's.

"Sit, you two. The cake will be ready in a few minutes. As soon as I mix up the icing, Jade will spread it over the cake, and then I'm cutting big slices." Mrs. Colter buoyed around the kitchen like the popular mom she was. All the kids liked her kitchen.

"I told you I'd see you Sunday," Dustin said into Jade's ear as he leaned over the counter.

She gripped the front of his PCM letter jacket, rising up until her nose almost touched his. "You're a liar."

"About what?"

"Hey, what are you two whispering about? Kendall, can you find the electric beaters in that drawer over there?"

Jade's jaw tightened as her limbs started to tremble. "Everything."

"Dust, so what are you guys planning on tonight?" Mrs. Colter asked, ignoring the exchange between her son and Jade.

"Kendall's never seen *Strange Brew*." Dustin backed away, holding his hands wide, as if daring Jade to challenge him.

"Really? Good. You know, Dad's always dying to show a movie on his new projection screen. Oh, that thing makes me seasick. I have to watch from the basement steps."

Pain burned the base of Jade's throat. *Strange Brew*. The make-out movie. Dustin popped it in the video player for their sixth date. She quickly became bored with the antics of Bob and Doug and surrendered to Dustin's sweet kisses and caresses.

"The guys call it the make-out movie . . . ," he'd confessed, driving her home. "Most girls don't last past the opening scene."

"Oh, really?"

"First time I've tried it, though."

"I cleaned the basement today too." Mrs. Colter fired up the beaters and whipped together the contents of her bowl. "Jade, are you staying to watch? You've seen the movie, though, haven't you?"

"Actually, no, Mrs. Colter." And please, shut up. All was not right with the world, no matter how cheery she tried to make it. Jade shifted her weight; the tops of her thighs had started to ache from leaning on the rim of the hard-top stool.

Kendall stood tucked in the corner between the fridge and the door. The only sound was the whir of the mixer and beaters bumping against the bowl.

Jade waited. She wanted him to do something, drag her off to his room and explain. Tell her he was sorry, he'd lost his mind for a moment, then lock the door and lay her back on his bed.

"Well, well, there's another pretty girl in my kitchen. Must be my lucky night."

Kendall waved from her chicken-liver hiding place. "Hey, Mr. C."

"Carla, how about that cake?" Rowdy thumped the counter by Jade with his palms, grinning down at her.

"Hold your horses, it's coming. Rowdy, why don't you set up the TV for Dust? He and Kendall want to watch a movie."

"When I come back, I want to see a big slice of cake right here." He jabbed his finger on the granite, demonstrating where he expected to see a plate of cake, then elbowed Jade. "You're staying for the show too?"

"We spoke vows, Dustin." The confession simply came, as if the words were destined to be said. Jade slipped off the stool, her chest rising and falling with each shallow breath.

The mixer went silent. Mrs. Colter's smile faded.

"You made a promise to me." Jade fingered the claddagh ring in her pocket. Blood rushed through her ears again, white-capped with ire. "You promised forever."

"Jade." His voice was flat and firm. "You're making something out of nothing. It's a movie."

"The make-out movie."

"What in the world?" Mrs. Colter glanced from face to face. "Now look, Jade, I know it's hard when your ex-boyfriend moves on, but—"

"Husband. He's my *husband*, Mrs. Colter. Your son proposed to me, and I said yes. We're married."

"Jade—"

"Tell her, Dustin."

"That's impossible. You're underage."

"We forged your signatures. Stu was our witness over the age of eighteen."

"Oh my land." Mrs. Colter fell against the counter, hand to her forehead. "Dustin, is it true?"

"Mom, listen—"

Mrs. Colter thrust her hand at him. "Give me your keys."

"What for?" He scoffed. "You're taking my truck?"

"Dustin, hand them over."

His cheeks reddened as he dug the keys from his pocket. "Mom, listen, let me—"

Mrs. Colter tore the keys from his hand and slapped them into Kendall's.

"Go on home, Kendall. Give us a chance to smooth this out. And please, don't talk about this. It's a private, family matter."

"Yes, ma'am." Kendall was out the door without a backward glance.

Mrs. Colter faced Dustin and Jade with a hard-set jaw and fire in her eyes.

Jade couldn't stop the tears even if she wanted, nor the sense of dread gathering between her ribs. Her blunt confession had just cost her the home of her heart.

"I won't let you do this to your future, Dustin. If you don't take the scholarship, you won't be able to afford college."

"We can make it together, Mrs. Colter." *Jade, listen to yourself. Stop talking.* "We had a plan. He'll work until I graduate, then we'll go to school—"

"It's not that simple, Jade. To work, earn enough money. You'll get distracted, forget to go. Wrestling is here and now. It offers far more opportunity than just scholastics. What if you get pregnant? What if you walk out on him? Then what? Who will want to give him a wrestling scholarship then?"

Dustin had yet to move or speak. Except he stared at Jade with wet eyes. "Mom, I love Jade. I asked her to marry me."

Jade exhaled, the pressure easing out of her spine. "We can make it, Dustin."

"And waiting to go to school with her is the plan?" Mrs. Colter bubbled with indignation.

"Yeah, it is." He walked over to Jade and kissed her. "I'm sorry. Guess I got lost for a second."

She watered his sleeve with her tears. "It's okay."

"Rowdy!" Mrs. Colter stormed to the basement door. "Rowdy, get up here. Your son has done an unbelievably stupid thing."

Twenty

The last thing Judge Harlan Fitzgerald expected to do on his way home from an intense day in a Washington, D.C., court was detour by a church. But today's testimony had disturbed him.

White slavery. A mother selling her six-year-old daughter to the traffickers. For heroin.

The slimy explanation of the wasted, needled-pricked woman poisoned him. He felt physically ill, polluted, and debased. The idea of talking to God, or one of His representatives, was the only tonic that promised relief.

The crimes and sins he presided over today were not committed by him, but by his fellow man—or woman as the case may be—and Harlan accepted guilt by association.

He would repent for this mother and people like her. For himself. At sixty-four, he was starting to believe what he never thought possible.

Man was *not* basically good. There was reality called sin. The world needed redemption. He himself needed redemption. Perhaps Jesus *was* the only true escape.

In his twenty years in Washington, he'd seen what man could do. Dark, evil, selfish. Fed up, Harlan was curious to see what God could do.

He made good time as he drove down Constitutional. Most of the D.C. traffic was heading out of the city instead of in.

At four o'clock, the New York Avenue Presbyterian Church grounds were quiet. He slipped through the front doors, signing his name in the guest book, making a mental note for his wife, Diane, to send a contribution.

During the Civil War, Abraham Lincoln had worshipped in this sanctuary, and Peter Marshall had exhorted parishioners to hold fast during the Second World War.

Standing on the edge of the sanctuary, Harlan tried to absorb the exhortations of great men who now watched from beyond the veil. After a few minutes, and a modicum of release, he eased toward a pew in the back of the sanctuary.

With his eyes closed, he located the portion of his soul that believed. The image of the cross from the front of the sanctuary floated over the depths of his heart.

God, forgive me. His prayer felt awkward and foreign. It'd been years since he'd attended church for anything other than a social function. But it was worth his pride to gain peace and some hint of restoration, of hope.

As Harlan sat in the silence, his meditations drifted from court to his latest Google search on his children. Aiden was doing well. Not surprising. He was a freelance photographer hopping the globe. The mental snapshot of Aiden wandering the Iowa farm with Harlan's Nikon around his neck was permanently framed and hung in a corridor of his soul where Harlan visited alone from time to time.

Since he'd started searching his kids' names a few years ago, he'd discovered his pride in them. Undeserved, but pride nonetheless.

Jade ran a vintage shop, and she was getting married in a couple of weeks. Today's testimony stirred his longing for her, his need to know she fared well growing up with Beryl.

He pressed his fist to his lips as his shoulders jerked forward with a burst of emotion. What kind of man left his children? What kind of man abandoned his beautiful, trusting little girl?

The picture of the blue-eyed, cherub-faced girl the prosecutor had displayed in court ripped his heart. So innocent, so trusting.

But really, was Harlan any better? No, he didn't deliver Jade to slavers, but he wasn't there to make sure she was safe. So caught in his pride and blind ambition, afraid of his own emotions, he never counted the cost of Washington prestige.

His daughter was getting married, and he would not have the honor of walking her down the aisle.

Harlan deserved to have his peace taken. Opening his eyes toward the ornate ceiling, he wondered what Diane would do if she found out her husband had children he'd never mentioned?

Ah, he was horrible with the emotional stuff. Always had been. Weak and self-serving.

Lord, I don't want anything for myself. But bless my girl, Jade. Please.

In the quiet, Harlan's river of peace started to rise as he beseeched God, not for himself, but for his girl.

~

"The contractor is going to refinish all the wood."

Beryl followed Max's hand as he gestured toward the trim and molding, the inlaid bookshelves and the floors.

From the tenor of his descriptions, Beryl sensed Max's pleasure in the Begonia Valley Lane house.

"Jade said all the woodwork was handcrafted by an Italian carpenter,"

Beryl said, feeling a bit like she was on a museum tour. But the house was Jade. Vintage and ripe with a sense of story.

"It was, so we want to preserve all of his work."

Jade didn't move with the tour when Max headed around the upstairs corner. Willow followed, but Beryl slowed her pace, one eye on Jade, the other observing the skylights cut in the roof above the hall. The shadows of blowing tree limbs danced along the plaster walls.

"These rooftop eyes are my favorite parts of the house so far, Jade." Beryl traced the light, streaming in from all angles and spreading like a feathered fan down the hall, spilling over the banister like a lucent waterfall and speckling caramel color on the foyer floor.

Below the open stairwell, Jade's dog, Roscoe, slept in the middle of the sun pool. Beryl liked the nearly all-black Shepherd. He was old and wounded, like she was, and a bit beat up by life.

"The house is much brighter and more open than I imagined from seeing the outside," Beryl said, resting against the top rail next to her daughter. "I expected those big oaks to shade away all the sun."

"It's an architectural marvel." Jade glanced up at the skylights, then down at the marble floor. "Guess we'll have to keep the trees trimmed."

Despite their years of distance, Beryl sensed when her girl was bothered. Willow referred to yesterday's blast from the past as Jade getting "T-boned." Beryl had apologized, but her words landed on a parched, hard heart.

"Will you hire help to keep it clean?" Beryl asked. *Come on, Jade, open up.* "I'd think you would need—"

"Wouldn't that grate on you, Mama? Your daughter, one of the elite, with domestic help?"

Tenets of Beryl's past soapboxes about the working class and equality colored part of her daughter's makeup. "Is that how you see me? A reverse snob?"

Jade's laugh surprised her. "Isn't it how you see yourself?"

"Maybe, at one time." Beryl ran her hand along the smooth surface of the banister. "But it's not how I feel about you. This home is lovely, and you deserve a place like this."

If Beryl hadn't fought Harlan's success so hard, maybe, just maybe—

"We'll need a gardener or something." Jade leaned with her arms on the banister. "I don't have Granny's gift with growing things."

"She kept that one all to herself. Good thing she's not around to see her manicured lawn turned into an overgrown field of weeds." Jade's shoulder was a few inches away. Beryl wanted to reach out to her, but touching was a hard barrier to cross.

Beryl searched her memory. The last time she remembered hugging Jade, the girl clung to her, crying, vomiting, confessing.

Max's phone rang, jolting Beryl's thoughts forward and into the present. His professional, deep, "Benson," rumbled in her ears.

Willow appeared from a room down the upstairs hall and hopped on the banister for a ride to the bottom. *That girl could conquer the world if she ever got focused.*

"I'm going to the little girls' room," Willow said, jumping off the end of the banister before she toppled to the floor. "I think I saw TP in the bathroom off the kitchen."

"Check the toilet for snakes," Jade said, hanging her arms over the landing rail, laughing.

"Ha, ha, you're very funny, Jade." Willow put extra wiggle into her narrow backside as she walked off. "I was only six."

"She'll never forgive you and Aiden for that trick."

"It didn't quite work out as we planned."

"How'd that go again?" Sometimes Jade let her guard down when they reminisced. Sometimes. "You and Aiden put a fake snake in the toilet—"

"Aiden and I put a fake snake in the toilet, then waited in the living room, watching TV with Willow until she had to go potty. Meanwhile, rotten, mean Boon-Doggle—"

"At thirty, he's still mean." His adventures with whisky were Prairie City legend. "Just like his dad."

Jade exhaled. "Do you want to hear the snake story or not?"

"Go on." Beryl focused on Roscoe, his paws twitching in his sleep.

"Boon-Doggle snuck in and replaced the fake snake with a real one. When Willow finally trotted to the potty and lifted the lid, the snake slithered over the seat, hissing." Jade shook her head, standing away from the banister. "Willow screamed into next week."

"She had nightmares for a month, and it set her back on sleeping without a light on for a time." Beryl spoke with authority, but she'd been on the road most of that year, working or touring with her third husband, Gig. The relationship and experiences weren't worth the price her kids had to pay.

"If Granny could've taken a strap to him, she would've. She called his dad, and for once, he thought Boon-Doggle had done something funny and clever."

"I thought Gig's band was going to make it that year." Beryl walked to the window at the end of the hall. "So foolish . . . stayed too long on the road. Missed too much."

"Mama, don't get old and come around apologizing for your life, what you did or didn't do. We've grown, moved on." Jade slammed the reminiscing window shut.

Beryl figured it wouldn't stay open long. She walked around Jade and descended a couple of steps to sit, feeling light, as if she swam through air. She hung onto the banister and gathered her breath.

Max appeared and whispered to Jade. Beryl peeked at them from the corner of her eye. Jade had become good with her masks. Not that Beryl blamed her.

Willow returned and tried to slide *up* the banister. She nearly toppled off twice but caught herself each time. Then, by some feat, she managed to fall backward and ended up hanging by her knees. "Help."

Jade jogged past Beryl and grabbed Willow's hand, pulling her upright. "Goofy."

"Woo, head rush." Willow dismounted from the banister and balanced herself with a hand on Jade's arm. "I'm hungry. Anyone for Froggers?"

Max descended, looking serious. "We could eat in the living room on the old moving blankets."

"An in-house picnic. I like it." Willow headed for the door. "Max, are you buying?"

"Willow." Beryl's rebuke carried no authority.

"What? I don't have any money." She barged into the fading evening light on the veranda. "Max, let's go."

"She's not shy about much," Beryl said as Max passed.

"It's refreshing," he said, smiling.

It was a solid smile, though a bit too much on the perfect side. Beryl preferred a little character in a man's teeth, if not his soul. Learned those lessons the hard way. However, Max she liked. Mostly because he appeared to adore Jade.

"Babe, the usual for you?" Max asked from the bottom of the stairs. "Beryl?"

"The usual," Jade said.

"Nothing for me, Max, thank you."

"Beryl, you haven't eaten all day." Willow stuck her head in from outside. "How about a burger and a chocolate shake. Sent me and Linc for one about a half dozen times last month."

"Jade's been drinking chocolate shakes lately too." Max's fancy-shoe heels clapped against the foyer marble on his way out. Roscoe lifted his one-eyed head.

"I'm fine, Willow," she said. "By the way, did you call Linc like I told you and make sure he's seeing to your passel of dogs?"

"He's on it, Beryl. A few weeks ago you were ready to cart them all off; now you're worried over them."

Max escorted Willow down the walk. The clap of their car doors echoed in the air. Jade wandered into the living room. Beryl gripped the banister to pull herself up, easing down the stairs.

"The contractor is already dragging in dirt." Jade picked leaves from the room's corners. Roscoe trailed along, his claws clicking.

"I like this room. Wide, long, open, and a stone fireplace," Beryl said. "The built-in bookshelves in the back are lovely."

"Reminds me of settings in old movies. I started looking for furniture this week."

Beryl crossed her arms and moseyed to the window. Guess now was a good time. "I drove down three weeks early on purpose."

Jade walked through the foyer and out the door. Beryl watched her dump the leaves from her cupped hand into the yard. When she returned, she folded her arms and leaned against the arched entry.

"Why did you come?"

"I came because—" Tears surprised Beryl, and she turned toward the light of the window. She'd rehearsed what she wanted to say. How she wanted to say it. She'd waited almost two weeks to be alone with Jade, for the right moment to deliver her speech with her practiced dramatic inflection. Beryl knew when to sigh. When to look into Jade's eyes.

Now it seemed morose and melodramatic.

"Because? What'd you do? Burn the house down? Rob a bank? Ooo, get married again?"

"Because I'm sick, Jade." The direct approach worked when drama seemed a bit much.

Jade furrowed her brow, pinching her eyes into a squint. "What kind of sick?"

"Dr. Meadows diagnosed me with chronic leukemia four years ago. It's been mild and manageable until recently. The war is going to the other side."

"So, what . . . you're dying?"

The idea seemed unreal. Beryl Hill, dying? She was too young.

"Nice and slow, like a pig over a spit."

Jade moved from the wall, opening her arms then closing them again. "I don't know what to say."

"I'm not dropping dead tomorrow, so you'll have time to think of something."

"You act like this is no big deal." Jade walked the length of the room, slowly, her back to Beryl.

"Oh, it's a big deal." The news was out, and it drained her. Beryl walked back to the stairs, needing to sit. The floor was too far down.

Her bones ached. Her bottom hit the second step up with a thump.

"Are you okay?" Jade appeared on the other side of the banister but faced toward the open door.

The western-floating sun painted the sky just beyond the rectangle frame of the door. A watercolor scene of brilliant gold and orange: the side of a porch post, the tip of the walkway, a tuft of weeds surviving under the swing of the iron gate, all lined by a row of looming, dark tree sentries.

Carlisle would bring out her paints if she were here. Of course, she'd want the marble floor to be her canvas.

"I've imagined you saying a lot of things to me someday, but 'I'm sick and dying' wasn't one of them." Jade looked around, her body stiff and still facing the door.

"That makes two of us." Beryl leaned against the banister spindles. "One day I was seventeen, free, a part of a new generation. Then one forty-two-year-long day later, I'm my parents' generation, middle aged, my body killing itself."

Beryl struggled against a new wash of sorrow.

"Are you in pain? Nauseous?"

"Tired mostly. My bones ache. I'm restless. Can't sleep some nights. Not much of an appetite. Can't work."

"You've been through chemo, surgery? What?"

"Nothing so far, but in the last six months, my white blood cells have been doing a number on me. Dr. Meadows wants to start chemo and meds." Her chin quivered and her voice wavered.

"What did Willow say? And Aiden?"

"They don't know yet." Beryl peeked at Jade through the carved stair posts. "I've only told you."

Jade snapped around, her eyes wide, her lips pressed into a line. "When are you going to tell them?"

"I don't know." Beryl sighed. "Maybe at the funeral."

Jade's laugh sparked her own low chuckle.

"I can see Willow saying, 'Why wasn't I informed? Just because I'm the youngest, doesn't mean I should be left out.'" Jade sat next to Beryl on the step and hammered her fist against her palm like a gavel.

"You'll take care of her, please. For me." Beryl covered Jade's gavel-fist with her hand. "She's a kite in the wind. Don't let her get caught in the trees."

"I've always taken care of Willow, Mama." Jade cupped her other hand over Beryl's, gazing out from the steps. Her tender motion stirred a warmth inside her. "This explains why you've been so different, kind of docile."

"I suppose." Was she docile? Beryl considered it fatigue.

"Are you scared?"

"I've tried not to think on it too much. What it means, death." Beryl curled her hands in her lap. "So far, it means I can't work. Dr. Meadows took me off the truck, Jade. Rolf doesn't have a place for me in the office. Not that I'd want it. No one else in Prairie City knows except Sharon. I got tired of keeping it to myself. How much joy can one woman contain?"

"Does Bob Hill know? You two have been divorced—"

"Six years. He doesn't know, nor Mike. Nor your dad. Only you, Jade, besides Rolf and Sharon."

"This is surreal, Mama." Jade shook her head.

"I'd like you to be my executor." Beryl drove easily in the practical, emotionless lanes. "Aiden's on the road so much, and Willow, well—"

"She's the kite in the breeze."

For a while, they sat shoulder-to-shoulder on the step, silence a buffer between short bits of conversation.

"What's going on with Dustin? The annulment?" Beryl ventured onto sandy ground.

"Seems he's disappeared. Max contacted a lawyer in Des Moines who will handle the proceedings as soon as we find him. If we don't, Max and I won't be able to get married."

"Max will find him." Beryl patted Jade's knee. "Think Dustin will give you any fuss over the annulment?"

"He'd better not," Jade scoffed. "After what he put me through . . ."

"I saw him around town a bit after his dad died, but then—"

"Rowdy died?" Jade's eyes were wide, her mouth in a surprised *O*.

"It's been eight years, I guess."

"Wow, Dustin, that feels weird. I still see him as the calming force between you and Mrs. Colter, as the one who tried to defend me. Why didn't you tell me?"

"Probably thought you wouldn't want to know, Jade. We weren't speaking much in those days." *In these days.*

"June, Ward, we're home." Willow held up brown bags of food, entering the foyer ahead of Max. The pink scarf around her neck matched the hue of her cheeks.

Jade met her in the middle, taking one of the bags with a glance back at Beryl. "Where's Max?" she asked Willow.

"On the phone again. Beryl, I brought you a burger and a shake. You need to eat, young lady."

"I am a bit hungry after all." Beryl pulled herself up by grabbing onto the banister and followed the girls into the living room.

Willow and Jade sorted out the orders, chatting about Froggers' good food. Roscoe stood between them, tail wagging. The aroma of grilled beef made Beryl's mouth tingle and her stomach contract.

"Beryl." Willow handed her a wrapped burger and a tall shake. "Roscoe, we didn't forget you either."

Trying to lower herself to the carpet, Beryl almost toppled forward, then Jade's hand reached under her arm, helping Beryl ease down to the floor. A white napkin appeared over her shoulder. "Do you want salt or ketchup?"

"Now you're talking." Beryl peeled away the burger's paper. "Any fries over there, Willow?"

"Hot ones, coming up."

Beryl couldn't chew fast enough. Willow was on target. She'd needed to eat. Willow laughed at something, sounding altogether like her Granny. Rolling and merry. Jade was more like, well, Jade. Steady and even, as if merriment from her must be earned.

Tears rose again, causing Beryl's heart to thump. She tossed Roscoe a fry. She'd miss them, her girls and Aiden, even in death. Though she hadn't earned the privilege.

"So what's up with the whole Dustin thing?" Willow dropped to the blanket, legs crossed, food arranged in front of her. "Here comes Max." She held up his burger. "It's getting cold, dude."

"Jade." Max stood at the edge of the room, an intensity in his eyes. "We found Dustin."

~

It was raining again. In the Blue Umbrella's office, Jade worked through the bank statement, listening to the water drops smack the window every few seconds—*thump, thump-thump*—to the lullaby of Roscoe's snore.

In the nighttime quiet, memories surfaced. Jade propped her chin in her hand and stared at the black window. Mama's confession remained on the outside of her soul like an *oh-by-the-way*, finding no ledge on which to land.

Eating her burger before Max came into the room and dropped his own bomb, she thought about talking to him. Should it bother her that Mama's news didn't bother her?

Jade would have time to deal with Mama after the wedding. She was used to boxing up her feelings about her. But Dustin? She had to deal with him now.

Jade slid open the top right desk drawer. The Froggers napkin scrawled with Dustin's cell number sat on top of her sticky notes.

Seven working days left to get the annulment. Max said the Iowa attorney he contacted was set to move the moment Dustin signed the papers.

Set to move. Jade slapped the drawer shut. Max made it sound like a business merger. But it was the ending of a marriage that once encompassed her heart. Did the fact that it was a dead, ultimately painful marriage change that reality? Or the excitement of his touch, the swing in her heart when he'd glanced at her down the high school halls?

Jade scraped her hair away from her face. She wanted a hot shower and her warm bed. She hated Prairie City showing up in Whisper Hollow. And why did Willow get to be the kite in the breeze?

"Are the answers out there, in the alley?" Max fell against the doorframe, his phone in his hand.

"Maybe?"

Moaning, he reached his hand around to his back and took the rickety metal chair. "Long day."

"Is your back bothering you again?" Jade twisted to face him.

"Feels like it might catch."

Jade's gaze landed on the wildflower poster. "I'm trying to imagine what I'll say to him."

"Don't overthink it, Jade. It's a phone call. 'How are you? Can you sign the annulment papers? Have a nice life.'"

Jade's fingers spun the pen sitting in the middle of her desk. "Sounds rude."

"Babe, seven days. If we can't get to the judge by the thirteenth, the fourteenth isn't happening."

"You're mad. You're blaming me for this."

"Did I say I was? It's just frustrating." He angled forward with his elbows on his knees, arching his back. "Shouldn't have gone to the gym the other day."

"Because it's a detail. A bump in Max Benson's smooth road. Something you can't control." Jade swallowed the emotion stinging her eyes and nose. "It's not about me or what happened thirteen years ago, but about you getting what you want."

Max was silent, and Jade's heartbeat picked up the rhythm of the rain. *Thump, thump-thump.*

"Maybe."

"Maybe what?"

"I don't like my future with you being out of my control." His voice wavered. "When I met you, Jade, you were like . . . like this fragile bird. I could tell one of your wings had been wounded, but you fought so hard to fly, high and straight. I wanted to make life easy for you, to help you."

Jade rolled her chair over to him and slipped her hand into his.

"The more I knew you, the more I wanted to be like you," he said. "Fly with my own wounded wing." He twisted her diamond around her finger.

"What is your wounded wing, Max?"

"That I actually lived a life without you."

She answered with an airy, breezy exhale. "Mr. 'Chattanooga's Most Eligible'? I don't believe it."

He gripped her arm, pulling her chair between his knees and kissing her. Closing her eyes, Jade released into the moment. "I can't lose you, babe. You're on every page of my future. I'm ready to settle down, have a family, be one with a woman."

"I'm yours." She stroked her hand over the contours of his face. "You have to believe me."

"The past is the past, over, gone, locked door. Right?"

"Nothing back there but a bunch of broken skeletons." She wrapped her fingers around his. "How mighty can a bunch of skeletons be, anyway?"

"Exactly." He lifted her chin to see into her eyes, letting her see into his. "I can endure back pain, the antics of an intrusive mom, and a hectic law practice, but Jade, not a life without you."

The rain hit harder and faster on the window. *Thump-thump, thump-thump.*

"So do you want to hear the rest of the story?" So much of her past had spilled on her present path, why not get it all out, picked through, then swept away.

"If you want to tell me, yes."

"By November of '96 . . . wow, and here we are getting married in November. I didn't put it together until now."

"Good, we'll erase his horrid memory with our own beautiful one."

Jade ran her thumb over his fingers. "After the night I blurted out the truth in his parents' kitchen, things went well for a few days, but . . ."

Twenty-one

The Colters' house, November 1996

"If you'd stay in town once in a while, Beryl, instead of gallivanting all over God's green earth, you'd know what your daughter was up to or not. Are you married now? Oh, right, a musician. I heard the girls talking at the PTA."

Jade hunched against the overstuffed cushion of the Colters' family room sofa and stole a peek at Dustin. Two weeks ago in this same room, he'd stood toe to toe with his dad, defending her, their marriage.

But then he disappeared. He changed his hall routine and transferred out of Mrs. Glenn's math class to Mr. Hancock's. Jade hadn't seen him in a week.

"What's your excuse, Carla?" Mama shot to her feet. "You're home all the time, apparently gossiping, while your son talked my daughter into forgery."

"She seduced him."

"He's lucky she even looked his way."

"Carla, Beryl," Mr. Colter interjected, his words sharp at first, then soft and slow. "Blaming one kid over the other isn't going to solve this."

Mama smacked her gum and jutted her hip, acting like a floozy, showing the plump of her breasts over the cut of her top. Jade's cheeks burned when she caught Mr. Colter looking before he dashed his gaze to the floor.

"All right, Rowdy." Carla crossed her arms. "What's your solution?"

"Get an annulment. Straightforward and simple."

"Annulment?" Mama fired. "Without asking the kids? Rowdy, they got married on purpose."

"They are too young, Beryl," Carla interjected, powering each word with emotion. "They don't know what they want in life, what it takes to make it in the world. Dustin has a wrestling scholarship to Northern Iowa."

"Jade isn't going to stop him." Mama whirled around. "You want to go to college, too, don't you, baby?"

Oh, Mama. Don't be so trailer trash. "They know, Mama." *Dustin, please, look at me.*

He remained slumped in his chair, swinging his knees to and fro with his chin in his hand, memorizing the carpet pattern.

"Didn't we raise you better?" Mrs. Colter swatted at him.

"Yes," Jade said, surprised by the sound of her own voice. "That's why he wanted to marry me. Because you raised him to respect women."

"Oh, mercy." Mrs. Colter exhaled, hand to her forehead. "Do I even want to ask what that means?"

"Mom—" Dustin spoke for the first time since Jade walked into the house.

"If the kids want to be married, let them be married." Mama spread her hands, peering around, waiting for the bandwagon to fill up. "We raised them to think for themselves, be decent human beings—who are we to tell them they're wrong?"

Mama, can you please not be a '60s hippie for once? It's 1996. The world has changed. Give a real argument.

"Beryl," Carla started, "you've been married three times. Do you really want to give these kids relationship advice?"

"Bite me, Carla."

Carla had better watch stepping in the ring with Mama. With one cutting glance, she could leave a person bleeding.

"Hold on now." Mr. Colter worked to be the neutral, wise party, but have mercy, he was about to step into a catfight. *Ain't safe, Mr. C.* "I think we can find a compromise here. Beryl makes a good point, Carla. The kids did get married. Legally or not, right or wrong, they made a gutsy move. Must have been for some reason."

"Well, then," Carla quipped out of the side of her mouth, shooting her husband a look. He'd pay later for not backing her 100 percent.

But when Mr. C smiled at Jade, she felt his heart to defend *her*.

"All right, Jade, Dustin, what do you say?" Mama barreled down the open communication lane. Gig waited for her at Granny's, not too happy about cutting the last week of their bar-hopping musical tour short to deal with his wife's teenage daughter. "Jade, speak up. Do you want to be married to Dustin?"

More than anything. She peeked at him, wanting some kind of clue before she wandered onto the high wire without a net. But his eyes were still aimed at the floor.

"Dustin?" Mr. Colter shoved his son's shoulder. "What about you? You proposed, gave her a ring. Do you want to be married?"

Mr. Colter, don't, please. Couldn't you leave us alone, let us talk about our relationship in private? If she'd learned anything in their brief marriage, it was to let Dustin brood for a bit, then he'd open up enough for her to dig down to the true intent of his heart. She knew Dustin better than she knew herself.

"Dustin, think about this, son. You're too young."

"Carla." Mr. Colter broke in hard.

After a second, Dustin stood. The knots in Jade's gut multiplied like crazy. *Say it, Dustin. Say, "Dad, let Jade and me talk alone."*

Instead he reached for his hat and slipped it over his head with the bill in the back. "No, I don't."

The last thing Jade ever heard from Dustin Colter was the bang of the kitchen door.

~

Mama slammed the driver's side door shut and cranked the truck's engine. "You're better off, Jade, better off. What in the world were you two thinking? If he wanted sex . . . That's it, isn't it? Mother's religious crap got to you. 'Wait for marriage.'"

"I told him he didn't have to marry me." Curled on the old floorboard, dirt crunching under her legs, Jade buried her face in the torn vinyl bench seat and let go of the sobs she'd been holding in her chest.

"Listen, it's going to be all right." Mama popped the clutch, manhandling the truck down the drive. "Cry it out, cleanse your soul."

"Mama, please stop." Jade popped open her door before Mama had a chance to brake and hung her head out the door, emptying her stomach. When she eased back into the cab, Mama gently drove forward again.

"You'll get through this." The gears whined as she powered up the engine and shifted.

Jade shivered as her sobs waned. But silent tears flooded her cheeks. "I don't want to get through this, Mama. I want to be married to him. I love him."

He was home. Now where would her heart live?

"Then why didn't you say so? Goodness, Jade, speak up for yourself. Do you want me to turn around?"

"No—Mama, no." The idea of facing Mrs. Colter again cut a deep swath through her heart.

"Well, maybe he'll come around." Mama fished in her purse, producing a napkin, shoving it under Jade's cheek. "Are you pregnant?"

"Mama—"

"You did have sex with your husband, didn't you? And by the way, I'm not ready to be a grandma."

"Can this not be about you for once?" Jade clenched her jaw as she wound the napkin around her fingers.

"You know what I mean." Mama thumped the wide, round steering wheel with the palm of her hand and muttered a few four-letter words. "Can you believe that Miss Priss, Carla? Hasn't changed one bit since high school."

The old engine rattled as Mama slowed for a stop sign, grinding the gears when she shifted into first.

"She was nice to me."

"Sure, until you married her son. Boils my butt she acted like it was all your fault."

"I'm not pregnant."

"You sure?"

"Yeah—" Pretty sure. Dustin didn't have any condoms the last time. He kept forgetting to buy more. Jade talked to him about visiting the free clinic in Des Moines so she could go on the pill, but once summer football started, time got away from them. Dustin assured her that condoms were doing the job. Then school started, and he began ever so gradually to drift. And forget.

"If you are, let me know. The sooner, the better. We can get it taken care of. It's no way to keep a man, Jade, being pregnant. He'll go off to college, and you'll be stuck slinging hash at a truck stop from midnight to seven, growing old and tired before you turn twenty." The truck gained speed as Mama made the final shift into third. "He's a cruel, stupid boy, Jade. I'm shocked you fell for him. You seemed to be so keen about people. In a few months, you'll be moved on."

Jade wiped under her eyes with the napkin, then blew her nose. "I'm not you, Mama. I can't just move on."

"You'd better learn. Don't waste your life pining. You'll turn pathetic."

Jade shoved off the floorboard, plopping down on her side of the old bench seat, moving away from the torn, sharp-edged vinyl poking through her jeans and biting her skin. "Are you mad?" She pressed her face against the window. The cold glass felt good.

"No. It's not like I didn't do things that shocked my mother when I was your age."

"Or now."

"Hush, because I can be mad if you want. I wouldn't have legally tied myself to a thughead jock, but I did a few things that would've curled your Granny's hair if she'd known."

"Like what?" Jade had heard Granny arguing with Mama over her choices, but the details had never been colored in. "When you were my age?"

"Sleeping in Golden Gate Park with my cousin Carolyn during the Summer of Love, getting high, doing whatever we wanted whenever we wanted. There was this one soldier on his way to 'Nam—"

"Okay, okay. I don't want to hear more."

"I fell in love."

Jade situated against the door. Mama cruised right by Granny's place. "With who?"

"A marine named Andrew MacGregor. He was wounded in Danang and got to spend the rest of his life in a government-issued wheelchair. Thank you very much, Lieutenant MacGregor, for your sacrifice; here's your consolation prize."

"What happened?"

"We met in the Panhandle, where the Diggers handed out breakfast to whoever wanted. He wheeled along beside me for the rest of the summer." Mama's story drifted. "My first love."

"Did you want to marry him?"

Mama drove on in quiet for many miles. "He shot himself. A few months after I came home to finish school. His death sent me on a journey. Who was I in this big universe? What did I believe? Who did I want to be? What was my generation doing to make things better for the next? I graduated from high school and spent a year at Iowa U, then got caught up in protesting and sit-ins, marched on Washington against the war, went to Woodstock, didn't even know what a legendary event that would turn out to be, drifted, tried to find myself." Mama's palm made a squeaking sound against the wheel. "Gig is probably driving Granny crazy."

The engine inhaled as Mama worked the clutch and downshifted. She muscled the truck down a narrow gravel road to turn around.

"Mama, do you ever think of dying? Like what really happens—?"

"He isn't worth it, Jade. No boy is ever worth your life. Andrew was disturbed about the war and, I can admit this now, really strung out on drugs."

"I'm not going to do anything, Mama. I just wondered, what happens when we die?"

"Women become queens of their own planets with gorgeous male servants." Mama shoved the cigarette lighter into the dash. "Hand me my cigarettes, Jade-o."

"Har, har." Jade hunted around in Mama's purse for her cigarettes and tossed them to her. "Do you think Granny's church is right? That we have to know Jesus to get into heaven?"

"Does it look like I believe?" Mama cracked her window, dragging deep on the fiery stick.

"Aiden said Jesus made a difference in his heart and stuff doesn't bother him anymore." Jade tried to escape the sinking sensation in her middle. *If true love doesn't last, and hearts can be broken over and over, what's the point? Was Jesus for her?*

"Good for Aiden. Whatever it takes to get you through life, do, believe." Mama tapped her ashes out the window. They jumped and twisted in the truck's wake like red-hot fireflies. "But that's not you and me, Jade. We're like the gemstones we're named after. We make our own destinies, our own way. People and things don't define us; we define ourselves. Don't let Mother cram her religion down your throat."

"What if we don't know how to define ourselves? What if we make wrong choices?"

"There are no wrong choices. Just a series of journeys and adventures."

Exactly what Jade feared.

"Granny made homemade pot pie"—Mama's tone fluctuated—"and a chocolate cake." She jabbed Jade's leg lightly. "You love pot pie and cake."

"Can you take me to Rachel's?" A ghost sob shivered across her shoulders.

"If that's what you want." Mama flicked her cigarette into the passing night. "It's going to be all right, Jade. You're destined for a beautiful life."

"I didn't even get to be Jade Colter. Not even for a day. I really wanted to be Jade Colter."

"You practiced your signature, didn't you?"

Why did she have to make fun? "When will I know it's been annulled?"

"Don't you worry about it. Go on with your life as if Dustin Colter never existed. The Colters and I will see to it."

As Jade leaned against the window, a fresh batch of tears spilled down her cheeks. Go on with her life? It would be easier to fill a jar with moonbeams.

Twenty-Two

The Blue Umbrella was busy. Tourists flooded the streets for the last day of the Hollow's Fall Festival. Max called every hour. "Only six working days left, Jade. Call him."

Cradling the phone on her shoulder, she handed a purchase to a customer with a smile. "I will, I will," she muttered into the receiver, "but the shop's been really busy."

"The moment Lillabeth comes in, call him. Jade, please, every minute that goes by gives him time to think of how to complicate our case."

"And why would he do that? He walked out on me, Max."

"Thirteen years as a lawyer . . . I've seen the unbelievable when it comes to relationships."

"Okay, okay. When Lillabeth comes in." Jade pressed End and shoved her phone into her pocket.

By the time Lillabeth arrived an hour later, business had settled down, but the shop was a mess. Lillabeth started straightening right away. "Was it double coupon day?"

"Panicked Fall Festival tourists." Jade smiled, taking a pull from the register and stuffing it into the money bag. "I'll be in the office."

Easing the door closed, Jade pulled her phone from her pocket and opened the desk drawer for the Froggers napkin. Under her desk, Roscoe slept, curled and comfy over a heat register.

After calling Dustin, she'd feed him and then find his leash for a walk. She needed the time and space.

Before she could dial the Iowa number, her phone rang. Must be Max. An hour had passed.

"Jade, Sean Dunham. Did I catch you at a bad time?"

"No, no." Jade kicked around her desk chair to sit, tossing the money bag on the desktop.

"Final week before the wedding. Hope all is going well."

"Did you need something, Sean?"

"As a matter of fact, I do. Put your name on the River Street property deed."

"Ah, very clever. To be honest, Sean, I haven't even thought of it."

"Understandable, but if you're interested, I can bring the papers up to you."

Jade took the money from the bag and started separating cash from checks. "What's going on? Why are you so intent on selling me this property?"

"Just want to see a good businesswoman get a break."

"I appreciate your concern, but I don't have the time or money." At least that kind of money. The big pile of green on her desk made her happy. This month's bills would be paid.

"Jade." Lillabeth poked her head through the door. "Someone's here to see you."

"Look, Sean, I need to go—"

"June put up the money, Jade."

She stood so fast her desk chair shot into the file cabinet. "What did you say?"

"It's already purchased. Just sign the papers. A wedding gift, I imagine."

"No! No, no, no." She snapped her phone closed. Who did she think—She dialed Max. "Your mom bought the River Street property."

"What are you talking about?"

"The Dunham property, on River Street, the one your mom took me to see the other day."

"So she bought it? Did you call—?"

"She's trying to force me into taking it, Max. I guess she needs a project after the wedding." Jade didn't need this today. Not the imprint of June Benson's nose in her back. She'd listened to her once. *Send your Mama the invitation, Jade.*

Now look . . .

"Sean is ready to drive the papers up here. What is wrong with her? Why does she have to manipulate people into doing what she thinks they should do?"

"Did it occur to you that she might want to do something nice for you?"

"By forcing me to expand my business after I told her I wasn't ready?" Jade was too worked up to cry.

"Let's make a deal. I'll talk to her. You call Colter."

"Sure, take the easy one for yourself."

"Jade, babe, please. I know it's hard. Like diving into icy water on a really hot day. Hold your breath and jump."

A knock resonated from the door. It eased open. "Lillabeth, just a second—" Jade reached for the knob as the door swung wider. She lowered the phone as Dustin Colter walked into her office.

"The girl, with the, uh"—he motioned to the top of his head—"sunglasses said I could come on back. I told her I was an old friend."

"Max, I'll call you back." Jade slipped her phone into her hip pocket. "Dustin."

"Long time no see, huh?"

"What are you doing here?"

"I had to see you." Dustin had the same blue spark in his eyes, only deeper and more intense. The aura of his strength was tempered by a distinct meekness.

"How did you find me?"

Roscoe snorted, poking his head out from under the desk. Spying a visitor, he crawled out and sniffed Dustin's shoes.

"Once your fiancé called, it wasn't too hard."

"I was about to call you." She motioned to the Froggers napkin on her desk.

"You look good." He kept his gaze tight and polite. "Still beautiful."

"You didn't drive from Iowa to see if I looked good." She folded the napkin and put it back in the desk drawer.

"I live in Saint Louis now." He twisted, glancing around. "Can we go someplace . . . to talk?"

"Jade?" Lillabeth knocked, then entered. "Mrs. Sparks wants to talk to you about her mantel clock on consignment. She claims I'm not doing my job as a saleswoman and directing customers to her merchandise."

"I'll be right there." Jade stepped around Dustin. "Can I get you anything? The bathroom is directly across in the storeroom. We have a soda machine out front, free coffee next to it. And, oh—"

"I'm good, thanks." He hesitated with his smile.

"Be right back." She exited the office, inhaling Dustin's woodsy fragrance. As she walked across the shop, her legs wobbled and her heart wondered where to go from here.

Dustin waited for her on the bottom step of the loft stairs with Roscoe's head on his knee. "What happened to his eye?"

"Hit by a dump truck. Max and I rescued him." Jade stooped to touch her nose to the dog's. "It was our first date."

"Lucky dog."

Jade grinned—smoothing her hand over Roscoe's snout. "Max drove to the vet like a man on fire, Roscoe wrapped in his Armani button-down, bleeding on the imported leather of his new Mercedes."

When she glanced up, Dustin's attention wasn't on the dog but on her. Jade rose, taking a step away. "Let's walk over to the park." Through the shop to the front door, she called, "Lillabeth, call if you need me. Oh, feed Roscoe, then take him out, please."

The slate gray day was stiff with cold. Midnight blue clouds floated over Whisper Hollow. A fortress against the sunlight. Pulling on her jacket, Jade led Dustin across Main and down Broadway toward Laurel Park.

They walked in silence until Dustin said, "Lovely little town."

Crossing the park oval, she motioned to a cluster of benches nestled against an evergreen. "We can sit here."

"Whisper Hollow is you. Jade Fitzgerald of Whisper Hollow, Tennessee." His deep laugh was fast and short.

"What makes you say that?" Jade sat on the bench a good foot from him.

"Unique, quiet, classic. American." Dustin leaned with his elbows on his thighs. "And I liked the sound of Jade Fitzgerald of—" He stopped, staring out over the park. "I remember when you worked at Mr. Wimple's Country Store."

"Rachel and me."

"You still in touch with her?"

Jade huddled against the nip in the air, tucking her hands under her arms, sniffing away the sting in her nose. "Not since college."

"I haven't seen Stu since the summer after graduation."

"The friend you met in fourth grade? Who would be your best friend for life?" She leaned against the back of the bench. Dustin had been overconfident about what he wanted in life—Stu's friendship, Jade's love. "Give up on me, sure, but Stu? That's low."

"I didn't give up on him. We just drifted."

Jade stood. "I need a hot drink." His presence knocked too hard on the closet door protecting all her tossed-in skeletons.

"Sounds good." Dustin walked with her to Froggers, quiet. Probably wondering what possessed him to drive down here on the spur of the moment. Jade ordered a tall hot tea for her and a coffee for Dustin, then took a seat at the round table.

"I saw Aiden a few years ago at Wal-Mart." Dustin poured a small creamer and a packet of sugar into his cup.

"He never mentioned it." Jade slapped a Splenda packet against her fingers before ripping it open. "Mama said your dad died."

"Yeah, heart attack." Dustin cupped his hands around his coffee. "Hit us all pretty hard. Mom closed up the house and moved next door to Sydney."

"I'm sorry, Dustin."

"I was hoping you'd come to our class reunion last year." He picked up his coffee and rose from the bench. "Can we walk?"

"It was my first summer in the shop." Jade matched his stride, staying beyond the circle of his fragrance.

"About half the class came." Dustin drank, shaking his head. "We got to telling football stories and—"

"Dustin, why'd you come here?" She stopped at the edge of the oval and gazed out over the park. Workers were already putting Christmas decorations on the giant evergreen at the center of the oval.

"I told you. I wanted to see you."

"Just like that? Thirteen years of silence, and suddenly it's like, 'Hey, I think I'd like to go see the ex'?"

"No, I never expected to see you again. At least not up close, maybe at a distance. Then I got a call telling me I was still married to you." He took a step, pausing to see if she was moving with him.

But Jade's cell blurted from her pocket. She tugged it free, wanting it to be Max. He chose now to stop calling. "It's Willow. I'll call her later." Jade slipped the phone into her hip pocket.

"Take it if you need to."

"It won't be a short call. She's in Chattanooga with Mama getting her dress for the wedding altered. Probably wants to gripe at me, and—"

What was she going on about? Jade started forward, crunching dead leaves underfoot as the wind skidded them across her path.

"I've thought about that night at my parents' house a thousand times." Dustin fell into step with her. "My stomach has been in knots, and I'm ashamed." He swirled the contents of his cup, took a gulp, then tossed the remainder on the ground. "I drove by your house every night for a few months, hoping to work up the courage to knock on the door and ask your granny if I could see you."

"Your mom wouldn't let me talk to you when I called."

"She was convinced you tricked me into marriage. For a few months, she met me at the door every night with this pained expression, expecting me to tell her you were pregnant."

"Lucky her. I wasn't." Jade sipped her tea, the drink hot on her tongue. Dustin angled toward a trash bin and tossed in his cup.

"A few times, I hoped you were. We weren't exactly careful toward the end."

"What would you have done?" She thumped the bottom of her cup, her pulse sounding in her ears. *This isn't happening.* "If I'd told you I was pregnant?" Jade motioned to the merry-go-round and cut to the right. Mr. Hannity was bringing up the lights.

"I'd have done the right thing." Dustin gazed at her, his thick hair falling over his forehead, tousled by the wind. "Stayed."

"You promised me forever, Dustin. Not with conditions. Not until-I-get-a-scholarship or only-if-you're-pregnant."

"I know, and I'm sorry, Jade. You should've seen my house once the wrestling scholarship came. Everything changed. My parents talked of nothing else. Especially Mom. I think she felt really guilty for spending my college money on Sydney's wedding." He zipped up the front of his jacket and ran his hand over his hair. "If you'd have been pregnant, Mom and Dad wouldn't have fought me."

"You had a chance to stay with me. Dustin, you walked out. You left me."

Jade's words powered through her, scraping the sides of her soul with a sharp, twisting pain. Her abdomen burned. Light began to fade from her countenance, and for the span of a hundred heartbeats, she couldn't get her bearings. Tiny needle pricks stabbed at her lungs until she couldn't breathe, and her thoughts swam through brackish emotion.

In an instant, she wasn't walking next to Dustin, but standing in the background, watching herself from a distant corner of the park. Her knees buckled, and she dropped to the concrete, throwing open her jacket, gasping for cool air.

Dustin knelt in front of her, his lips moving, *Jade, Jade*, but she couldn't hear him. His grip was strong on her arms, but she jerked away. Her cup tipped from her hand, and the warm tea splashed on her jeans.

Brainwaves fired: *Run. Panic.* But she couldn't command her limbs. The park spun around her. Dustin was talking to someone. People were staring.

Jade gripped her praying hands medallion. The surface was warm against her skin. *Help me, God, if You can. Help me. I can't be crazy.*

One pure breath. Then another. She faced the ground, struggling to think of good things—Max, Roscoe, her shop—until the murk in her soul began to recede. Sounds clarified. Her soul no longer stood on the edge of the park, watching from a distance, but was back in the oval, with Dustin next to her.

People weren't staring, only passing by. Looking down, Jade dabbed the tea spot on her jeans and picked up her cup from the grass.

While her hands still shook from the residue of fear, her pulse returned to its normal rhythm.

"Jade, are you okay?"

"Fine, yeah." Blinking, she focused on his face, the square of his chin and the blue concern in his eyes.

"I should've called. I'm sorry, Jade. I jumped in the truck and drove here. I didn't mean to upset you."

She walked to the trash bin and tossed her cup. "Dustin." She whirled to face him. "You're here. Let's just move on to why."

"Yeah, well." He slipped his fingers into his pockets. "I wanted to talk to you about the annulment."

The music from the merry-go-round lured Jade. Walking backward toward the ride, facing Dustin, she addressed him. "Like, 'Sorry it didn't get done'?" She wanted away from this moment, the panic, and the source of it all. Dustin.

"Are you going to keep throwing daggers?"

"Until they equal the size of the spear you chucked at me the night you walked out without a backward glance or good night."

"If I'd looked at you, I'd never have been able to leave the room."

"Then you should've looked at me."

"I told myself you'd be fine and that the scholarship was the first door to many great opportunities in my life. If I turned it down, I'd be stuck, working at the plant like my dad, farming on the side. When I proposed, I thought wrestling was over for me."

"You thought I'd be fine? What gave you that idea? I was ready to fly with you, Dust. Get out of Prairie City. I loved you." She gripped her hands into fists, pressing them into her chest. "I gave you my heart, my soul, and my virtue, and you sold me for a scholarship."

The merry-go-round whirled under an array of candy-colored lights, the molded horses gliding up and down without riders to the tinny music.

"Didn't seem like it at the time, Jade." Dustin stopped at the gate. "I couldn't sleep, so I went to Coach and told him everything. He started talking about the legalities and taxes of being married, even thought we could face criminal charges for forging our parents' signatures. Stu could get in trouble. Suddenly, my wild idea felt foolish and stupid. My rock turned into my ball and chain."

"If you'd fought for us, no one would've known the signatures were forged but our parents."

"Coach rattled off stats about failed teen marriages while hyping the fun and benefits of college, and how I needed an education and I was doing my parents proud. I thought I'd take you with me, live in married housing, but to get the scholarship, I had to live in the dorms."

"Semantics, Dustin. We could've worked those things out. It was you and me, and we could've done anything if we'd stuck to our love and our pledge." The fire of her words burned away the residue of her panic. Words she'd stored for thirteen years glided to the tip of her tongue—the argument against him she'd made while walking across her college campus, while shopping in downtown Chattanooga, when her mind drifted during a marketing meeting, in the cab of her truck, driving from estate sale to estate sale.

But Dustin's pale blue eyes reflected regret and doused Jade's fire.

"When the attorney contacted me about the annulment, everything surfaced. I had to see if the feelings I felt were still real. Jade-o, maybe we're still married for a reason."

"Hey, Jade, you and your friend want to hop on?" Mr. Hannity leaned over the red sleigh as the ride circled. He watched them with a smile, disappearing around the corner.

"Dustin, we're still married because your parents didn't file the annulment. That's the reason. The *only* reason."

"I know, I know. But is this serendipity? Dad went to a lawyer for help and found out we could've been criminally charged for forging the signatures. So they freaked and backed off, intending to do it later, when I was eighteen. Truth is, Dad always felt bad about what happened, and while he never admitted it, he wanted to ignore the annulment, hoping we'd find our way back to each other."

"I need you to sign the papers, Dustin."

Mr. Hannity circled around again, this time sitting on a horse, backward, his hat over his eyes.

Dustin watched the ride, resting against the fence, his hands in his jacket pockets, his legs stretched long and crossed at the ankles. "I think we could've made it."

"Do you hear yourself, Dustin? We didn't make it. Unless five months is forever." Jade fiddled with the gate latch, opening, closing, swinging the gate to and fro.

"Jade, I signed the papers." He looked at her. "The lawyer said we should hear from the judge in a few days."

"Thank you." Her heart softened, and it seemed the merry-go-round lights brightened. *He's moving on.*

Mr. Hannity rode by, standing on the chocolate steed, balancing on one foot. Jade smiled at him.

"Is it true, Jade?" Dustin stood away from the gate.

"Is what true?"

"I thought you'd tell me, but—" He put his palm against the ends of her hair lifted by the breeze. "Were you pregnant?"

"Did you see me pregnant? I was in school every day." Almost. "Even avoiding me, you'd have found out sooner or later." Jade zipped up her jacket, flipping the collar up around her ears.

"Rachel told me a few years ago that you were."

And he's just now asking? "Rachel should write soap operas." Jade jammed her hands in her jacket pockets and pulled out a naked, dirt-dotted peppermint.

"Maybe so, but that doesn't answer my question. Were you pregnant?"

"Dustin. Go home. Move on. Be glad we took a different path than the one we started on. How's that for serendipity?"

She strolled away from the merry-go-round, the sound of rattling bones in her ears.

Twenty-three

Women's Awareness Clinic, Des Moines, December 1996

Staring at the ceiling tiles, Jade counted. Twenty down the length of the small room, twelve across the width. When she finished, she began again.

Counting took her mind off the cold, steely room and occupied her thoughts. The pain had been almost unbearable at first. She writhed when the doctor began the process, almost rolling off the table.

The doctor apologized and backed away. "We'll wait a bit longer," he said, setting a long tubelike instrument on the stainless steel cart and leaving her exposed with her feet in the stirrups.

That thing was . . . inside her? The thing that would end . . . this ordeal? Jade closed her eyes, swallowing the taste of grief burning her throat. She wanted this day, this moment, to be over. This saga of her life to be over. Whatever pain she had to endure.

"Sorry for the delay." The nurse's touch was warm on Jade's arm, and their eyes met. She didn't want to be in the room any more than Jade did.

"I'll stay with you," she said, more to the room than to Jade.

"Thank you." Tears rolled from her eyes to her ears.

"Are you sure you want to do this?" the nurse asked.

Jade wiped her face with the sleeve of her gown. "What choice do I have?"

Mama's exhortation on the drive to the clinic was reasoned and well-spoken, convincing Jade she was doing the right thing. Really, did she want to carry the child of a man who didn't love or want her?

"I don't want to be responsible for ruining his chance for college. I don't want to sling hash at a truck stop, nor be tired and old by the time I'm twenty," she told the nurse, echoing her mother's words.

The nurse patted her hand. "The doctor will be right with you."

She tried not to, but Jade wondered what Dustin was doing on this fine December Saturday. Hanging out carefree with his buddies? Going on a date with Kendall? Walking into his mama's warm kitchen, draping his arm over her shoulder, and stealing a fresh-baked cookie?

"How are we doing?" The doctor sat at the end of the table and reached for his instrument.

The nurse squeezed Jade's shoulder.

With her eyes shut, Jade winced as the whir of the vacuum filled her vacant thoughts. The doctor tugged and jostled her insides until the distinct slurp of suction sounded. The baby. A sensation of "too late" circled her heart like a hungry wolf. What had she just done?

God, I'm sorry.

He repeated the routine, again and again, with Jade locked down, refusing air and light to her soul. Bile rose in her throat, and she swallowed it down with her last ounce of determination. It was too late for regret.

The doctor wheeled backward and the nurse moved away from Jade, reaching for a tray, hurrying out of the room without a word, blood dripping on the white tile floor.

Oh God, I'm so sorry.

~

Talk to me, Mama. Say it's okay, it's going to be all right.

Jade struggled for a sense of self, a sense of the everyday, of the girl she was six months ago before this nightmare began. But Jade felt vacant and hollow, sad. Unanchored thoughts and fears climbed through her ribs and choked her heart.

"Ooo, Jade-o, did I tell you Gig got the band booked in Chicago?" Mama smiled as she ran her fingers through her hair. "That man knows how to work a deal. We're leaving in a few days, picking up some other bookings along the way, but Gig thinks this might be their big break."

So what about Gig and his big chance? She'd just killed her baby. Dustin's baby. He'd hate her for sure if he knew. Outside her window, barren and brown December fields flashed past. Along the horizon, a row of houses flashed red and green Christmas lights.

Mama zipped past a cross street, and Jade caught a familiar flash of blue at the stop sign. She twisted against her seatbelt to see out the back window. *Dustin?*

"Mama, turn around."

"It wasn't him."

"Yes, it was. Turn around."

"And do what? Say what?" Mama gunned the gas a bit harder. "As I was saying, we'll be back on the twentieth, I promise." Mama's promises were hollow and meaningless. Like Dustin's.

"Whatever." Jade collapsed against the cold door. Christmas was for children. For babies. She slammed her fist against her temple. *Forget about it, Jade. It's over.*

"Let's do Christmas up big this year, what do you think? My first one with Gig. Lots of presents and tinsel. Money's tight, but oh well, it's only money, and it is Christmas."

The woman rattled on as if nothing unusual had happened today, as if she'd taken Jade for a root canal. Which would've been a thousand times more pleasant. Mama hummed and tapped out the beat of a song that only played in her head.

"What's up for you next week, Jade-o? Anything fun in school? Tests? School holiday program?"

"They counted body parts, Mama." Jade buckled forward, enduring a sharp cramp. The numbness was starting to wear off.

"Don't go there, Jade. Your mind will play tricks on you. Let it go, let it go."

"I heard them, Mama, on the other side of the partition. The nurses couldn't find one of the baby's legs."

"What is the point of this?"

"So they sent the doctor to check me again. With the vacuum thing—"

"Jade, it's over. What is the point of rehashing how it happened?"

The rest of the ride home was silent. Even the radio playing in Mama's head went dead. When she parked in the barn, she mashed the emergency brake and cut the engine.

"Not a word to Granny. She's old school and will have a coronary if she finds out." Mama touched Jade's chin. "Don't sulk, or she'll ask questions. This is no big deal. You'll get over it. Having a kid now is not right for you. In a few days, you'll be your old self, running around with Rachel and the gang like nothing ever happened. This ordeal will be done."

"Like nothing ever happened?" Jade's body was awakening from a numbed sleep, questioning, wondering. *Who had invaded?* "Something did happen, Mama, whether you want to admit it or not. For the rest of my life, I'll know. I was pregnant with Dustin's baby."

"I'm simply trying to remind you, life is a journey, it moves on and—"

"Is that how you felt after your abortion?" Jade arched forward, sensing the pad the clinic gave her fill with blood. "Did you just go on like nothing ever happened?"

"No, no, I guess you're right." Mama stared quietly through the windshield at the battered wall of the barn. "It wasn't easy. I thought about it . . . for many years."

"Who was the father? The lieutenant you met in San Francisco?" Another cramp rippled through her abdomen. Good. She deserved pain and punishment.

"Jade, why do you want to know?" Mama ran her hands around the steering wheel. "It's not important."

"It is to me." She needed a friend standing next to her on this desolate island.

"No, it wasn't Andrew."

"Then who?"

"I don't know . . . there were several men about that time, and—"

"Never mind." Jade jerked on her door handle and stepped out of the truck.

~

Roscoe stood in the closet with Jade as she searched the top shelf, his one eye following her as if he wanted to help.

"It's in here somewhere, Roscoe." She knocked sweaters, handbags, shoeboxes, and photo albums with no pictures inside to the floor.

Then the UT throw blanket slithered to the floor, exposing a flowery box with a white card taped on top. *The Dustin years.*

Carrying the box to her bed, Jade lifted the lid. It seemed incredible now that she'd kept such a box of horrors. Inside was a mixture of photographs and letters, doodled napkins, his varsity football letter, and various silly souvenirs like ticket stubs and fair passes. The claddagh ring.

The picture Rachel took of Jade and Dustin on their wedding day sat on top of the pile. Jade stared at the image, searching for the sense of love and safety that had exploded in her heart that day. The emotion lived somewhere in her. It had leaked out when she told Dustin's story to Max. But all she felt was a loss of innocence and hope. Sixteen was too young.

Roscoe stretched his nose to the top of the bed, sniffing.

"Smell something rotten, buddy?" Jade rubbed his ears. Why had she bothered to keep this stuff? It was a mystery. Did she think one day she'd look back on it with nostalgia? Who was she going to share it with? Her husband? Her children? Jade picked up a picture from the wedding. "This is the boy who obliterated your mom's life, sweetie. Isn't he handsome?"

Jade ripped the picture in two. *Burn it.* Tugging open the nightstand drawer, she found the matches and touched one half of the wedding picture to the tiny flame.

The image of her cradled in Dustin's arms, laughing with her head back and legs in the air, began to melt. If she'd known then what she knew now . . .

"Ouch." Jade dropped the burning Kodak halves to the floor. Roscoe barked and growled. She stomped it out with her foot, but the burning picture charred a spot in the carpet. "Just great. A scar."

Angry and frustrated, she stooped to pick up the picture. The first sob rolled up from her chest, stealing her breath. The second hit like a boulder.

Snatching up the box and the matches, weeping, Jade ran to the bathroom and tossed the box in the tub. The pregnancy test stick popped up from underneath a corsage.

Collapsing to the toilet seat, cheeks flooded with tears, Jade bombed the box with one lit match after another. *Burn, burn. Good riddance.*

Reaching behind the commode, she found the stick handle of the plunger. Raising it over her head, arms trembling, Jade shouted until her gut ached, beating the burning box over and over, grinding soot and ashes into the white bathtub porcelain.

Twenty-four

Max flipped through channels while Jade folded a small load of laundry. Despite the laughter of a *Seinfeld* rerun, the room was silent. She kept waiting for him to ask if she'd called Dustin, but he didn't. Frankly, she was relieved. Today bore the weight of a hundred years.

Jade carried the basket of clothes to the bedroom, put her jeans in the dresser drawer, and hung her tops on hangers. After the great box-burning, she had reassembled the demolished closet and, except for the splinter in her palm—she broke the plunger handle—no one would ever know anything went on here today.

When she turned around, Max was sitting on the bed.

"Tired of channel surfing?" She closed the closet door.

"What happened to the carpet?" He stomped his foot on the sooty spot but kept his gaze on Jade. "And the bathtub."

"What'd you do? Come in with your spyglass?"

"Big, black spots are hard to miss."

He's crazy. Jade had scrubbed the tub with Clorox and carried the ashes out to the Dumpster. Going into the bathroom, she pulled back the shower curtain and peered at the tub. Okay, so a second scrubbing might be in order. Beating black ashes into porcelain might have been overkill.

"I found this. By the storeroom door." Max held up a black and dented claddagh ring.

"I burned a box of Dustin's stuff." Jade reached for the ring. "He gave this to me on our wedding day."

"I've been sitting in front of *Seinfeld* for an hour, waiting for you to tell me Dustin was here."

"Who told?" Jade rubbed the soot from the ring.

"Lillabeth."

"She's so fired. Why didn't you ask? You called me every hour right until he showed up."

Max lowered his chin, regarding her from under his brow. "I could tell I was getting on your nerves."

She sighed softly, leaving the bathroom for the kitchen. "I'd have gotten around to it."

"What happened? Seems there was a pretty brutal ritual with a box of matches today."

She retrieved the blender from the bottom cabinet. "In a way, yes. He reminded me of the worst year of my life." And the ugly, enduring aftermath. There'd best be some ice cream in the freezer.

"Did he sign the papers?"

"Yes." Half a carton of vanilla. Jade snatched the ice cream scoop from the utensil caddy and filled the blender jar. "How I trusted that big galoot is beyond me."

Max was beside her, offering up the milk and the chocolate syrup. "Love doesn't always lead our hearts in the right direction."

Jade stopped squeezing the syrup. "Then how can we know?"

"We don't."

Setting the syrup down, she faced him. "Tell me you know, Max. I won't marry you if you don't. Forget annulments; forget teenage heartbreak or ex-husbands and fiances. If you're not the real deal"—she slipped his diamond from her finger—"you can take this and go."

Max gently slipped the ring back on her finger. "I've never been more sure of anything in my life. Jade, after a year, I'm more in love with you than I've ever been with anyone. I think about you in the middle of depositions. Sometimes, I get a sense of well-being, wholeness, and I pause to wonder why. It's you. Nights on the sofa watching movies or playing Scrabble with you are like a rocket shot to the moon."

She fell into him, looping her arms around him. "I don't deserve you."

His hand caressed her back, hugging her tight. "I'm all in, Jade."

"Thank you for being patient with me."

"It's not easy, knowing you've been married before."

"But you and I are nothing like what I had before. There was no real ceremony, no one knew except Stu and Rachel. Dustin and I never lived together. I didn't change my name. Everything with you is new. There will be so many firsts, from the ceremony to—"

"Our first child."

Jade turned to the counter and uncapped the milk, splashing a gulp into the blender jar. "Sure, our first child."

"So, the past is the past."

"Nothing before we met each other existed."

"Everything is new."

Jade covered the shake concoction and pressed the Liquefy button. Max retrieved the fountain glasses, and when the mixture was the right texture, Jade poured.

"Mm, best in town, babe." Max's kiss was wet and cold. He fell against the counter. "As long as we're coming clean . . ."

Jade lowered her milkshake, licking the chocolate mustache from her lip. "What do you mean?"

"That business with Mom, and kicking you out of the kitchen . . ." Max opened the silverware drawer and pulled out a long, skinny spoon. "I was addicted to pain meds a few years ago, Jade. It started when I was in high school, and I reinjured my back playing basketball during law school. I went to the doc, and he gave me Percocet and . . . I was feeling no pain."

"Just like that, you were hooked?"

"Not overnight, but my back would tighten after a long study session, with hours still ahead of me. Percocet took the edge off and didn't make me drowsy. Over time, I started thinking I needed them for the long nights in the law library."

"I see." Jade stirred her chocolate shake. "Are you struggling now?"

"No, but I can't convince Mom. She's afraid it'll happen again. She only gave me four pills from that prescription." He stirred his drink. "Then, when I was with Rice, I'd taken on a big divorce case that got a lot of media attention. I was in constant pain. Or so I thought." He checked her response with a deep gaze. "I learned how to get what I needed."

His confession made the atmosphere of her heart feel normal again. "Do I need to worry?"

"No." He tipped up his glass. "I don't want to do that to you, Jade."

"That's what Rice meant . . . you were in denial."

"We broke up, and I got help."

"Then the relationship fell apart because of your issue with pain pills? Not because you realized it wasn't going to work?"

Max set his milkshake aside and pinned Jade between his arms, hands locked on the counter behind her. "My problem was just the catalyst. But like I told you, Jade, Rice had always been more of a buddy. She was one of the guys. We started hanging out, then dating. Mom said to me one night, 'You're all but engaged, Max.' For the first time in my adult life, I realized I was old enough, responsible enough to get married. I ran out and bought a ring, convincing myself she was the one."

"Rice said something about wanting to work things out with you."

"Who cares what she said, Jade? If I wanted to be with her, I would be. Period. Truth is, she doesn't want to be with me either."

She tapped her forehead to his chin. "What a mess, you and me."

"But we're going to make it."

They carried their shakes into the living room and curled up on the sofa, Jade tucking her cold toes under his leg. Max flipped to ESPN for SportsCenter.

"Remember, tomorrow is my bachelor day with the guys. Six a.m. tee time."

She tipped her glass to scoop out a melting clump of ice cream with her tongue. "All day?"

"All day. Why don't you do something fun with your mom and Willow?"

"Oh, sure, you get a great day with the guys, and I get stuck with Mom and Willow."

"Then call Daphne and Margot."

"Actually, Willow's going hiking with a group she met in the park."

"You're kidding? A bunch of strangers? Scary—"

"Tell me. And Mama seems content to sit and listen to records or talk to Lillabeth. I don't think she feels well."

"Has she said anything more to you about the leukemia?"

"No. I just let her be. Seems to work for both of us." She leaned across the sofa for a slow and passionate kiss. "Go, have fun with your boys."

He brushed his fingers through her hair. "I love you."

"I know." Maybe for the first time, she really did.

~

Daphne and Margot waltzed into the Blue Umbrella the next morning. "Spa day, let's go. Max called Daph at six a.m. and said to take you for a spa day. His treat." Margot did a jig around the office. "We're ready to be pampered."

"Can't." Jade carried the cash drawer out to the register. "I've got a lot to do today."

"Girl, it's your last weekend of freedom before Ball and Chain Day." Daphne held a cashmere sweater to her torso. "This is gorgeous."

"Remind me not to come to you for relationship advice, Daph." Margot draped her arm over Jade's shoulders. "Come on, for old time's sake. Max is paying. How can you not?"

"This isn't fair, and you know it. I'd love to spend the day at a spa with y'all, but I've got so much to do before the wedding. I wouldn't be able to relax."

"Did you see her desk, Margot? It's been attacked by lime green sticky notes." Daphne handed Lillabeth her credit card. "What's my discount, Jade?"

"Zero." Jade didn't even hesitate.

"What? No friend discount?"

"Hey, two-hundred-bazillion-dollars-an-hour headshrinker, pay the full price and tip the cashier." Margot winked at Lillabeth. "We agreed no discounts until Jade got on her feet, remember?"

"She looks like she's on her feet to me."

Daphne purchased her sweater and Jade walked them out to Margot's car, promising a spa day when she got back from her honeymoon. The girls had yet to hear the details about Mama, Dustin, and the battle of the mighty plunger against the burning box.

Jade wanted their full attention when she doled out the details.

But her stomach contracted and deflated like a day-old balloon when she waved good-bye and Margot and Daphne pulled away. They'd been a trio for so long.

Mama arrived at the Blue Umbrella shortly after opening and sat in the storage room, listening to a Beach Boys LP.

"Jade, this woman wants a consignment form." Lillabeth pointed to a well-groomed older woman with an air of Southern aristocracy.

"Certainly." In the office, Jade was fishing a form from the file cabinet when her cell rang from her pants pocket.

"Aren't you off with the boys? Golfing?"

"Yeah, but I just wanted to say I love you and I'm sorry about everything. Being stupid about Dustin, not telling you about the meds."

"I love you, and I'm sorry for being stupid about Dustin too. But I like a little bit of the jealous Max from time to time." Sometimes she craved the way Max made her feel. Loved, wanted. Worthy.

"I'll see what I can do."

When she hung up with him, her cell rang again. Jade answered as she walked the consignment form out to the customer.

"What now?" she said, laughing as she pictured Max leaning on his 3-wood.

"Hello? Is this Jade Fitzgerald?"

"Yes." She swallowed her humor. "Can I help you?"

"Jade, it's Lynette Simpson."

"Lynette, hey." Jade scanned her to-do stickies. Seems she had one here with Lynette's name on it.

"What time will you be here today? My daughter has a rehearsal tonight for the children's Christmas choir, and—"

"The Lugger estate." Jade ripped the sticky from her desk. It'd been moved to the top row when it should've been on the bottom. "Lynette, I'm sorry, I forgot."

"Jade, you have to come today. I can't hold your pieces any longer. I'll have to sell them."

"I gave you a deposit."

"Then come get the inventory."

She needed the Lugger inventory. Well, wanted it, anyway. Jade had passed on other estates to save for this one. She'd fallen in love with the Lugger's antique French sofa and begged Lynette to hold it for her. The Italian pasta service and the jewelry were worth the trip over, nevermind the rest of the inventory she'd selected from the sale. *Shoot, shoot, shoot. What time is it? Eleven. Okay. Roughly two hours to Nashville.* "How about one thirty, two o'clock. Is that okay?"

"Three at the latest, Jade. I've got to run some errands and get dinner before the rehearsal."

"I'm on my way." She'd have a full truck bed when she returned home tonight.

"Guess wedding details can mess with a girl's schedule." Lynette's tone softened.

"You might say that." Jade snapped her phone shut, grabbed a bite of the cinnamon bun that had been there all morning, and rounded the office door to the shop. "Lillabeth, my darling, dear, beautiful employee."

"Nothing good ever starts with those words."

"I've got to run to Nashville and pick up the Lugger estate items. They're too valuable and unique to let them go. Can you handle the shop by yourself?"

"I'm your girl. I'll even open tomorrow for you if you want, after church. You can have the afternoon off."

"Still begging for more hours? What's up, Lillabeth? It's not like your parents don't have money."

"I owe someone, like I said." Lillabeth walked from behind the counter and started straightening the pumpkin display.

"Owe who?" Jade dusted crumbs and sugar icing from her fingers, reaching under the counter for a wet wipe.

"A friend." Lillabeth's eyes glistened.

"Did you borrow money? Lose her favorite top?"

"I wrecked *his* car."

"Oh, honey." Jade stepped closer. "Was it bad?"

Lillabeth nodded, wiping her eyes. "Fifteen hundred dollars' worth."

"That's a lot of vintage."

"Every time I think of it, I get all watery." Lillabeth's laugh was weak but buoyed with hope. "I gave Alex my savings, but I still need eight hundred dollars. My parents were pretty mad. They're making me earn the money to pay Alex back." She kicked at the largest pumpkin, knocking over a little pilgrim man. "I stayed up all night to figure out a plan, going over what I had saved, what I could earn here. My dad is *big* on having a plan."

"What about basketball?" Jade stooped to set the man on his buckle-shoe feet.

"I quit the team."

"Lilla, no—"

"I wasn't having fun anymore, Jade. When I smashed Alex's car, the only way I could pay him was to try to work more hours, so I left the team. Coach understood."

"Then work all you want. I'll contribute to the cause. And I'd be grateful if you'd open tomorrow for me."

Lillabeth brightened. "I'll be here right after church. Thank you, Jade."

Back in the office, Jade grabbed her purse and the shop checkbook. Keys? Got them. Office was all good. She surveyed her desk and shelves to make sure she hadn't forgotten anything. Flipping off the light, she closed the door behind her.

"Count down the drawer when you close, and put the money in the bag. I'll worry about the deposit on Monday." Jade gave a few other last-minute instructions to Lillabeth. Not that she needed them. "Oh, Roscoe. He's up in the loft. Can you walk him in an hour or so? Feed him about five?"

That was it. She remembered everything. Jade headed for the storeroom door.

"Jade?" Lillabeth's call was soft. "What about your mama?"

Mama. Right, she'd forgotten Mama. Willow was off hiking, so there was no one else to keep her company. "I'll just, you know." Jade exhaled, glancing toward the storeroom. "Take her with me."

"Have fun."

"Right." Four hours in the truck with Mama? *Fun* was not the word Jade had in mind. Opening the storeroom door, Jade was fairly confident Mama would say no to a road trip anyway.

She was reclined in the pea-green and brown wooly chair, wearing the headset even though the turntable wasn't turning.

"Mama?" Jade lightly jiggled her foot. Her eyes popped open, and she sat up with a start.

"Jade. Sorry, guess I dozed off." She slipped the headset off.

"It's okay." Given Mama's circumstances. "Listen, I'm going to Nashville to pick up some inventory for the shop." If she didn't say anything else, maybe she could just slip out the door with a casual good-bye.

"Are you inviting me along?" Mama lowered the footrest, rubbing her hand over her eyes. Strands of gray hair freed from her braid floated around her head.

"I'll pull the truck to the door."

~

Beryl watched the hills of Tennessee out her window as Jade sped along I-24 toward Nashville, the old International truck rattling and shimmying.

Light flashed over her arms and legs, the rays of sun fighting a thick blue army of clouds rolling in from the north.

"Think it'll snow?"

Jade leaned over the wheel and peered out through the windshield. "In the mountains, maybe. It's a little early for down here."

"Reckon so."

Jade hadn't said much since they started out. Other than, "Want a coffee? I'm stopping at 7-11."

Maybe she should've said no to Jade's offhand invitation. The recliner was comfortable, and the music eased the ache in her bones and puttied the cracks in her heart.

"Max," she ventured. "What's he up to today?"

"Golfing with his buddies, then doing some kind of bachelor party in the city. One of them has a house on the river."

"Does he golf much? June said he had bad back problems from time to time."

"June should mind her own business."

"What did he think of Dustin?"

"They didn't meet. But he's happy Dustin signed the papers."

"Was it hard, Jade, to see Dustin after all these years?" A bit of music would be good. Beryl pushed the radio button, but no sound came.

"It's broken." Jade gazed out her window for the span of a few mile markers. "Seeing him wasn't hard. It's the remembering."

"I wouldn't want to see any of my exes." Beryl shuddered. Got rid of most of them as soon as she could. Except Harlan. She'd like to see him again. It took a bit of mental scrounging to add up the reasons for their demise.

"Not even the lieutenant?"

"No." The simple answer lingered between them. "Your dad, though. I was just thinking I'd like to see Harlan."

"Not me. He can kiss my—"

"Yeah, I get it."

"I heard you arguing that day I got lost in the cornfield."

"What day? When were you lost in the cornfield?" Her memory wasn't what it used to be. Willow claimed it was because she spent a few too many years smoking weed.

"Don't you remember? I was gone most of the night. The sheriff's deputies came. Snoops the hound dog found me. I was eight."

Beryl shook her head. "You'd think I'd remember."

Jade sighed. "Yeah, you'd think."

"Don't get huffy. We all store different memories."

"Not remembering the solo I sang in fourth grade is understandable, but having your kid lost in a cornfield?"

"You sang a solo?"

"No, Mama, I'm just saying—"

"What were your dad and I arguing about?" There'd been so many around that time. A few of the reasons she let Harlan go tapped her mental calculator.

"He was going to Washington, and neither of you wanted Aiden and me."

"Never. Jade, what kind of accusation is that? I was angry at him for taking the job without talking to me—he had a way of leaping before consulting—but we loved you two." Beryl looked at Jade. Out her window, there was a patch of blue sky showing between the storm clouds. It was so low, it almost appeared even with the truck.

"I heard both of you." The truck surged forward as Jade pushed harder on the gas. "He said he didn't want kids, you said it was your turn to do for yourself."

Beryl stared out her window, her chin resting in her hand. Fragments of the conversation replayed in her mind. "Your dad and I loved you and Aiden."

"Could've fooled me."

Beryl adjusted the lap seatbelt and repositioned. Her leg was falling asleep. "Was it so bad? With me as a mother?" She was sick, dying. What the heck. Ask the hard ones.

"Sometimes, yeah. You left us with Granny a lot, Mama. It felt like we were such an unbearable burden to you." Jade glanced at her, then back at the road, shifting in her seat, reaching for the radio's power knob.

"It doesn't work, remember?"

"Got to get that thing fixed."

"You weren't a burden . . . you kids." Beryl ran her hand over the weave of her braid. Dr. Meadows said she'd most likely lose her hair during chemo and suggested she cut the braid before her hair thinned to nothing. "Seems I was a burden to you though. I remember you stopped having civil conversations with me. One day we were talking, the next we weren't."

"Is that how you see it?" Jade gripped her hands tightly around the wide wheel. "Just one day, boom, I stopped talking to you?"

"Seems so." Beryl remembered being close to Jade during her breakup with Dustin and the subsequent ordeal. Then . . .

The cab was hot. Fog crept up the windshield. Beryl cracked open her window.

"The defroster is busted too."

"Why don't you have Max buy you a new truck?" Beryl said. The chilled air felt good on her face.

"I'm not marrying him for his money."

"Did I say you were? But this old rattle trap . . . reminds me of Paps' old junker. I'm surprised this thing runs."

"It runs great. Just had it in the shop, and Zach said it'll outlive us all."

"Okay, Jade. Didn't mean nothing by it. Max seems like a generous man, that's all." *The girl wrestles. Best leave her be, let her settle.*

The truck lurched, hesitated, then fired forward. "What's going on, Petunia?" Jade clutched and downshifted, patting the dash to the rattling of the engine. "Come on, girl, keep going. Did you hear me say what Zach said? You'll be running long after I'm gone."

"Maybe she doesn't like that, Jade." Beryl held onto her door handle, sitting up straight.

Petunia choked and gurgled, the motor gasping and losing power. Jade flipped on her hazards and eased onto the berm. I-24 traffic zipped past. Steam hissed out from under the hood.

"Want me to take a look? I've been broken down a few times in my life."

"I just had her in the shop. How can this be?" Jade clicked off the engine, smacking her fist against the wheel.

Beryl popped open her door. "All old things must die, Jade, sooner or later."

Twenty-five

"Water pump's broke."

"We figured." Mama had called it. Jade angled around to read the name stitched on the man's shirt. "Clem, how long to fix it?"

He patted his hand over his sewn-on name, then smoothed it down over the too-large shirt. "Name's Wayne, but my shirt got a hole in the front so I borrowed Clem's. He's off today, left this hanging in the washroom."

"You should've gone with the holey shirt, Wayne," Jade said. The one he wore was covered with grease. "But anyway, the truck? How long? An hour, two, three?"

"No, no, got to get the part in." He walked over to the body shop's office. "We don't stock the part you need. This here truck is too ding-dang-dong old. An International. Ain't seen one of these in years. Parts come up from Atlanta. In fact"—he took a skipping kind of step—"I'll go do that right now."

"And *awaaay* we go." Mama bent forward, hiking her left foot up to her right knee, and with a pump of her fists, skipped after Wayne.

"What are you doing?" Jade frowned.

"Jackie Gleason. 'And *awaaay* we go.'" Mama did the move again.

Jade raised her eyebrows, then popped the air with her fist. "'To the moon, Alice, to the moon.'"

Mama laughed. Then the two fell silent. Standing in opposite corners at the garage.

"All righty, the part's ordered," Wayne said, finally returning. "Hope to have it Monday by ten, get it fixed. Then you gals can get back on the road. Sorry for the delay."

"Monday? By ten? Wayne, seriously, there's no way you can get the part today? I'll be happy to pay extra. Can we drive to Murfreesboro? Nashville?"

"No can do. Part is shipped in from Atlanta. You all need a ride somewhere? We ain't got much for motels and hotels here in Beechgrove. I can drive you into Murfreesboro for a hotel or you can hole up at Miss Linda's. She's got a nice bed-and-breakfast. Want me to get her on the horn?"

"Yes," Mama quickly agreed.

"No," Jade insisted.

Jade and Mama faced off. "What's wrong with Miss Linda's?"

"I'd rather find a hotel in Murfreesboro." Jade turned to Wayne. "How far to the nearest hotel?"

"Fifteen, twenty minutes. I can drive you out, but Monday I'm the only one here, so you'll have to take a taxi."

"Where's Miss Linda's?" Mama asked.

Wayne walked to the edge of the bay and pointed toward a fiery golden maple tree with a gingerbread cottage sitting beneath it.

"Right there. You can walk. If she were on her stoop, I could holler a conversation with her."

"Jade, she's right there." Mama motioned. "If we go to Murfreesboro, we'll have to eat out . . . We'll have no way to get around. I can't walk very far, Jade. I'm sorry."

"Miss Linda makes a mean pot roast and rolls."

The idea of a home-cooked meal certainly appealed to Jade. But a weekend in a bedroom with Mama? She sighed.

"Get Miss Linda on the horn, Wayne."

Wayne whipped the portable phone from his pocket. Five minutes later Jade stood between twin beds in a room that looked like a flower garden had exploded—on the walls, on the bedcovers, in the picture frames.

"Towels are in the closet." Miss Linda motioned to the bathroom. "I serve snacks at ten and four except on Sunday, and then only snacks at four. Will you all be attending service with me tomorrow?"

"Service?"

"Church, of course."

"No," Mama said, easing down to her bed by the windows.

"I'd love to." Jade dropped her handbag on her bed. She'd need something to break up the day. "What time?"

"Meet me in the kitchen at ten." Miss Linda was bright and cheerful, with sapphire eyes peering out from under permed, red-rinsed hair and brown, drawn-on eyebrows. "Dinner is at six." The door clicked behind her.

"Your worst nightmare, stuck in a room with me?" Mama asked.

"Don't be a martyr." Sitting on her bed, Jade dug in her bag for her phone. "I'm going to ask Miss Linda if there's a store nearby, see if I can get some toiletries, a pack of underwear."

"We can wash our undies in the sink."

"*You* can wash *your* undies in the sink."

Jade called Lynette, hoping she'd give grace on picking up the inventory. "Lynette, hey, it's Jade. You're not going to believe this, but my truck broke down. Yeah, I know. Feels like, 'My dog ate my homework.' No, I won't . . . Yes, I do want the inventory . . . another buyer? Already?

Lynette, I can't help it my truck broke down . . . Well, send back the deposit then. Yeah . . . sure . . . I understand. Have a nice night."

"She's not keeping the inventory for you?" Mama asked.

"No."

"I'm sorry, Jade. But things always have a way of working out."

Sometimes. Maybe. "I'm going to give Max a call." Jade ducked into the bathroom and eased the door shut.

If she asked Max to drive to Beechgrove for her, he'd come. At least she thought he would. But this was his bachelor day, with the boys. How could she ruin it? It wasn't his fault she forgot the appointment in Nashville, or that the truck broke down.

June wouldn't come, she had a charity event with Rebel. Margot and Daphne were having their spa day, lucky girls, and would laugh all the way to Beechgrove and back if she called them.

Sighing, Jade stared at the bathroom door. Mama was on the other side. She'd been prepared to spend an afternoon with her, but an entire weekend? No.

Pressing the phone's buttons, she hesitated before finally calling Max. Maybe it would be all right to spend an extra day with Mama, discover they had something in common. Truth was, they barely knew each other.

"Baaabe," Max answered, very, um, exuberant. "How are you? It's my babe, fellas, shh."

"Have you been drinking?"

"No, no, just had a taste of champagne. Having fun with my boys, right?" Their raucous cheer filled Jade's ear.

"Just the boys, huh?" Max's tone and the influence of irreverent men pinged an old feeling. *The guys want to watch game film.* Surely it was just a disturbance from Dustin's abrupt visit. "No girls?" No silky-haired sisters?

"If there're girls, they're the ugliest I've ever seen. How're you? Did Daphne and Margot come get you?"

"They tried, and thank you for that, by the way." Jade touched the lacy trim of Miss Linda's hand towels, wishing she'd let Margot and Daphne kidnap her. "I had to run to Nashville for a pickup I'd forgotten."

"Nashville?"

"The truck's water pump blew, and the mechanic has to get the part from Atlanta. Mama and I are in a bed-and-breakfast in Beechgrove."

"Ah, sweetie, I'm sorry. Want me to come and—"

"No . . . no. Have fun. This is your bachelor party. If I drag you away, who knows, you might resent me twenty years from now."

"Never." He laughed softly. "But I hate to see you stuck in Murfreesboro. Can't you rent a car or truck to do what you need to do?"

"I need a truck and by the time I rent one, go to Nashville, pick up the inventory and drive back to Whisper Hollow, return the rental and pick up my hopefully-fixed truck . . . I'll have missed the wedding." Sighing, Jade blinked away a wash of tears. "I'm tired, Max. With all that's happened in the past few weeks . . . not even a gorgeous antique French sofa is worth my time right now. I just want to get *married* and go on our honeymoon."

"This time next week, Jade, this time next week. Sweetie, relax, have fun. Don't let your mama or the situation get you down. We'll find another antique French sofa. Ten times better than this one. In the meantime, your mama's here, trying to make amends. A day with her won't be so bad, will it? Shoot, the Dustin cat is out of the bag. What could be worse? Sliker . . . wait for me. No, man, no, not my woods. Jade, I need to—"

"Go, babe." She pictured him running after the dark, mischevious Sliker. "Have fun. I love you."

"Love you, too. Sliker, man, stop, you're going to pay—"

Jade clapped her phone shut with a weighty exhale and slouched against the toilet tank. *A day with her won't be so bad, will it?*

~

The afternoon light had shifted when Beryl woke from her nap. The room was eerily quiet.

"Jade?" She rose from the bed, thirsty. Gaining her bearings, she shuffled toward the bathroom, catching herself against the bathroom door.

Beryl hated this part of being sick. Weakness. Being submitted to the whim and will of disease, leukemia braking her life even though her will wanted to hit the gas.

Filling a Dixie cup with water, she made her way back to bed. No TV. All right, she appreciated quiet. Beryl propped the pillows against the headboard and peeked in the bedside table drawer.

A Stephen King novel. Good enough. She nestled into the pillows. A cigarette would taste good about now. She tried to read, but she couldn't concentrate on the tiny words on the page.

Head against a fat foam pillow, eyes closed, her thoughts wandered. Life was a series of journeys and adventures, and her train was pulling into the station too soon.

But she'd change nothing. How could she? Good, bad, otherwise, she had come to this moment, stranded with Jade in a flower-powered B&B.

~

Prairie City, December 1996

Mother's rocking chair creaked when she sat down. "The snow's sticking."

"We'll have a white Christmas." Beryl stretched her legs the length of the sofa.

"You want to tell me what's going on with Jade?"

"Other than being sixteen?" Beryl smacked the throw pillow by her legs with the flat of her hand, plumping and fluffing.

"It has to do with the Colter boy, doesn't it?"

"She'll be all right, Mama."

"She went through two boxes of pads while you were gone."

"Rough month, so what?" Headlights bounced along the wall. Good, Gig and the kids were home.

"Beryl, was she pregnant?"

"Mother, mind your own business." Beryl hopped off the couch, tugging her jeans straight. "I'm going to make some cocoa to drink while we put up the tree. Can you put on some Christmas music?"

Mother rocked silently, eyes straight ahead. Beryl bent to her ear.

"I did, *we* did, what was best for everyone."

"Really? Is that what you did?"

Okay, if she wanted to throw down, then throw down. "Yes, Mother, that's exactly what we did. How was she going to raise a kid with Dustin off in college having a grand time? Her friends going on to school or getting jobs, traveling. You want her stuck here with a baby on her hip, fighting with the Colters for control?"

"How was it a choice if you gave her no choice?"

"We did what was best for Jade, Mother."

"You've gone too far this time . . ." The woman began to shake. Her eyes narrowed and her face flared a bright red.

The kitchen door banged. "We got a tree, we got a tree." Willow's excited voice came from the kitchen.

"How do you sleep at night?" Mother's jaw was tight with the edge in her voice.

"Quite well, thank you."

Willow darted into the room, rosy cheeked and grinning, her wavy hair dotted with snow. "We got a tree, a big one." She jumped onto her granny's lap, stretching her arms out as far as she could. "Like this, but bigger."

"I love a big tree." Mother kissed the little girl's cold face and patted her bottom. "Go find your sister and tell her to come help us." When Beryl returned to the living room, declaring the water was boiling, Mother grabbed her arm.

"I've never seen Jade like this. She doesn't eat unless I make her. All she does is school and work. Spends every night in her room studying or sleeping. Won't even go out with Rachel."

"It's hard to get over a broken heart." Beryl pulled free.

"And losing a baby?"

"Mother, don't make—"

"And before that, having her father walk out on her, then her mother running off whenever she felt like it. Beryl, you're so busy telling the rest of us how to live, you never stop and look at yourself, evaluate your actions, see the trail of pain you're leaving."

"The kettle is about to steam. Gig, is that you and Aiden? Bring the tree in here by the front window."

Mother blocked Beryl's exit, stepping in her path. "I've held my peace for a long time, Beryl. Harlan left. Then Mike. You hopped on the road as soon as Carlisle called, the ink on your divorce papers still wet, leaving those kids with me. I was in no shape after Paps died. I worked all the time, was barely home to feed and bathe them at night. You know why Jade won't eat a peanut butter and jelly sandwich, don't you?"

"They were safe with you, and I knew it."

"Safe? Jade's never felt safe. Didn't you see? She never had a moment of confidence until that boy came into her life. Now he's gone, along with the child he created with her. Once again, off you go without a word to me." Mother pointed her long arm toward the upstairs. "She needed you, and I had no idea. Beryl, you didn't even call her. She must have asked me two, three times a day for the first week, 'Did Mama call?'"

"Don't you dare try to guilt-trip me."

"Mercy, no, why would I want to spoil all your fun? I'm just giving you an update on your daughter. When we did know where you were, she left a voice message with the hotel. Did you call her back? No. I heard her crying at night, and my heart crumbled into a million pieces because I didn't know how to get invited in. I'm ashamed, Beryl." Mother shook her head and pressed her lips tight. "Ashamed of what you've become. How did I raise my girl to be a mother like you?"

"How dare you judge me."

"Make way, make way." Aiden came in carrying the front half of the tree with Gig sporting the back.

Beryl whispered hotly to her mother. "Are you finished?"

"I pray, Beryl. I shut the door to my room and pray. 'God, lift her soul, heal her hurt.' If Jade survives the life you handed her, it's because He's good, because He loves her. Not you."

"Then what's your worry? Holier-than-thou. You've covered all the bases. She'll be fine."

"Yes, Beryl, but a broken-winged bird can still flitter away. Don't think Jade will forget this easily."

~

Jade was back in the flowered room, loaded with Wal-Mart bags. "I guessed at your size." She dropped a few bags at the foot of her bed and handed another to Beryl.

"You didn't have to do this." She set aside the King novel, still on page five, and peered inside the bag. Toothbrush and toothpaste, a brush and comb set, a packet of underwear, a top and a pair of jeans.

"Everyone feels better in clean clothes." Jade gathered a couple of bags, motioning toward the bathroom. "Are you done in there? I'd like to take a bath."

"Go ahead." Beryl stared at the door when she heard the click of the lock, the tiny sound trumpeting in her soul. *Keep out.*

Reaching for her Dixie cup, she sipped the last bit of water, trying to think why Mother's voice was so prominent in her thoughts. Did she dream about her when she drifted off?

Beryl reached for the book, but Stephen King just didn't appeal at the moment. She went to the window and peered out, brushing her hand over her forehead. Had she abandoned her children? In retrospect . . .

Was Jade still upset about the choice they'd made? After the drive home that day, they'd never talked about it again. What was there to say? Then Jade was off to the University of Tennessee and here they were . . . eleven years later and a week from her wedding.

Could she blame the strain between them on Dustin? His sudden reappearance sure didn't move Jade toward Beryl with tenderness.

Jade had called those days after the abortion. She'd left messages. A twinge of regret snapped at Beryl. Half the time she probably didn't even get them. The motels Gig booked weren't known for their amenities.

But the ones Beryl did get . . . the twinge twisted tighter. She'd ignored them. Mercy, those were wild days with Gig. She was kind of relieved when he wanted to plant roots in L.A., but not with her.

At the sound of a light knock, Beryl turned from the window. "Girls, dinner. We're eating in the dining room tonight."

"We'll be right along." Beryl searched the floor for her shoes, wishing she were hungry. She'd caught a whiff of roasting meat about an hour ago and thought it'd been years since she'd eaten a good slice of pot roast. "Jade, dinner."

No response. Beryl knocked softly. "Jade?"

A muffled, moaning sob crept from under the door.

"Jade? Are you all right?"

"Go away." Tears washed her words.

"What's going on?" Beryl gripped her hands at her waist, checking the temptation to try the doorknob.

"Go. Away." Water splashed, with the echo of a deep tub.

"Miss Linda called us to supper. The pot roast smells wonderful."

"I'm not hungry."

"All right." Beryl's appetite had diminished even more now, but she didn't want to leave Miss Linda eating alone in the dining room. Sounded like such a special deal when she announced it. "If you change your mind, we're in the dining room. Miss Linda seemed to think it was a special treat."

Beryl waited a few seconds. "Jade?" Okay . . .

Miss Linda waited at the head of the table, beautifully set with white-and-blue china and tall, tapered candles.

"One more and we can say grace." Miss Linda motioned for Beryl to sit.

"I'm afraid my daughter isn't feeling well."

"Should I set aside a plate for later?" Miss Linda crinkled her face with concern.

Then Jade appeared, pink and fragrant, her wet hair combed and tucked behind her ears. Beryl's gaze caught on the praying hands medallion lying against her soap-scented skin. She hadn't thought of that old thing in years.

"It smells delicious." Jade spread her napkin over her lap with a smile for Miss Linda, but not so much as a glance toward Beryl.

Twenty-six

After dessert on the patio, Miss Linda scrubbed her kitchen, refusing help, then bade Mama and Jade a smiling goodnight and dimmed the lights.

At eight thirty Jade paced over to the window. Stuck in this warm, still-air room with a woman looking to make God happy before she dies.

"All right, Jade, let's have it out," Mama said, sitting on the foot of her bed.

"I'm not in the mood for your drama." Had Miss Linda turned on the heat? So hot . . . Jade shoved aside the curtain to see if she could crack the window.

"Drama? I wasn't the one sitting in the tub crying."

"Mind your own business." Max was saluting his bachelorhood with his buddies while she was stuck in No Place, Tennessee, with a piece of her life she didn't treasure. Was there no justice? "I'm going for a walk."

"Mind if I come along?"

Jade snatched up her jacket as she walked out, leaving the door ajar. "It's a free country. For now."

The cold night air felt good. Mama hurried to keep up, but Jade didn't break stride, following the moon's pearly path down the dark, unfamiliar street.

A cranking, tired engine was the melody in the breeze.

"It's not healthy to keep things bottled up, Jade," Mama said, winded.

"Oh really?" Jade stopped short, zipping up her jacket. "Want me to spew my emotional baggage? Because most of it has your name on it."

She shivered from the inside out. Mama waited in front of her, huddled in her jacket, hands in her pockets, not flinching. The wind pushed and pulled the ends of her hair.

Did Jade want to go off on her? What was the point? Mama might be trying to get in good with God, but Jade didn't want to risk any more of His wrath. She'd tempted Him enough already. How many pardons does a girl get?

"Bad day, Mama." She exhaled. "The truck breaking down was the last straw. In Wal-Mart, it all started to hit me. Getting married, you showing up, then Dustin, some issues with Max." *The escalating anxiety attacks.*

"But my presence is more than just a tipping point."

"Are you surprised?" Jade started walking. "When have things been any different between us?"

"When you were a girl, you'd beg to ride the tractor with me." Mama's laugh was low. "I can still see your little hands hanging onto that big wheel, so brown and strong from playing in the sun all summer."

"It's been a long time since I was eight, Mama." Jade remembered those days like an ancient, lost civilization that had somehow self-destructed. Once, she'd been the girl growing up on a farm with parents who loved each other. With parents who protected her. Loved her.

"True, but you grew into a strong, capable girl. I could trust you."

"How convenient." Jade skidded to a stop. "I grew into a strong, capable girl right when you wanted to be a wild and irresponsible woman."

"I wasn't irresponsible."

"Says you, Beryl Hill. Mama, why didn't we go with Daddy to Washington? Would it have killed you to think of someone else besides yourself?"

"Why don't you ask him?"

"I'd love to, if he ever bothered to call his own kid."

"You could always call—"

"Stop, Mama, just stop." Jade sliced the cold with her hands. "I was eight when he left. Eight! My relationship with you two was not my responsibility. You were the parents, and you both left us."

"I was around when you needed me."

"Oh sure, to argue with Carla Colter, call her a few choice names." Jade walked a few paces off. Mama waited on the edge of a moonlight shadow, half in, half out.

"You were the one who ran off and married that boy. You forged the signatures."

"For the first time since I could remember, I felt loved and wanted. Safe. Dustin was my whole world. I could breathe when he was around; I could see beyond the boundaries of Prairie City and imagine a life for myself. Outside of Granny and Paps, no one ever really loved and cared for me."

"I always loved you, Jade. Aiden and Willow too."

"Don't tell me of love, Mama. Show me." The lid on her emotions rattled.

"Watch it, Jade. Who turned things upside down to come home and take care of the mess you created with Dustin?"

"You want a medal?" Jade clapped her hands, the popping echoing through the trees, and walked over to Mama. "Well, thank you, Beryl Hill, for cutting your husband's two-bit, roadside tavern rock-n-roll tour a few days short. Has the music world recovered?"

"You'd not be standing here, Jade, mocking me, if I'd not taken care of things. Do you think Dustin would've stayed with you if he knew you were pregnant?"

"Yes, he said so. When he was here."

"Oh, Jade—you believed him? And what was his response when you told him that you were?"

"I didn't tell him."

"Because you know it wouldn't have made a difference, Jade. Maybe he would've been the one driving you to the clinic. He would've left you, Jade, sooner or later. Fine for him to sound heroic with nothing on the line. Did he tell you what he's been up to?"

"Actually, no."

"Nothing. He moved to St. Louis last year and still doesn't have a steady job. His great college education, the one he had to leave you for, going to no use." Mama swerved into a little neighborhood park, taking a bench.

Jade sat on the opposite end, inhaling cold air that tingled her lungs but boiled in her middle. "You want to know why?"

The slice across her heart was sharp and quick, surprising. Jade balled her fists, battling tears and anger, lightly pounding her thighs. She'd carried the pain alone, through panic and depression, shame and guilt, talking to no one.

Jade shot to her feet, her tone sharp and boisterous. "You drove me to the clinic, waited while they scraped my womb, then drove me home and went on your merry way. I had nightmares. I was cramping and bleeding, with no one to talk to, no one to help me. I felt completely and utterly alone."

Her confession hung in the air like crystals, falling slowly to the ground, pulling a curtain of silence behind them. Jade walked to the two-seat swing set, leaning against the cold metal pole. For a blip of a second, fear trickled over her as she remembered the angst of feeling so abandoned.

"I didn't know it was so hard for you," Mama said finally, low and slow. "I thought you were mad at Dustin, thus the rest of the world, me included."

"You never bothered to ask."

"You were sixteen. What sixteen-year-old doesn't hate her parents from time to time?"

Jade turned around. Mama sat gathered to herself, shivering. "I didn't want to hate you. But I'd lie in bed at night . . . hurting. I just hurt, Mama. All over and inside out. Every time I closed my eyes, I was in the clinic, the doctor asking me if I was numb. Then my heart would race and I'd bolt out of bed, fussing around, going for long walks at one or two a.m."

"What do you want me to say, Jade?"

Tears spilled down the curve of her nose. "If I have to tell you . . ." She walked back to the street. "It's getting too cold."

"Why did you come to me instead of Granny?" The words followed Jade as Mama hurried to catch up. "You knew what I would say, what my advice would be."

"You're my mother. Why wouldn't I come to you? But you didn't even ask me if I was sure. Talk about options."

"Neither did you. You were sixteen, old enough to find options if you wanted."

Sobs rolled up from her chest. "Because . . ." She shook her shoulders. "I wanted you to help me, Mama. Despite everything, I thought you were so worldly and wise. I wanted your attention. I believed you'd know the right thing to do."

"And I did."

Jade covered her face with her hands, shaking her head. "No, Mama. No."

The memory contained hurt. The knowing contained slicing pain. She'd agreed with her mama to abort her child. To remove what remained of her life with Dustin.

Jade lived with the cement-feeling of regret every day. And the heart-blinding shame.

Jade knelt on the pavement, chilled and shivering, sobbing. Her emotions swelled; her breathing felt constricted. "I just want the hurt to end."

Mama rested her hand on her head. "I'm sorry you hurt."

Jade dropped the rest of the way to the street, wiping her face. Miss Linda lived near the end of a quiet neighborhood with small houses and large yards. But if a car came along . . .

Jade took a long, weepy breath. *No.* She hadn't thought of death in a long time. She had so much life ahead of her. Brushing her hair back, she gazed toward the orange line of the horizon.

"After Dustin walked out on me, I felt so numb, so unworthy. I hated myself. I hated him, hated you."

"I didn't make you go, Jade." Mama's hand pressed against Jade's shoulder as she knelt next to her in the street. "But it's done. Why dwell on it? We can't change anything. Don't bring this into your life with Max."

"You don't think I've tried to forget?" Brushing the pavement with her fingertips, Jade picked up pebbles and tossed them to the curb. "Every once in a while, out of the blue, I'll catch my reflection in a window and wonder, Is my life worth sacrificing a baby? Who would she be now? How would her life enrich mine?"

"Jade, that kind of thought process is fruitless."

"The answer is no, always no. Nothing I am or will be is worth my child's life. If I live to be a hundred, find the cure for cancer, and save all the starving children in Africa, the answer will still be no." Jade stood, knocking the dirt from her jeans, feeling stiff from the cold. "You'd think an avid war protestor like you would've thought of that, Mama."

Mama lifted her hand for help getting up. "If only life's questions and answers were so straightforward."

"People like you make them hard because the answer always has to be what's best for you." Jade pulled Mama to her feet, then started for Miss Linda's. "How do you do it, Mama? You don't seem to struggle with any of your life choices—being divorced, leaving your kids for your mother to raise, having an abortion. Why does my body, my soul remind me from time to time, but you don't seem to struggle at all?"

Mama peered at Jade, then looked toward the street. "I never had an abortion, Jade."

"Excuse me?" A trembling sensation crept from Jade's middle to her arms and legs. The confession couldn't find a soft place to light. "You told me you did."

"When we came home from the clinic, you looked so lost and broken, so sad."

"So you lied to me? Oh, why am I surprised? What kind of mother does that! You're a horrible, horrible woman." Jade spun around, pointing behind her, keeping Mama at bay. "Don't follow me."

Jade vanished into the darkness of the trees, her heels crunching the street pebbles.

Twenty-seven

Sitting in her truck cab, in Wayne's garage, Jade auto-dialed Max and blew her nose into a McDonald's napkin.

"Answer your phone, Max. Answer." On the third call, his voice mail picked up again. She clapped the phone shut without leaving a message. "Where are you?"

Jade dropped her head against the seat. How could Mama do such a thing? Could she be more cruel? Lying about an abortion. Not that she didn't have one, but that she did. Who does that? The woman is certifiable.

She caught the trail of her tears with the back of her hand. Tired. She was so tired. Of lies, of hurting, of being alone. Of fear. Once in a while, in the late hours of the night, she'd wake up with a sense of loneliness, as if her life was going nowhere, feeling like she'd be in her bed, in her loft, alone, for the rest of her life.

Even rolling onto her side and dreaming of Max didn't comfort her.

She dialed him again, but his voice mail answered. *Where are you?* She pressed auto-dial for Aiden.

"The bride-to-be." Aiden's cheery voice settled her agitation. "Can't wait until Wednesday to see me?"

"Your mother is a freak, freak, freakity-freak."

Silence. Jade felt like a mini freakity-freak as her exclamation echoed in her mind. Aiden doesn't even know what happened during the fall of '96. "Aiden, forget—"

"She's sick, you know." His voice was tender. Even.

"How did you know?"

"Dr. Meadows called me. He didn't think Mom was letting anyone know and wanted to make sure her affairs were in order. I was going to talk to her after the wedding."

"She asked me to be executor since you travel so much."

"That's fine, at least she's thinking ahead." Aiden had a Bing Crosby quality to his voice. Yeah, everything was going to be all right.

"She came to Whisper Hollow to right all of her wrongs before she meets the Big Guy."

"Anything in particular, Jade?"

The cab of the truck was claustrophobic and airless, and the windows were completely fogged. Jade cranked down her window. "Dustin came to see me."

"What'd he want? Tell you he was stupid to leave you?"

"Basically. The annulment never happened. He wanted to see me, so he drove to Whisper Hollow."

"What did you do?"

"Nothing. Walked the park . . ." She didn't have the emotional energy to recount the conversation with Dustin.

"So is that the big angst between you and Mama?"

Moonlight broke through a stand of trees on the edge of the garage's pavement.

"Aiden, I—" She ran her fingers through her hair and shifted in her seat, envisioning the black-and-white sketch of her ordeal. What would he think of her? Her big brother, the one who came into her room at night when he discovered the truth about Dustin, and prayed good night and encouraged her to find her destiny. "I was pregnant."

"I see."

The temperature in the cab rose a degree. Jade kicked open the door and stepped out. "Mama took me to a clinic . . . in Des Moines. She told me she'd been through the same thing, before Daddy, and that it was no big deal."

Aiden whistled down the digital line. "Jade, I'm sorry."

"I've been so mad at her for so long. Hated her really. Hated myself."

"So what happened tonight? Why are you telling me this now?"

"She lied, Aiden. She never aborted a baby. She just told me that so I'd feel better. Then she dropped me at Granny's and ran off with Gig. I thought I was dying. I needed her to put a soft hand on my hot skin and tell me I was going to be fine."

"Did you ask her to stay?"

"Do you think she would have?" Jade pressed her forehead to one of the square glass panes of the garage bay's door.

"Whether she would've or not isn't the question. Did you ask her?"

"Whose side are you on? You know darn well she wouldn't have let Gig go to Chicago without her."

"You didn't ask her because you were already ticked."

"So what if I was? She made me go to the clinic."

"Jade, I'm sorry for what you went through, but since when did Mama make us to do anything? Granny was the one with all the rules. Mama would come home and say, 'Leave the kids be, Mother. They're doing fine.' She had three life platitudes: 'Stand up for yourself, stand up for your fellow man, and follow your heart.'"

"Then she should've stood up for me, her daughter."

"What are you saying? She dragged you to the clinic? Come on, Jade. You got in the truck and went with her, didn't you?"

"I was sixteen." Jade tucked her chin to her chest. "Dustin walked out on me. I was devastated." A whiff of grease made her queasy.

"Why didn't you go to Granny? Or a teacher? Why Mama?"

"Stop, stop. I call you for help and you condemn me. You sound like her, like it's all my fault!" Jade's voice bounced against the garage walls. "Well, it's not. Everyone abandoned me. Even you abandoned me . . . for Jesus. And when I got in a bind, I was left to suffer on my own."

"Pity isn't your shade, Jade. The first step to healing is being honest with yourself. You made the decision to go."

"He walked out on me, Aiden. He chose wrestling over me. Why are you being so mean?" Jade fired the phone across the garage, rage careening through the canyon of her soul.

~

Jade bolted awake, gasping, her hair clinging to the side of her face and neck. She exhaled in short puffs. Where was she?

The garage. Wayne. Right. The cab of her truck. She crawled out, her eyes burning, her muscles without power. Did someone get the license plate of the Mack truck that hit her?

The cold air of the garage chilled her warm skin. Shivering, Jade zipped up her jacket as her eyes adjusted to the darkness. If she had the truck keys, she'd turn on the headlights. But she'd given them to Wayne, and the office door was locked.

She needed to find her far-flung phone. Getting on her hands and knees, Jade searched the grimy floor by the soft illumination from a distant street lamp. She moaned when her hand landed in an oil slick. Ah, her phone. In the back right corner.

Checking to see if it still worked—it did—Jade exited Wayne's shop by the back door and stepped into a solemn, hushed night.

Two a.m. How many nights had she been awake in the early morning hours, wrestling with the ghosts of condemnation and fear?

The cold pushed her into a jog toward Miss Linda's, and Jade's conversation with Aiden came alive in her mind. He'd blamed *her*. All the years Mama ran off, having a fun ol' time, neglecting her responsibilities, and he had the nerve to indicate Jade was the one responsible for their estrangement, for the drive to the clinic, for her own pain?

Her brother was crazy. Did he not see the picture she'd painted? *Baby, abortion, no choice.*

Pausing outside Miss Linda's gate, Jade called Max again. Still no answer. He always had his phone with him, on, charged up, ready to go. Her heart thumped with the idea that something might be wrong. His back? Who knows what those overgrown frat boys had talked him into doing?

Lifting the gate latch, Jade followed the walkway around to Miss Linda's back patio. She gently tried the sliding glass door, but it wouldn't budge.

Wrapping her arms around her waist, Jade curled up on the bench swing, laying back so her head rested on the swing's arm between the chains.

She couldn't blame herself for that day. No. Not. Her. Fault. Mama made the appointment, and—

Jade shot upright, catching the ends of her hair in the chain's links.

Besides, she alone was her heart's final port of call. A haven when all else failed. When safe places turned off their cell phones. When safe places ran off with musicians. When safe places moved to Washington, D.C., and never looked back. When safe places chose a sport where men wrestle men instead of loving her.

Anxiety bullied her sanity and reason. Jade absently set the swing into motion, back-and-forth, higher and higher, her fingers gripping the varnished seat slats. The chains creaked and moaned as they wore against a heavy, gray beam.

A nightingale sang. Jade gripped her medallion as her heart rhythm increased. A heavy, almost liquid breeze blew past her. Goosebumps tightened the skin on her scalp and down her arms.

"Hello?" She slid off the swing, anticipation burning in her chest. This was it. She was finally going crazy. "Who's there?"

The wind gusted again with a distinct, other-worldly chill. Jade dropped back onto the swing as if it made her untouchable and safe. Her eyes darted around the porch as she strained to hear.

"Who's there?" Her skin prickled. If someone answered . . . This was crazy. She was alone, completely alone. There was no one here.

Me.

She swallowed. "Okay, what if I did decide? What if it was what I wanted? Not to have Dustin's baby. Not to be humiliated for nine months. Not to raise a child alone."

The wind gusted again, against only her face. Not even the ends of her hair moved. Adrenaline pumped her pulse, and she wanted to run.

"Is that what you want me to say? I did it. I got in the truck and went to the clinic."

Bile burned the base of her throat and hot tears warmed her cheeks. How could she stand before the court of heaven and testify against herself?

If possible, the air thickened even more, and Jade labored for each breath, feeling as if she might jump out of her skin. The force inside her churned, warring with the power outside, the one in the wind. Jade fired off the swing's seat, stumbling into the yard weak-kneed. The swirling air, alive with energy, followed. A suffocating scream swelled in her torso.

Let go, Jade. Come to Me.

Under the moon's milky eye, Jade spread her trembling arms wide and screamed, thumping her chest. "I chose . . . me." *Thump.* "I got in the truck and went with Mama. I chose me over my child. I did it."

Dropping to her knees, she sobbed, covering her face with her arms. "Forgive me."

The Wind snapped, but instead of a distinct chill, a searing heat formed in the bottom of Jade's feet and crawled up her legs, into her chest, down her arms—hotter, hotter—creeping up her neck, burning along her cheeks to the crown of her head. The Wind had become Fire.

Purifying fire.

"Oh God, oh God, please, I'm sorry, so sorry." Jade drummed out her confession.

Intense and gripping heat engulfed her, and every pore of her burned. She couldn't move or cry out.

Then, as quickly as it came, the heat vanished, leaving a cool river of peace.

Jade mentally walked through the memory of that day at the clinic, seeing herself on the table, and anticipated the throb of decade-old shame and hurt. Instead, she felt free of her sadness and grief.

For the first time in thirteen years, Jade wept for her child.

I was always with you.

Closing her eyes, Jade felt the hand of Jesus as she drifted along the current of a sapphire-blue day with cotton-candy clouds and lemon-drop sunbeams.

She was finally free.

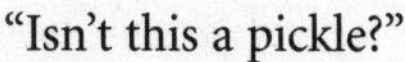

"Isn't this a pickle?"

Jade bolted upright, banging her head on the swing chains—again—and surveyed the porch in the bright white of a new day.

"I suppose you'll want a refund for sleeping on the back porch?"

"Miss Linda, hello." Jade rubbed the spot on her head where she'd lost a clump of hair to the swing's chain, eyeing the caught dark strands billowing in the early morning breeze.

"Good morning. Did your bed have bugs?" Miss Linda was perky and dressed for church.

"No, well, maybe . . ." Jade raked back her hair, waiting for the familiar dull ache to remind her last night was a freakish, emotional moment. Did she dream it all? But there was no twinge. She felt light, as if she was floating. "Is Mama still asleep?"

"The bedroom door is closed. Goodness, girl, didn't you freeze?"

"I was surprisingly warm." Jade ran her hand along the base of her neck where His fire had burned.

Miss Linda perched on the edge of the swing. "He comes here often. Never understood why. I just learned to appreciate it."

"Who comes here?" Jade jumped from the swing, jostling Miss Linda so she had to hang on.

"Jesus, the Spirit. In a wind, most often. Oh, the peace I've experienced out here. It was so pure and deep, I never wanted to move from my chair."

"I was out walking, and when I came back, the door was locked." Jade snapped a dangling, dead violet off the plant sitting on a plastic stand.

"He brought you here, Jade. He's been wanting to meet with you for a good long while."

Jade fixed her gaze on Miss Linda. "Why would He want to meet with me?"

"He loves you. It's why most people come here. Jesus and Wayne bring them around. I can see in your eyes that He's been with you. The pain is—"

"Does He forgive me too?" Jade smashed the dried bloom in her hand, letting the crumbled pieces fall to the floor. It was strange to breathe without that familiar catch in her lungs.

"Jade, if you sacrificed your life, gave everything you valued and loved to redeem another, wouldn't you forgive them just about anything if they asked?"

"Is that what Jesus did for me?"

"You, me, and all those who believe." Miss Linda made a gentle humming sound.

For Jade, last night was like nothing she had ever experienced before. Her broken-down truck had driven her to a place of healing.

"Well." Miss Linda clapped her hands against her legs and stood. "Breakfast will be in an hour. You still plan to join me for church?"

Jade's gaze met hers. "I think I'd like to stay here on the porch for a while."

"Can't say as I blame you." Miss Linda smiled, waving her finger in the air. "Let Jesus put His seal on what He started."

~

In the pink-and-gray light of the flower-power room, Mama slept. Her form was barely visible under a mound of blankets. Jade peeled off her coat and stepped out of her shoes.

"Mama?" Jade gently touched her arm and smoothed her hair away from her face.

"Jade?" Mama stirred but couldn't open her eyes. "I'm so cold."

"Cold? It's an oven in here." Jade pressed her cheek to Mama's. Her lips were pale, and she was shivering.

"W-where were you? Are you-you all right? I'm s-s-so sorry, Jade—"

"Shh, it's okay." Jade slipped underneath the blankets, molding her body against Mama's, rubbing her hands along her thin arms. "Let's get you warmed up."

Compassion bloomed in the ravine of Jade's heart where thorns once grew.

"I've b-b-been thinking, Jade. You're right, I-I-I wasn't there—"

"Mama, it's okay. I did choose to go with you. I've been mad at myself but blaming you. I'm sorry, Mama. Now, let's get you warm. Later, I'll tell you all about my night."

"Was it good?"

"Strange, but good." Jade nestled closer, memorizing the scent of Mama's skin, wondering how to describe an encounter with the Divine.

"Nehru jacket."

"What?"

"N-Nehru jacket." She shivered. "I have one in the attic. An original. In-in great shape. For your shop."

"My shop? For me, shoot."

The encounter with Jesus didn't remove all of Jade's obstacles. Liking Mama might not happen overnight, but being free compelled her to love. And that had to be a real fine place to start.

Twenty-eight

Monday evening, when Jade and Mama pulled into the Blue Umbrella's alley, the truck bed loaded with items for the store—turns out Mama was an excellent antiquer—Max was waiting for her.

"You're a sight for sore eyes." Max wrapped his arms around her, his kiss hot on her lips. "Evening, Beryl."

"Max." Mama hugged Jade, then brushed her hand over her hair. "I'm going to get on over to the Magnolia Tree, see what Willow is up to, and take a nap."

"See you tomorrow, Mama. And . . . thank you."

"Thank . . . you, Jade-o."

Unhooking the tailgate, Jade gazed at Max, Mama's taillights flashing red over his face. "Where have you been, cowboy? I tried to call you a hundred times."

"Babe, I'm so sorry. The guys took my phone."

"I see you had a mature, responsible weekend then." She lifted the Dutch boy and girl porcelain set. "I thought something might have happened to you. But June hadn't called, so I didn't panic."

He moaned, rubbing his hand over his head. "I told them, but they never listen. They like to play keep-away . . . the bachelor from his fiancée." Max tried to draw her to him again.

"Want to help unload? Hey, Roscoe, buddy." Jade bent to touch her nose to his. "Lillabeth, my hero, thank you for covering the shop all weekend. Are you getting closer to that eight hundred?"

"Well, if you give me a raise—" She hugged Jade and reached inside the truck bed. "I should get extra pay for dealing with your anxious fiancé. He's been hanging around all day waiting for you. I almost had to put him to work."

"You should've." Jade glanced at Max. A weekend-old beard darkened his jaw, deepening the shadows under his eyes.

"I tried to call you, Jade. All day." He unloaded a box of frameless paintings from the truck.

"Irritating, isn't it." Roscoe led the way inside. "My phone battery died. Lilla, put that stuff over there. Max, bring the paintings into the office."

It was good to be home. Jade dropped her bag on top of the lime green stickies and collapsed in her chair. Max leaned against the edge of the desk, stiff and distracted.

"Vegas," he blurted. "They hijacked me to Vegas."

"Vegas? The bachelor party went to Vegas?"

"They blindfolded me, took my wallet and phone. Burl has a plane, so . . ." Max swooped his hand toward the ceiling. "Off we went. Bunch of goofballs."

Jade regarded him a moment. His countenance seemed sad. Low. "It's okay, Max."

"Is 'What happened in Vegas stays in Vegas' pertinent here?" he asked.

"What happened in Vegas?" Her middle knotted. *Don't do this to me, Max.*

"Relax, Jade." He smiled. "Nothing, I'm just teasing. The only thing that happened in Vegas was I lost a bunch of money."

"How much?" Tension eased out with her next exhale.

"Let's just say we'll need to keep the money from the dinner party."

"Max, that's ridiculous."

"Tell me, I know." He started to pace. "Once you start at the tables, it's almost impossible to quit. Of course, it didn't help that the guys were tossing money down on my behalf."

"You need new friends."

Roscoe trotted in, burying his head between Max's knees, giving him a Roscoe hug. "Hey, old boy. Did you miss me?"

Lillabeth ran a continuous shop update, helping Jade and Max unload the rest of the truck. "We were swamped until closing on Saturday, then when I opened yesterday, there were people waiting."

"Tell you what, take anything you want from the '70s rack, on me."

"Now you're talking. Thanks, Jade."

Letting Lillabeth close up, Jade ordered pizza and climbed up to the loft with Max. "I need to tell you something. More gunk from my past."

"R-really. What happened with letting the past be the past?"

"I met Jesus, Max."

"What do you mean you met Jesus? Was He hitchhiking?" He closed the door behind him, yuk-yukking, his humor fading when he peered at Jade.

"Max, when Dustin walked out on me, I was pregnant."

"Pregnant?" The word hung in the air between them.

"I didn't know until after he'd walked out."

"Okay, what happened to the baby?"

She expected to see his jaw tighten, but it didn't. Jade thumped her palms against her thighs. "Well, I'm not proud of this, but Mama took me to a clinic

. . . I-I went to a clinic. In Des Moines." She collapsed on the couch. Wasn't the week before a girl's wedding supposed to be stressed with wedding preparations, not heart-wrenching confessions?

"Oh." Max sat on the couch and brushed her bangs aside with the tip of his finger. "Wow. I'm sorry, Jade."

"Max, look, I thought a lot about this on the drive home. I've told you a lot of lies. If you don't want to marry—"

"Wait, Jade, please don't." His tone was tender. "I wasn't expecting this news, but it doesn't change how I feel. Nothing can change how I feel. I love you. Just . . . are there any more surprises?"

She slipped her hand into his. "Last one, absolutely, I promise. Well, from my past anyway."

"Look, Jade, the past can still be the past. In fact, we can start clean, right now, today. Five minutes ago, yesterday, last week—ancient history."

"I need to tell you, to finish the story, because this is where Jesus comes in."

"Then tell me."

~

On the Bensons' enclosed patio, overlooking the fading gold-and-red valley, Jade sipped fresh-squeezed lemonade from a Baccarat crystal glass and reviewed the final wedding preparations.

She read the list the wedding planner, Betsy, handed her, but without focus. The first time Max came to her loft for dinner, she served him sweet tea in a mason jar, and he said it was the sweetest tea he'd ever tasted.

"Jade, I heard you were stranded with your mama in Beechgrove." Betsy tapped on her iPhone, sticking out her tongue. "If that was me and my mom, someone would've died."

June regarded Jade. "You don't seem any worse for the wear."

"I took your advice." Jade sipped her lemonade.

"Really?" June squared her shoulders, smiling. "You let go of the issue with your mother?"

"Yes, by letting go of an issue with me." She wasn't all the way there yet, but the train was on the tracks. All aboard.

Who knew sending a ruby red invitation to Beryl Hill would result in her redemption and freedom? Jade *Freedom* Fitzgerald.

"We should have Max confirm the honeymoon details, flight, reservations." Betsy's fingers flew over her iPhone keypad. "Max . . . confirm . . . hon-ey-moon . . ."

"Bridesmaids' gifts, Jade. Done?"

"Antique jewel boxes."

"Check." General Betsy. "The quartet for the wedding is confirmed, but we need to confirm with the reception band. They're coming over from Nashville, which makes me nervous. I've had bands not show before." Betsy started another text. "I'll have my assistant confirm."

"Final head count, two-ninety." Betsy slid Jade the final list of names. "Your sister asked to invite a few of her friends."

Jade reviewed the handwritten names, smiling. Willow. That girl.

Betsy moved on to bridesmaids' and groomsmen's arrival times, confirming rooms at the Magnolia Tree. June assured her the rehearsal dinner was all set at the club, with a local bluegrass band for entertainment.

"Jade, have you thought about your gift for Max?" Betsy jammed a baby carrot in her mouth.

"My heart isn't enough?"

Betsy peeked at Jade from under her brow, then laughed. "Cute. I thought you were serious for a moment."

"I'm not?"

"No, Jade, it's okay. We get it. The gift is a private matter." Betsy sent off another text. "Best to remind Max. He *is* a man."

"He bought me a house, Betsy, and a diamond ring."

"Can't wear a house around your neck, and I'd have killed him if he proposed without a ring. Let me see it again." She leaned over the table. "Hm, the man did good."

"Rebel is so good about birthdays and anniversaries. Even brings me gifts just because," June said, reaching for the lemonade pitcher.

"Come on, June, Rebel is the biggest philan—" A pink hue crept across Betsy's face. "Flowers. We're set with calla lilies. Jade, remember, the boutique called and we can pick up all the dresses tomorrow. Yours I have, but I need to get your sister's and your mother's."

"Rebel is the biggest what, Betsy?" June's voice cut like a razor.

"Philanthropist." She gulped her lemonade. Ice slipped forward in the glass, spilling the drink on her blouse.

June handed her a napkin. "He is, and it's important to him that the right hand doesn't know what the left is doing. Jade, you didn't know your father-in-law was so generous, did you?"

"No, June, I didn't. But I'm not surprised." Her gaze met Betsy's. What was she hinting at?

"Speaking of generosity." Betsy arched one brow. "Rebel arranged a surprise for you."

"Really?" asked June. "For Jade?"

"What kind of surprise?" asked Jade.

"Now what kind of surprise would it be if I told you, hm?"

They concluded the review with tuxes and limos, and arrival of out-of-town guests.

"It's so good to have your brother walk you down the aisle. So sad about your dad passing."

"Yeah." Jade shoved away from the table, folding the copy of the list Betsy had handed her. She'd have to clear up that topic another day. "I need to run. I have an appointment." She hugged Betsy, then June. "Thank you. For everything."

"You're marrying my only son. Of course . . ." June walked her to the front door, the heels of her leather pumps echoing in the bright marble foyer. "About what Betsy said."

"It's none of my business, June. Besides, I'm not one to judge."

"Reb's a good man. You know that, don't you, Jade?"

"I do, from all I can see."

"He's imperfect, as are all men, you know. Weak."

"Aren't we all?" Jade twisted open the door. "June, this day wouldn't have been nearly as lovely and special if it weren't for you. From the parties, the gifts, and the organizing to hiring Betsy and taking care of so many wedding details I didn't think were important. But most of all, for challenging me to have a ceremony like this one, and to invite my mother."

"What am I for if not for helping?"

Jade planted a soft kiss on her future mother-in-law's cheek.

~

The church sanctuary wasn't quiet when Jade entered; it was alive and buzzing with Thursday choir practice.

Reverend Girden called to say he was running late, but to wait for him in the sanctuary. Jade eased down on the front pew.

"Arthur, did you get a copy of the music?" The choir director held up copies in his hand.

After a response of "Yes" and "We're all good," the director settled the choir down to rehearse the first number.

When the first chords from the piano and guitar filled the sanctuary, Jade's heart swelled. Granny loved this song.

In the sweet by and by . . .

Jade hummed, eyes closed, swaying from side to side.

. . . we will meet on that beautiful shore.

The peace Jade encountered the night in Beechgrove at Miss Linda's deepened. She'd started reading Granny's old Bible instead of clinging to it like a stuffed toy.

"Jade, thank you for waiting." Reverend Girden crossed over to her, hand extended. Today, he was the soft, unassuming man. Not the mad dog with a bone. "I'm blessed today. First I had some time with Max, and now you."

She stood. "Max was here?"

"He was. Just wanted to talk over some things."

"About me?"

"Actually about him. He's about to get married, make a big commitment, and he wanted to make sure he's on the right course to be a stand-up guy and go the distance with you." The reverend started for his office. "He really loves you, Jade."

"I don't know what I did to deserve him, but I'll take it."

"Good for you." As before, the reverend sat behind his big oak desk, and Jade took the leather-and-wood chair opposite him. "What can I do for you, Jade?"

"I'm here because of your boss."

"As in the board or the Lord Himself?" He folded his hands on top of the desk.

"Yes, the . . . the Lord." Jade angled forward, smoothing her thumb over her fingernails. "I think something happened."

Her news didn't seem to surprise him. "Can you tell me about it?"

"At first, I thought I might have been going crazy. But the more I think about it . . ." Jade shivered, remembering the burn of His fire. "I did something I'm not proud of, Reverend, and it has caused a lot of pain. For years I blamed my mom, but when I finally faced my part . . ." She made eye contact with Reverend Girden. "Do you think God would be with someone in their darkest hour? No matter what?"

"If not in their darkest hour, then when? God is always with us. Dark and light are the same to Him."

"Even if the person doesn't believe?"

"Do you know the story of Paul, Jade? He was a passionate young man in his day, running around Jerusalem arresting and beating Christians in defense of the synagogue. One afternoon, right in the middle of his mission, God dropped by for a visit."

"What happened to him?"

"He became a great lover of Christ. More passionate *for* Him than he had been *against* Him."

"But this is a different day, a different era."

"But He's the same God. He doesn't change. He's the same yesterday, today, and forever. If they needed to know Him in Paul's day, we surely need to know Him now."

"Does He love everyone?"

"You know that verse, Jade? 'For God so loved the world . . .'"

"I do." A few times, she woke up with the verse in her head. "I haven't forgotten every Sunday school lesson."

"Did He visit you, Jade?"

"Yes, I think. Mama and I broke down in Beechgrove and stayed at this woman's home. She claims God visits her there often."

"Sounds just like Him. He loves relationships. We make it about religion, rules, and regulation. But God, He loves to be in a relationship with people. So were you distressed at the time?"

"Very." She pressed her fingers to her eyes to block her tears. The first since confronting Mama. "Dealing with what I'd done."

The melodies of the choir practice seeped through the walls. The reverend waited.

"I felt heat." Jade motioned to her body. "From my toes to my crown. Well, first I felt a wind. It blew only on my face, or at my feet. After I told God I was sorry for what I'd done, then the heat came. Searing heat. Then the burden of pain was gone, and I felt this incredible peace."

"Jesus comes to take away our guilt and shame, Jade. Why not yours?" The reverend smiled. "We like to put God in a box, determine when and how He can speak to us, but He can relate to us any way He wants."

"Guess I thought I'd disqualified myself." She exhaled. "I feel . . . free."

"Nothing can separate us from the love of God. We all mess up, make mistakes, but if there's a yes in your heart to Him, you're on the right path."

Jade laughed. "My Paps and Granny are dancing in heaven. They were quiet in their prayers for us, but I have no doubt that's why I'm sitting here now."

The reverend folded his hands on his desk. "Max asked me this morning to do a religious ceremony, weaving your faith and God into the vows. I'm honored to do so. Jade, anytime you want to talk, my door is always open to you."

She stood. "I was thinking I could sign up for those classes you mentioned."

"We meet every Monday night at seven."

Twenty-nine

The white room with yellow buttercup trim was too quiet. Beryl longed for Willow's exuberant presence, but she'd gone off with her new friends.

That girl. She'll never be lonely.

Dr. Meadows had just called. Wanted to know if she was feeling all right, if she had any weakness or pain. The weight loss and weather contributed to the night at Miss Linda's when she was so cold. Beryl was just glad to not have the flu the week of Jade's wedding.

Then he told her he'd schedule her for chemo the week she returned home.

Stretching out on her bed, her silver hair splayed across the starched pillowcase, Beryl reached for the brass ring that may have only existed in her dreams and closed her fingers around it. *Don't let me go.*

She wondered if she could experience what Jade had in Miss Linda's yard. A healing heat. She might believe if she did.

Drifting in the twilight between awake and asleep, Beryl was young again, dancing in the moonlight with Harlan. Planting corn. There were Mother and Paps, around the red-and-chrome kitchen table. Little man Aiden taking her picture while Jade jumped up and down in the kitchen, begging for her to make cookies. Willow, cherubic but ornery, swung up on Beryl's hip.

Call him.

Beryl's eyes popped open. *Call him? Who?*

Call him.

Beryl sat up, leaning her back against the headboard. *Call him.* But she didn't want to call *him*. It'd been too many years. Too much silence. She wouldn't begin to know what to say.

Call him.

Hesitating only a half second, Beryl picked up the phone and followed the instructions for making a long-distance call.

~

Sunlight washed her bedroom window as Jade kicked her legs from under the covers and dropped to the floor next to Roscoe's bed. He snored in a smooth, even rhythm. "Roscoe," Jade whispered, "I'm getting married today."

His feet fluttered and a muffled "ruff" billowed his lips.

"Get that old rabbit." Jade rubbed his brown and black head. "Even with one eye, you're better than the best German Shepherd hunter."

As if he had heard, Roscoe opened his eye and touched his nose to Jade's.

Rolling over on her back, Jade stared at her white ceiling. "Max was so sweet last night at the rehearsal dinner, Roscoe. He's getting it, you know? He stayed with me all night, never left my side, even when those bozo friends of his tried to get him outside for a cigar.

"I'm doing the right thing, Roscoe." The dog nudged her shoulder. "Time for breakfast and a trip outside."

Jade tugged on a pair of jeans and a T-shirt, finding her sneakers by the door.

Ten a.m., and it felt like an eternity until six p.m. Down the loft stairs and out the storeroom door, Jade and Roscoe stepped into a cold, blue-sky day. Shivering, she urged Roscoe to do his business quick.

It was weird seeing the shop dark and the sign announcing, "Closed for the Owner's Wedding."

Back up in the loft, Jade scooped Roscoe's breakfast into his bowl, then stood in front of the open fridge trying to decide if anything sounded good to eat.

"Big sister." A knock echoed and Willow let herself in. "Breakfast from Sugar Plumbs. Daphne and Margot gave me Bridal KP. Did you know Margot is bossy?"

"Really? I had no idea." Jade opened the box Willow handed her. "Mm, an omelet."

"Mae cooked your breakfast herself. Said she figured you'd need something to stick to your ribs. All they'll serve is bunny food at the bridesmaids' luncheon." Willow hunted through Jade's cupboards. "Where do you keep the napkins?"

Jade pointed her toe at the pantry.

"Beryl's still asleep," Willow said once they hit the sofa, cartons propped on their laps, feet against the coffee table. "She's sick, isn't she?"

Jade's eyes met her sister's. "She has leukemia. Four years now."

Willow swirled her eggs around her box. "That makes sense. She's been losing weight, sleeping a lot, not working. When did she tell you?"

"When we toured the house."

"Wow, I suspected something was wrong but never thought it was real." Willow set her food on the coffee table and walked to the window. "Is it serious?"

"Dr. Meadows wants to start her on chemo. Mama said she's losing the war."

"For a long time I didn't think I'd care that much if she died. That sounds awful, doesn't it? It's not like when Granny went. I felt like my childhood died with her." Willow peered back at Jade. "But it's Beryl, isn't it?"

"Yeah, it's Mama, with all her ups and downs, marriages and parties." Jade patted the cushion, calling Willow back to the sofa. "We can do the right thing and forgive all she's done, help her through this."

Willow bit off the end of a sausage link, then give the rest to Roscoe. "I'm sad for Beryl. She seems so alone." Willow tapped her food with her fork.

"That's why we'll be there for her."

"I should go back to school, shouldn't I?" Willow tore off a bit of bacon.

"Yes. Mama's been wrong about a lot of things, Willow. But she's right about you and the potential you have." Jade set her food aside. "Don't waste yourself on a bunch of men, partying, living like there's no tomorrow."

"Jade—" Willow broke her biscuit in two, biting one half, giving the other to Roscoe.

"It only destroys your self-esteem, not to mention how physically dangerous it is. Now that I have Max, I wish I'd never been with anyone else. Those experiences don't matter or help. At all."

"So the sinner becomes the preacher." Roscoe scooted closer to Willow and dropped his chin on her foot. She handed over a whole sausage link.

"More like the fool becomes wise. I'm not judging you, Willow."

"I know I act all crazy sometimes, but when I stop moving, it's like I can't breathe."

"Was it awful after I left for college?" Jade never asked before because she didn't want to know. She had enough guilt, thank you very much.

"Granny was my mother, Jade. She took good care of me until she died. We had some good times." The tip of Willow's nose reddened. "I miss her."

"Yeah, me too. I'm sorry I left you, Wills. But I had to get out of Prairie City in the worst way."

"It's okay, I understood." She peered at Jade. "Beryl's your only parent, Jade. I have Mike, but Beryl is all you and Aiden have."

"As parents go. But I have you and Aiden. And now Max and the Bensons."

"You are going to be the most beautiful bride, Jade. Inside and out."

"I hope Max thinks so."

"Are you nervous? I'd be petrified."

Jade pictured Max, the reverend, Willow, Mama, Daphne, Margot, and the Bensons. She pressed her hand over her middle where the ache always used to be.

"It's about faith, Willow, and I've already taken the leap. I'm in midair, doing a somersault, believing love will catch me if I miss my mark."

Thirty

First Baptist Congregation, November 14, 5:30 p.m.

In the bridal room off the large slate and marble foyer, Jade waited with Roscoe. It was Betsy's idea to dress him up in a doggy tux. Jade refused until she saw him in a bow tie, wagging his tail as if he understood it made him part of the wedding ceremony.

Betsy shooed Willow, Daphne, and Margot out of the room to allow some "peace and quiet time" for the bride.

The air felt thick and heavy. Jade inhaled deep. She wondered if her heart would race today as though she were being chased by a thousand enemies. But so far, not even a flutter.

Her gift from Max sparkled on her wrist—a diamond bracelet. His note made her heart well up and her eyes mist. "Diamonds are forever, so is my devotion to you. Always yours, Max."

The parking lot was filling up, and guests in formal attire hurried toward the sanctuary.

"Jade-o?" The door creaked open.

"Come in. Oh, you let them fix your hair." Mama's braid was coiled around the back of her head and adorned with baby's breath. "You, with your flowers in your hair, look beautiful."

Mama stood back, smiling, eyes glistening. "Thank you for inviting me, Jade. If I'd have missed this, well . . . You are beautiful. Simply stunning."

"It took a beauty team to get me like this."

"Max's eyes are going to fall on the floor."

"I hope not. He has to drive me to my honeymoon."

"Paps and Granny would be very proud."

"I hope they're watching." Jade touched the spot on her neck where the medallion usually laid.

"Can we sit a moment?" Mama motioned to the long white couch.

Jade pointed to the back of her dress. "I don't want to wrinkle."

"I've done something." Mama remained standing, wringing her hands, her brown eyes glossy. "I thought I was supposed to . . . now but I'm not so sure."

"What did you do?" After the past three weeks, Mama's news didn't rattle her much.

"I figure you won't kill me on your wedding day."

"Mama . . ."

Aiden poked his head inside. "Hey—"

"Is it time already?" Jade whirled to see the clock. Betsy promised a five-minute warning.

"Mom, he's here," Aiden said.

"Who's here?" Jade said.

"Your dad, Jade." Mama's smiled wobbled. "I called him and suggested he might regret missing his daughter's wedding. Oh, I went too far, didn't I?

Stepped over my bounds. He said I shouldn't butt in, and he refused to come without an invitation from the bride, but . . ." Mama gripped Jade's hands with a growing boldness. "I can't face chemo and leukemia knowing I'm your only parent. He's been a shabby excuse for a father, but still, he is your dad. You remember him a bit, don't you?"

"Max. Aiden, get Max."

"Jade, I'm sorry."

"Are you sure?" Aiden asked, hand on the knob. "You're in your dress."

"Aiden, get him. Now."

"He'll be your only parent. I thought I could help mend things, do something right by you kids for a change."

"Are you kicking the bucket tomorrow? Honestly, Mama, I'm about to walk down the aisle."

"I'm sorry—"

"Mama, stop saying 'I'm sorry.' Let me think."

She called Harlan? He came? Oh, Jade didn't want to deal with this now.

"Jade, what's wrong?" Max burst into the room, worry wrapping around his eyes. "Are you okay? Beryl, what's wrong? Aiden said to come quick."

"My father. He's here. Mama called him, and he came."

"Here, in this place?" Max pointed to the floor, gazing between Mama and Jade.

"Just got here," said Beryl.

"Do we have to deal with this now?" Max asked.

Jade leaned into his chest, careful of her makeup against his white shirt. "He wants to see me." She batted away tears.

"Jade," Aiden said low. "I talked to him. He's fine if you want to wait for another time."

She dabbed under her eyes with the tissue Mama pressed into her hand. *Jesus, what do I do?*

Peace was an amazing tonic. Forgiveness, a powerful tool. "Tell him to come in."

"Are you sure?" Max asked, slipping his hand into hers.

"Yes, yes, I think I am." Jade laced her fingers tight with Max's, a buzz and a bubble in her middle. One word, and she might laugh. Another, and she'd weep.

What was he like fifteen years later? Still dashing with coal black hair and gray eyes? Had he gained weight? Did he wear glasses? A toupee?

At the end of all her questions, Harlan Fitzgerald was still the same man who'd rescued her from the cornfield.

Max touched his lips to her ear. "Jade Fitzgerald, you are breathtaking."

She peered up at him. "Sorry I ruined the grand entrance."

"I'll still be stunned." His kiss to her temple was tender and warm.

"Jade?" Aiden checked with her, then stepped back. "Come on in, Dad."

A distinguished, silver-haired Harlan Fitzgerald barely entered the room. He stood just inside the door, watching Jade with humble eyes. "Jade. Thank you for letting me see you."

"It's, uh . . ." She swayed as if the room had tilted. Max gripped her hand tighter. Roscoe sniffed around Harlan's shiny shoes. "It's good to see you."

"You're lovely."

"Maxwell Benson." He stepped forward, pulling Jade with him, offering his hand to the judge. "I took your ethics course when you guest lectured at Duke."

"Yes, Beryl said you were in the law."

"Okay, Jade . . ." Betsy burst through the door. "Oh, my stars above, what have we here? Who are all these people? Max, jumping catfish, what in the world?" She smacked her hand over her heart like this was the big one. "You're not supposed to be in here, with the bride."

"Extenuating circumstances, Betsy. Meet Jade's father, Harlan Fitzgerald."

"There's a father?" She gripped her clipboard for dear life. "Isn't he dead? I thought the brother was going to walk the bride down the aisle."

Jade's cheeks burned when Harlan looked at her, surprise and wonder in his eyes.

"Long story."

He grinned, the smile that lived in her memories. "I bet."

"Are you walking her down the aisle now?" Betsy tapped his arm like a drill sergeant.

"No, no," Harlan said, holding up his hand. "Just saying hello."

"Well, it's good to know you're not dead."

"Tell you what, Betsy," Max said with a glance at Jade. "How about the groom walks his bride down the aisle? But only if you want to, Jade."

"Max, really?"

"Absolutely not." Betsy waved her hands and clipboard, shaking her head. "The groom cannot walk the bride down the aisle. The dog here, yes. But *not* the groom."

"New rule, Betsy." Max linked Jade's hand through his arm. "Aiden, you don't mind?"

"Anything for Jade. It's her day." His crinkly gray-eyed smile was the image of a younger Harlan.

"Max, your mother is going to freak, just freak." Betsy's high-pitched voice had Roscoe tipping his head to one side.

"She'll live."

"What's going on? The music is starting." Willow popped her head around the door. "Wow, party in here. Max—"

"The music." Betsy's eyes popped. "Everyone out. Places. Max is walking his bride down the aisle. No time to argue." She backtracked to Max before following the others out. "If your mom doesn't pay me, I'm coming to you."

The room emptied, but Daddy hung back a bit. Starting to tremble, Jade kept her eyes on him, the proud Washington judge with an air of contrition.

Just before he stepped out the door, he glanced at her and she broke. "Daddy—"

Jade fell into his embrace, not caring about her hair and makeup or Betsy's clipboard schedule. Her Daddy had come.

His whisper warmed her ear. "I'm sorry, baby, I'm sorry. I just didn't know how—"

"You came for me. I knew you would. I knew you would."

~

Blades of sunlight sliced through the surly November clouds, falling in glittery white streams over the valley as the church bells chimed.

Listen all, come and see, hear the good news. Maxwell Charles Benson married Jade Freedom Fitzgerald.

Jade clung to Max as they scurried down the portico steps through a confetti rain. Reverend Girden's exhortation reverberated in her heart. "Love is patient, love is kind, love keeps no record of wrong."

Mama watched from among the throng of guests wishing them well, tucked away as if she didn't deserve to be noticed. "Wait, Max."

Jade reached into the wedding crowd and pulled Mama forward, kissing her cheek. "We can't change our yesterdays, but we can change our tomorrows. Max and me, Aiden and Willow. We'll be there for you."

Mama's brimming eyes spilled over. "Go on now. It's your wedding day."

"Jade, let's go." Betsy appeared, shoving her in the back. "You can talk at the reception."

Max led her to the end of the walkway, and a horse-drawn carriage rounded the corner of Divine. "Dad's gift."

Six perfectly matched white horses—not one or two, but six—pulled a white-and-burgundy open Victorian carriage. The driver pulled them to a stop and tipped his top hat before hopping out to lower the brass steps. "My lady."

She was Cinderella again, and by the depth of Max's hazel gaze, she wouldn't wake up Monday morning to be just the girl-with-the-shop.

Jade had believed in forever once, and as the carriage swerved out of the church drive, the guests waving and cheering, she believed in forever again.

Epilogue

December 24

The Christmas lights in the Blue Umbrella window splashed red, blue, and green puddles on the floor. Over the speakers, Dean Martin crooned, "Baby, it's cold outside," and a Christmas tree grove bloomed where there had once been a pumpkin patch.

A sign was pasted in the window: The Blue Umbrella Celebrates Christmas. Closed December 24–25.

"The paper goods for the party are on the shelf, ready to go." Lillabeth came from the storeroom wearing a Santa hat. "If you don't need me, I'm going to go get changed and come back."

"Your debt all paid?" Jade shoved the table in the center of the store under the front window.

"Almost."

"How much more?"

"Two hundred. I sort of took some money for Christmas."

"What do you know?" Jade handed Lillabeth an envelope. "Merry Christmas."

"Really?" The girl smashed Jade with a hug. "Thank you! Oh, it's too much . . . really . . . thank you."

"Go on now, or I'll regret abusing you for the party."

Jade finished closing up business so she'd be ready for the party, glancing out the window every now and then. *Max, hurry home.* Her stomach flip-flopped. Finally, she could give him her wedding present.

Mama and Willow were back in town, but not at the Magnolia Tree B&B. June insisted they stay at their house on the hill. "You're family."

Willow was making noise about moving down and attending UT. And the latest from the contractor was that they'd be finished with the Begonia Valley Lane house by February.

"Honey, I'm home." Max breezed in the front door with a cheesy grin.

"Did you bring it?" Jade ran around the counter, gave him a quick kiss, and checked his hands.

"Right here. What do you want with this thing?" Max handed over a Benson Law wall calendar and stooped to greet Roscoe. "The year is all but over."

"You'll see." At the counter, Jade hunted in the pencil drawer for a Sharpie. *Hello, Sharpie, present yourself.* There it was. She'd assign Lillabeth to clean this drawer next week.

Snapping off the cap, she circled the 24th of December and printed: *Wedding Present to Max.* "Come on."

"What's going on?"

Jade drew him to the storeroom and the row of calendars, hooking hers on the nail she'd hammered into the wall, extending the tradition. Then she faced her husband. She shook the nervous tingle from her hands.

"I was so excited, but now I'm nervous."

"What's going on?" Max grabbed her for a kiss. "By the way, the Thompsons said to 'tell your wife' they're coming to the party tonight."

"I love that word."

"So what's with the calendars? Are we starting a new tradition?" He gazed down the wall. "We're keeping a tradition. What's this? 'Wedding Present to Max'?"

"The Sorges started this tradition. The wall of calendars. The wall of reminders. When I bought the Five & Dime, I decided to keep the tradition, adding significant years, ones that mean something to us."

"So you hung this year." Max fastened his hands behind her back, low around her waist. "One of the best of my life."

"Max." Jade leaned back to see his face. "I hope it's going to get a bit better. We're . . ." She paused, her voice betraying her. "We're going to have a baby."

His eyes rounded. His back stiffened. "What?"

"I'm pregnant, Max. I just found out yesterday." Her heart fluttered as she pointed to the date. "A child is my wedding gift to you. And to me, I guess. And Merry Christmas and Happy New Year."

Max snatched her from the ground and whirled her around, his hoot exploding against the ceiling and raining down joy. "Thank you, thank you." His kisses were wild but tender, landing on her nose, eyes, cheeks, then lips.

"I love you, Jade Benson."

"Forever, Max. Forever."

Acknowledgments

From Sara

This book is dedicated to my daughters, my sisters, my girlfriends, my mother-n-law, my step-mother, my Granny, and my Mother . . . and all the women in my life who have helped make me the girl I am today. With love . . . Sara

I want to thank Rachel for truly hearing me and "getting" me and helping me put my story to words on paper. I'm honored . . .

From Rachel

Special thanks to Ami McConnell, friend and editor. Thanks for seeing the beauty amid the rubble. I thank God for you.

Also, I offer my thanks to:

The great visionary Allen Arnold and the team at Thomas Nelson. Thanks for your ideas and amazing insights.

Katie Sulkowski and everyone at Creative Trust.

Jennifer Stair, for your insight and edits on this book.

Susan May Warren, for your friendship and constant wise counsel. And my InGeorgia girls, Christine Lynxwiler, Tracey Bateman, and Susan Downs. You make me laugh.

My family, who cheered me on.

Chelle, Anna, Lin, Esther, and Helen—the Tuesday night Dream Team—for being such prayer warriors and a wonderful support system.

My husband, Tony, for giving me room to fly.

My friend, Jesus, who makes all things new.

And many thanks to these kind folks who gave advice:

Chelle Tapper, for candid answers to deep, personal questions.

CJ Casner, for tales from her teen years.

Timothy Greene, for Iowa legal advice.

Jeff Breese at Inter Mat Wrestling.

Gary Brown, for help understanding teamsters.

Donna Kletting of Prairie City, Iowa.

Diane Southwick of the Prairie City, Iowa, City Hall.

Steve Scholfield at Northern Iowa University.

Danny Hayes, my brother, for advice about trucks.

And Crystal at the Read House Starbucks.

Reading Group Guide

1. In chapter one, Jade struggles with sending a wedding invitation to her mother. A deep wound has distanced them. Have you or anyone you've been close to struggled with inviting a parent to a personal and family-oriented event? Is there ever any benefit to not inviting a parent to a child's wedding? Is there a benefit to putting the hurt aside for the day?
2. In chapter two, Mama—Beryl—struggles to open the back door of her parents' old farm house because her arms are full. What does this symbolize? Are there physical things in your life that symbolize your emotional or spiritual life? Are they positive or negative? Can you change them?
3. In the pastor's office, Jade has an odd experience. What did you think of this experience? Have you ever had something similar happen? How long did it last? How did you respond?

4. Jade and Max decide to let their pasts stay in the past. Is there wisdom here? How can letting the past stay out of the present benefit your heart and relationships? How might it hinder? When is it right to talk about the past? When is it best to let issues of the past go?

5. Beryl is a product of the '60s and the Summer of Love. How did the philosophy of the day impact her life as a teenager and adult? Was there a significant event that began her spiritual journey? Did you have a moment like this? How has it impacted you over the years?

6. When Jade was eight, her father Harlan left the family. How did this event shadow her through life? What is the significance of a father's presence in a son's/daughter's life? How has your life been impacted by the presence or absence of a parent?

7. Jade met Dustin in high school. How did this relationship impact her? What did he bring to her? Did you have a significant relationship as a teen? Think about how such a relationship can help or hinder. Would you do what Jade and Dustin did?

8. As an adult, Jade runs a vintage shop. What does this symbolize? How does her physical and external life reflect her emotional, internal life?

9. When Jade takes Beryl with her to Nashville, what is symbolized by the truck breaking down? As you read the story, did you sense the significance of the moment for mother and daughter? Share an event from your life that permanently affected you.

10. What created the wedge between Jade and Beryl? Do you and someone you care about have an unresolved issue? Do you want to resolve it?

11. Why didn't Jade want to admit her part in the abortion? Do you have issues you are hesitant to face because you don't want to take responsibility for the part you played? If you've lived through and overcome a hard situation like abortion or addiction, can you share your success with the group?

12. When Jade is on the porch at Miss Linda's, she senses a presence manifested in wind and heat. Have you ever had a supernatural encounter? How did it impact you? Did Jade understand in this moment that God loved her and forgave her? Do you realize this?
13. Why does Harlan show up at the wedding? What do you think of Jade's response?
14. It is important to remember the good years. In the epilogue, Jade hangs a calendar on the shop wall to represent a good year in her life. Consider setting up a monument in your heart (or on a wall in your home) to note the blessings you've received. If you are in a group, talk about the kind of year you're having.

Jade is moving from her past to a bright future. Until someone close reveals a secret that changes everything.

Excerpt from *Softly & Tenderly*

One

Along the first of spring, when winter began to ease its grip on Whisper Hollow mornings, the word barren began echoing over the shadowy recesses of Jade's mind.

"You're quiet." Her mother-in-law peered at her from the passenger side of Jade's truck. She looked out of place perched on the faded red, torn vinyl seat wearing an haute couture pink suit.

"Thinking." Jade forced a smile just as the tires hit a bump in the road, jostling the passengers from side to side.

June grabbed the dashboard. "Mercy me."

"Sorry . . ." Jade urged the truck up the hill to Orchid House, her husband's childhood home. "You feel everything in this truck. No matter how new the shocks."

Truck shocks aside, Jade had managed to hit all the holes today. Holes in the road. Holes in her business. Holes in her heart. With a slow exhale, she propped her elbow on the door and pressed her fingers against her forehead.

Today it seemed that every woman, *every* woman who came in to Jade's downtown shop was pregnant. Nearly picked clean Jade's retro maternity clothes. She'd been folding and hanging the remaining items when June called and asked Jade to give her a ride home.

"It's beyond me why you still drive this old bucket of bolts, Jade. Why don't you just buy a new truck?" June brushed a piece of foam from the crumbling ceiling off her skirt. "You're a Benson now. A successful business owner in Whisper Hollow and river front Chattanooga. Surely you can afford a vehicle better than this. Max would buy you one if you asked. I'm quite sure he—"

"Your pink suit is beautiful," Jade interrupted. "Did you get it on your girls' shopping trip in Atlanta?"

June cut Jade a glance. "Paris, last spring. I figure I could risk wearing it another season."

"Do I get dibs when it's out of season twenty years?"

"Shug, this thing will be completely out of vogue in three months. And by the end of summer, sold at the club auction." June ran her hand along the three-quarter sleeve, finally smiling. Ever since Jade had picked her up from the Read House Starbucks, she'd been fuming beneath a stone-face.

"So Rebel got tied up with a case or something? Couldn't bring you home?" Jade asked. June had yet to say why she was stranded at Starbucks, and so steamed.

"Oh, who knows? That man. He can be so self-focused. I specifically told Rebel that Honey Andover could not drive me up to the house when we returned from Atlanta. Her granddaughter's birthday party is up in Knoxville, so she wanted to get back on the road. So . . ." June fiddled with the air conditioning vents. "Rebel agreed to meet me at Starbucks."

"The truck doesn't have air, June."

"Well, why not? Mercy, Jade, buy a decent truck. What's this thing, a hundred years old?"

"Thirty-eight. So what happened with Honey? What's got you riled?"

"Nothing happened with Honey. She dropped me off at the Read House Starbucks like planned, right by Benson Law, right by my husband, where he agreed to be. But Rebel's nowhere to be found."

"You tried his cell?"

"I'm angry not addled, Jade. I called his cell and his office. Gina didn't know where he was—and if she doesn't know, he's gone. Vanished into thin air." June twirled her hands in front of her.

"Maybe Reb hit the golf course, taking a break for the class action suit their firm's been handling. That case has Max preoccupied and bleary-eyed."

"Nice try, Jade, but Reb hasn't *worked* a case in years. He just *oversees*. Charms. Asks a few tough questions in court when they want to intimidate someone." June snatched her handbag from the seat and stuffed it in to her lap. "He's probably schmoozing someone in the governor's office, hoping he'll get a special appointment should one ever open up."

"Reb has political aspirations?" Jade crested the hill and rounded the bend toward the Bensons' white brick estate.

"Jade, have you learned to tune out his ramblings already? Reb wants to run the universe from his throne on the moon."

A fawn suddenly leaped onto the road from the cluster of trees tucked into the curve of the bend. Jade hammered the clutch and brake.

"Sake's alive." June smacked the dashboard with her Gucci bag.

Stiff-arming the steering wheel and mashing the brake, Jade winced as the truck drifted into a blinding patch of sun. Anticipation drilled a hole between her ribs.

When there was no impact, breath exploded from her lungs. Just beyond her windshield, a black-eyed doe and her two spotted fawns crossed the road into the woods on the other side.

"My heart is thumping in my throat." June spanked the dash grit from the smooth leather of her handbag. "Can you imagine if you'd not seen—"

"I wouldn't have been able to sleep for a week." Jade watched the doe as she led her young to the other side, her head high, her steps neat and sure. Joy pressed the clutch and shifted into first with a final glance at the creature.

In the grass, just beyond the trees, the doe turned and fixed her polished gaze on Jade. *Yes, I know. . .* A motor roared and the doe dashed into the trees the moment a car whizzed around the bend.

"Farrel Lawrence," June said. "She's got a lead foot."

Run, girl. Run. Jade eased off the clutch and the truck chugged up the last few feet of the hill, the heart of the doe and the sensation of beauty resonating in her heart.

~

The Bensons' foyer was cold. Jade shivered as she followed June inside, carrying a few of the bags and boxes her mother-in-law had collected from three days of shopping in Atlanta with Honey.

"Constance?" June clicked on the table lamp. The soft yellow light caught the gloss and glimmer of the polished mahogany.The wood grain matched the banister of the sweeping, curved staircase that spilled from the second floor into the Italian marble foyer. "You here, Constance?"

Jade dropped the packages at the base of the staircase, rubbing the bend of her arm. "What did you buy? Bricks?" She peered into the Neiman Marcus bag. "Christian Louboutins? Don't you have like four pairs already?" Jade sat on the bottom step and lifted the lid off the shoe box, inhaling at the sight of dark red patent leather heels. "Wow."

"And now I have five pairs." June scouted the formal living room for signs of life. "I bought them for the club's Christmas ball. Reb? Constance?"

Barely emerging from winter's gray, and June was already planning for Christmas. Jade could learn something here . . . What, she wasn't sure, but the moment sure felt teachable.

"How much?" Jade dug around for the receipt.

"Didn't your mama teach you it's impolite to ask 'how much'? Get your nose out of my bags." June gazed into the family room on the other side of the foyer. "Well, the place looks tidy."

"Six hundred dollars?" Jade dropped the shoe back into the box and let the receipt go, fluttering into the bag. "You can buy a lot of food for the poor with that kind of money."

"For Pete's sake, Jade, don't preach to me. Reb and I give plenty to the poor." June turned for the kitchen, her low heels beating a rhythm against the marble. "Why don't you call Max and have supper here? Run quick to pick up your mama too. Mercy, I pay Constance for a full day's work and I want a full day. Whether I'm here or not. Constance!"

"Max is working late." Jade sauntered into the kitchen. "Mama's still recovering from the last round of chemo. Why don't we try for another time?"

"Well, if you're sure, fine . . . another time." June stood in the middle of the arching, stainless steel kitchen, looking disconcerted.

Jade leaned against the ivory and green island. The kitchen was like a structural hug—cozy with June's Southern hospitality and dabbled with yellow and gray Smoky Mountain sunshine dripping through the skylight.

"How about we get Reb to fire up his grill this weekend?"

"He'd love that. . . we can thaw the kobe steaks." June opened the fridge and then closed it without looking inside. "Tell Beryl I'll be over tomorrow for a game of hearts."

"She'd like that. June?" Jade peered into her pinched eyes. "Are you okay?"

"Of course I'm okay. I've just been shopping for three days. Now, how about some hot tea? The house is freezing." June walked over to the basement door. "Constance?" June shoved the door closed. "That girl . . . I'm docking her pay a whole day."

"Why don't you hear her out first?" Jade slipped onto one of the island chairs and watched June fill a kettle with water and drop it onto the stove with a clank.

It was nearing five. Jade would have to leave after this cup of tea to get Mama's dinner. The latest round of chemo had zapped her energy more than the previous treatments. She slept most of the day, eating only when Jade urged her. Leukemia was a cruel taskmaster.

June set two mugs in front of Jade. "So what's new with you in the three days I've been gone? Have you and Max made any decisions?"

June never hesitated to dig around in Jade's life, prying open internal windows. Didn't Honey empty June of all her idle words? Didn't the woman just want to relax in a hot bath, order a Mario's pizza, and curl up with Rebel and a good TMC movie?

"A decision? In three days? I've hardly seen him." Her sorrows over the plethora of pregnant shoppers at the Blue Two this afternoon surface, gasping for air.

Perhaps June had a right to know if she would ever be a grandmother. Or not. Jade's private life with Max was private. And if Jade was . . . barren . . . then she needed to deal with that first, on her own, without her mother-in-law peering into her heart.

"What about a surrogate? The Bidwells had great success—"

Or without offering myriad unwanted solutions.

"June, please, Max and I have talked ad nauseam about the options." Jade pressed her fingers into the taut muscles along her shoulders and propped her elbows on the light-kissed granite countertop. "I can get pregnant; I just can't stay pregnant. And I'm sorry, but I'm not open to using another woman's womb. It would be like . . . like having an affair, inviting another woman into our marriage. Either Max and I make a baby together, or we don't have a biological child."

"Then you'll adopt." June set tea bags and sweeteners on the island.

Jade exhaled. "If and when we decide. You can't just pick up a child like a Jiffy Mart stop for a gallon of milk and loaf of bread." Didn't she just have this conversation with Max the other night? His response and tone had been almost identical to June's. Matter-of-fact, devoid of an emotional response or commitment. But the Bensons made things happen. There was a fix for everything. "Why can't a family just be a man and his wife? Do children validate us? Prove we make love? Make us more complete? What if we're happy . . . just Max and me?"

"Are you?" The kettle rumbled from its perch on the gas flame. June reached for it and filled the cups. "If you're happy, then I'm happy." She smiled. "But every time we talk about children, I can see the pain in your eyes, hear the longing in your words. You want what you never really had growing up. A family."

"I have a family. You and Reb, Mama, Aiden and Willow." Jade tore open a packet of sweetener and dumped the white powder into her tea.

"Is that good enough? Max wants children, Jade. He doesn't care if they're biological or not."

"June." Jade fired her name with a caustic edge. "We'll have children if we are meant to have children. Maybe Max and I aren't meant to be parents. What if God doesn't find me trustworthy? Why would He give a child to a woman who—"

"Why would God decide you aren't . . ." June dipped her head to see into Jade's downcast eyes. "Oh, I see." Her spoon tapped out a beat against the ceramic mug as she stirred her tea. "You think God would choose you out of all the women in this world who've had abortions to say, 'No baby for her; she blew it'"?

"Feels like it sometimes." Jade sipped her tea to hide her emotion. She ignored the yearning most of the time. But it had been stirred today, by the pregnant women, by the doe with her fawns. If she could finally carry a baby to term, not miscarry again, she'd feel like her past was truly forgiven and God was smiling.

"You're young, Jade. It'll happen." June's words brought little comfort.

"Sure, I know." Jade sipped her tea.

"I've got just the thing for you." June motioned for Jade to pick up her tea and follow.

Jade carried her tea up the stairs behind June, whose narrow hips swung from side to side. She'd spent her entire marriage, the past two and a half years, trying to convince herself that children didn't matter. Max completed her. God, as she was beginning to know Him, completed her. But a child . . . one of her own. Jade could imagine the joy.

She'd lost their honeymoon baby after ten weeks. It was a long eighteen months before she got pregnant again, only to lose the baby last summer, two weeks before Mama came down for a short visit.

But her August visit never ended. Mama's leukemia symptoms had intensified since Jade had seen her the Christmas before, so she refused to let her return to Iowa to live in the old farmhouse, alone.

Between managing the shops, The Blue Umbrella in Whisper Hollow and The Blue Two in downtown Chattanooga, Jade cared for Mama, driving her to doctor appointments and chemo treatments.

Into the crisp, golden fall and blustery holiday season, the busyness of the shop and town celebrations kept Jade's yearning for babies at bay. When she discovered she was pregnant at Thanksgiving, she lay awake that night in bed, pools in her eyes, crunching her fingers around Max's fisted, sleeping hand. The God of mercy bestowed favor on her.

"So, June, where are we going?" Then she had her third miscarriage in January. "What's this *thing* you have for me? Stuffing envelopes for the club's Spring Life Auction and Dance? Or licking stamps?"

"Jade, really, no one licks stamps anymore."

At the top of the stairs, June stopped short. Jade nearly sloshed her with tea.

"What's wrong?" Jade peered around her mother-in-law's shoulder. The pink hue of her suit brightened the dim light of the landing. The media room door was ajar with an eerie blue tint emanating from the flat-panel TV screen. "Is someone here?"

"Constance?" June thudded toward the door, a matronly authority in her stride. "You best not be napping. I warned you—"

"June," Jade hurried behind her, hoping to cushion the clash between Constance and her mistress. "So what if she fell asleep? It's not like she ignored her chores. The house is immaculate."

"I don't pay her to sleep." June raised her voice as if giving Constance one last chance to wake up and feign dusting before June crashed through the door and flipped on the light. "Constance Filmore—"

Jade hung back. Constance didn't need an audience when June reamed her out. *Be awake, Constance . . .*

"Oh, my, oh, oh—" June crashed backward into the door, her tea cup toppling to the plush cream and beige carpet. The golden-brown liquid spread through the fibers, sinking into the pile, creating a sprawling stain.

Jade surged into the room, accosted by the pungent scent of day-old cologne and sweat. As she stooped to pick up June's mug, her gaze strafed a bare-breasted woman standing on the other side of the U-shaped sofa. Her tangled, bleached hair stood high over her head and her unfastened jeans rode low on her hips. Surprise shoved the woman's name through her lips.

"Claire?"

Wasn't she one of June's best friends? What's going on? Jade averted her eyes from Claire's form and glanced at June.

Her mother-in-law's high, rosy cheeks faded beyond pale, her eyes fixed, and for an insane moment, Jade wondered if she even breathed. "June," Jade whispered, gathering June's cup by the tips of her fingers.

"June . . . we didn't know . . ." Claire Falcon tugged on her cotton top, then hunted around for her shoes. "We thought you were—"

"We? Who's we?" June's blank, unblinking gaze matched her monotone.

"I gotta go." Claire peered down at the sofa before darting for the door, her bra, socks, and shoes clutched to her chest. A sour bile burned at the base of Jade's throat as she moved aside for Claire to exit.

Suddenly, there was Rebel, standing, smoothing his hair, fixing his belt, and fastening the bottom buttons of his blue shirt.

Jade dropped June's mug, barely having presence of mind to set hers on the edge of the wall table just inside the door. *Rebel?* Her knees buckled.

"Maybe you should go, Jade." Rebel stepped around the couch. "I'm sorry you had to see this."

"In my own home, Rebel?" June's tone sent chills over Jade's skin. "My. Own. Home."

"You weren't supposed to be here." Rebel casually walked between the women and out the door.

June dashed after him as he descended the stairs. "Don't you *dare* walk away from me." She smashed her fist into his back.

Flinching, Jade tucked in behind the wall. For a short moment, she was eight again, watching her daddy leave their Iowa farm in the middle of the night, Mama hollering after him.

But June and Rebel? The benevolent king and queen of Whisper Hollow?

"My . . . own . . . home."

The smack of June's hand against Rebel's cheek shocked Jade's heart. Tears swelled in her eyes. She expected infidelity from her Mama, but not from the refined and dignified Bensons. Rebel was a church deacon. June chaired the woman's auxiliary.

"You disrespect me so much you bring your filth into my home? Forty-one years, Rebel, I've been faithful and—"

Back to the wall, Jade slid down until her bottom hit the hardwood.

"Forty-one, June? Are you sure you want to stick with that number?" Jade waited for Rebel's chest-rumbling "Ah, June bug,"'paired with a contrite apology. She listened for his tender begging, pulling her into their room to talk in private. But instead he spoke as if June railed on about petty things—a towel on the bathroom floor. A forgotten dinner date with old friends.

"I don't deserve this, Rebel, not in my own home. Where's Constance?"

"I sent her home. Didn't need her interfering."

"Never again, you hear me?" June's voice rose with command. She would be obeyed. "Never. In my home. Do you hear me, Rebel Benson?"

Dread filled Jade's belly. Never *again*? Max never mentioned his dad's affairs. A door slammed. Footsteps hammered down the stairs and tapped across the marble.

"Jade—" June's call carried up from the foyer and bounced around the hollow pockets of the second floor.

She couldn't move.

"Jade!"

Pushing off the floor, Jade scrambled for the stairs. She peered at June as she inched her way down.

"You might want to keep this to yourself." June gripped her hands together at her waist, squeezing her fingers.

"To myself?" The chill of the encounter lifted, but her bones rattled beneath her skin. "What are you saying? Max doesn't—"

"Jade, you heard me." June's olive-green eyes pleaded, red and swimming. "To yourself."

The inspiring conclusion to the Songbird Series

Also from Rachel Hauck, co-author of

The Songbird Series

Available April 2012

Visit RachelHauck.com

About the Authors

Multi-platinum recording artist Sara Evans has been honored with numerous accolades, among them the 2006 Academy of Country Music's Female Vocalist of the Year and the Country Music Association's Video of the Year for "Born to Fly." Evans has been named one of *People Magazine*'s "50 Most Beautiful People" and won the hearts of television viewer's as the first-ever country star to compete in ABC's *Dancing with the Stars*. Sara is a Cabinet Member of the American Red Cross.

Best-selling and award-winning author Rachel Hauck lives in Florida with her husband, Tony, a pastor. A graduate of Ohio State University, she left the corporate software marketplace in '04 to write full time.